'das haus'

the house and

the Son of the Rabbi

a novel by

Sean Ryan Stuart

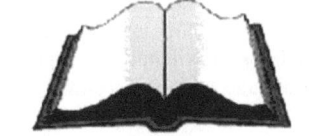

CCB Publishing
British Columbia, Canada

'Das Haus' the house and the Son of the Rabbi: a novel

Copyright ©2008 by Sean Ryan Stuart
ISBN-13   978-0-9810246-4-6
First Edition

Library and Archives Canada Cataloguing in Publication

Stuart, Sean Ryan
Das Haus: the house and the son of the rabbi: a novel /
written by Sean Ryan Stuart.
ISBN 978-0-9810246-4-6
1. Holocaust, Jewish (1939-1945)--Fiction. 2. World War,
1939-1945--Germany--Fiction. 3. World War, 1939-1945--Fiction.
4. Fascism--Fiction. I. Title. II. Title: House and the son of the rabbi.
PS3619.T8325H38 2008   813'.6   C2008-904570-X

The author wishes to thank Ryan Laughey for his assistance on the book cover.

Disclaimer: Although this book is partially based on real characters and events; the
characters as outlined in this novel are fictitious, and in no way represent living or
deceased individuals. An effort was made to include actual events and stories for
dramatic effect, but using fictitious stories and persons in the plot. This is a novel
partially based on true events. It is up to the reader to interpret what is real or fiction.

Extreme care has been taken to ensure that all information presented in this book is
accurate and up to date at the time of publishing. Neither the author nor the publisher
can be held responsible for any errors or omissions. Additionally, neither is any liability
assumed for damages resulting from the use of the information contained herein.

Publisher: CCB Publishing
             British Columbia, Canada
             www.ccbpublishing.com

Dedication

This book is dedicated to all of the victims of the Holocaust, and those who survived. I would also like to include my grandfather Adolfo, whom I never met, due to his untimely execution, and my five other uncles and aunts who perished due to Fascism and war.

In particular, I would like to remember my favorite uncle Rolando who recently passed away at the tender age of ninety. He unlike many victims never gave up and fought the Fascist in Spain and in North Africa during WWII. He was the bravest man I ever met.

Contents

Prologue

'DAS HAUS' is a story spanning over six decades, two continents, many tears, jeers and almost as many years. It is a story based on some "true events" and some real characters. Although the names, some locations and events have been fictionalized at the request of our main character Erik Goldmann (fictitious name), a majority of the Goldmann story is based on events, incidents and memories of those who participated in its story. Additionally some of my direct family members are still living in Das Haus, and in the past were threatened by current day neo-Nazis and their sympathizers. Erik Goldmann wishes to protect his family and the memory of the survivors of that long ago HOLOCAUST, known as WWII. Erik expressed direct concern about revealing his true identity.

I have in fact **changed** some of the story line to protect Erik, his family, my family and confidential sources. It is a sad event in our history, that sixty-two years after the end of WWII we still must fear the Nazis or their cohorts. While researching this book, members of my family and myself were threatened with death. Das Haus was burglarized on several occasions, and many of us had our cars vandalized by neo-Nazis or their friends.

Their favorite method of intimidation was to carve large swastikas on the hoods of our cars, scratch our paint and or destroy the car lights. Additionally, we would also receive mysterious and threatening phone calls. Soon after any vandalism took place, these hateful messages were left on our answering machines. They threatened to kill or injure us, if I did not stop my research. The German authorities were unable or unwilling to do anything about it. Ironically, one of the German police officers investigating one of these complaints was the son of the former Chief of Police who so heroically stood up to the Nazis sixty-nine years earlier.

The son was not cut from the same mold as the father. The German powers to be did not even take it seriously enough to

1

make an earnest attempt at trying to catch the perpetrators, nor to take a written report. They kissed it off with the following statement, "Ah, don't worry about it, it's just a bunch of hotheads, if they really wanted to harm you, you would be dead by now!" With that statement, I now understood the evil truth of what was really going on in modern Germany.

I was amazed at the amount of fear and apprehension still permeating throughout the village. I happened to be visiting my family in early November 2000, and I participated in a remembrance ceremony in front of the old burned down synagogue. I started taking pictures of the ceremony and was immediately asked to please stop taking photos by some of the older participants. Knowing that my presence there was not welcomed anyway, I stopped being so obvious, but still managed to get some good shots from a better and less obtrusive vantage point. I later spoke with one of the participants, and was told, "We don't like to have our pictures taken in front of the memorial, it might lead to trouble for us?" Stated the somewhat offish resident of Niedergeyer (fictitious).

Not wanting to insult my intelligence any further, I quietly disappeared in to the shadows, and observed from afar. Unfortunately it seemed that a new generation of bigots and quasi-Nazi sympathizers grew up where none existed before. Research on this book later revealed that **only** one-one hundredth of the eligible voters in Niedergeyer cast their vote for Adolph Hitler in 1933, when he first came to power. The only known Nazi was the future mayor of the village. Yet it appeared today that many more were either flirting with the right wing or openly supporting them. When I say right wing, I don't mean conservatives, I mean neo-fascists, fascists or their supporters.

I must quantify the word "many." My estimation of right-wing supporters is in the neighborhood of 10 percent of the adult population. In the age range of 15-32 years old; as many as 12-15 percent of the younger generation, were involved. Supplementary research indicated that many young adults from the former East-Germany were heavily involved in "Skinhead, and neo-Nazi organizations." It appears that those under the former communist regime were also willing to be Nazi sympathizers. This may not be a majority, but way too many for a country with Germany's checkered past.

A recent news report in 2007 by Fox News stated, "That as many as twenty-five percent of German citizens praised Hitler for some of his accomplishments such as the Autobahn system, family values, no unemployment etc. Another 18% somewhat supported the Nazis, but no mention was made of the Holocaust! Can it be that 43% of the population still supported or admired Hitler? These figures are amazingly high in the year of 2007?

There was a famous incident in the late 1970's or early 1980's involving a large bomb attack on the famous festivities at the Oktoberfest in Munich. A neo-Nazi group claimed credit for it, and its leader was later apprehended and jailed. He confessed to the German authorities; informing them of a large stash of weapons and munitions on the border to East Germany. The authorities allowed this individual to show them this alleged cache. While the police were digging a giant hole near the East German fence, a slow moving train just happened to come down the tracks, right along the East German border. This neo-Nazi waited until the train was parallel to him and ran across the train tracks, through the minefield, through the hidden automatic machine-guns and through an opening in the fence and escaped into East Germany.

West German authorities filmed it, but the East German government denied any knowledge of this incident. It was later discovered through informants, that the Russian KGB and East German STASI had in fact knowingly assisted him to escape. They wanted to embarrass the West German intelligence community and perhaps cause a major political rift in the government. This participation between opposite political spectrums was similar in nature to Stalin and Hitler's partition of Poland in 1939 and their alleged non-aggression pact.

However, I do strongly believe that many of the post WWII era inhabitants of this area have strong ties to the current wave of "Xenophobia" that permeates many European countries, particularly Germany and France. There have been horrible examples of anti-foreigner discrimination all over Europe, especially in Germany, Austria and France. This new form of Nazism is no less menacing than the old one. Many of today's Germans refuse to admit to this inherent Germanic problem. Even though the Nazi party is officially forbidden in modern day Germany, the NPD is an auxiliary legal party that holds many of the same common beliefs as the former Nazi party. In some German states they have achieved as many as 10-12% of all the votes cast, in both local and national election results.

These recent barbaric acts seem to be in stark contrast to the many brave and heroic deeds performed by the villagers of the 30's and 40's. It is of these brave souls and the Goldmann's that we will speak of. Although I am highly critical of many Germans of today's generation, I do not wish to be as "Xenophobic" as they are. Many of the villagers were and are very brave and courageous citizens. It is important to note that I have many friends and relatives who do not fit this "Xenophobic" mold, and in fact were very sympathetic and tried to help those who were oppressed by the Nazis.

I often wonder how I would have acted under similar circumstances? It is far easier to criticize than to relive the horrors they endured under Hitler. Most modern Germans are honest, hard working and socially democratic, however the other 10-12% are dangerous, evil and aggressive in nature. One has to only watch some of the large sporting events between Germany and some third world countries. Many of the banners and placards carried by German soccer fans are openly Xenophobic and racist in nature. It is also amazing to me that discrimination is legal in Germany! They can and do openly advertise; "Foreigners need not apply, Americans, Turks etc." These statements were often posted in newspaper ads, and journals.

This is why it is so important for me to tell this incredible story. A story of hate, fear, betrayal, gloom and misery. And yet sandwiched between those strong sentiments were desperate feelings of hope, heroism, love, honor, friendship and respect.

Every new development brought about a new and startling paradox in emotions and thoughts.

As a writer I initially objected to this form of novel writing. However after speaking with our main characters and thoroughly researching these events, Erik and the other participants convinced me to use this style of a **<u>novel</u>**. I agreed to their desires and altered the story just enough to protect his family wishes, the memories of a heroic father, his family and the victims of the Nazi holocaust.

I have written this book in the form of a **novel** based on some true events, liberally sprinkled with some Hollywood drama for effect. It is my hope that younger generations will not be so easily swayed from the path of rightfulness and justice. I do not wish to convey the idea that *all* events happened exactly as I described them. I am telling it as it was told to me; with some dramatic license to help it along when needed. One thing we must remember, this is **not** a trial that we are conducting, but the telling of a human tragedy and the rebirth of a courageous man.

Germany is a beautiful and majestic country to the casual tourist or observer, but deep in its subconscious lays a sleeping dragon waiting to once again wake up, and swallow Europe? Maybe not in the same context as WWI or WWII, but perhaps using political and economical might? A prime example of Germany's love with authority is the former East Germany, aka DDR. Their communistic form of government was even more repressive than their puppet-masters the Russians. The East Germans had more secret police agents and spies than the KGB. When the wall finally came down, over four million secret files were found on many West/East Germans, Americans and other NATO allies.

A warning must go out to all of those who flirt with these unhealthy and undemocratic ideals. The world is watching and we cannot allow a repetition of those past experiences.

Our story takes place in the 20th and 21st centuries, a time in which such horrors cannot and should not occur again, and yet, we see that in fact they come to pass, again, again and again. Some of the most recent example being the genocide committed against the

Muslim minorities in the Balkans and the horrors against the people of Kosovo, Kuwait, Iraq, Darfur Sudan, Lebanon (by Syria), Rwanda and especially the continuous attacks on Israel by the Hezbollah and Hamas terrorists supported in great part by Syria and especially Iran.

In fact one could say that the fanatic zeal of today's Islamic terrorists are reminiscent of yesterday's fascists. Large crowds all chanting in unison, preaching their twisted beliefs and calling for the deaths of Jews and Christian. It seems as if the world has forgotten the pre-WWII historical events leading up to the holocaust. Thank God that Israel is strong enough to defend itself. Hopefully we in America; will continue to support Israel.

This plot started over thirty-three years ago, when a young American, living and working in Germany, purchased an "old" house, Das Haus, in a small city in Germany, near the Belgium/Dutch border. At the time, he had no idea what he was getting himself into.

Das Haus had a way of growing on you, and as circumstances later developed, it became an obsession to find out what really happened to its original occupants. His first impression was not favorable. The once beautiful facade of the house had been severely damaged by hundreds of bullet and shell fragment holes. The sides of Das Haus were even worse; over twelve hundred bricks would have to be replaced during the renovation. Over two decades of research, work, agony and many tears finally led to a form of finality. A totality for some and not for others. No one, but the original Jewish inhabitants of Das Haus will ever know the truth. Das Haus was to become the house of death for all the Jewish inhabitants of that and many nearby villages. It was also the birthplace of freedom, courage and bravery for one heroic man, rabbi Franz Goldmann (Fictitious).

It was not the perfect answer to a very difficult question, but at least the discovery and location of our hero Erik Goldmann, made the effort worthwhile. My investigation led me to the Holocaust Museum in Washington D.C., and after many hours of research, I also found the final resting place of Rabbi Goldmann (fictitious name) in Izbica, Poland. Izbica was a sort of staging area used by the Nazis, until they could decide what to do with you. Some Jews were executed on the spot and never sent on to camps. The Nazis butchered Rabbi Goldmann, and thousands of others in 1942.

It was a very emotional, yet fulfilling moment in my life. To know that I had perhaps helped his son come to term with the loss of his brave father, a real hero.

I was later informed by Erik of his pilgrimage to Izbica, Poland and the feeling of relief he felt when he visited the spot where his father, a brave, honest and good man; was so viciously murdered by the Nazis. Strangely enough, we found no record of his beloved mother. She simply disappeared like so many others, never to be heard from again.

One of the many reasons that it took so long to locate Erik was the fact that he had slightly altered his name. If it had not been for the *Internet,* and its endless capabilities, I would probably still be looking for him. For obvious reasons, Erik also made very little effort in maintaining contact with anyone in that village.

The only exception was one individual, who has since passed away. That individual received an occasional phone call every five or ten years from Erik. In return he rarely kept in touch with Erik. Although boyhood friends, too much had happened for them to keep up an artificial friendship. However, this individual was instrumental in our final success, because he had a clue that led me to Erik.

This human being happened to be my now deceased father-in-law. Dieter, (fictitious) had been for many years the sole caretaker of the long forgotten Jewish cemetery in our village. He hoped that his small gesture would someday reunite long lost friends, and perhaps rekindle a kindred spirit of his youth. Although Dieter freely admitted to me having been a member of the Nazi party in his youth, he showed me a true and genuine interest in what happened to his Jewish friends. Some of his neighbors and friends chastised him, but he dutifully cared for the graves of the ancient Jewish inhabitants until his death.

Despite his gruff exterior, he had a heart of gold. Dieter at times risked his life by actually helping two French POW's escape Germany. They were able to make it back to France alive, and after the war became good friends. On another occasion he helped some shot down American flyers find their way to Belgium and freedom. His wealth and prominence protected him from those who did not agree with his views, and hopefully those lost Jewish souls will remember him kindly for his deeds.

It must be remembered that although some of the events are true, or based on events as told to me. I have altered it enough it to make it a novel based on partially true events by those involved in this epic drama. However the courageous Rabbi Goldmann, Erik and his family's valorous deeds are true, to the best of my knowledge.

Sean Ryan Stuart

'Das Haus' the house and the Son of the Rabbi

Chapter 1

The Beginning

Cameron Clark is sitting in his new F-250 Ford Heavy Duty Turbo Diesel pick-up and loving every moment of it. He is driving westbound on an extremely busy Highway 50 towards his home near Sacramento, California. Traffic this time of day is just awful in both directions, and just to make matters worst today, a westbound big-rig truck flipped on its side, spilling twenty-tons of tomatoes. This swamp of future spaghetti sauce has ground the afternoon traffic to a halt. One hundred-five degrees has turned the tomatoes into a red, gooey mess, which no one can escape from.

As Cameron sits in this quagmire of pollution and red contamination, he reflects on his 'New' truck. *There is something magic about the smell of a new vehicle,* he thinks to himself. *There is nothing quite like it. Many deodorizer manufacturers have attempted to duplicate that new smell, but without much success. The odor is almost addicting,* he thinks to himself. He is brought out of his daydream when a bright red Mustang cuts in front of him and slams on its brakes. This sudden maneuver forces him to do the same, and allowing Cameron to find an open lane. Before you can say 7.3 Liter Turbo Diesel, Cameron is cruising along at just under seventy-five miles an hour and listening to his favorite talk show host on KFBK AM 1530, Sacramento, California.

Listening to the afternoon news and talk shows had become a daily routine. As a freelance writer he had the opportunity to pretty much choose his subject matter, and he relied on this popular news station for many of his tips. However today, he had some interesting news for his family. Jerry Kunstoff, the Chief Editor and owner of the Sacramento Daily Recorder, a major local newspaper, and several other newspapers both in the USA and abroad. Jerry had hired Cameron to write a series of expose articles on the "New Germany." Could a "United New Germany" once again pose a threat to the world?

Sacramento and the surrounding communities had recently been the target of several right-wing/neo-Nazi attacks, and there was a strong belief by Jerry and the newspaper staff, that Nazi sentiments still existed in Germany, and perhaps they were the puppet masters to these many acts of hate and terrorism. Was there a worldwide conspiracy? Were some of the European, American or Muslim radicals somehow united? Was there an international plot? Were some of the prison gangs such as the Aryan Brotherhood, (AB), White Order, etc. also involved? Jerry was extremely interested in finding out and he knew that Cameron was his man. After all, Cameron has spent nearly four years "in country" and he was also married to a German girl.

Cameron's new assignment had many interesting facets to it. It was in a political arena, which greatly held his interest, and he only hoped that he was up to it. His entire prior career was going to be sorely tested by this assignment. Cameron had made an effort to keep his overseas contacts alive and he was convinced they might come in handy one day soon.

This new adventure reminded him of one of those WWII black and white propaganda films. The plot was usually very simple, a tough young reporter is sent to Berlin a few months prior to our entry into WWII. The hero is usually chased by a great film Nazi character, played by such notable actors as Basil Rathbone or Hans Conreid and chased throughout Germany. Of course there always is beautiful girl involved, and it all happily ends on the Swiss border, steps ahead of the evil Nazis. However in this plot, Cameron now had to be worried about his wife and daughter and the reality of our turbulent world.

Cameron was personally very excited, and extremely surprised that his new boss, Jerry Kunstoff, was as ebullient as he was. Jerry, a forty-year veteran in the journalism wars rarely got excited, but today, he was as nervous and feral as a virgin on her first romantic interlude. Cameron was happy to have the opportunity for this interesting and stimulating job. It had been a long time since he had such a rewarding position and he was bound and determined to make the most of it.

Chapter 2

The Discussion

After what seemed like an eternity, Cameron pulled into the driveway of his modest two-story home. The drive home tonight had been particularly hectic and longer than usual. Cameron lived in a fairly nice neighborhood and knew most of his neighbors on a first name basis. His stay at home job gave him the opportunity to know everyone on his block, and he took the advantage to develop acquaintances, and most important of all, time with his daughter Jennifer and wife Ingrid.

"Is that you honey?" Asked Ingrid, as he walked through the front door.

"Sure is. Who were you expecting? The mailman?" Replied Cameron, as he walked through the living room entrance towards the kitchen.

Cameron stopped between the living room and kitchen doorway and admired his wife from behind. *Ingrid was of good German stock,* he thought to himself, and she looked like she would be more at home on a farm, than a Bank Operations Manager. The years had been kind to her. However she was always very secretive about her exact age. When Cameron questioned her, she would become very defensive and say, "It's none of your business. My age is a secret." She would then make a joke of it and change the subject. Cameron always wondered why she was being so secretive, but he eventually accepted her coyness, and did not discuss it anymore.

When Cameron first met her in Germany forty-years earlier she had been a tall buxom statuesque blonde. Despite having Jennifer late in life, and a very busy life; both at work and home, she had not gained more than twenty pounds in the past four decades. She was still very beautiful, athletic looking and Cameron was delighted in his wife's vigor and good looks.

Ingrid took the news of their upcoming trip with both joy and trepidation. On one hand she was very happy to see her family again, but on the other hand she hated to leave her home in Dixon. It had taken many years to decorate and landscape their yard in such a way that she was the envy of the neighborhood. *Starting all over again in Germany would be difficult for her*, she thought. And yet the excitement of returning to her **Heimat** (Homeland) excited her more than she expected.

Although born and raised in Germany, she had married Cameron in her early twenties and spent most of her adult life in California; except for her semi-annual trips to the **Vaterland**. Cameron and Ingrid never really discussed politics, but Cameron could tell that she was very proud of her Germanic ancestry.

Dixon had become her new home and she was positive that her daughter would greatly miss being taken out of school. Jennifer was actively involved in her school and in the community. Ingrid expected that this assignment would not last more than a year or two, and they could always lease out heir home for the twelve or twenty-four months, during their absence.

When Ingrid first met Cameron, while he was serving as a young military intelligence officer in Germany, he had told her that there would be times when their lives could be uprooted on a moments notice, and I guess this was one of them.

Cameron's daughter Jennifer like most teenagers was very unhappy. Not only because she did not want to leave her friends behind in Dixon, but over the past seventeen years, Jennifer had become very popular, and did not want to leave just now. She had finally made the cheer leading squad and was really looking forward to the football season, and especially spending time with her new puppy love, James "Jimmy" Prepp, the star running back of the football team. Jimmy was the most gifted athlete in the school's history and was by teenage girl standards a dreamboat.

Jimmy was six-foot tall, muscular and quite intelligent. He had every major college and university hot on his trail with football scholarships. Jennifer was devastated at the thought of losing him.

It was her first true love and she was not about to lose him! She thought of devious plots in order to escape her dreaded trip to Germany.

It is easy to understand why young families moved to this community. Dixon is and was a small bedroom community on the outskirts of Sacramento. However it is near enough to the Bay Area and Silicon Valley to make it worthwhile for the diehard commuter.

Ingrid sat in the living room reflecting on their upcoming move and hoped that their decision would be a wise one. There was so little time left and so much to do. Ingrid knew that Jennifer would be her toughest challenge and she feared it the most. Deep in thought, *Ingrid drifted off and thought about her happy childhood in Germany.*

Just then, a very angry and upset teenager stormed into their house and yelled at the top of her voice.

"I am not going to any 'Fricken' Germany! No way, and you can't make me! I am not a little child anymore. I have rights too!" Stated a rather angry, distraught and emotional Jennifer.

Her young face was beet red. Her mascara ran down her cheeks, and giant teardrops cascaded down her face. Ingrid had never seen her daughter so upset.

Both her parents stared at her in disbelief. Jennifer had never used that kind of language, or for that matter any fervent outbursts of that sort. She had always been a rather shy and quiet child; both parents were taken by surprised. Neither one of them knowing what to say, until Cameron attempted to reply.

"First of all young lady, you owe us an apology? I am sorry you are so upset, but my job requires me to go." Answered Cameron.

"Your mother and I did not raise you to behave in this manner! We can understand that you have issues, but I am sure we can work them out? What do you think, Jenny?" Stated Cameron once again with a little more authority in his voice. Jenny was the name he used when she had done something wrong.

Jenny turned and glared at him. Not knowing what to say or

do. Her eyes darted back and forth.

"How could you do this to me, without even asking me? I am not a child!" She stuttered, clenching her fists as she did so.

"I had to find out from Jerry's daughter, Donna at school!" She continued as large tears ran down her face.

His attempt to placate his daughter did not achieve the effect he wanted, because Jenny ran upstairs to her room. All the way screaming and crying, "I hate you, I hate you both of you!"

Both parents stood there in shock and amazement and tried to gather their thoughts together before they had another confrontation with her.

"Well what do you think, Ingrid? How do we handle it? I think its time for a deep mother to daughter talk, don't you?" Stated a confused Cameron, with a sly grin on his face.

"Sure, sure. You cause the trouble and leave little poor me to solve your mess!" Quipped Ingrid, as she slowly walked up the stairs towards her daughter's bedroom.

The mother and daughter talk did not go as well as she would of liked. Her daughter was in no mood to listen or understand what her mother was saying. All she knew was that she was being torn away from everything and everyone she loved. Mrs. Clark tried in vain to console her distraught daughter, but nothing helped. Ingrid ran out of the room and begged Cameron to come and help her. After all she reasoned this was all Cameron's fault, and he should take care of the problem.

"I need your help! She won't listen to me at all! Maybe you can manage to do it. I am giving up for now! She is just like you, stubborn, stubborn and stubborn!" Yelled an upset and angry Ingrid, as she ran out of the room.

Cameron went upstairs and spent the better part of an hour calming his daughter down. It took every bit of negotiating skill he had to come up with an armistice between them. It was agreed that she would be able to spend two months of her vacation in California, and her boyfriend would be able to visit her twice a year. She eventually understood, how important it was for Cameron to go and work in Germany!

"Let me make sure I understand? You are going to allow me to visit California twice a year? And you are going to pay for it? In addition to that, you are going to allow my boyfriend to visit me? As long as you keep your promise, I will go with you to Germany." Stated a much calmer Jennifer.

Chapter 3

The Adventure Begins

As Cameron prepared to enter his editors' inter-sanctum a series of brilliant and vivid flashbacks appear before his eyes. He reflected on everything he knew about *Jerry Kunstoff: Jerry is an old-timer by any standard, and is a veteran of over fifty-years of journalism. Both as a writer-journalist, and as an anchorperson for some of the major networks around the world. His assignments have covered every part of the known world, and some that were not that well known. He had traveled extensively in the past five decades, and covered more than a dozen major wars. On at least two occasions Jerry Kunstoff was severely wounded and barely made it out alive. As a matter of fact, he was once shot in the head by a Vietminh sniper, while covering France's Indochina debacle in 1954. He now proudly wears the crease on his skull as his "Red Badge of Courage."*

Cameron knocks loudly on the door and no one responds. He knocks a second time, and a gruff sounding voice bellows from the other side.

· "What do you want? If it's not important, don't bother me."

Not waiting for any further instructions, Cameron walks in. Although small in stature, a mere five-foot four in his socks, Jerry could party with the best, and had a command presence in many ways reminiscent of an Edward G. Robinson tough guy character. Perhaps it was the ever-present large cigar in his mouth that reminded him of Robinson or USAF General, Curtis LeMay.

"So you finally showed up? Where have you been all morning?" Asked a somewhat grumpy Jerry.

"Excuse me, sir? But you said to be here at nine-o'clock sharp and it's only eight-forty-five." Replied Cameron, a slight tone of amazement in his trembling voice.

Once the initial jousting was over between both men, they sat down to business. Jerry was very specific in what he wanted out of Cameron and wished to make sure there were no misunderstandings between them. Jerry was able to provide Cameron with an initial list of leads and references, but also expected Cameron to come up with his own clues and above all, be creative and flexible. After several hours of further discussion, both men felt more comfortable with their future development of this story.

"Don't forget Cameron, you are representing me and my paper in Germany. I am a ninety percent stockholder in that newspaper and I expect them to give you all the help you need. While you are there, you are the acting manager. Is that understood?" Stated Jerry, in a gruff voice.

"Tell me Cameron, have you decided how you are going to get to Germany?" Asked Jerry as he slowly twisted his cigar in his yellow stained, stumpy fingers.

"I will probably fly nonstop to Cologne airport. Ingrid and Jennifer can join me in a week or two, once everything is settled at home." Replied Cameron.

"I want you to get started as soon as possible, and please keep me informed at least twice a week of any new or exciting developments." Stated Jerry as he stood up and extended his hand.

"It's a deal. I promise you Jerry; we are going to get a great story and maybe even a book out of it? What do you think?" Replied Cameron as he walked out the room towards the outer office.

"I would be delighted with a book, but let's first concentrate on this story. One thing at a time." Replied Jerry as he bent over his desk and pressed the intercom.

"Miss Harris, would you please give Cameron his salary advance on the way out." Asked Jerry to the still silent black box.

"Of course Mr. Kunstoff, I will be glad to." Replied Gladys Harris, head administrative assistant to Jerry Kunstoff. Gladys was a short and squatty fifty something brunette. What she had lost in good looks, she made up in efficiency and discipline.

As Cameron walked out into the outer office, Gladys reached into her right-hand drawer and withdrew a large eight by eleven manila envelope. She handed Cameron two hundred one hundred dollar bills, a receipt to sign and a set of written instructions on how to apply for more spending money when needed. He silently counted the money and signed the receipt for her. He had never held that kind of cash in his hand at one time. At least money that he could have direct access to and spend on a project.

Cameron drove home thinking about the future, his family and what lay ahead of him in the next twelve months. He was so embroiled in his thoughts that he didn't even notice the time and drove by the first exit to his house. He concentrated a little more and managed to hit the next one on the button.

His wife Ingrid had made him a wonderful spaghetti dinner and he could already smell the garlic bread as he walked in the house. Ingrid had cleaned the house, put flowers on the table and had a great smile on her face.

"Wie Gehts, schatzie?" (How are you sweetie?) She said in German.

"Gut und selbts?" (Fine and you) Replied Cameron, looking at her oddly and wondering why after all these years, she spoke German to him again.

"I guess we should start practicing German again, what do you think?" Answered back Ingrid in English this time.

The rest of the evening was spent discussing their travel plans, their daughter's attitude and how best to lease their home. Inge had a very strong opinion about the Germans, and how they were treated after the war. She felt the Allies were unduly harsh with the German population. Whenever Cameron brought up the subject, there was a price to pay, and he was not up for it tonight.

Cameron wondered, *"whether or not she had already notified her parents of their upcoming trip?"*

"Ingrid? Have you spoken to your parents yet?" He asked Ingrid.

"Do you think this is the kind of news that one withholds from ones parent?" Replied Ingrid, her eyes smiling at Cameron.

"No, I guess not. I hoped to talk to your dad first and sort of feel him out about us staying with him, until we found a place." Replied Cameron.

"Cameron was surprised by the fact that his wife had not inquired as to his exact duties in Germany. Normally she would have asked numerous questions, but her short notice left her occupied with a million things to do, and it probably slipped her mind," he thought to himself. *Maybe it was better this way, just ignore the whole thing and she might not get angry with him?*

Cameron was successful in dodging the bullets, and actually managed to maintain a truce with both of the females in his life. His daughter was quieter now, but still prone to outbursts of hysterics, and his wife was actually looking forward to returning to her **Vaterland** (Homeland).

Cameron went about his business and within seventy-two hours he was all set to fly to Germany. His trip over was very uneventful, and the fact that he was flying first-class made it even more pleasurable. Lufthansa airlines had a sterling reputation and this trip was no exception. He arrived almost exactly eleven hours after leaving San Francisco International. Cologne (Köln) airport was one of the smaller airports in that part of Germany, but could on occasion be very convenient for the savvy traveler. Cameron had not wanted to disturb his father-in-law and rented a large BMW 740i sedan from the local Hertz counter. Traffic at that time of the day was very light and he managed to get on the northbound Autobahn 3 towards Aachen and the Dutch border. It took Cameron a few minutes to re-acquaint himself again with German driving style.

Drive as fast as you car will take you! No speed limit on the autobahn was something Cameron would have to master again. It was rather unnerving to be driving at one hundred-twenty mile an hour and have someone pass you at one hundred-fifty!

By the time he pulled alongside the city of Kerpen, he was doing just fine, and his BMW was humming along with the best of them. The distance from the airport to his father-in-laws house was around eighty miles, and he pulled in the driveway in less than fifty-minutes! Cameron found himself enjoying the excitement of the autobahn, however he always maintained a safe distance and did not drive too fast in inclement weather. Unlike most Germans who drove fast in any weather!

Chapter 4

Wilkommen
Welcome

Cameron pulled up to the driveway and admired Dieter's house. It was exactly as he had remembered it. Large, spacious and meticulously maintained.

"Hello." Shouted Dieter Johannes from the upstairs window.

Cameron got out of his car and walked the three steps towards the front door. He waved to Dieter as he did so. Dieter's home was built on a large corner lot near the woods. It was obvious that a rich man lived there. Compared to some the older homes in the neighborhood, it stood out and was in show room condition. His father-in-laws house was a beautiful modern two-story stone house. Dieter was a well-known architect and he had built his home to include a nice size office on the first floor. Dieter Johannes was a successful and well-respected architect in that part of northern Germany. Over the years he had come to specialize in restoring, building, remodeling old castles, churches, convents and hospitals for the Catholic church of Germany. His youngest son Peter and daughter Lizbet also worked in his office. They had both recently graduated from the university and hoped someday to take over the business.

Dieter opened the door and hugged Cameron so violently that he nearly passed out from the embrace. Dieter was by no means a large man, he stood five-foot ten and weighed a solid two hundred and ten pounds. However, even though he was in his late-seventies, he had the physique of a much younger man. He was built more like a fullback than an architect. Dieter had played soccer his whole life and had the legs of a weight lifter.

Cameron exhaled and stated, "Wow, Dieter! Please don't kill me, I just got here."

"I am sorry Cameron, I was so happy to see you again!" Exclaimed a joyous Dieter.

"How are my daughter and grandchild?" Stated Dieter without missing a beat.

"Just fine and they will be here in a few weeks. Ingrid and Jennifer will be flying out as soon as we lease our home in Dixon. Meanwhile, if you don't mind, I will be your guest until they arrive and we get ourselves situated here." Replied Cameron.

"Ja naturlich." (Yes, of course) Replied Dieter in German.

"I am sorry Cameron, do you still speak German?" Asked an inquisitive Dieter.

"Klar! Dieter." (Of course! Dieter) Replied Cameron in a matter of what tone.

"It's like riding a bicycle, once you get the hang of it, you will never forget how to pedal." Continued Cameron, trying to use the occasion to regain his composure and breath.

Just then an ebullient and lovely Kate walked in. Kate was a statuesque six-foot tall brunette. Although in her late-seventies, she still was a beautiful if introverted woman. Kate was a few years older than her husband, and never let him forget it. Dieter had married her during WWII and they had produced five beautiful children. Kate was a very talented chemist and worked for a giant German industrial concern in the field of toxic research. Although way past retirement age, she loved her work and still worked two days a week. Kate greeted Cameron in a friendly manner, but did not seem to be as happy as Dieter to see him. Cameron had always wondered why Kate was not as forthcoming as the rest of the family. He assumed that it was merely a reflection of her personality and left it at that.

Dieter showed him his guest room and made him at ease. Cameron unpacked and lay down on the bed. It did not take long for him to pass out on his extremely comfortable bed. His long trip and strenuous drive had exhausted him. He quickly fell into a deep sleep.

The next morning, fourteen hours later, Cameron woke up to the smell of good German coffee and freshly baked bread.

Cameron quickly showered and walked downstairs to the warm and friendly kitchen.

"Guten Tag." (Good morning) said Cameron. He was almost immediately answered with a chorus of "Guten Tag, Cameron."

"Well, I slept like a dead person. I was so tired, I did not even have a dream last night." replied Cameron, as he sat down to the table.

Kate had made several loaves of fresh bread, and everyone was greedily wolfing down the delicious bread and coffee. Cameron stared across the table and saw that only two of the kids were still there. Both Peter and Lizbet were eagerly eating their breakfast. They greeted Cameron, but seemed more interested in finishing their meal. Cameron enthusiastically joined them and quickly finished his meal. After breakfast, Dieter invited Cameron into his office and happily exclaimed, "I hope you don't mind if I get involved in your business, but I knew that Ingrid would feel more comfortable in her own house, and I started looking around for you?"

Cameron asked? "What do you mean?"

"Well, as you can imagine there are not many homes for sale in our village. There is actually only one house on the main street for sale. Das Haus is near the northern part of the village and has over three acres of land for sale. The house itself is fairly new by Niedergeyer standards, it's only one hundred-ten years old. However, it was heavily damaged in the last war, and it also has a very interesting history." Stated a smiling Dieter, as he looked at Cameron.

"Well Dieter, it sounds like a good idea, but I cannot possibly decide to buy anything without Ingrid being here? That would be tantamount to committing suicide." Replied Cameron, as he slowly put his index finger to his forehead and pretended to pull the trigger.

"Yes, I know what you mean, but the owners want to sell immediately due to health reasons, and the property might not be for sale by the time Ingrid gets here. We have to act quickly. Why don't you call her after we go and visit the property today?"

Asked Dieter.

"As a matter of fact, if you guys don't buy it, I might just buy myself." Said Dieter, as he stood up.

"OK, I don't have a problem with that, but I know Ingrid. I doubt if she will agree to buy anything without being here, but I can try. After all, we are not planning on staying more than a year or two, and I don't know whether or not we should buy a house." Replied a somewhat skeptical Cameron.

"*Ja,* OK Cameron. Let me call them and make an appointment for later on this afternoon. You guys can decide after you have seen the house." Stated Dieter as he picked up the phone.

"OK, everything is set for this afternoon at three. I think you will like it, although it will take some work to make it ready for you." Answered Dieter as he put the phone down and stared at Cameron.

"What do you mean work? Asked a curious Cameron.

"The house was damaged during the war, and it needs some modernization. A new roof, heating system, three new bathrooms, kitchen, insulation throughout, painting, windows, a new entry way, landscaping, but other than that, it's a great bargain!" Replied Dieter with a smile.

"OK, but that sounds like a whole bunch of work? Don't you think?" Asked Cameron, his mind racing to imagine the condition of the house.

"No, are you kidding? This property is the only one on the main street, and it has a beautiful view of the hills behind the house. It has over twenty fruit trees and a cellar. They only want one hundred and fifty thousand dollars! Can you believe that? If we don't act soon it will be gone, and you will be sorry. Don't worry, I will help you get it in shape, and for another sixty or eighty thousand, you will have a home worth five or six hundred thousand dollars, maybe even more? I am confident we can get all the work done in less than three months." Stated a confident Dieter.

"Well, since you put it that way. I guess, I will have to accept your recommendation and speak with Ingrid." Cameron thanked

Dieter and called his wife Ingrid.

After an extensive conversation with Ingrid, he finally got the approval to make a deposit on the home, but she insisted on having the final remodeling and decorating choices. Cameron was amazed at the fact that she had agreed. Usually, Ingrid was very set in her ways and not so easily convinced to do things without extensive research and investigation. Later that afternoon Dieter drove Cameron to Das Haus. As Dieter slowly drove up the main street of Niedergeyer, Cameron could not help but wonder about the history of this very ancient village. The village could trace its roots to the Roman era around 100 A.D. The Romans had installed a large brick and pottery factory in the village. The VII Roman Legion built a fort in the village and it remained there for several hundred years. They had even imported grapes and grew them for wine. As a matter of fact one could still see the wild vines growing in the woods today.

The village consisted of many very old *"Fachwerk"* style homes (massive oak beams for framing and filled in with mud, straw and twigs. One Catholic church, five pubs, a bakery, grocery store and butcher shop, and not much else. Many of the homes had large metal numbers affixed to the front of their doors showing when they were built. Cameron was amazed at the dates, 1472, 1561, 1611, 1727 etc. It seemed as if the average age of a home was around the sixteenth century. The church was actually built around the tenth century and there was one building still standing that was even older. He could not help but notice the numerous bullet holes and shell fragments which still adorned many of the homes.

Dieter and Cameron finally drove past the last curve on the main street and he immediately noticed Das Haus.

It was an imposing structure. Three stories high, plus an attic for good measure. It had that typical late nineteenth century style. It was called the, *"Luetische"* (Liege, Belgium) style. It somewhat resembled a Victorian home, but it had an ornate three-dimensional carved front of poured cement. The facade of the house, which paralleled the main street, had been severely damaged by large caliber machine gun fire (probably .50 Caliber) and mortars. Many of the ornate cement animal head carvings had been shot away or damaged. The sides of the house were made of bricks; they also bore many scars of war and conquest. Cameron could immediately see how this home had been an important fortress. It was the tallest building in the village, and was at the junction of three roads leading away from the village. From the attic, one could see 360 degrees in all directions. *It would have been a great observation point for an artillery observation post,* he thought to himself.

Cameron looked at the structure and was immediately struck by an immediate feeling of sadness and terror. He could not understand this strange emotion, but it bothered him. As his eyes moved across the impressive building, his view became fixated on the bottom floor, where large windows faced the main street. He suddenly thought he saw the face of a young man; with sad eyes staring at him through the bottom left front window. The boy's eyes had a haunting quality about them and it unnerved him. As suddenly as he had seen him, the boy vanished without a trace. Cameron was about to ask Dieter about the boy, when Dieter unexpectedly slammed on his brakes and parked on the main street across from Das Haus. Before Cameron could utter another word, Dieter was already out of the car and walking across the street.

They went around the large brick wall, which separated the courtyard from the sidewalk. Dieter knocked on the old and well-worn door. No one answered. Dieter tried again, and after two or three minutes, the door slowly creaked open. An extremely old and pale looking gentleman looked up at them. He could not have been more than five-foot two and weighed a maximum of one hundred and ten pounds. His hands were trembling and he had the look of a man who was already dead, but did not know it yet.

"*Ja,* what can I do for you." He stammered.

"Ah, hello Herr Johannes, I am glad to see you. This must be your son-in-law." He said, as he extended his scrawny white hands.

Cameron stepped forward and shook his hand, but made it a

point to take it easy on the old man. The hand was withered, pale and trembling. The old man, Herr Jacobi, was of slight build, bald and smelled like a rotten piece of Brie. His odor was so repugnant that it was physically uncomfortable to be near him. Cameron had never in his life smelled a more vile and disgusting individual. Herr Jacobi, for some unknown reason, was unable to look Cameron in the eye. As if he was somewhat aware of his body odor, and could not do anything about it.

Dieter stepped around Cameron and also shook the old man's hand. Dieter led the way in the darkened musty hallway and Cameron followed behind. Cameron had a difficult time seeing in this somewhat somber environment. It reminded Cameron of a black and white vampire movie. There were no visible lights, and the only means of illumination was a small shaft of light pushing through the dirty and stained glass window above the door.

Herr Jacobi slowly walked through the house; showing them every room. Cameron was somewhat amazed at the condition Herr Jacobi was living in. There was garbage, broken furniture, unopened boxes, junk, filth and stacks of old magazines throughout the house etc. Cameron had never seen a more disgusting and soiled abode in his life. Cameron thought to himself, *I am glad Ingrid is not here, she would never buy this rattrap.*

Dieter stopped and looked at Cameron.

"I know what you are thinking, but don't worry, I guarantee that we will have this home in a good condition by the time Ingrid comes here. Many skilled workers owe me favors, and I will pull a few strings." Stated Dieter, in off-handed sort of way.

"OK, I will take your word for it." Replied Cameron, as both men walked out of the house. Cameron was still haunted by the face of the small boy in the window, he stopped Dieter in the middle of the street and asked him.

"Dieter, who was that small boy, I saw in the window when we first drove up to the house?" Asked a curious Cameron.

"I think your imagination got the best of you my friend. And don't listen to any of those old wives tales about ghosts and evil spirits." Replied Dieter, as he walked over to his car, and got in. Cameron decided to drop the subject, maybe the sunlight played tricks or he was just imagining.

Both men had inspected Das Haus and left after an hour of thorough investigation. Dieter was convinced that he could restore this ancient home into a beautiful and cozy residence for his daughter. As they drove back to his house, Dieter told Cameron about his remodeling plans for Das Haus. Cameron on the other hand was not as sure that this was such a good idea, but was willing to give Dieter the opportunity to prove him wrong. After all Dieter had restored hundreds of old buildings in worst condition than Das Haus.

Cameron's mind now shifted to his current work assignment and hoped it would not be challenging as the restoration of Das Haus.

For the rest of the day, his thoughts were solely on his assignment and his first day at work. The excitement he felt was comparable to the first day of school. That sour queasy feeling in the pit of your stomach. No matter how hard he tried, that feeling would not go away. He hoped that his new colleagues were forthcoming and not to upset that an American would be their new boss.

Chapter 5

"Arbeit Macht Frei"
Work Will Set You Free
*(Quotation often seen at the
entrance to concentration camps)*

Cameron woke early, unable to sleep. The excitement and strangeness of the previous day had left him somewhat uneasy. Yet it stimulated him to the possibility of purchasing this new home, Das Haus. He only hoped that Ingrid would be as excited as he was. After all he thought to himself, *women are more sensitive to these types of things and may not see the mystery of it all.*

He glanced at his watch and noticed it was only five forty-five a.m. Cameron was sure that his office staff would not be at work this early in the morning. Germans were very punctual individuals, but not that punctual. He took his time while showering and dressing, and eventually wandered down to the kitchen by six-thirty. Both Dieter and Kate were already up and drinking coffee, their favorite pastime it seemed. He sat down at the table and joined them for breakfast, and ate in silence. Eventually Cameron broke the silence by asking Dieter for directions to his office in Aachen.

"No problem Cameron, I know exactly where it is. Just take the Europaplatz exit and follow it down to the intersection of Bismarckplatz. If you look to the right, you will see a four story modern yellow building. Your office is actually on the third floor and it faces the main square." Answered Dieter in a matter fact tone.

"Thank you, Dieter. I am sure I will be able to find it without problems. I think I will be leaving shortly." Replied Cameron as he got up and walked out to his car.

The trip to Aachen took around forty minutes. Cameron was

once again flabbergasted at the speed of the average German commuter, somewhere around one hundred and twenty miles an hour. Cameron knew he would have to practice high speed driving techniques again, because the Germans showed no mercy for unsuspecting Americans, they would simply be brushed aside like General Rommel going through El Alamein in North Africa.

Cameron found a convenient parking spot near the Kaufhof store and hoped it would be OK to park there all day. He glanced at his watch and noticed that it was only seven-thirty. He grabbed his attaché case and walked over to his office. *The building itself appeared to be of modern construction, but was actually over a hundred years old,* he thought to himself. The other tenants were mostly insurance companies, law firms or so they appeared to him. Cameron took the elevator to the third floor, and as he exited the elevator, he immediately noticed the doublewide glass door of his office, **Aachener Freies Blatt** (Aachen Free Press) was boldly emblazoned in three inch high letters across the center of the door. Jerry Kunstoff's name was boldly painted on the side of the door.

No question as to who owned it, Cameron thought.

He walked in and was immediately surprised at the modern décor of the place. The front lobby was right out of a Scandinavian furniture store. Pale colors and pine furniture everywhere. However, other parts of the office were less modern and were more baroque. Towards the back of the room, sat a majestic woman. She was by any standards extremely tall, and when she stood up she appeared to be at least six-foot three. Frau Rausching wore a navy blue suit and wore her hair on a bun, which even made her look taller. *She was by no means skinny, hardy German stock.* Cameron thought to himself.

"Guten Tag, Herr Clark." boomed a smiling Frau Rausching as he entered the office. Her English was impeccable, although a trace of Oxford grammar punctuated her sentences.

"Guten Tag to you, Frau Rausching." He answered as he approached her desk. Cameron extended his hand towards her and she took it like a fullback running for a touchdown. Her grip was extremely powerful and her stare even more so.

It took Cameron a few seconds to recover from this wrestling experience. He politely bowed and withdrew his crushed right hand from her deadly grip. *Wow! I am sure Frau Rausching wrestles professionally,* he smiled deep in thought. The images of a six foot three, two hundred plus woman in tights rushed through his mind like a derailed freight train.

"I am glad to see that you are early, Frau Rausching. I have many things to discuss, and I would like to get started as soon as possible." Stated an obviously confident Cameron.

"I am equally happy to see that you are also punctual, Herr Clark. One hears such unpleasant work ethic comments about Americans, and I am happy to see that they are not true." Replied Frau Rausching in a snickering sort of way.

Cameron was a little dismayed at her comment, but decided not to take it too seriously right now. He would have plenty of opportunity to put her in her place in the near future. Frau Rausching walked Cameron to his new office, and politely informed him of the office regulations. Cameron listened attentively, without interrupting her and finally decided he had heard enough of her bullying.

"Frau Rausching, you must understand that my assignment in this office is only temporary. However, as long as I am here, you will try to follow my protocol. Jerry Kunstoff has given me the ultimate authority to run this office as I see fit, is that understood, Frau Rausching?" Stated a somewhat displeased Cameron.

His tone of voice and mannerisms obviously caught her by surprise. It was not very often that anyone dared to talk to her in that manner. She quietly reflected his demeanor, but decided that discretion was the better part of valor. She quietly smiled and bowed her head, as she walked out of the room. Cameron realized that Frau Rausching would be a hand full, but he had won the first battle. The next few hours were a series of interruptions as various staff members came in to introduce themselves during the morning hours. There was Fraulein Ziggerman, a thirty- something good-looking woman with brunette hair. Beate as all her colleagues knew her, had a catching smile and a face full of freckles. Her charming personality was contagious, and her work ethic unsurpassed by anyone.

Hans Guenther Froemer was the kid of the group. He was barely twenty-two, and yet pretended to be much older. He was a university student, majoring in 'Journalism', and spent his non-academic time working for a living. One member of the staff was missing today; Reiner Devries was the senior editor, but had gone to Mallorca Spain, for a much needed vacation. According to all, he was the backbone of the office, and was sorely missed by all. Reiner had recently divorced his wife of fifteen years. In Germany where the 'No Fault Divorce Law' was invented, a vacation was the best thing for any male caught up in such a horrendous financial dilemma. Cameron was extremely unhappy about Reiner's absence, but they had to get started as soon as possible. Cameron asked the not so friendly Frau Rausching to get the staff together.

They all met in the official conference room, which was at the end of the office. It was in sharp contrast to the modern decor in the inner office. Cameron was instantly amazed at the magnificent adornments and opulence of this large meeting room. It had no resemblance to the rest of the building. It was right out of the nineteenth century. Heavy oak panels covered the entire room from floor to ceiling. They not only looked expensive, but permeated an aura of nobless and royalty. A huge Austrian crystal chandelier hung from the ornate twenty-foot high ceiling. It was so lavish that it appeared to be made out of diamonds instead of cut crystal.

At the northern end of the conference room hung a giant portrait of an elderly man beaming down on everyone in the room. A large figure of a man no doubt, his physical dimensions were only surpassed by his beautiful enormous gray handlebar mustache.

This lustrous facial appendage dominated his entire face, and the portrait as well. One could tell that the painter put a great deal of effort into this most telling feature.

Beate noticed Cameron intently staring at the painting and said.

"Herr Clark, that you are staring at is Herr Doktor Willhem Von Struebenz, the original owner and Direktor of our company circa 1929."

"Thank you Beate, I am glad to know. For a moment there I had a feeling the old gentleman was not happy to see me in this room." Replied Cameron in a half joking manner.

"Well I am sure he would not be happy if he knew the real purpose of our engagement." Answered Beate as she sat down next to Cameron.

"What do you mean?" Asked Cameron in an inquisitive manner.

"Herr Doktor Willhem Von Struebenz was the Nazi Gauleiter (Nazi political leader for that region) for Kreiss Aachen and a very dedicated party official from 1934 until his untimely death in 1945." Replied Beate pointing her finger towards the old gentleman.

"It's nice to know, but his evil puss is not going to change our mission!" Stated Cameron with emphasis. The room suddenly grew quiet as they all sat down.

Cameron began his presentation with an outline of their respective assignments, as he understood it. His outline and the many questions kept the meeting going until well into the late afternoon. After all was said and done, he felt comfortable with his staff and their respective assignments. Cameron was amazed at the length it took to brief them and what was expected of them. He had been so intense that they had skipped lunch all together, and the workday was nearly over. He let everyone go an hour early and apologized for his tardiness.

Cameron stayed behind and wrapped up the rest of his paper work. There was one more thing he had to do before he left the office. He walked over to the conference room, and slowly opened the door. He turned on the light and once again stared at the portrait of the old man. Herr Doktor Willhem Von Struebenz glared down from his lofty perch. By then, he was the only one left, and the office was deserted. *No witnesses*, he thought to himself. Cameron slowly raised his middle finger, in an act of defiance. This infantile and rude gesture had somehow made him feel much better. At least the old goat knew, who the real boss was now.

The drive home took a little longer than expected. Traffic was pretty fierce today, until he reached the Dueren exit. Once he got on the main **Landstrasse** (highway) towards the **Eifel** region, traffic slowed down, and the rest of the trip was pretty uneventful. He pulled up in front of Dieter's front door at around seven fifteen. Dieter and Kate were waiting for him. She had prepared a great German dinner and was dying to show off her culinary skills. In fact, Cameron had never tasted a better Goulash beef stew and noodles. The noodles were hand made and added to the incredible taste of the dish. Even his wife Ingrid's cooking, paled to Kate's cuisine. She had obviously spent a great deal of time on this sumptuous meal.

They all ate their meal in absolute silence. It seemed as if noise of any kind would somehow disturb their enjoyment and ruin their evening delight.   Dieter brought out a couple of bottles of **Spaetlase** (late bloom) sweet Moselle region wines. These vintage wines added to the absoluteness of this meal. In addition, Kate had baked a beautiful **Apfeltorte** (Apple cake) to finish off this one in a lifetime dinner. Although the meal was consumed in silence, there was a great deal of chatter afterwards. Both men complimented Kate and asked her if she wanted to join them in the living room for an after dinner drink. Kate thanked the men, but declined. She could not stand the smell of cigars, and she knew that her husband could not drink brandy, without smoking a stogie.

Dieter went to his bar and opened a bottle of German brandy. **Asbath Uhralt** was its name, and it was one of the better brands in Germany. After a couple double shots, both men mellowed out to the point of almost falling asleep. Eventually, Dieter brought up the conversation around to Das Haus. He started to tell Cameron about the historical, political and religious significance of his future new home. Das Haus was more than just a mere stack of stones, bricks and paint, explained Dieter to an exhausted Cameron.

"It is probably the most important house in our village." explained Dieter as he stood up from his comfortable chair.

"That is a pretty strong statement Dieter. Give me some more details." Asked Cameron.

Dieter started to tell him an incredible, but true story of a Jewish family tragedy. The story was all about the Goldmann family, and some of the other Jewish inhabitants, who inhabited Niedergeyer and the surrounding villages.

"Did you know that I was Erik Goldmann's best friend? I played soccer with him for many years? Erik was the best soccer player in our region. We were in kindergarten together and stayed friends, and close buddies until the day he was sent to Buchenwald. I knew him for over thirteen years." Stated Dieter in a mournful kind of way.

Cameron did not answer at first, but shook his head. Dieter paused for a few seconds; then continued with renewed vigor and determination. He hoped that Cameron would show some interest in this amazing saga.

Initially Cameron was somewhat jaded, but as Dieter continued to expand his tale, his interest grew. Dieter was a great storyteller and managed to capture Cameron's attention.

"This is a great story, incredible and fascinating. Who would ever thought that such an unbelievable event would have taken place in this little village? Who else knows about these events?" Asked a curious Cameron.

"Well, some of the villagers who are still living will remember the Goldmann family. But no one knows all the details like I do." Stated an obviously proud Dieter.

"You must tell me more." Finished an enthralled Cameron Clark.

Chapter 6

Krystalnacht
The Night of the Crystal

November 8, 9 and 10, 1938

Dieter continued telling his incredible, but true story. He realized that Cameron might not feel the same way he felt, but he plunged ahead anyway.

"The carefully planned and well executed attack on Germany's Jews was carried out on the nights of November ninth and tenth, nineteen thirty-eight. A scant ten months prior to the beginning of WWII; Hitler had already shown his true colors by taking back the Rheinland from the French in 1936, he sent troops to Spain, annexed Austria etc." Stated Dieter in a somber tone.

He continued to speak without waiting for Cameron to reply. Cameron sat in his comfortable chair and listened attentively.

Dieter stated. "Those of us who lived here were totally unaware of the historical importance of November 9th and 10th, 1938. To those of us living in Niedergeyer it was a great day in sports history. We had for the first time in almost a century of organized sports won the Divisional Soccer Championship. We were all proud of my best friend, Erik Goldmann. He had single-handedly scored all four goals, and won the game for us. We had no idea that today was also the beginning of Hitler's horrible plot to destroy all of the Jews in Germany and eventually Europe."

Dieter paused for a second to wipe a small tear from his right eye. Cameron was amazed to see this somewhat sentimental emotion from Dieter. Cameron had never seen him shed a tear, not for anyone or anything.

Dieter regained his composure, took a deep breath and settled in to his chair. He grabbed one of his favorite cigars and lit up.

He was so enthralled, that he forgets to offer Cameron one.

"On this evil and eventful day, Hitler had instructed Dr. Joseph Goebels, the Propaganda Minister, and then **Brigadefuehrer** (Brigadier+) Reinhard Heydrichs, Himmler's Deputy, to carry out the carefully planned and well executed attack on Germany's Jews. This obnoxious and cruel event took place on the night of 9-10 November, 1938." Continued Dieter with firmness in his voice.

"I am sure you know most of this, but it will give you a historical perspective to the whole drama that occurred on those dates." Stated a somewhat bombastic Dieter.

"A violent storm of anti-Semitism broke out throughout Germany. The well-coordinated attacks struck fear throughout the land. It seemed as if this horrible plot to destroy all Jewish businesses, places of worship and schools might succeed after all." Dieter continued without a single interruption from Cameron.

"As you know Cameron, they used the murder of a German consular official in Paris, Ernst von Rath was his name, and by a strange coincidence he was an avid anti-Nazi. The perpetrator was a deranged Jewish refugee, and his action was the excuse, justification and catalyst for the beginning of "The Night of the Crystal, AKA **Krystalnacht.**" Stated Dieter with passion and conviction in his voice.

"In retrospect Herschel Grynzpan, the Jewish assassin, could not have picked a worse time to commit this murder. Some historians have even hinted at the possibility of a German Nazi conspiracy in this hideous and bizarre plot." Dieter took a sip of his brandy and a puff of his cigar and continued without interruption.

"The unabated and violent action continued for more than two days. Just about every Jew in Germany was either directly or indirectly affected by this action." Stated Dieter.

"Do you know why it was called **Krystalnacht** (Night of the Crystal) Cameron?" Asked Dieter as he looked at Cameron.

"No! I don't, but I am sure you will tell me." Replied a curious Cameron.

"Just about every Jewish shopkeeper in Germany had his front window smashed or damaged by the Nazi goons. There was broken glass lying everywhere, therefore 'Night of the Crystal.' On those two nights there was around a hundred Jews murdered or seriously injured. The figures vary greatly, but one thing is sure, there was great devastation throughout the land. Approximately 200 synagogues were burned to the ground. Even our own synagogue in Niedergeyer was destroyed by fire. You could also say that these two evenings were the official 'Coming Out Party' for the Nazis." Finished a somewhat drained Dieter.

After taking another long swig from his brandy, Dieter looked at Cameron with a somewhat inquisitive glance.

"Are you really interested in hearing the rest of the story, as it really happened?" Asked Dieter.

"Of course I am. Maybe this will help me in my current investigation. The more I know about the past, the more it will help me in the future. I need to have a better understanding of what the German Jews went through, and also what the rest of the population suffered." Replied Cameron, as he sat back on his leather chair and stared at Dieter.

"I will try tell it like was, exactly as I remember it. My memory plays tricks on me sometime, but I will try to be as truthful as I can." Dieter finished with a sigh and a frown.

"OK, Dieter, I am sure you will do the story justice." Stated Erik.

Chapter 7

Forgotten Memories

A well maintained soccer field is hidden from view in the middle of the large forest. The only way to get to the playing field is through a large path in the middle of the woods. This athletic event could only be reached by climbing a steep hill at the base of the village.

The small town of Niedergeyer is located in an area called, the "Eifel." This location has often been used as a gateway by invading armies throughout history. This part of Germany is covered in rolling hills and some heavily wooded areas. The Romans, Gauls, Charlemagne, Nordic tribes, Swedes, Napoleon Bonaparte and many others have tried to invade its territory. In recent memory it was the site of two of the most famous battles in WWII, Battle of the Bulge and the battle of *Huertgenwald,* AKA by the GI's as "Green Hell." This whole region has a long a bloody history, and has been in constant turmoil for centuries.

The village of Niedergeyer can trace its roots to ancient Roman times. At one time around the second century AD, the seventh (VII) Roman legion had a fort and a ceramic factory in this small village. It also had the distinction of having Roman grapes planted in its numerous hills, and produced some of the best wine in the region. In addition to its famous wine and glorious past, it also had one of the best soccer teams in Northwest Germany. They had won the class B division championship four out of the last five years. This year would be of particular interest to the players because if they won the championship again they would be allowed to keep the beautiful permanent trophy in their village.

The entire village, and playing field was festooned with giant Nazi flags and streamers. Every pole, tree, and balcony was decorated with red white and black flags. The weather was extremely cold, overcast and windy; typical for this part of Germany in November. A well-disciplined Hitler Jugend band (Hitler's equivalent to the Boy Scouts) was playing a series of German martial music.

This very loud and stimulating music had the effect of energizing the entire stand. The small wooden stadium was packed to capacity, and many additional spectators were standing on the sidelines waving small Nazi, or home team flags. The mood was festive, despite the miserable weather. However this was very rypical for this part of Germany.

Erik Goldmann is Niedergeyer's star player. He was one of those wonderful soccer players who never seem to run out of steam. Although not very tall, he made up for it by his speed and agility. Additionally, he had the capability to jump up like a kangaroo, and could score many goals with headers. He was a perfect soccer player. He had speed, agility and an endless amount of stamina.

The home team ran out on the field and the local villagers erupted in thunderous applause. The volunteer fire department band, quite good by homegrown standards, started to play up a popular tune and everyone went wild with joy. When the opposing team from Kreiss Dueren finally ran unto the field they are met with good-natured boos and catcalls. A few minutes later the referee blows his whistle and the game begins.

Niedegeyer is the underdog, but no one counted on Erik Goldmann. In the second half, the score is already 3-0 in favor of the home team. The Dueren players and coaches are in shock. No one had counted on Erik Goldmann, he had pierced their defenses like General Guderian marching through Poland.

The right forward kicked Erik the ball and it landed over his right shoulder, and about one yard in front of him. He faked to the right; cuts suddenly to the left and manages to burst through the left defender as if he was invisible. The startled goalie did not have a chance. Erik kicked the ball on long high arc and it found its way into the net. It was one of those spectacular goals that goalkeepers have nightmares about and center forwards dream about. The partisan crowd erupted into a frenzied roar. The score now stood at four to zero for Niedergeyer and Erik had scored all four goals! Once the score reached 4-0, the coach brought some of the second string players, and even Dieter Johannes was able to play for the last twenty minutes. The game ended with the same score.

The winning trophy was brought to the center of the field, and all the players, coaches and fans go wild with joy. Both bands began playing joyous and cheerful music, even the losing team comes over to congratulate the Niedergeyer players.

Strangely enough, only one of his teammates, Dieter Johannes his best friend, came over and gave him a hug. Dieter and Erik had been best friends since they were in kindergarten.

Although Dieter was a member of the Hitler Youth, he had no time for politics and really admired Erik. Politics were of no interest to either boy. They just enjoyed playing soccer and talking about girls.

Dieter was convinced that under different circumstances Erik could have been a professional soccer player. Erik was a natural talent and was far superior to the rest of the players on either team. However being Jewish made his chances non-existent. Circumstances and world destiny would keep him from that goal.

Once the initial jubilation subsided, the rest of his teammates ignored him and ran off the field, without acknowledging his presence.

Many of the players, may have wanted to congratulate Erik, but they were afraid of what might happen to them. Being friendly with a Jew today, was not healthy. The only reason Erik was still on the team was because of his spectacular athletic ability. Nazi dogma preached that Jews were inferior to Germans, however Erik proved just the opposite. Dieter suspected that Erik would not be allowed to play again because of the current political environment. How true would Dieter's prophecy be? Today's victory would be the last time these young German boys would ever play soccer together again, or for that matter see one another for a long time. Sad as it was, providence would tear them apart.

Their fathers on the other hand, had both been friends and also served together in WWI. They had both served in Northern France, near the Champagne capitol of the world, Reims. Actually, three young men from their village had served together in the same unit, and on the same front. Erik's father, although much older than the other two boys, had risen to the rank of Sergeant Major. As a matter of fact, Erik's father was a highly decorated soldier and had been twice decorated for valor with the Iron Cross First Class. Erik's father had valiantly fought for Germany and always considered himself a German first. Although he was a Rabbi by calling, his profession was that of the village butcher. Many of the inhabitants could fondly remember his generosity and kindness to all in the village, particularly those in need.

On the other hand Dieter's father was more inclined to music and was an expert clarinet player. Unfortunately, during WWI, he was gassed by the British and never fully regained his health. He died at the early age of thirty-five in the year of 1933. Dieter never completely recovered, and always missed his gentle and talented father. The third boy who fought with them in France was Johann Krieger. Johann had been severely wounded, and was last seen in a French field hospital as a P.O.W. in late 1918. His fate was never known, as he was never seen again in the village. For over twenty years his destiny remained a mystery. Erik was puzzled and could not understand why the current Nazi regime mistreated all Jews. After all, being Jewish was just a religion and the Goldmann's considered themselves Germans. It was very typical of most German Jews to be patriotic and pro-German.

Back on the field of play.

The crowd slowly left the playing field and within a few minutes, only Erik and Dieter were left. Erik turned to Dieter and said.

"How would you like it and to come over to my house and have some coffee and cake with me?" asked Erik to a startled Dieter. Without even pausing to reflect, Dieter gladly accepted.

Both boys quietly walked down the path to Erik's house. By then dusk was gathering, and the walk down to Erik's house had taken on the feeling of a funeral wake. It seemed that despite all good intentions a small rift had developed between them. Neither Erik nor Dieter ever suspected that this final soccer game for the league championship would also be the beginning of a nightmare for millions of European Jews.

After about fifteen minutes of walking they arrived at Erik's home, Das Haus. Erik's mother was there to greet them at the door. The Goldmann family had already heard of the good news about the winning game, and they were very excited for Erik, and the rest of the team.

However their excitement soon changed to worry when they saw Dieter standing there. Both parents looked at each other in a way that only parents can. They excused themselves and went to the kitchen.

"Can you believe that Erik brought that Nazi boy home?" shrieked an angry Mrs. Goldmann.

"Well, there is nothing we can do right now, and besides Dieter is not a Nazi! Don't forget that his father served in my unit, and was a very brave, but gentle man." Answered Mr. Goldmann, shrugging his shoulders.

"I, I hope you're right, but I have a bad feeling." Replied a now visibly upset Sarah Goldmann.

Sarah began preparing a large pot of steaming hot coffee, and brought out a tray of delicious German pastries for the boys. Both young men wolfed down the cakes and cookies as if they hadn't eaten in a month. After thanking them for their hospitality, Dieter politely excused himself and left Erik's house. Dieter realized that being there could jeopardize all of them. As he walked away from Erik's home, he felt a thousand sets of eyes staring at him. Dieter lived less than eight hundred meters away, but it was the longest walk he ever took. He could not understand what was occurring, and yet he knew that something awful was about to happen. He quickened his steps, and arrived home in less than fifteen minutes. His door never looked so good in his life. The moment it shut behind him, he let out a sigh of relief. He went straight to his room and locked his door. He was both mentally and physically exhausted to the point of falling down. Dieter did not even bother to take off his dirty clothes; he just crumpled down on his soft feather bed and fell into a deep sleep. It was as if his mind was begging him for relief.

On the northern part of town, an equally tired Erik also resigned himself to an early nightfall. The weather was ideal for this type of scenario. November 8th, 1938 was a cold and dreary evening. Although winter was still more than a month away, the temperature had already sunk to five degrees Celsius below freezing. However there was moisture in the air. By eleven o'clock, the humidity was so heavy that a thin sheet of ice had already coated everything white. It made walking and driving particularly difficult. Nonetheless at this time of night there was very little vehicular traffic throughout the village. As it was customary in this part of Germany, everyone had already shuttered their windows for the evening, and were all preparing themselves for bed.

A shadow appeared on the street corner. It hugged the walls of the houses as it carefully made its way southward on the main street towards Das Haus. The only thing that gave his position away was the crunching of the ice beneath his feet on the sidewalk, and the phantom like footprints left behind on the ice.

This apparition was almost invisible. He wore dark clothing and stayed close to the doorways. It was obvious that he did not want to be seen by anyone. His furtive moves were in fact almost cartoon like. Those over-exaggerated movements almost resembled an early Disney cartoon. After a few moments of silence, he made a dash towards his target, Das Haus.

The last sprint towards the doorway had taken his breath away, and he was panting heavily. The cold night air was about to give his position away. He stood there frozen for a few seconds, pressing his black leather gloves against his mouth in an attempt to conceal his breath. After furtively looking around, the covert figure finally approached the door and knocked.

Franz Goldmann, Erik's father, had just finished stoking the coal-fired stoves in the bedrooms. He knew from experience that this was a vain attempt at heating their rooms, but this was their only source of heat. The knock surprised Franz and his wife Sarah. They looked at each other and wondered who could be calling on them at this hour? No one in Niedergeyer would normally intrude on their privacy. Franz hoped that the sudden noise had not awakened the children.

Rabbi Goldmann told his wife to stay in bed, and he went to answer the door. He asked?

"Who is there, please?" When no one answered, he asked again.

"Hello, who is there?"

"Machen Sie auf! Geheime Staatspolizei (Open up, German Secret State Police, AKA ***GESTAPO).*** " Answered the rather subdued voice from the other side of the door.

Franz was horrified, but he could not figure out what they wanted with him at this hour of the night? Franz attempted to peek through the peephole, but the porch light was not working. *Strange* he thought. Why is the light not working? He eventually mustered up enough courage and opened the door.

Johann Krieger who was hidden in the shadows, immediately shoved his way past Franz, the porch light bulb still clutched in his hand. His actions were so swift that Franz was unable to react until Johann was well in to the hallway. Johann instructed Franz to quietly close the door and turn off the hallway light. When this was done, Johann turned and faced Franz, handing him the outside hallway bulb as he did so. Franz was totally taken aback by this strange action. Both men looked at each other for a few seconds, and Franz finally murmured.

"Who are you and what do you want?" Asked a now trembling Franz.

The mysterious figure stood in the frame of the doorway and glared at Franz. "How dare you speak to me that way?"

"Shut up you fool, you are going to wake up the dead!" Answered the Gestapo man.

Franz noticed that the stranger was wearing a black leather trench coat, a Nazi party officials pin and had a white and black

48

swastika armband around his left arm. This Gestapo agent impressed Franz. *He looked the part,* thought Franz as he glanced up and down. It took Franz a few more seconds to completely gain his self-control. When he did, he observed a tall blond man in his early forties, with striking blue eyes. Good looking at one time, but he now carried a horrible seven-inch scar from the corner of his left eye, downwards to his jawbone, and series of smaller scars radiating from his eyes upwards towards his hairline. The disfigurement was so complete that Franz could not help, but stare at him. Franz thought, *he had experienced war, but this man had experienced hell!*

Before Franz could do or say anything else, the figure reached in to his coat pocket and pulled out an oblong metal disk and flashed it before Franz's face. The sudden motion made Franz jump back in terror. He thought the man might be pulling out some type of weapon.

"I said Gestapo, and that should be enough reason to let me in, you fool." Blurted out the Gestapo agent.

"Please forgive, Sir. I was a little surprised by your actions and this late visit. What can I do for you?" Asked the rabbi.

"It's not what you can do for me, but what I can do for you." Replied the still unidentified man.

"Do you think, we could perhaps go into your living room and talk?" Asked the Gestapo man.

"But of course Mein Herr, I am terribly sorry." Answered Franz as he pointed to the living room.

Franz led the way down the hallway into the living room. It was small, but yet cozy. The large metal potbelly stove was still purring heat, and it gave the room a warm and comfortable feeling. The Gestapo agent looked around the room and noticed several interesting items on the far wall. On top of the cupboard were several military decorations, photos, awards and two regimental battle flags. Additionally in a glass case, there were two high ranking German medals and the written citations to those medals.

"So you are a veteran? Are you?" Asked the Gestapo man with a sneering tone in his voice.

"Ja, that is correct. I served from 1914 to 1918 as a Regimental Sergeant Major in France." Replied Franz, his chest expanding with pride.

"I see you were awarded the Iron Cross First class?" Asked the stranger.

"As a matter of fact, I received that award twice." Replied the now boasting Franz, as he waived his hand over his many awards.

"Quite a honor for a Jew. Don't you think?" Mocked the scarred man.

"I am a German citizen first, and a Jew by birth, religion and heritage. What does my religion have to do with my military service? My family has lived in this area for almost three hundred years, and many of my ancestors also served in the armed forces with distinction." Stated Franz in a rather forceful tone.

"You are still the same stubborn Sergeant Major, I knew in France." Replied the now smiling Gestapo man.

"France? France? Do I know you? Did we serve together in Reims?" Asked Franz.

"Yes to all the above. As a matter of fact, I am the reason you won that second Iron Cross, you fool. Don't you remember the last attack on Fort La Bombelle? It's me! Dieter Krieger, your lieutenant!" Stated the scarred stranger.

"Oh my God! It's been so long. I did not recognize you. We, we, had heard you ended up in a French P.O.W. camp after the war." Replied Franz.

"No news from you in nearly twenty years, and now this?" Stuttered Franz, as he extended his arms out towards his old comrade.

"Well it's true. But they treated me pretty good, except for the scars. I guess I can't complain, they saved my life after all. After the war and the long stay in their hospital, I just did not want to come back looking like this. I ended up in Munich, and drifted around until I met some old friends from the 316th Bavarian Reserve Regiment. They helped me out, and eventually I joined the National Socialist German Workers' Party, AKA NSDAP. Later to be known as the Nazi Party, of course." Finished Johann

Krieger, almost out of breath.

"Well it sounds like you have had an exciting life, but what brings you back home to Niedergeyer this evening?" Replied Franz as he pointed to the large overstuffed leather chair near the stove.

Johann took the hint and made himself comfortable.

He seemed to be at a lost for words, until Franz reached into the cabinet and pulled out a bottle of Dornkaart corn liquor and offered some to Dieter.

"Here my old friend, this should help warm you up." Quipped Franz as he poured a generous portion of the powerful drink into a large tumbler.

"Thank you, I needed that." Offered Johann as he raised his glass towards Franz.

"*Prosit* (cheers)!" Replied Franz, as he stood up.

"Cheers to you my old friend. I am really happy to see you again, but I am sure that this nighttime intrusion is not a social call? Is it now?" Asked an inquisitive Franz, his eyes looking straight into Johann's face.

"No, you are correct in your assumption. I don't know where to begin? I am actually stationed at the party's headquarters office in Dueren. We received orders today from Berlin to take action against all Jewish agitators, their businesses, homes and synagogues." Stated a somewhat subdued Johann. His voice quivering with emotion.

"What do you mean? Take action? Asked a troubled Franz.

"Where have you been for the past six years? Don't you know what is going on in Germany? Our Fuehrer has ordered us to round up all the Jewish troublemakers, and that includes you Franz!" Stated an obviously distraught Krieger.

"What are you talking about? Troublemaker? I am a loyal German citizen, and I have never done anything wrong, or for that matter caused any trouble in my entire life." Complained Franz, as he suddenly sat down to catch his breath.

Johann stared at him, knowing full well that his old friend was right, but there was nothing he could do about it, other than to warn him.

"Franz, get a grip on yourself and face reality. No matter what you say or believe, the powers to be are going to take action. You are powerless to stop them! Listen to me! Tomorrow, I will be back with some of my comrades, and I will be forced to burn down your synagogue and arrest anyone who gets in our way!" Stated a somewhat reluctant Johann Krieger.

Franz was in shock. He could not believe what he was hearing. His country and their leaders were going to betray him and his faith.

"But, but, but Johann, isn't there anything you can do?" Asked an emotional and teary-eyed Franz.

"You fool! What do you think I am doing now! Do you know what would happen to my family and me if I were to be found out? Yes, I would end up in the same place you might be going unless you leave this evening! Is that understood? All of you must be gone when I return tomorrow morning! I have no choice Franz. You must flee to Belgium this evening and never return! If you pack your belongings in the next hour, you could be in Liege by three in the morning and to Oostende by morning. There are ferries to England on the hour, and by this time tomorrow evening you could be in London safe and sound?" Stated a pleading Johann.

Franz gazed at his old comrade in arms, but no words could come out of his mouth. This paralysis lasted a whole minute or two. Both men just stared at each other without saying anything. Finally Franz broke the ice.

"I, I, I can't believe this is happening to me. We don't have a single enemy here. Why are they doing this to us?" Asked a confused Franz.

"I am sorry you can't understand what is going on, but I have risked my life and the lives of my entire family to try and save you. If you are unwilling to do anything about it, you will be responsible for the consequences! Franz, I owe you this much. You saved my life on two separate occasions, but if you do not follow my warning, you will have to answer to your God for your actions and consequences." Finished a somewhat angry Johann Krieger.

"I sincerely thank you for your interest in my family. I will have to discuss it with them and come to a conclusion this evening." Answered Franz, as he showed Johann the door.

"Don't be a fool Franz, tomorrow will be too late, and please never repeat to anyone what happened here tonight! Understood? Don't call or discuss this matter with anyone except your family! Finished a somewhat desperate Johann.

Johann stood there transfixed and reflected. *After all, Franz had been there for him on several occasions in the trenches near Fort La Bombelle in northern France, 1914-1918.* He once again pleaded to his old comrade to leave the country.

"I shall never forget what you did for me in France and I hope by warning you tonight, my debt will be paid in full. There is not enough time to explain our political differences, however I do know that you were a brave German soldier and fought for your country. I implore you and your family to leave tonight. You may not survive what may happen to you tomorrow or in the next few weeks. Please, I beg of you listen to me and get out of the country. I don't have time to go into all the details, but sometime tomorrow officials of the Gestapo, the police, and SD members will be coming around and arresting all Jews in this village and all the neighboring villages.

Additionally, your synagogue will be burned down." Stated Johann, running out of breath as he spoke.

"What, what are you saying? Is this for real? This can't really happen to us, I'm a German, and I'm a loyal German." Shouted Franz, his voice sounding strangely aggressive for this usually mild-mannered man.

"As you know Johann, my family has lived in this village for nearly three hundred years and we have always been patriotic and supportive of Germany. Why are they doing this to us? stated a somewhat dismayed and embittered Franz.

"I am not the man to talk to about this problem. As I already informed you, I'm coming here at great personal risk and you must listen to me. I don't have time to discuss all of the political ramifications with you, however I do know that if you and your family don't leave tonight you may never get another chance. I will not argue the point with you now. I don't intend to spend too much longer here. This is the one and only chance you will get from me. When you see me again tomorrow, I must follow orders and do my duty. Please, I beg of you for the sake of the children and your wife. Do the wise thing and leave now! After tomorrow the borders will be more difficult to cross, and Belgium is only 32 km away. If you and your family left in the next hour, you could be there by morning." stated Johann, his voice rising in anger as he walked out the door into the darkness. Johann had mixed emotions, but he felt that he had done the best he could, and if Franz chose to stay, it was his own doing.

Before Franz could utter another word, or finish his thoughts, Johann turned off the hallway light and sneaked out into the night. His muffled footsteps were barely audible, and within a few seconds he had vanished into the night like a vampire stalking his pray. Johann quickly walked away into the cold night. His black hat and black leather coat blending in with the darkness, and within three seconds he was invisible. This sudden action caught Franz by surprise. Franz stood in front of the darkened door and attempted to reflect on this horrible news. Only the cold air finally brought him back to reality and he quietly closed the door.

His brain was not accustomed to handling this type of information. Franz attempted to plan a course of action that would benefit his family.

"What does that mean? What are we going to do? Are we the only ones who know? Should we tell the others? Oh, Franz I am so scared." Stated an extremely upset Sarah.

"Calm down, and let's discuss it." Whispered Franz.

Sarah had been listening to the whole conversation through the closed bedroom door. The moment Johann Krieger left the house, she came out into the hallway pale as a ghost. Her whole body was trembling, and she began to cry uncontrollably.

Before he could come up with a satisfactory answer, his wife tapped him on the shoulder and shocked him back to reality. Franz had never seen his wife in such a worried state.

"Franz what does that mean? What are they going to do? What is going on? Are we the only ones who know? Should we tell the others? Oh Franz, I am so scared." Stated an extremely frightened and distraught Sarah Goldmann.

"Calm down, calm down, and let's discuss it. However, I believe the children have a right to know? Don't you think so? Asked Franz as he turned and hugged his wife.

"Yes, I guess so, but this is so frightening. I am worried about my father and grandfather in Kerpen." Stated Sarah as long streams of tears ran down her face. Deep concern was written all over her face.

"Oh, don't worry. Everything will be all right. Krieger only spoke of us, and our synagogue. We don't know what they have planned for Kerpen? Let's sit down and talk about it." Replied Franz as they both walked into the living room.

Just then both children, Erik and Esther walked into the living room and sat down next to their parents.

"What is going on? Asked Erik. Esther just sat there her big brown eyes fixed on her father's worried face.

"Why are you still up and why is mama so upset?" Asked the youngest child, Esther.

Both parents sat there in silence; not knowing what to say or do. Finally Franz said:

"We just received some bad news, children. Some very bad news! An old army friend has told me in strict confidence that the Nazis are going to take some kind of action against all Jews living in Germany. This will take place tomorrow morning, and he has advised me to leave for Belgium tonight and never come back!" Stated Franz with emphasis.

Sarah and the children remained silent, but Erik finally stood up and asked his father a question.

"Do you think this is serious? What could they do to us? Work camps? Or worse? Concentration camps?" Asked Erik, his voice quivering as he mentioned the words.

Almost on command, both women started sobbing uncontrollably again. Their tears growing in size and rapidity.

Within seconds, both of them were hysterical.

"Quiet, and don't worry. Papa will know what to do. He is the one to make the decision." Stated Erik, standing up and facing his father.

"Thank you for your confidence, but this decision affects more than just the four of us. Remember our flock consists of around 12 Jewish families, and thirty or forty family members! We can't abandon them without notice. Let's try to contact them tomorrow and come to a joint agreement. If we go, they should also go. What do you think Erik?

"I will do whatever you say, but I hope it won't be too late." Replied an anxious Erik. Both Sarah and Esther nodded their heads in agreement.

"OK then, lets put our faith in our God, and he will lead us down the righteous path. Let's all try to get some sleep now, goodnight children." Finished Franz, as he kissed both of his children on the forehead.

Both children slowly climbed the stairs to the second floor, neither one of them had ever seen their parents this upset. The twenty-one stairs up to their bedrooms never seemed so long in their short lives. By the time they entered their second story bedroom, Esther was once again crying hysterically. Her whole body was shaking like an autumn leaf in November. Erik was so moved by his sister's dilemma that he decided to do something to calm her down.

"Esther, why don't you quiet down. I promise everything will be OK. Would you like to spend the night with me?" Offered a protective Erik.

"Yes, yes, yes! Would you mind?" Replied a tearful, but grateful Esther.

Both children quietly went to bed. Although their minds raced ahead with horrible thoughts of what might happen to them, they eventually fell into a deep, but restless sleep. Meanwhile Franz and Sarah sat in their living room in silence. The events of the last sixty-minutes had both of them in a state of shock. They just stared at each other unwilling or unable to move.

Both parents had that thousand-yard stare, the same look that shell-shocked combat veterans have after extended periods under fire. Their long and wonderful life was slipping away, and they had no control over it. After what seemed like an eternity, but actually was only ten-minutes; both of them turned and embraced each other. Never in their twenty-six years of marriage had they held each other closer than today. It seemed as if their souls were trying to bond into one magical unit. As if on queue Sarah began to cry; Franz tried to comfort her as best he could.

"Don't worry dear, everything will be fine. Our God will protect us, and those around us. We must pray for our family, and the other members of our synagogue. We Jews have endured many other tribulations throughout history, and we shall survive this." Finished a somewhat emotional Franz.

Sarah nodded in silence, but still had the foresight to ask him one more question.

"Franz. do you still think we should prepare? Just in case? Please tell me what to do! Please?" Asked an emotional Sarah.

Well, I guess we could take some precautions. Let's prepare one small suitcase per person. Additionally, we should perhaps take some of our gold coins with us. You could sew them into the lining of our coats. Better yet! Be sure to spread them out evenly between us. That way we could prevent losing them all at once," Replied an anxious Franz.

Sarah nodded her head and stood up. She walked the twenty feet to the kitchen and bent over near the stove. She reached down and pried up a large board near the corner. Using both hands she pulled up a heavy wooden box. Wrapped inside a fine Belgian cotton pillowcase, was a heavily gilded wooden box. Sarah carefully unwrapped the contents. Inside the box were forty, mint condition, twenty-mark gold pieces. These coins had been given to them as a wedding present. They had been carefully preserved over the years, and had risen in value. Each coin was worth around four hundred Reich marks. Currently these coins represented a substantial sum. Sarah decided to also stash her three diamond rings, given to her by her grandmother.

Under normal circumstances these coins represented a small fortune. Sixteen thousand marks was enough money to purchase a house, a car and have some left over. Sarah walked over to the vestibule and retrieved her children's coats. After carefully splitting the seams, Sarah sewed fifteen gold coins in each coat. She also took her three platinum and diamond antique rings and sewed them into Erik's lining. After examining her perfect handiwork, she proceeded to sew five gold coins into her and Franz's coats. Once she was satisfied everything was undetectable; she packed two suitcases and placed them near the front door. Franz sat the whole time in the living room and silently watched his wife. He did not know or have the courage to say anything meaningful to her.

He eventually stood up, and walked over to his wife. He stooped down and kissed her on the cheeks. His tenderness caught Sarah by surprise. Franz was not normally an affectionate man. She stood up and embraced him. The more she held him, the less she wanted to let him go. After two minutes of silent hugs, they reluctantly went to bed. Franz lay in bed and silently prayed every prayer he had ever memorized. He prayed for his family, children, wife and his flock, as he was so fond of calling them.

His thoughts raced ahead. *What is going to happen tomorrow? What will they do with us? What will our neighbors think? How will they notify us? Why are they doing this to us?*

As it turned out, destiny took care of the events, and before long all Jews and non-Jews would suffer the consequences of a madman.

Chapter 8

The Real Heroes

The morning could not come soon enough for Erik and his sister. They both got up before dawn and took a quick shower and hurried downstairs. Both of their parents were actually still sleeping when they loudly knocked on their bedroom door.

"What, what? Who is it, and why are you waking us so early?" Asked a still groggy Franz.

"It's us, Vater." Replied Erik.

"OK, OK, OK, I know it's you, but why are you up at this ungodly hour?" Asked Franz, as he got out of bed and put his housecoat on.

"Please don't be angry, we only thought that after last night, it might be a good idea to get up early and leave town, before, before, before?" Stuttered Erik.

"Well son, it's probably a good idea, but I have decided to wait and see what happens? I just can't leave town without informing the rest of the families. You do understand? Don't you?" Asked Franz, looking directly into his son's big brown eyes.

"No, no I don't! That, that man last night warned us. And I am afraid Vater." Replied a nervous Erik.

"Sometimes we must leave our destiny in the hands of our God. You have every right to be afraid, but God will show me the way." Stated Rabbi Goldmann.

Erik looked downwards and then away from his father. He was thoroughly confused, but he trusted his father and did not want to upset him. His mother appeared and told the children to go to the kitchen and wait for breakfast. Both of them answered in the affirmative and walked into the cold room. A few minutes later, Sarah walked in, still dressed in her nightgown and lit the stove. Within minutes the kitchen was warn and cozy, as they had always known it. She made a pot of coffee with lots of milk and sugar for the kids. She wanted to make sure that everyone had plenty to eat today.

Sarah boiled eight eggs, cut eight crunchy breakfast rolls, served fresh cheese, sliced roast beef and homemade marmalade. This was a feast, and she smiled when she saw her children devour every bite on their plate. Before she could finish the dishes, the church bell began to ring in an unusual but, rapid fashion. This was the signal for the volunteer fire department to report to the firehouse. Both of the kids looked up to their mother as if asking permission to go to the fire.

"No, no, no! Don't even think about! Today is not the day to go and get lost. You need to stay close to home. Please, don't look at me with those puppy eyes. I am not changing my mind! What do you think Franz? Asked Sarah.

"Well, for once I agree with you." Replied a smiling Rabbi.

"Oh, you are incorrigible. You will give them the wrong impression." Stated Sarah as she stood up and walked towards the open window.

"Franz, Franz. Maybe you should go and see what is going? Half the village is running towards the church." Begged a now concerned Sarah.

"OK, OK. Calm down. I will go now, but all of you stay nearby and don't wonder away! Is that understood?" Stated the ex-Sergeant Major. His voice booming across the whole downstairs.

"Yes, yes. Just go and see what is going, please." Asked a concerned Sarah.

Franz dressed hurriedly and ran out unto the street. Most of his neighbors had already left their homes and were halfway down the street. As he caught up with them, he asked a man next to him if he knew what was going on?

"No I don't, but it must be important because everyone is there!" Screamed the stranger as he outdistanced him.

* * * * *

60

Back in the present time.

"Wow, that is an incredible story. I had no clue that this house had such a historical and religious background. Please continue you have me in suspense." Stated Cameron to an excited Dieter. OK Cameron, let's continue, finished Dieter. His father –in-law resumed the story.

* * * * *

November 9th, 1938

By the time Franz got to the corner where the church and synagogue stood, he suddenly had a horrible thought. Those armed SS *Sicherheitdienst* troopers, and Gestapo agents were not there for a picnic. A large throng had gathered in front of the synagogue. Four members of the SS and Gestapo were heatedly discussing with members of the volunteer fire department. Rabbi Goldmann mingled in with the crowd and listened.

A rather large and balding man was shouting at the top of his lungs to a gathered group of volunteer fireman. His erratic behavior only made matters worst.

"You will burn it down, and you will do it now! That is an order! Do you understand?" Finished the out of control *Sturmbannfuhrer* (Major).

Hans Ebberhardt, the volunteer fire department's acting chief, slowly looked up at the screaming madman and said in a calm, yet firm voice.

"We are firemen! Not arsonist! We put fires out, not start them! We will not burn the synagogue! I don't care what you say!" Shouted an irate Ebberhardt.

The mad Sturmbannfuhrer glared at the firefighters, his eyes bulging out of his skull like a crazed Chihuahua dog in heat. He nervously circled the area, his arms and hands waving about like a crazed individual. Eventually he calmed down, long enough to shout.

"Do you realize what you are doing? This is an order from higher headquarters. I have full authority to take whatever measures I see fit! And if I were you I would not push it too far! Do you understand what I am saying?" Continued the irate Nazi.

"I hear what you are saying, but I still cannot order my men to burn down this holy shrine. This is an unlawful order and we cannot in good conscience follow your command." Replied a still defiant Chief Ebberhardt.

Rabbi Goldmann stood there not knowing what to say or do. He was in a trance, not wanting to believe that his own countrymen were contemplating burning down his house of worship. Before he could react or make a move, the crazy Nazi continued screaming at the top of his lungs.

"OK, you have had all the chances you are going to get. If you refuse to burn down this filthy house of Jews, I will put all of you inside, and your families, and burn you up alive! Screamed the enraged despot. Even this threat did not move the firemen to action.

The crowd suddenly grew quiet, as Rabbi Goldman walked out and stood in front of his synagogue. He had a serene, yet strong presence about him. He waived to the brave firemen, as if to tell them, *Thank you for your heroics, but it is my duty now and I will assume all responsibility.*

The Nazis, firemen and spectators were all taken by surprise. Rabbi Goldmann stood there defiantly, his arm folded; glaring at the storm troopers. His action was more symbolic than useful. How could one man stop the inevitable? Was it the first open act of defiance against the Nazis? Was he the first Jew to say enough? He was not going to allow this madman the burn down his synagogue!

"Don't you think that you are going to stop us. I am going to Dueren to get reinforcements, and you will all pay the price!" shouted the bald Nazi as he stormed off towards his vehicle.

Just then, Niedergeyer's only police officer and chief, Wolgang Baume, appeared on the scene and wanted to know what was going on? Rabbi Goldmann and Chief Ebberhardt told him the whole story. Chief Baume was outraged and told all present to disperse and that he would handle it from now on. He mumbled under his breath that if anyone attempted to burn the synagogue, he would personally arrest them for arson! He proceeded to scatter all of the remaining spectators by loudly blowing on his police whistle and frantically waving his arms back and forth. Once he was assured that the crowd was under control, he returned to his home.

Rabbi Goldmann took the opportunity to return to his residence. On the way, many of his neighbors congratulated him for standing up to the Nazis, and not allowing them to bully them.

Franz's old war buddy, Johann Krieger; current Gestapo agent and Nazi party member, purposely maintained a low profile. He hid behind a grove of antique oak trees and made himself as inconspicuous as possible.

Krieger stood around in the background, and actually appeared to feel embarrassed by the ongoing events. After all, Johann was a hometown boy and he knew most of the inhabitants. However, no one had immediately recognized him. His disfiguring WWI scar had made it difficult to directly distinguish him from the many other WWI veterans.

Chapter 9

The Beginning of the End

The events of the past few hours spread like a wild firestorm throughout the small village. It was the biggest event to take place in Niedergeyer since the Romans invaded the village in the second century A.D.

Rabbi Goldmann slowly walked back to Das Haus. *What would he tell his family?* He thought to himself. His mind raced ahead of himself. Was this the beginning of the end? Was this the first step? As he was deep in thought, *he almost missed Simon Denlon waving at him.*

"What is going on? What has happened?" Screamed the visibly upset Simon, the village baker and small shop owner.

Rabbi Goldmann, came to a screeching halt, and stared blankly at Simon. It took him a few seconds to regain his composure. Although Simon was standing but a few yards from him, his thoughts were far, far away. Eventually his memory refocused, and he was able to walk over and speak with him.

"I am sorry, Simon. I was in a hurry to get home. We have a difficult time ahead of us, and I would like you to come over to my house as soon as possible; bring as many of our fellow Jews you can contact. Do this, and do it now. I can't explain at this instant, but I will, when you come over. Please, please, do it now." Shouted a somewhat shook-up Rabbi.

Simon Denlon had never seen the rabbi so upset. Simon knew of Franz's wartime achievements and was surprised by his obviously panicked demeanor. However, he decided to follow his suggestion and make contact with as many Jews as he could. By the time Goldmann reached his home, many of the Jewish villagers were already notified and anxious to find out what was going. Even some of the Jews in the neighboring villages were notified of the events in Niedergeyer.

Franz ran into his house completely out of breath. His wife Sarah looked at his pale face and knew the news was not good. It took Franz a few seconds to regain his composure. By then his children had come downstairs and were equally anxious for the news.

"Well *Vater,* what is going on? Please, please tell me what happened." Begged a visibly upset Erik. The rest of the family just stared at him, waiting for the facts that would alter their lives forever.

"OK, OK, OK! They, they tried to burn down the synagogue! They tried to burn it down! Can you believe it? Shouted Rabbi Goldmann.

His wife Sarah was the first to speak. She slowly stood up and spoke to the family.

"Your comrade Johann Krieger was right? Wasn't he? Asked a visibly distressed Sarah Goldmann.

"Yes, I think he was, but things still may change for the better." Replied Franz as he walked towards his wife.

"Let's not panic and wait for the others. I have passed the word along and hopefully they all should be here shortly." Stated Franz as he bent down and gave his wife a hug.

"What do you mean the others? Who else is coming here? Why are they coming here? We need to leave now!" Screamed a hysterical Sarah.

"We cannot allow our emotions to take over. Now is the time for peace and calm. Hysteria and panic will not help us." Replied Franz in a chiding way.

As if by magic, the extremely loud front door bell rang, and someone simultaneously knocked on the back bedroom window. Franz went to answer the door, and sent Erik to see who was at the back window. Franz opened the door and saw three of Niedergeyer's Jewish families standing there. He asked them in. They all walked in as if they were in a funeral procession.

Erik opened the back bedroom window and saw no one at first, suddenly Werner Schlemke and his girlfriend Lisa Lottie from the neighboring village, jumped up from behind a large bush and asked to come in. Erik pointed to the front door and they both shook their heads in unison. Erik shrugged his shoulders not knowing what to do; before he could come up with a solution, both Werner and Lisa jumped up on the windowsill and hopped into the bedroom. Their actions were rather unusual to say the least. Confused by their strange behavior, Erik could only point towards the hallway.

"Erik, who was that?" Asked Franz from the living room.

"Oh, don't worry *Vater*, it was only Werner and Lisa from Schlicht." Replied Erik as he escorted them to the front living room area.

By the time Erik brought the two youngsters into the living room, there were fourteen anxious villagers assembled there. Rabbi Goldmann looked around at this group and asked them all to sit down. He tried to explain to them what he knew, but was continually interrupted by various individuals asking questions beyond his capabilities to answer them. He eventually raised his hands and voice; asking them all to be quiet for a few seconds. That did the trick. All of them looked up to him for guidance and counseling. A deathly and eerie silence engulfed the room.

"Look, I have told you all I know, and the decision will be up to you. I could have left last night, but I decided to stay and hope for the best. After all, what do we have to fear? We are loyal German citizens and we have not committed any crimes!" Stated Franz to the assembled group.

Most of the adults seemed to nod their heads, but the younger members were not as willing to go along with crowd. No one in the crowd seemed to have noticed that he said, "last night." His son Erik however, stood frozen in terror, staring at his father. Still no one said anything except Werner!

"No, no and hell no! Answered an angry Werner. Haven't you heard about the concentration camp? Thousands of German Jews are disappearing on a daily basis! I listen to foreign broadcasts and they report monstrous things are going on in our country. I for one, am not going to wait to be transported away. Lisa has an aunt in London, and we are leaving immediately." Replied an agitated Werner, to the stunned crowd. Lisa just sat there, tears streaming down her pretty face.

"That is your decision Werner, but what about you parents, and Lisa's parents. Do they agree?" Asked Franz looking at the gathered assembly.

"With all due respect Herr Rabbi Goldmann, Lisa and I are both over eighteen and we must do what is best for us. If you were smart you would let your children leave now and never look back!" Stated an excited Werner.

"I respect your desire to leave, but what about your parents? Both your parents may not feel as you do? Don't you feel an obligation to them? What if you are right? Are you just going to abandon them? Asked Franz.

"Actually they encouraged me to do the right thing and leave. My father has given me his motorcycle, and it's parked behind your property, at the edge of the woods. If I leave now, we can be in Liege in ninety minutes. Once we reach Liege, I will sell it and use the money to go to England or America. If we catch the four o'clock from Liege, we can be in London by midnight." Stated an emphatic Werner. Lisa nodded her head in agreement, but tears continued to stream down her face.

"I admire your courage and determination, but there are some of us that have responsibility in our community. However, if my son wants to go with you, he has my permission." Answered Franz, as he looked at Erik.

Erik was shocked by his father's statement. His first reaction was to say, "Yes, I'll go," but he then reflected on his whole life, and could not find it in his heart to leave his parents and sister at this time.

"Thank you *Vater* for thinking of me, but my place is with you and the rest of the family. I have no wish to leave now!" Stated Erik, as he stood up and faced everyone.

"I admire Werner and Lisa for their courage. However, I feel I should stay here with my family and support them. I may regret this decision later in life, but now it's the right one to make.

However, I would appreciate it, if you could give me your aunt's address and I will give you my uncle's address in Chicago, USA." Stated Erik as he looked at his parents.

Werner reached in his pocket and withdrew a piece of paper and handed it to Erik in silence. Erik grabbed a notebook and wrote down his uncle's address also in silence. Both boys stared at each other intently.

"Thank you son, that is a good idea, and I am sure you won't regret it!" Replied Rabbi Goldmann as he looked to the gathered crowd.

Before he could say anything else, the church bell rang once more. It had that same nervous tone that they had heard earlier that day. Everyone in the room seemed to stop breathing for a second, except for Werner and Lisa. They looked at Rabbi Goldmann, and fled out the back window. Their actions were so sudden that one had a chance to react.

"Don't, don't leave!" Franz was unable to finish his sentence. Both of the teenagers were running across the backyard towards the tree line and the woods. A few seconds later the loud roar of the BMW motorcycle was heard speeding away from Das Haus. Within seconds the loud roar was no longer heard as it melted into the medieval forest.

"I wish them and the rest of us luck, we are going to need it." Stated Franz in a melancholic way. This statement seemed to shake the gathering.

The rest of the congregation looked to Franz for comfort and solace. It was a difficult and unnerving time. Rabbi Goldmann seemed to be the only one with a calm heart and a cool head.

"I recommend that everyone go home, pack a bag and await further developments. Only bring what is absolutely necessary. Don't do anything rash, but be alert and cautious in the next few days. Stay indoors, and if you are a shopkeeper, close your store for now. If you can, contact everyone you know and tell them what is going on." Finished Goldmann as he ushered the rest of them out the door. For a moment, the crowd just milled about the hallway not knowing what to do. Finally, Rabbi Goldmann showed them the door and they reluctantly left.

As the last visitors left his house, Rabbi Goldmann reflected on his earlier decisions. *Should he stay? Where should they go? Maybe his younger brother Jacob in America could help them?* Jacob had left Germany in 1927 and now lived near Chicago. He was a successful chicken farmer and often wrote Franz of his wonderful life in America. He decided to write him a letter as soon as possible. Franz was happy that he had given Werner his brother's address.

"*Vater, vater* I see smoke!" Screamed a terrified Erik from the second-story window.

"I'll be right up, son." Answered a now panicked Franz as he scrambled up the twenty-one stairs to the second floor landing.

Without pausing to take his breath, Franz gazed out the large East-facing window and saw a large column of black smoke rising up into the sky from the vicinity of the synagogue. He could not believe his eyes. How had they gotten back so fast? Were they really burning down his holy shrine? Or was it just another nearby house going up in flames?

No! He thought to himself, *this has to be my worst nightmare!*

He ran back down the stairs, nearly bowling over his wife Sarah. Franz grabbed the door handle to leave, when his wife begged him not to go.

"Please, please, please. David, Don't go! Who knows what these terrible men are capable of doing?" Supplicated a concerned Sarah.

"Please don't call me David, my name is Franz David and I have not been called that since my youth." Shouted an obviously upset Franz.

"I need to make a stand! We cannot allow this to happen to us, without some form of resistance! We are not sheep! God would want us to at least protest these horrible events? Don't you think so?" Asked Franz as he ran out the door, closely followed by Erik.

Sarah was convinced that her resistance was futile and that Rabbi Goldmann was on a quest, a holy quest! One filled with honor, dignity and goodness. She returned to the living room and sat quietly in a corner, hoping for the best.

Rabbi Goldmann ran down the sidewalk as fast as he could. Within a few seconds, Erik was alongside of him. Both men sprinted the eight hundred meters to the synagogue. Before they could turn the corner in to what used to be the courtyard, a large crowd of bystanders had gathered to witness these horrible events. The now useless fire department stood by with their hoses still in their hands, looking on in disgust.

The over one hundred year old synagogue was in flames. Bales of hay were stacked around the synagogue and were fiercely burning. Some of the Nazi hooligans had Jerry cans (gasoline cans) filled with petrol and were adding fuel to the fires. Some of the firemen had tears on their faces, and were being forcibly held back at gun point by the Nazis. The many spectators stood around and shook their heads in disbelief. Just when things seemed to be out of control, a loud cry was heard coming from the Catholic Church, at the end of the courtyard.

"Schanda! Schanda! (Shame, Shame!) What next? The Catholic, and Protestant churches?" Shouted the incensed Catholic priest as he ran down towards the synagogue.

Father Reiner Rushner, an avid anti-Nazi and community leader came running out of his church and screamed at the firemen. His voice sounding a lot harsher and meaner than anyone had ever heard before. Everyone just stood around and stared at him and at the Nazi officials. It was as if everyone knew the right thing to do, but lacked the courage to do it. Father Rushner ran over to the fire truck and started to unravel some of the fire hoses in a vain attempt to get someone motivated enough to actually do something.

"Do your duty, you cannot let this happen! You must stop them!" Bellowed the extremely agitated Catholic priest. The Chief of Police came running out of his house and also attempted to stop the Nazis. Both the Catholic priest and Police Chief were immediately detained by the Nazis, and actually temporarily locked up in the one room police station. Krieger later released both men after a severe threat and warning.

Just then, an out of breath Rabbi Goldmann came running

around the corner and observed the destruction of his beloved synagogue. The flames had already reached the upper windows and they were violently exploding. Hundreds of pieces of broken glass were sent screaming throughout the area. Even the Nazi thugs took cover behind the large fire truck. The bald Nazi official shouted at everyone to stay away from the synagogue, and as if to emphasize his authority, he pulled out his 9mm Luger pistol and waved it at the crowd. Rabbi Goldmann ran forward in a vain attempt to stop the annihilation of his hopes and dreams. Everything that he believed in, was being turned in to ashes; blowing away in to the far reaches of heaven. How prophetic that the demolition of his synagogue would also mirror the destruction of over six million Jews in the next seven years.

All who witnessed this travesty on humanity will never forget it. Although Niedergeyer only had a few die-hard Nazis, they too were similarly shocked by the brutality of their regime. This village has existed in harmony for hundreds of years, and they could not accept this type of violence. The only vocal and local Nazi was the ***Burgermeister*** (mayor) Heinrich Schniztler. Schnitzler was a short and stocky WWI veteran, who never amounted to anything in his life until he became a Nazi. He strutted around like a peacock; always wore his Nazi party members button, carried a wooden stick and often boasted of the Nazi Party's many accomplishments.

The ***Burgermeiser*** looked at Rabbi Goldmann, his short and quivering fat body shaking with rage. He stared directly at Franz and shouted at him.

"You, you Jew! What are you trying to do? Are you interfering with Party matters? This is a serious offense! I warn all of you to stay out of this business, or you will face similar consequences, isn't that so Herr Krieger?" Said a boisterous and vicious ***Burgermeister.***

For the first time since this event happened, a quiet and up to now uncommunicative Krieger, stepped out of the shadows and made himself known. He raised his head and stared at the crowd.

"That is correct Herr ***Burgermeister!*** Anyone who interferes with our duties will be arrested immediately!" Growled the revived Gestapo man. Although his voice sounded harsh and authoritative, he failed to look Rabbi Goldmann in the eyes.

Many in the crowd, turned in shock and looked at the dominating Gestapo man. The name sounded familiar, but his face was almost unrecognizable. The scar, the ugly scar made him almost impossible to identify.

Finally after a few seconds, the crowd reacted to his statements and began to withdraw away from the scene. Slowly at first; faster and faster they disappeared down the small streets of Niedergeyer.

"As of today, all Jewish inhabitants will report to me. Since the local jail is not big enough to house all the Jews in the area, I will have them report Rabbi Goldmann's house. Anyone found aiding or hiding Jews, will also be arrested. All Jews must register within twenty-four hours! We will have some officials there to facilitate this process." Screamed the Gestapo man.

Everyone in the crowd seemed shocked by this pronouncement. While pointing his stubby finger at the crowd, the despicable and tormenting ***Burgermeister*** re-iterated Krieger's statement with emphasis.

As if by magic, everyone began to segregate themselves from Franz and Erik. Although many of the good citizens of Niedergeyer wanted to support their neighbors, the fear of imprisonment forced them to retreat.

It was a time in history when prudence was a better part of valor for most of the citizens of Niedergeyer. Most of them were courageous; yet unwilling to risk their lives. Many of them openly supported Franz and the rest of the Jews, however the Fascist still instilled fear in everyone.

Chapter 10

Auf Wiedersehen!
Goodbye!

Cameron sat there fascinated by this incredible story. The more he heard, the more it captivated him. This was a more personal and touching tale, not only affecting him, but his family as well. He could not believe his good fortune by stumbling in to this marvelous epic. He hoped that it would assist him in his assignment. Dieter spoke up and it snapped him back to reality.

"Cameron, you seem to be drifting away from me? Are you still with me? Do you want me to continue?" Asked a perplexed Dieter Johannes.

"I am sorry, I am having a difficult time staying focused on reality and the past. This family tragedy is somewhat reminiscent of my mother's past. She had a similar misfortune which affected her, and lost six of her siblings in the war." Stated Cameron, in a matter of fact way.

"What do you mean, Cameron? I did not know your family was Jewish? I thought they were all Catholics?" Asked Dieter, leaning forward in his chair.

"Well, I guess you could say I was partly Jewish. My mother was born in Spain to a Spanish-Basque Catholic father, a Jewish French mother and an Italian Catholic paternal great-grandmother. I have a very interesting and varied heritage." Replied Cameron, as he took another sip of his brandy.

"It sounds like it. Tell me about your father? Where was he from? Is he American?" Dieter asked.

"Yes, he was. His family has roots going back to the eighteenth century. His family came from Scotland, and his mother came from Ireland. My mother was raised as a Catholic and her grandmother was originally from Italy and was very religiously motivated, and had a staunch Catholic background. My grandfather on my mother's side was a well-known attorney who was executed by the Fascists and Germans in Spain in 1937. Her family suffered horribly and eventually escaped to Morocco in 1937. Unfortunately, the Fascists/Germans invaded Morocco in 1940, and one of my uncles spent several years at various concentration camps. He was fortunate to escape on three separate occasions, and because of this, he was my childhood hero. My uncle hid out in the hills until November 1942 when the Americans and the allies invaded North Africa. He later joined the Free French Army and fought throughout Morocco, Algeria and Tunisia. It was at this time that my father met my mother in Morocco." Cameron finished with a long sigh.

"That is quite a story. I had no idea. Does my daughter know this?" Asked Dieter, staring at Cameron.

"Well, I don't think so. I don't think I've ever told anyone except you. It was a very personal and difficult time in our lives and I wanted to keep it that way." Cameron replied.

Dieter Jonannes stood up and walked over to the bar area and grabbed himself another drink. He looked at Cameron but, he shook his head, he had had enough to drink.

"I can understand your feelings, but perhaps you should tell her someday. I think it might interest her. Would you like me to continue with the Goldmann story." Asked Dieter with emphasis.

"Please, go ahead. I can't wait to hear the rest of it." Continued Cameron, leaning forward for emphasis.

"OK, then. I will carry on." stated Dieter. He sat back down in his comfortable leather couch and continued with the story.

The rest of the Jewish inhabitants were rounded up one by one and brought over to Rabbi Goldmann's house. It took the Nazis almost all day to locate them and drive them to Das Haus. With the exception of Werner and Lisa, who had fled to England, all of them obeyed orders and allowed themselves to be taken without resistance. By nightfall approximately forty-two Jewish members of the community were crammed in Das Haus. Conditions to say the least were miserable. Das Haus had only one bathroom and an unused outdoor outhouse. Within hours it would be back in operation, and was rapidly being used by all inhabitants.

Around seven P.M. a loud knock sounded at the front door of the now de-facto mini-concentration camp. All of the residents reacted in unison by freezing in to a mummy like trance. They all looked at Franz for inspiration. He slowly walked over to the door, trying very hard to maintain his composure, and opened it. Standing there in his full Gestapo regalia was his old comrade Johann Krieger. Near him stood six heavily armed Nazi goons.

"May I come in." Asked Johann.

"But of course, Sir! You have the ultimate power, and we are here to follow your orders. Can you please answer one simple question? Are we being detained because we are Jews, or have we committed any crimes?" Asked Franz, as he looked his old buddy straight in the eyes.

"Don't be so impertinent! It will go easier on you if you follow orders and don't ask too many questions. Do you understand me?" Replied Johann, as he growled at Franz.

Franz was surprised by his old friends' nasty temperament, but he knew that being surrounded by his soldiers, Krieger had to play the role. He ordered most of the adults in to the living room, hallway, stairwell and kitchen. The crowd was so large that many of them stood on the stairs and foyer and tried to listen in. Those that could not fit, gathered outside in front of the door.

"Listen and listen well. I do not have the patience or the time to repeat myself. Higher headquarters has ordered the deportation of all Jews to work relocation areas. Those of you between the ages of thirteen and sixty years old, will be immediately sent to various camps throughout Germany. Those of you over sixty, or twelve and under, will remain in this house until we decide what to do with you! Is that understood?" stated a serious and harsh Johann. Rabbi Goldmann will be responsible for all of you. You must obey him and give him all the information I require. These soldiers will be on duty to prevent any of you from escaping. Any attempt will be met with harsh punishment.

Before anyone could ask questions, or complain. Johann turned around and started out the door. Franz felt the urge to speak with Johann, and gathered his courage once more.

"Sir, sir. Excuse me? What is to happen to our homes and property. Are we to leave everything behind?" Pleaded Franz to his old friend.

"I don't have all the particulars worked out yet, but when I know I shall inform you. You, you there the Rabbi. Come with me." Ordered Johann as he pointed his finger towards Franz.

Both Franz and Johann walked outside and stood near the backyard. Franz was extremely uncomfortable, and did not know what to expect. Johann turned his back away from his soldiers and whispered.

"You fool, you stupid fool! Why did you not listen to me! My hands are tied now! I cannot disobey or I will be following you to those camps. I warned you last night!" Screamed a visibly upset Johann Krieger.

"Franz! You must yell when I strike you in the face." Stated Johann as he suddenly struck the Rabbi across the face with the back of his hand. Although the blow was not hard, the suddenness of it caught Franz by surprise. Franz dutifully obeyed his orders and let out a loud piercing scream.

Franz whispered to Johann, "Why did you do that?"

"I had to make them believe that I really hate you, otherwise I would find it difficult to help you and get away with it." Replied Johann as he looked away. It was the first time in many years that anyone had struck Franz, and it brought back strange feelings of hate and revenge.

Rabbi Goldmann looked at his old friend and was speechless. He knew his position was very tenuous, but he prayed to God that a miracle would happen and save them from this horrible nightmare. After a few seconds, Krieger asked him one more question.

"Franz, how old are you?"

The question caught him by surprise. What on earth could his age have to do with the current situation. Before he could answer, Krieger growled at him again.

"How old are you!"

"I am fifty-nine eleven months and a few days." Answered a nervous Franz.

"Good!" Replied Krieger.

"May I ask what my age has to do with my situation?" Asked a somewhat bolder Goldmann.

"It has a lot to do with everything. I am obligated to ship all Jews between thirteen and sixty years old, to a work camp within two weeks from today. Since you are within a few weeks of being sixty, I will make an exception for you, but there is nothing I can do for the rest of you. I warned you last night! You did not listen, and now you must pay the price." Finished Herr Krieger with emphasis.

"You mean all members of my family who are under sixty will be leaving Niedergeyer within two weeks?" Asked an incredulous Franz.

"Yes, and as a matter of fact, I am going to require you to get me a list of all Jews and their ages. However, you cannot inform anyone of what is going on. It will only cause panic and hurt everyone. Do you understand?" Asked Krieger.

"I can't do this thing you are asking of me. It would be the same as Pontius Pilote in the bible. This is too horrible to even contemplate. Why are we being treated this way?" Cried Rabbi Goldmann as he stared at his old friend.

"I guess you are right. This could be a bible story, and I am one of the Roman soldiers following orders. Try to make the best it and help your people get through this mess. If things work out, you might come home one day soon and resume your life." Stated a somewhat irate Krieger. He hated to lie to his old comrade, but he truly believe that he had done everything within his limited power.

"No, I don't think so. Our lives have been changed forever. We could never feel the same way about Germany, but we still would be proud of our German heritage." Replied Franz his voice trailing off in to a sob.

"I am truly sorry, Franz! You should have listened to me, and you would not have been in this situation! I am angry with you for putting me in this dilemma. Enough of this, just follow my orders and things will take their course." Stated Krieger as he walked away from Rabbi Goldmann without looking back.

The die was cast. There was nothing that Krieger or Franz could do now. Events would take place beyond their control. Both men wished that things had happened differently, but circumstances had dictated otherwise.

Krieger returned to his barracks in Dueren and finalized the assault on Niedergeyer. He had to plan the final removal of most of the Jews from Niedergeyer and the surrounding communities, and Rabbi Goldmann had to reflect on a poor decision he had made.

As he re-entered the house, his wife pleaded with him, "Franz, Franz what is happening to us? Why did he strike you in the face? Are you OK?" Begged his wife.

"Don't worry, all is well. God will protect us." Replied the rabbi.

Chapter 11

Life Goes On

Things went from bad to worse. Before the week was out a total of forty-two lost souls were crammed into Das Haus. No one knew how long they would be there or what their future held for them. The inhabitants of Das Haus were fortunate to have Rabbi Goldmann as their spiritual and practical leader. Once the initial shock wore off, he organized them into sleeping, working and kitchen details. Everyone had a job to do. The Nazis initially allowed them to go work in the garden and continue growing the multitude of fruits and vegetables in their backyard. However, at least four heavily armed guards watched over them.

. Like most Germans the Goldmann's had a large potato patch, some beets, a small amount of wheat, various types of leafy plants, cabbage and twenty fruit trees. As long as they still had money, Rabbi Goldmann had worked it out with Dieter Krieger, they could twice a week, under armed guard, go to the local grocery store and purchase necessities. The Nazis did not provide them with any food or water, at least for the first few weeks anyway.

However, the inhabitants of Das Haus had to be careful. Their funds would eventually run out and hunger would set in. Sarah Goldmann had for years canned most of her fruits and some vegetables and had an ample supply of each. Franz was also the local butcher and had hundreds of already made sausages and other culinary delights in his cellar. All in all they managed to take care of themselves. Except for the occasional spat over this or that, their lives were filled with daily chores and plenty of anxiety.

The biggest problem seemed to be keeping the younger children occupied and out of mischief. Franz assigned the older teenagers the task of finding ways to keep them busy. It wasn't before long that shrill laughter was once again heard in the

Golmann household. Hordes of children were seen running up and down the stairs, from the attic to the basement. It was a comforting sound despite the horrible situation they were in. Children have a way of coping with circumstances a lot better than adults.

What appeared to be a nice routine, was in fact the quiet before the storm. On a quiet, but cold evening Johann Krieger once again came knocking at the door. He seemed only to appear in bad and cold stormy weather. His appearances were reminiscent of old vampire movies. He skulked around in the shadows and disappeared just as quickly. As it was customary only Rabbi Goldmann or his wife Sarah were allowed to answer the door. This would keep the nervous inhabitants in the dark until such time they needed to know. Rabbi Goldman had purposely devised this plan to attempt and control those who might have wild ideas of escape or other schemes. The Gestapo man had made it very clear. "Anyone attempting to escape would cause the immediate execution of all forty-two souls."

There were some who doubted the sincerity of this threat, but Rabbi Goldmann kept reminding them on a daily basis not to jeopardize their already tenuous situation. It was a constant battle on his part to maintain order and discipline. His previous military training came in very handy at times. Some of the inhabitants resented his new-found authority, but most accepted it.

On this faithful evening Johann Krieger asked to see Franz alone. Both men asked all inhabitants to go upstairs or to the cellar. Once this was accomplished Krieger said.

"Franz, do you have the list I asked for two weeks ago?" Asked Krieger in a somewhat grouchy tone.

"Well, I, I, I don't have it ready yet." Replied a frightened, yet courageous rabbi. In his own way Rabbi David Franz Goldmann was trying to stand up to this Nazi.

"What do you mean? You don't have it yet? You have had plenty of time, and my hands are tied, Franz! You either provide me with the list, or I send all off you to Buchenwald concentration camp tomorrow morning!" Screamed an irate Krieger.

Franz did not know what to do? He in fact had a list. He had gotten all the names together on the first evening, but was too afraid to turn it in. It burned a hole in his pocket, and he wished to be rid of it.

"Tomorrow morning, tomorrow morning? What do you mean? Has it come to that?" Asked Franz, tears slowly rolling down his cheeks.

"Tomorrow?" He repeated as if not wanting to believe this horrible yet inevitable event. His right hand reached in his pocket grasping the note. Although too afraid to say anything, his motion gave away the hidden message.

"OK, OK! Let's play a game. I accidentally reach in to your pocket and discover the list? You are therefore not responsible, and the matter is settled? How does that sound?" Asked Krieger, his lips smiling like a toad.

Before Franz could respond, Krieger shoved his right fist deep in to Franz's pocket and fished out the list. He held it high in his right hand, waving it back and forth like a trophy. Franz was too shocked to say or do anything. He let out a heavy sigh and bowed his head in shame.

Krieger started reading the names of those individuals who were on the list. Pausing occasionally to catch his breath. Franz eventually turned his head away and began sobbing.

Name	Date of Birth	Place of Birth
Anders, Jakob	June 27th, 1898	Moers
Anders, Anna	July 1st, 1903	Embken
Anders, Samuel	April 4, 1921	Embken
Anders, Bertha	September 9th, 1923	Embken
Alexander, Daniel	June 7th, 1896	Dueren
Alexander, Ida	May 11th, 1901	Niedergeyer
Denlon, Simon	June 21st, 1886	Niedergeyer
Dingelmann, Hermann	August 8th, 1883	Guerzenich
Dingelmann, Klara	August 2nd, 1889	Niedergeyer
Goldmann, Erik	April 19th, 1921	Niedergeyer
Goldmann, Esther	June 21st, 1924	Niedergeyer

Goldmann, Sarah	June 13th, 1883	Kerpen
Goldmann, David Franz	October 25th, 1879	Niedergeyer
Hirschfeld, Thomas	November 3rd, 1899	Weilerwist
Hirschfeld, Johanna	January 23rd, 1904	Niedergeyer
Hirschfeld, Elsa	May 1st, 1923	Niedergeyer
Hirschfeld, Samuel	June 12th, 1924	Niedergeyer
Hirschfeld, Rosanna	June 12th, 1924	Nierdergeyer
Luegen, Melanie	July 16, 1889	Niedergeyer
Luegen, Lothar	September 2nd, 1887	Dueren
Luegen, Abraham	October 3rd, 1918	Kreuzau
Luegen, Martha	April 2nd, 1920	Nideggen
Luegen, Heinrich	May 8th, 1921	Kreuzau
Meyers, Fritz	August 1st, 1881	Soller
Meyers, Lisalotte	February 28th, 1889	Niedergeyer
Meyers, David	May 21st, 1909	Guerzenich
Meyers, Claudia	May 7th, 1911	Guerzennich
Schmitz-Perlmann, Franz	August 6th, 1915	Kreuzau
Schmitz-Perlmann, Kate	September 1st, 1917	Dueren
Waltmann, Samuel	June 4th, 1888	Kerpen

(Please note: These are not the real names of those sent away to the concentration camps.)

Krieger screamed in rage as he saw Franz's name on the list.

"How could you put your own name down, after I offered to help you? Don't you want to stay?" Asked Krieger in a more relaxed tone?

"Well actually, I do not want to stay if my family leaves tomorrow. I would have nothing to look forward to. Life would be meaningless without them. I have made up my mind, I wish to go with them, and that is final!" Stated a determined Rabbi Goldmann.

"Well I am sorry you feel that way, but I must keep you here at gun point if necessary. I need you to stay and take care of the remaining fifteen. Who are either too old or too young. Higher headquarters has not decided yet what to do with you guys yet?"

Krieger stated, as he looked Franz in the eyes.

"Jews, Jews, Jews you mean! Don't you?" Screamed an irate and out of control Rabbi Goldmann. Krieger was caught by surprise. He did not expect Franz to react so forcefully. He took a few seconds to reflect upon this outburst of emotion.

"Yes Franz, Jews! You must face your circumstances and learn to cope with it. Tomorrow morning at seven a.m., I will be here with a squad of soldiers and I will transport those folks on the list to the train station in Dueren. From then on I relinquish all control to higher headquarters. They will be transported to Koeln, Frankfurt, Munich and then on to Buchenwald concentration camp. Some may be sent to other locations, but I have no control or knowledge of their final destination. I pray to God that all goes well for your family, but I am merely an expediter." Stated Krieger turning away from his old comrade in arms and walking towards the front door.

When Krieger reached the hallway, he turned around once more and stated. "Franz, don't forget to tell everyone to bring on bag and one bag only! Anything more will be thrown away. Also remind them, that everyone will be thoroughly searched upon departure and arrival at their respective camps. Thoroughly searched!" Stated Krieger as he stepped through the front door.

The moment Krieger left the house, Franz Goldmann was overwhelmed with strong feelings and emotions. He slowly started to cry, and his body began to shake uncontrollably. Within seconds, his wife, children and the rest of the inhabitants of Das Haus surrounded him. All of them were severely distraught by his obvious loss of emotional control. His wife Sarah approached him and slowly spoke to him.

"What is wrong Franz? What is wrong Franz? Why are you crying." She asked, tenderly holding his shaking hands in hers.

"It's tomorrow, tomorrow, tomorrow!" Replied Franz, his body shaking like a leaf in a hurricane.

"Tomorrow, tomorrow, OK, we will deal with it. As long as we are together, we can handle anything." Stated, a confident Sarah.

"You don't understand, I am not going with you!" Screamed Franz his voice becoming more rasp as he spoke. They have decided that I, and fifteen others will stay here until such time as they can decide what to do with us. Everyone over sixty, and under-thirteen must remain in Das Haus. Every one else will leave tomorrow morning, no exceptions!

It took several seconds for this information to sink through her brain. She heard what Franz said, but her senses were not quite in tune with the rest of her body. She suddenly screamed and wailed at the same time. This expression of grief was so loud that everyone in Das Haus heard it and came running. Within seconds the hallway, parlor, living room and kitchen were filled with anxious inhabitants. Everyone asking the same question, over and over.

"What is going on?" Asked Herr Hirschfeld in an excited voice.

Before he could reply, an over-anxious Sarah blurted out.

"They are taking us all away tomorrow, tomorrow!" She screamed and collapsed on the ground.

This statement caused many others to react in a similar way. Wails, moans, screams, hysterical laughter suddenly broke out throughout Das Haus. Everyone was talking at once, and all of it directed at Franz.

"Wait, wait, wait!" screamed Franz at the top of his voice. His strong presence finally brought everyone under normalcy.

"There is nothing we can do right now. Lets figure out the best way to handle it. Don't do anything stupid, they have the house surrounded and any attempt to escape will bring instant death to all of us. As long as we are breathing, we still have a future. Is that understood?" Stated a Rabbi Goldmann, in a firm voice.

His controlled presence and emotional stability seemed to calm everyone down, except for the occasional moan or wail from someone in the crowd. Rabbi Goldmann continued.

"You older children, I want you to take the younger ones upstairs in the attic, and stay there until we call you! Is that understood?" Ordered the former Sergeant Major. His firm demeanor and military bearing got the point across.

"Yes sir." Responded the teenagers in unison.

"Common kids, lets go upstairs and play." Shouted Erik, Esther and several other older kids. At first, the younger ones were somewhat hesitant, but one by one they followed them upstairs.

Once all the children had left the area, Franz ordered the remaining adults to cram themselves in to the living room/kitchen area. Once that was accomplished, he began to inform them of what Krieger had said. He read the list and one by one they answered as their names were called. Some were surprised that Franz's name was on the same piece of paper. He explained the circumstances and they seemed to accept his explanation.

"We must now figure out a way to best help ourselves and survive. We cannot just fade away like worms in the garden. Let's do what we can for the children, and for ourselves. We only have less than twelve hours before dawn tomorrow. Those of us left behind will have to manage somehow, however those leaving tomorrow need our support." Explained a determined Rabbi Goldmann.

Some of the more timid members raised their hands; reminding Franz of his schooldays. "Yes, what can I do for you." replied Franz, his hand waving towards Herr Hirschfeld.

"Give us some details, what is going to happen to all of us? Has Krieger said anything to you? Is he the same Krieger from Niedergeyer?" Asked an embolden Herr Hirschfeld.

"Well if it's details you want, I can't help you. Krieger only said, tomorrow morning at seven a.m. That is all I know, and yes to your second question. Krieger is the same Krieger who went to war with my father in WWI. Answered Franz. That statement seemed to create a stir in the crowd.

Franz formed them into five groups. Each one had a task to accomplish.

Group A: was responsible for collecting and distributing warm clothes to all that were leaving tomorrow. Group B: collected all of the food that they would need on their trip.

Group C: Made sure that everyone had their ID cards, passports, birth certificates etc. Group D: was made the security detail, they would watch over everyone and try to protect each other as best they could, and finally Group E: they made sure everyone had complete a will and collected a list of names of relatives and friends. This entire procedure took almost five hours. Meanwhile the younger children and teenagers were still entertaining themselves in the attic.

At around midnight Franz gather the section leaders once more for a final briefing. "So how are things going? Everything under control?" Asked Rabbi Goldmann.

One by one, they all nodded their heads. Franz asked one last question?

"What are you going to do with your money and gold? Have you thought about it? Krieger made it a point to emphasize the fact that everyone would be thoroughly searched before and after. If you have any valuable you want to leave behind, or pass on to your remaining family or friends, you had better do it now, because tomorrow will be too late."

That statement seemed to wake everyone up. The group leaders all went to their respective sections and informed them of the news. For almost an hour there was silence as each group secretly huddled together and discussed their individual plans.

It was nearly two in the morning when everyone had finished stashing their loot. Three of the leaders came over and asked Franz if he would be willing to hide some of their money and jewels, until such time as they might need it. Franz gladly accepted the responsibility and took all the bundles to the basement. In the far corner of the sausage storage and curing area, he dug a hole two feet deep. He carefully placed all three bags on the bottom and covered the whole thing with a heavy flagstone. He checked out the area and sprinkled dirt and dust over everything. No one would ever know what was buried in his basement. Upon returning to his living room, he reflected on his own family's gold coins, *should he have buried them as well? Would they need them?* Krieger's warning raced around in his head like a spinning top.

No, the children will need them more than me, I will just keep the five coins and perhaps one or two rings. He thought to himself. Keeping that in mind he called his children and wife to his bedroom.

"You all know what will happen tomorrow, however we don't know what the future holds for us? We need to take care of ourselves and protect what we have from the Nazis. Listen, and listen carefully. Tomorrow you will be thoroughly searched, and when you arrive at your destination, you will be searched again! It is vital that they do not find your gold coins or the jewels. Is that understood?" Stated Rabbi Goldmann.

"If at anytime you suspect a full body cavity search? You must swallow the gold coins or hide them someplace where they will not be found? Is that understood?" Growled Franz, as he looked down upon his terrified family.

"Swallow coins? Can we do that?" Asked Erik.

"Yes, no problem. Make sure to drink a large quantity of fluids, and obviously do not each much for a couple of meals and eventually, they will all pass your rectum." Stated Rabbi Goldmann with confidence.

"Have you ever done that, Vater?" Asked an incredulous Erik?

"Well, yes in fact when I was a child, I ate three coins, and they all passed within two days. As a matter of fact Erik, when you were a young boy of two or three years of age. You swallowed five marbles, and passed them also within a couple of nights. The trick is to drink fluids, and have a safe place to recover them." Stated Rabbi Goldmann with conviction.

"That is right, that is right. I remember now." Answered Esther as she replied and nodded her head at the same time.

"It's time for bed now, tomorrow will be a long day for all of us, and we should get some rest now." With that statement, Franz gently prodded his children upstairs.

Franz took his wife Sarah to their bedroom. It would probably be a long time before he would ever sleep with his wife again and he wanted to have a few quiet hours with her. He was sure that all over "Das Haus" the same events were taking place for the last time?

It had been a long time since they had had intimate moments together, but they both embraced each other with desperate passion and love. They lovingly fell in to each other's arms and slept like they had not slept in a long time. Although their dreams were restless and agitated, the night seemed to last forever.

Chapter 12

Terror!

Sarah Goldmann woke up screaming in terror. She knew this would be the last time she would ever see and touch her loving husband. Franz grabbed her by the shoulder and gently caressed her.

"Don't worry "*Schatzie*" (sweetheart), everything will be OK. We must maintain our faith, and pray to God! He will provide the answers." Answered a very sad Rabbi Goldmann.

Although he tried to maintain his composure, the tears just started to flow, and before long they both were sobbing uncontrollably. A loud knock on their bedroom door interrupted their self-pity trip.

"Vater, Vater, Vater! Come quickly, please! It's Herr Hirschfeld, he is dead! Please come now!" Screamed a hysterical and obviously upset Erik.

Franz jumped out of bed and quickly threw some clothes on. His son Erik was patiently waiting for him in the hallway.

"Come on Vater, he is blue in the face. He hung himself in the rafters last night. No one saw or heard him do it. He took an overdose of his heart medicine, and then let the noose do the rest. Frau Hirschfeld was so upset yesterday evening that she took a sleeping tablet and was totally unconscious herself until this morning." Explained Erik to his father as he ran up the stairs to the attic

The large two level attic had been cordoned off with bed sheets and blankets giving the different families a semblance of privacy. When Franz and Erik arrived upstairs, total chaos reigned supreme in the attic. The parents were trying to protect the children from the awful vision of Herr Hirschfeld hanging from the far corner rafter. He had his best Sunday suit on, and pinned to it was a handwritten note to his wife and Rabbi Goldmann. His lifeless eyes bulged in their sockets, and his swollen blue tongue was sticking out for all to see. It was a frightening and disturbing vision.

"OK, get everyone out of here, especially the children and the family Hirschfeld. But before we do, lets say a prayer for him and his family." said Rabbi Goldmann as he began reciting an ancient Hebrew prayer for the dead. Before he could finish, a loud knock was heard at the door.

"**Raus, Raus, Raus aus dem Haus**! (Out, out, out of the house)" Screamed a Nazi Untersturmfueher.

"Everybody must gather in the courtyard, and do it quickly. You have five minutes to assemble or else!" Screamed the irate Nazi. Behind him stood a large group of heavily armed storm troopers all pointing their weapons in the direction of Das Haus and its occupants.

"All of you who are leaving today, have your one and only suitcase in your possession. Remember you will be searched. Do not, I repeat bring any weapons or illegal contraband with you. You will be severely punished. Is that understood?" Shouted the Gestapo man as he walked up the stairs.

Franz waved at Krieger and asked him to please come inside. Krieger nodded his head and pushed his way past the terrified hordes of residents trying to get out. Franz motioned Krieger into the now empty living room, and explained to him what had happened that morning in the attic.

"Coward, cowardly act. How could he leave his wife and family behind? They still must go without him. There is nothing I can do." Explained Krieger, shaking his head in disgust.

"I beg of you, in the name of humanity. Please allow his family a few days to bury the man, and then you can do whatever you wish with them." Pleaded a begging Rabbi Goldmann.

"I guess you don't understand the words coming out of my mouth? There is nothing I can do! As a matter of fact, I will have hell to pay explaining the missing man! After all, I am accountable for all of you." Stated Krieger, his voice rising in anger.

"Take me instead and your count will be correct. Just allow the Hirschfeld family a few days to bury their father." Asked Franz, as he stared at Krieger.

"It's of no use Franz, I can't do it and don't ask me again!" Screamed Krieger, catching the rabbi by surprised.

"Besides, who else would bury him tomorrow? If not you? You must stay here and handle everything. Don't argue anymore and go to the courtyard with the others for now." Said Krieger to a sorrowful Franz.

One by one everyone slowly assembled in the courtyard, their pitiful belongings in one hand or sitting on the ground in front of them. The smaller children were oblivious as to what was happening, and had a hard time sitting still for the final roll call. As the names were called, the families were forever separated. Some responded in a brave and courageous fashion; others were more emotional and could not separate themselves from their loved ones.

The Nazi soldiers were quick to prod them their bayonets and eventually both groups were apart. The ones remaining were so shocked and upset that they ignored the heavy icy down pour, which had suddenly started. It was one of those horrible windy rains that soaked through your body. Before long, everyone was shaking uncontrollably. Even the hardened soldiers looked at their leaders for guidance. Krieger finally gave the order and allowed the remaining inhabitants to re-enter Das Haus.

Once the lucky fifteen had re-occupied Das Haus, Krieger approached Franz and allowed him to go outside again and wave goodbye to his family. Rabbi Goldmann saw the unlucky ones board the trucks, and he had a last glimpse of his brave son Erik clutching his hysterical mother. As hard as Erik tried to control his emotions, a wave of nostalgia swept over him. *Was this the last time he would ever see Das Haus again?*

Everyone in the truck was sobbing, crying or generally whimpering in one form or another. His sister just sat there, unable to comprehend the reality of their situation. Although her eyes were open she could not see her father frantically waving at them. The shock had been too great for her. The last thing Rabbi Goldmann saw of his family, was the tail end of the army truck rounding the bend and his son desperately waving at him.

"Franz, do not allow anyone to go to the attic until I contact the Chief of Police, and we can prepare services for Herr Hirschfeld tomorrow." Stated Krieger to a sobbing Franz. Krieger's order, helped bring Franz back to reality. He still could not believe the fact that his beloved family and the rest of Niedergeyer's Jews were no longer among them.

"Franz, Franz, Franz!" shouted an angry Krieger.

"How do you know we can arrange everything so quickly? It takes time to arrange a funeral." Replied Franz, in a sad voice. His thoughts finally focusing on Krieger.

"Don't worry Franz, everything will be arranged by tomorrow afternoon. You just make sure that no one else does anything foolish. I hate doing all of this paperwork." Snickered Krieger, as he looked at Franz.

"Herr Krieger, I do not think that levity is appropriate now. Please forgive me if I do not laugh. I have too much on my conscience right now, and I cannot accept your bad taste." Replied an angry and defiant Rabbi Goldmann.

Krieger was surprised by the outburst, but did not wish to heighten the tension or make the situation worst than it already was. He pretended not to hear his last statement and turned away.

"Oh, by the way. I have something for you. It came in the mail today and I am giving it to you on one condition. You cannot tell anyone where you got it! Is that understood?" Stated a somewhat grouchy Krieger.

Krieger reached in to his black leather jacket and pulled out what looked liked a postcard. It was addressed to Rabbi Goldmann, Hauptstrasse 192, Niedergeyer, Germany. It had an English stamp on it and no return address. It took Franz a few seconds to realize whom it was from. *Werner, of course!* He thought to himself. It had the following message:

"Have arrived at aunt's house, all is well. I was able to contact the chicken farmer and he sends his greetings. Will try to do something from home. Never fear, we love you and pray for you. Please let my folks know that I am well. Love, Renrew............."

To say the least, it was a little confusing at first. This cryptic message from Werner was an unexpected surprise. Franz had to laugh at Werner's childish attempt at deception, "Renrew" was of course Werner spelled backwards, and the chicken farmer was Franz's brother in America. It brought a smile to Franz's sad face; poor Werner would never know that his parents were among the first group to be shipped away today. The always-observant Krieger, noticed the grin and asked Franz who was Renrew was in England?

"It's my mother's cousin, Matilda Renrew in London. They left Germany after the first war and we keep in contact." Replied Franz, trying to keep a straight face.

"I need to ask you a favor? We will have to have regular food rations delivered to us on a regular basis. Additionally, the ladies have asked for permission to run a clothesline between my house and my neighbor Frau Scmitdken. It's the only place to hang a line and keep the clothes off the ground? When the weather is nice, that is. It really would help us?" Asked a pleading Rabbi Goldmann.

"I guess that would be all right. I am sure the soldiers would appreciate not having to escort them outside every time they want to dry clothes. I will tell Frau Schitdken to run a line over today or tomorrow. You must now concentrate on the funeral, and I will make sure that you are provisioned with an adequate amount of food." Stated Krieger as he walked away.

As if he had an afterthought, Krieger turned around and once again emphasized, "don't touch the body, and the Chief will be over shortly!" Reminded Krieger as he left the area.

Franz grunted and nodded his head. By the time he re-entered Das Haus, Krieger was already around the corner and gone. The rest of remaining fifteen inhabitants were curious as to what had transpired outside. They were all still upset and disturbed by the day's events. Franz looked at the assembled group and motioned to them to come closer. Once in the living room, he pulled out the postcard and read it out loud. The Oohs and Aahs resounded throughout the living room. Everyone had questions, but were thrilled none the same, to receive news from the outside world. Although they were not quite sure what it meant, at least Werner and Lisa were safe, and they could tell the world the truth. Before anyone could really absorb the news, a loud knock was heard at the door. Rabbi Goldmann told everyone to be quiet, and jerked the door opened. Standing there was Chief Wolfgang Baume, escorted by three soldiers.

"Hello Franz, I am here to look after Herr Hirschfeld. I understand he is upstairs in the attic? Is that correct?" Stated a somewhat uncomfortable Chief.

"Yes Herr Baume, he is upstairs. I will show you the way, if you would like?" Replied a somewhat hesitant Rabbi Goldman.

"No, I know the way, however, I would like to have any witnesses come forward and give me a statement." Asked the Chief, as he slowly ascended the stairs.

"Well Chief, if you want any statements, you are going to have to go Buchenwald and get them. Everyone who was upstairs is now on an army truck en route to the train station. Even his own family members were deported by the Nazis." Replied Franz, as he gazed upon Baume.

The Chief just shook his head and kept walking. Rabbi Goldmann now noticed that the Chief's uniform was torn in three places; he also had a couple of bruises on his face and was not carrying his duty Luger 9mm Parabellum pistol. Franz wondered, *have they been getting even with him for his earlier statements concerning the synagogue? Are they exacting retribution for his anti-Nazi sympathies? One thing was sure, the Chief had seen better days!*

Ten minutes later, Chief Baume and the three soldiers came marching down the stairs, carrying the already stiff body of Herr

Hirschfeld wrapped in a large quilt. They did not do a very good job of wrapping his body. His right arm had popped out of the quilt, and was now banging on the railing as they proceeded downwards. It made a horribly loud sound. Katonkk, katonkk, katonkk all the way down the stairs.

"Chief, can I please say a quick prayer before you take him away?" Asked a distraught Rabbi Goldmann?

"OK men, let's take a small break at the foot of the stairs." Stated Chief Baume, in a more inquiring rather than a direct order sort of way. To make matters worse, one of the men dropped the front end, and Herr Hirschfeld's lifeless body fell out and slid down at the foot of the stairs.

Everyone gasped in horror as they saw his face once again. The bulging eyes, protruding tongue and purple color were a reminder of how horrible death can be.

"Please, please, please let me pray for him?" begged Rabbi Goldmann as the soldiers tried to regain their composure and cover him up. "Yes, go ahead." Stated a now more authoritative, Chief Baume.

Rabbi Goldmann started to say his prayers out loud, but was interrupted by the butt of a gun to his stomach.

"Don't say that filth out loud or you will be joining your dead Jew friend!" Screamed the nearest Nazi soldier. Everyone froze, in their tracks. After a few seconds, the ranking soldier picked up the body and they all walked out the door towards the waiting truck.

Chief Baume turned around and said. "I am sorry. I will be back tomorrow at three p.m. We will keep him in my facility until then. Please have everything in order for the ceremony.

Franz looked at Chief Baume and nodded his head. Just when things seemed to be at their worst, a smiling and friendly Frau Schmidtken came over and offered to hang up the clothesline. Franz thanked her, and asked one of the men to help her out. Franz suddenly noticed Frau Schmidtken putting something in his front pocket without anyone else noticing.

When no one was noticing, Franz pulled out the piece of paper and read it.

"We are all with you. We will do what we can. The clothesline is attached to a wheel and can be reeled back and forth. Be sure to only use it at night, and when no one is watching. Our sympathies are with you. Frau Schmitdken and friends. PS, Be sure to destroy this message!"

Franz instinctively shoved the paper in his mouth and swallowed it in one gulp. This simple message had invigorated him, and gave renewed energy to continue his struggle for survival.

Once Herr Hirschfeld had been removed from Das Haus, a sense of calmness and tranquillity overtook all remaining inhabitants. Rabbi Goldmann spoke with them and asked them to all pray for their lost friend. The rest of the evening continued without any further incidents. Everyone had their evening meal and went to bed early. The dawn broke over Das Haus like a Gothic painter's canvass. The bright sunshine stroked Das Haus with renewed energy and hope.

Franz once again heard someone at the front door. The banging grew louder by the minute. "Hold on!" Shouted Franz as he ran towards the door. Standing there, looking as if he had just swallowed a canary was Krieger, the Gestapo man.

"Franz, Franz, do you have anything to do with this? I can't allow it! It would cause a great deal of trouble for all of us, don't you understand?" Screamed an irate and obviously upset Krieger.

"What do you mean? I do not know what you are talking about? I have been here locked up all night; protected by the mighty German army!" Stated Rabbi Goldmann in a factual tone of voice.

"You mean you don't know what is going on? I have been told that almost the entire population of Niedergeyer will show up for Herr Hirschfeld's funeral later on today! The priest, Chief of Police, volunteer fire department, school teachers and just about everyone else insisted on showing up! It would be a disaster if this got out!   Don't you understand?" Shouted Krieger at Rabbi Goldmann.

"Calm down and reflect on your options.   Are you going to arrest a thousand German citizens simply for attending the funeral of a neighbor?   Just think how bad it would look if some sort of riot broke out and someone else was hurt?   You would held responsible!" Rabbi Goldmann said to the Gestapo man.

"Well, I guess you make sense after all.   However, I can only allow you and two others from Das Haus to attend.   Is that understood?" Shouted a now visibly upset Krieger.

"Oh!   So you mean you going to have your brave German soldiers carry the casket of a Jew?" Replied Goldmann in a mocking manner.

"Don't push it Franz.   Our friendship has long since been repaid in full!   But I guess that makes sense after all.   OK, you may have six mourners, and no more!"   Huffed the Gestapo man, trying to show his authority.

"I think that is a fair and wise compromise.   I will make sure here is no trouble from any of us."   Said Franz with a smile.

"OK then!   I will see you at two-thirty in front of your house!" Replied Krieger as he walked out the door.

Most of the inhabitants came into the very crowded living room and politely asked what was going on?   Rabbi Goldmann explained his dilemma and asked for volunteers to carry the casket. All of the remaining inhabitants, including the very young and very old raised their collective hands in unison.

"I am truly moved by your enthusiasm, but unfortunately Krieger will only allow six of us to go.   Since this is a solemn occasion, I will automatically rule out any of the younger ones. That leaves ten adults; in order to placate everyone I will conduct a lottery and draw out the name of those who will be going with me later on." Stated Rabbi Goldmann in an official sounding voice.

. Everyone seemed to agree with his decision and nodded their heads; without saying a word. Rabbi Goldmann wrote their names on small pieces of paper and placed them in a coffee pot. A young child was asked to pick out the names. Within thirty seconds all six names had been drawn, and those selected were agreed upon. The selected ones left the room and went to put on some more appropriate clothing. Twenty minutes later, all of them had returned and were anxiously waiting in the foyer. Krieger suddenly opened the front door and abruptly notified them that it was time to leave. Rabbi Goldmann and the six inhabitants stepped out on to the main street and were immediately overwhelmed by the sight before them. It seemed as almost, every-single resident came to pay their final respects to a good man, friend and neighbor. The crowd rapped itself around the corner of Das Haus, spilling over unto the neighboring side streets and yards.

The army truck carrying the body pulled in front of Das Haus, and the whole convoy of the truck, cars, and humanity began the short trip to the Jewish cemetery, less than four hundred meters up the road. The cemetery was visible from Das Haus and normally a quick eight minute walk, however today due to the large crowd it took nearly twenty minutes for everyone to reach the small iron gate that surrounded the ancient burial ground. Rabbi Goldmann was amazed to see that a plot had already dug and was waiting for Herr Hirschfeld. The body was brought out of the truck and carried to the site by the six selected participants. Although the brave citizens of Niedergeyer had shown courage and determination by simply coming to the funeral, most of them were very quiet, and showed little emotion. The Catholic priest had in fact been a great influence in convincing so many of them to show up. They were damned if they did, and damned if they didn't. The fact that a heavily armed platoon of SS soldiers stood around the cemetery with their weapons pointing at the crowd probably had a great deal to do with the crowd's mood.

Everyone suddenly grew quiet as Rabbbi Goldmann began the "Mourner's Kaddish, or prayer to the dead. He started off in German by asking all present to participate. In a beautiful, yet mournful voice he prayed out loud:

"Magnified and sanctified be God's great name in the world which He has created according to His will. May He establish

His kingdom soon, in our lifetime. Let us say: Amen"

At first only a few of the mourners recited the prayer, but an inspired Catholic priest began preaching the prayer in loud voice. Suddenly many of them began to follow his lead, and before long they were all following in his footsteps

"May His great name be praised to all eternity."

"Hallowed and honored, extolled and exalted. Adored and acclaimed be the name of the Holy One, though He is above all the praises, hymns, and songs of adoration which men can utter. Let us say: Amen".

The mesmerized crowd were now following his every word with interest and respect. He was amazed that so many recited his Jewish prayer. Rabbi Goldmann continued:

"May God grant abundant peace and life to us and to all Israel. Let us say: Amen."

"May He who ordains harmony in the universe grant peace to us and to all Israel. Let us say: Amen."

Once Rabbi Goldmann finished, the Catholic priest said the "Lords Prayer", and again everyone stood in silence and repeated the words with great fervor and enthusiasm. Once he finished the casket was lowered and ceremony was over. Everyone began to dissipate down the main street away from the cemetery. It seemed as if everyone was anxious to get back home. Only Rabbi Goldmann and the pole bearers hung around for a few minutes and began reciting the "Kaddish" in Hebrew.

"Yit -gadal v'yit-kadash sh'mey raba, b'alma di v'ra hirutey, vyam-lih mal-hutey b'ha-yey-hon uv'yomey-hon uv'ha-yey d'hol beyt yisrael ba-agala u-vizman kariv, v'imru amen".

Before Rabbi Goldmann could continue with his prayer, the senior Nazi non-commissioned officer in charge of the detail, slammed the butt of his K-98 Mauser rifle into the stomach of the still praying rabbi. The blow was so strong that it sent him sprawling to the ground. He lay there panting and gasping for air. He never stopped praying, the other six Jews continued as well. The Nazi sergeant was about to deliver another blow, this time to the head, when a voice whispered in his ear.

"If you do that, I will take measures to forever ruin your career and tell the world of your homosexual tendencies, Sergeant!" Stated a serious and commanding Krieger.

"But, but, but Sir, I don't know what you are talking about? I am not a homosexual and you cannot prove it!" Stated the somewhat defiant sergeant.

"Is that a fact? How about private Reinhardt? Do you remember him? Guess where he is now? Buchenwald, that's right the same horrible place where these unfortunate Jews are ending up. If you don't want to go there yourself, you had better stop now!" Finished an irate Krieger, leaning over the sergeant's ear.

"Yes, yes Sir, it won't happen again, I promise!" Stated a humbled and embarrassed Nazi sergeant.

Rabbi Goldmann and the six pole-bearers, watched fascinated as this dramatic event unfolded in front of them. They continued to pray in Hebrew as they walked back to Das Haus.

"Y'hey sh'mey raba m'varah l'alam ul'almey alma-ya.

Yit-barah v'yish-tabah v'yit-pa-ar v'yit-roman v'yit-na-sey v'yit-hadar v'yit-aleh v'yit-halal sh'mey d'kud-sha, b'rih hu, eyla min kol-bir-hata v'shi-rata tush-b'hata v'ne-hemata da-amiran b'alma, v imru amen".

As the small crowd slowly made its way back to Das Haus, Rabbi Goldmann never stopped praying

"Y'hey sh'lama raba min sh'ma-ya, v'ha-yim aleynu v'al kol Yisrael, vimru amen."

"Oseh shalom bim-romav, hu ya-aseh shalom aleynu v'al kol yisrael v'imru amen".

"Oseh shalom bin-romav, hu ya-aseh shalom aleynu v'al kol yisrael, v'imru amen."

Just as Rabbi Goldmann finished his prayer, the procession stopped in front of Das Haus. An apologetic Krieger tried to speak with Franz, but Goldmann would have none of it, and simply walked into Das Haus.

Everyone gathered in the living room and warmly hugged each other. It was as if their "Kaddish" prayer had given them a renewed sense of pride, self-worth and renewed their faith. This was the first of many sad events that would befall the residents of Das Haus. However it also was the first sign of rebellion. They had in fact had gotten their way, and stood up to the Nazis. Rabbi Goldmann was very proud of his flock, and prayed to God that they would continue to maintain solidarity, now and in the future. *This merely was a small skirmish, but that is how battles are won! One at a time,* "He thought to himself."

Chapter 13

"Visitor"

"Wow! This is certainly an incredible story, keep going, and keep going." Stated an anxious Cameron.

"Slow down Cameron, I need to take a bathroom break. All of that beer, wine and Schnapps has gone to my kidneys. I will be right back." Answered his father-in-law as he walked out the door. Just then the phone rang several times. After a few minutes Kate came in and had a confused look on her face.

"There is some strange woman on the phone; speaking incoherently in a combination of English, French, Spanish and gibberish. I can't understand a word she is saying except, Cameron, Cameron, Cameron!" Stated a visibly upset Kate.

"My guess is that it is my mother, Maria Theresa. She has a habit speaking at a fast pace and gets her foreign languages all mixed up. Let me handle it." Replied Cameron as he got up to go to the phone.

"Hello, hello." Said Cameron.

"Is that you mama?" Stated Cameron once again. Before he could ask anything else, a torrent of various languages and words came out of the other end of the phone line. *Yeah, that has to be my Mamacita,* he thought to himself.

For the next few minutes he was unable to say anything, because Maria Theresa was like a rapid-fire machine gun. She went on about her visit to the Holy Land, Egypt and Morocco and Spain, and that she decided she was going to stop and visit for a few days before going to France and visiting the rest of the relatives. She was especially happy to meet Dieter and Kate. She had never met them in person, and was looking forward to this opportunity. Cameron knew what an effort it was for her to visit Germany. Maria Theresa was not particularly fond of Germans or

German things. She had sworn never to come to Germany and buy anything made in Germany. Her family had suffered greatly under the German bombs in Spain, France and Morocco. Her father and six of her siblings had perished between 1937 and 1944, all directly or indirectly caused by the Germans or their lackeys. However, this was a special occasion and he was glad that she had come.

"OK mama, I will pick you up at the airport in about forty-five minutes. Lufthansa terminal number two at the Köln airport." Answered Cameron, as he hung up the phone.

Just then, Dieter walked in and asked what was going on? "You are never going to believe who is at the airport? My mother! She decided to stop by and say hello before going on to France! I can't believe she did it?" Stated Cameron, a whimsical look on his face.

"But why? Why shouldn't she come and visit? Asked a confused Dieter.

Cameron tried to explain his mother's hatred for Germany and anything German. Dieter nodded his head, and explained that at one time he had similar feelings about all Americans and the English.

"Let's try to make her feel welcome, and please Cameron. Do not talk about your investigation. It would only confuse her and reinforce her beliefs. Let's make her stay as pleasant as possible." Stated Dieter.

"Sounds good to me. I agree. It might spoil her trip. Let's go to the airport. I told her I would be there in fort-five minutes or less. Please do not talk about Das Haus and those strange happenings." Replied Cameron as he walked towards the front door.

"Don't worry Cameron, I am going with you, and I know a short cut that will save us at least twenty minutes. Lets use my Mercedes, it's faster." Stated Dieter as he grabbed his keys off the table.

"Let's do it then." Answered back Cameron, as he sped after Dieter.

The ride to the airport, was one that Cameron would never forget. Cameron had always chided Dieter for his lead foot, but this was the ride from hell! Dieter mostly used country roads, highways and eventually got on the autobahn. The average speed was over a hundred miles an hour, and up to one hundred and forty on the freeway. Cameron tried to explain to Dieter that Maria Theresa did not like high speeds, and he would have to slow down on the way home.

"Ja, ja, ja! Don't worry, on the way home, I will drive like an American." Dieter replied, laughing as he did so.

"Don't forget, she is truly petrified, and I don't want to ruin her vacation, please? Asked a pleading Cameron.

The Mercedes, a beautifully restored silver metallic 1963 280SL coupe, screeched up to the Lufthansa terminal. Dieter stayed in the car while Cameron went looking for his mother. After few minutes of walking around in the giant hall, he finally located his tiny four foot eleven mother sitting on her suitcase near the female toilet. The reunion was very loud, joyous and extremely Mamacita. Her words rolled off her tongue, one hundred miles an hour, and as was her habit she kept switching languages. Cameron thought to himself, *Charo the Spanish entertainer, and my mother have many things in common, they use their hands when they talk and speak as if they are trying to break a world record!*

Dieter was outside the terminal trying to explain to a very irate policeman why he should not get a ticket. The officer was very upset and was in the process of writing it when a very calm and charming Maria Theresa grabbed his writing hand. She then proceeded, in her usual fashion, to speak to him in three or four languages. The officer looked down upon her and shook his head in despair. She continued to rattle on, not making any sense at all. He finally looked in supplication to both Dieter and Cameron for assistance, but none was forthcoming. Both men smiled and shook their heads. The disgusted officer took the ticket and tore it in a million pieces. He turned around one last time and shook his head in desperation; walking towards another illegally parked automobile, and hoped that he did not encounter another wild woman from Spain.

Both Dieter and Cameron helped Maria Theresa with her luggage. They then proceeded towards the A3 Autobahn north, which would lead them towards Aachen and home. Cameron, in German, reminded Dieter about the speed limit. His father-in-law grumbled something under his breath and slowed down to one hundred twenty kilometers an hour (a mere 72 m.p.h.!). Traffic was very light that time of day and they arrived back in Niedergeyer in an hour. The only comment from Maria Theresa was,

"Germany is very clean and also very green. However everyone drives way to fast and I am glad to see that Dieter is such a good driver!" Cameron and Dieter both laughed out loud, which confused Maria Theresa. The rest of the trip all three were silent, which was unusual for Maria. She maintained her silence until Dieter pulled up to the driveway.

"What a beautiful house." She stated.

"Thank you Maria. I built it myself after the war." Dieter replied with a certain sense pride.

Just then, the front door to the house, and Kate stepped out and greeted everyone. Maria looked back at Cameron and then back at Kate. She whispered at Cameron in Spanish, **"Que grande la vieja!"** (what a tall old lady). Cameron bent down to his mother and said, "Mama, you are not the only one who speak Spanish. Please be careful what you say, they both understand Spanish. Dieter owns a summer home near Barcelona, and they spend at least one month a year there.

"OK, OK! I will be careful. I promise." Replied an indignant Maria Theresa as she walked in the front door.

"Welcome, welcome, Hertzlich wilkommen." Stated Kate as she showed Maria Theresa in to the living room.

"What a lovely home you have Mrs. Johannes." Stated Maria as she entered in to the spacious and elegant room.

"Please call me Kate, after all we are family, aren't we?" Replied a somewhat cold Kate.

Maria Theresa picked up on the cold shoulder and replied. "Please call me, Maria, Maria Theresa, Terry, Theresita, or Mamasita. Whatever is easiest for you." Said Maria as she walked over to the window and looked out unto the well-kept backyard.

"Do you do your own gardening Kate?" Asked an inquisitive Maria.

"Yes, yes of course. It's my hobby. I love to spend time gardening. Gardening and painting are my two favorite pastimes." Answered Kate, waving her hand across the window for emphasis.

"I also love flowers, but I have such a small yard and so little time. I spend most of my time writing poetry, songs, lyrics and music. I have written over five thousand poems and songs in my lifetime." Stated Maria with obvious pride. Her tiny frame stretching to five feet tall in the process.

The sparring session continued for five minutes until Cameron and Dieter joined the ladies in the living room. Cameron could tell that Mamacita felt very uncomfortable and uneasy. Dieter was also conscious of the bad blood between them. In an attempt to pour water over the boiling flame, he offered Maria Theresa a glass of wine. Which she graciously accepted. She did not realize how tired she was until that wine hit her exhausted brain. She could barely finish her glass and asked to be excused. Cameron took her upstairs to the guest bedroom where unpacked her things and told him she needed some rest. However, prior to going to bed she informed him that Frau Johannes was a total and cold-hearted bitch!

"Well Mamacita, you are probably right. Dieter is a very kind and friendly individual, but Kate is a cold fish. She is a typical Nordic type. Just try to make the best of it. By the way, what is your scheduled? Do you have any definite plans?" Asked Cameron.

"I will only stay a few days. My flight leaves Paris in nine days and I still have to see all my relatives there. I only came to see you because I had a bad feeling something was going to happen to you, and I was worried." Answered Mamacita while reaching up to give Cameron a hug and a kiss.

"Mama, everything is fine. As a matter of fact I just bought an old house up the road and I am going to restore it. It's a beautiful old house with a lot of history." Replied Cameron.

"What do you mean, you just bought an old house? You are not staying in this damned country are you?" Screamed an emotional Mamacita.

"No Mamacita, don't worry. I won't stay here more than a year or so. This was a great bargain, and Dieter said I could more than double my money if I restore it. It's strictly an investment, nothing else." Replied Cameron to an anxious Maria Theresa.

This calming statement seemed to put her at ease. She started to unpack her toiletries and stopped midway and asked Cameron a question.

"Do you think I could visit this house of yours tomorrow?" Asked Maria Theresa.

"But of course Mama. We can a take a nice walk to the other end of the village tomorrow after breakfast. How does that sound?" Asked Cameron, as he was walking out the door.

"Don't wake me up too early, you know I hate to get up before eleven. However, due to the time change my body clock is all screwed up. Just wake me up around ten or eleven, and we can go from there. OK son?" Stated Maria Theresa.

"Sounds good to me, I don't have to work until Monday anyway." Answered Cameron as he left her room.

Both Kate and Dieter were waiting for him at the foot of the stairs. He could tell that they had been arguing. Dieter's face would get red blotches around his neck area and a large bulging vein on his forehead would throb like a drowning snake. Kate on the other hand would turn pale white, as if a vampire had drained every bit of blood from her body. Cameron looked at them and stated:

"I sure hope my mother's presence hasn't caused any grief between you guys. She will only be here a few days at the most. Her flight leaves from Paris in a few days and she still has some relatives to visit." Stated Cameron in matter of fact voice.

"Not in the least. It's a pleasure to have her here in my house." Replied Dieter, with an emphasis on "my house."

That last statement did not go unnoticed by Kate. She turned around and stormed off towards the kitchen. Dieter looked at Cameron and shrugged his shoulders. "Women." He said as he walked away towards the living room.

"Common on Cameron, lets go and have a few more drinks before dinner. Do you think your mother is up to coming down for supper?" Asked a gracious Dieter.

"I don' really think so. She seems to be really exhausted, and that last glass of wine really knocked her out. She has been flying around the world non-stop for the past month and she has a bad case of jet lag." Answered Cameron as he sat down in his chair.

It was less than thirty minutes later when Kate announced. "Dinner is served." Once again she had outdone herself. A pork roast in a thick gravy sauce; covered in mushrooms and red cabbage and boiled potatoes. As they sat down to eat, Dieter made the comment that it was too bad that Mamacita could not join them. Two seconds later a now refreshed and starving Maria Theresa walked in, and exclaimed.

"I am so hungry! I could not sleep! The wonderful smell of your cooking kept me from falling asleep." Stated Maria Theresa.

Everyone wolfed down the meal in almost complete silence. The participants exchanged very few words. However when the meal was over, Mamacita expressed amazement that Kate could maintain her slim figure after eating such wonderful food all the time. That simple statement seemed to break the ice between Mamacita and Kate. There never would be great love between them, but Cameron felt that an "Armistice" had now been reached, and would shortly be followed by a complete cease-fire.

Desert was as good as dinner. A fresh fruit baked torte covered in heavy German whip cream. Mamacita once again congratulated Kate on her wonderful skills, and she really seemed to enjoy the evening. It was decided by all, that going to bed sounded like a like a great idea. Everyone headed to their respective rooms except Cameron who escorted his mother to her room.

"Thank you Mama for being such a wonderful and forgiving person." Stated Cameron to his mother as they entered her room.

"I am glad you think so. I did it for you. I know you can't help whom you are married to. Or even who Kate really is? She is an obnoxious, giant pain in the ass and probably a Nazi too!" Finished Mamacita with a great theatrical flair.

Cameron ignored the statement, "Who you are married to." He knew his mother had never approved of Ingrid because she was German, but tolerated the marriage as long as Ingrid was good to her baby boy.

"Don't you think you are being a little harsh? She maybe a pain in the ass, but a Nazi? I don't think you have any grounds for that kind of statement." Replied Cameron, hoping that the whole thing would simply go away.

"Son, if there is one thing I know, it's Nazis! Don't forget all those years I spent working for the French underground in Morocco and Algeria during the war! My most important job was to track down Fascist Vichy French collaborators and their Nazi handlers. If you remember, I was very successful, and I caught my share of them all over North Africa and France. As a matter of fact, I was awarded three "Croix de Guerre" medals for those same accomplishments!" Stated Maria Theresa with vigor and pride.

"Yes Mamacita, I know all of that, but you could be wrong about Kate? Don't you think? After all she is almost eighty-two years old?" Asked a concerned Cameron.

"What does age have to do with anything? I am almost #$$%%^^&& (garbled) years old and I can still smell a Nazi a mile away! I only came to visit you, and I hope you don't stay longer than you have to in this damned country!" Replied a now visibly upset Maria Theresa.

"Is that so? So you can smell a Nazi a mile away? What if I told you that Dieter was former member of the Nazi party when he was eighteen years old? What would you say to that?" Queried Cameron.

"Well I knew that already! He told me that as a young architect he had to join to get a job. He also told me that he never served in the military! Is that true?" Asked an inquisitive Maria Theresa.

"Yes that is correct. He had a severe case of stomach cancer when he was eighteen, and was excused from military service. Towards the end of the war they were going to draft him anyway, but he managed to avoid it." Replied Cameron, looking down on at his agitated mother.

"It doesn't matter, I think he is a good man. As long as he is good to you, I will forgive his past, but Kate is definitely still a Nazi!" Replied Mamacita in a high-pitched voice.

OK Mamacita, lets change the subject. You need to get some rest. Tomorrow will be a long day. Go to sleep now!" Cameron finished in a more forceful way than he really wanted to.

His mother glanced up at him. She was trying to decide whether to continue the battle or go to sleep. After a few seconds delay, sleep won over; she kissed Cameron on the cheek and asked him to leave. Cameron took the hint and was glad at the opportunity to make a quick exit. He left her alone, and returned to his room. It did not take long for him to fall in to a deep coma like sleep. However visions of Das Haus, concentrations camps, Nazis, tortured souls all kept spinning through his restless mind.

Cameron awoke the next morning around eight. He knew his mother would still be sleeping and did not bother to go to her room. Instead he went to the kitchen, and had a cup of coffee with Dieter.

"So how did you sleep?" Inquired a pleasant Dieter.

"I slept fairly well, but I had some horrible dreams about Das Haus, Nazis etc. I tossed and turned most of the night." Stated Cameron.

"I am truly sorry about yesterday evening. Sometimes Kate forgets her manners." Stated Dieter in an apologetic way.

"Well it must run in the family. Ingrid also loses her temper once in a while. However lately, she is doing it more often and for longer periods of time." Stated Cameron, nodding his head in the process.

"Really? I am surprised? Ingrid has always been a level

headed person, not prone to hysterics like her mother." Replied Dieter, a questioning look in his eyes.

"Maybe it only happens after they approach that time in life, you know. Hot flashes, back pain, headaches etc." Stated Cameron, more seriously now.

Dieter looked at Cameron, and nodded his head in acknowledgment.

"Dieter you have always been very honest with me about your past and former Nazi party membership, but you have never told me about Kate? Did she ever belong to the party? I am curious." Asked Cameron to a very quiet and nervous Dieter.

"Why do you ask? Is there a reason? What happened sixty years ago is of no consequence today!" Answered a very emotional Dieter, his voice cracking as he spoke.

"I guess you are right, but I would like to know just the same. I sometimes feel that Kate does not like me or any foreigner for that matter." Continued Cameron, pressing Dieter for an answer.

"That's ridiculous, Cameron. She really loves you and often has nothing but good things to say about you and America." Replied Dieter in a half-hearted manner.

"Not that it matters. But yes! Kate was a member of the *Jungmaedel* group until she was fourteen, after that she became a member of the **BDM**, or **Bund Deutscher Maedel,** until eighteen years of age. These groups were the female equivalent to the Jungvolk and Hitler Jugend for boys. As you already know, I was a member of the Hitler Youth until I became of age. After that, if you wanted to get a decent job anywhere, you had to join the party or else. Kate went on to nursing school, and worked at a hospital for a while during the war. Yes, she also joined the party in 1940. She later on went to the university and studied chemistry; becoming an engineer at the tender age of twenty four." Explained Dieter to a curious Cameron.

"Not that it matters, please don't mention it to Kate that I told you. She would be very upset if she knew I told you. As a matter of fact, no one but Ingrid knows about this. We have kept it secret from our other children. Their political views don't quite coincide with ours, and they might say something mean to their mother." Stated a somewhat reticent Dieter.

"Ingrid knows about this? Asked Cameron.

"Yes, we told her when she was around fourteen years old and was studying history in high school." Stated Dieter.

Cameron paused for a few seconds, and reflected back to a conversation he had had with his wife many years ago. *"No, no, absolutely not! My parents were never members of the party!"* Ingrid had passionately exclaimed to her new husband, when they first met. "

"Oh don't worry, I............." Cameron started to say, when an irate and extremely furious Kate, came around the corner.

"How dare you! How dare you, tell anyone about my private life! It is no ones business but mine. And you Cameron, why are you inquiring about my past? It's none of your affair!" Screamed an out of control Kate to both Cameron and Dieter.

Kate looked at Dieter and pointed her very long index finger at him. She said in German to him. "Let's go upstairs to our room and discuss this matter in private, now!"

Dieter started to say something, but thought better of it and nodded his head. Cameron had never seen Kate so angry, or Dieter so submissive in his life. Dieter got up and started walking towards the hallway leading upstairs to their room. Every time Dieter started to say something, Kate would raise her voice and drown him out. She screamed and yelled every obscenity in the book at him. This tirade lasted all the way up the stairs and continued in their bedroom. For over thirty minutes a continuous non-stop verbal assault rained down on Dieter. Eventually things calmed down and Dieter returned to the kitchen. His face was once again flushed and displayed red spots all over his face and neck. Dieter looked at Cameron and said:

"I am so sorry Cameron. My wife has lost complete control of her senses, and the best thing we can do is go for a walk. What do you think?" Asked a pleading Dieter.

"I think that is a marvelous idea. Let me see if my mother is awake?" Replied Cameron, as he started to walkout of the kitchen he nearly bowled over his mother.

"Good morning everyone, I see we are all having fun this morning! Exclaimed an unusually joyous Mamacita.

Dieter stood up and greeted her with a big bear hug and apologized for the ruckus this morning. "Don't you worry Dieter, in our house in Spain things like this happened every day. It's part of life." Stated Maria Theresa in a calm voice.

"Please, please Maria, sit down and have some coffee. Cameron and I wanted to go to Das Haus, and thought you might want to go along?" Inquired Dieter, as he looked Mamacita in the eyes. Their eyes met for a split second. She knew that he was in fact, pleading with her to go along in an attempt to calm things down.

"Si, si, and si! I think that is wonderful idea. Let me have my cup of coffee and we can go." Agreed Maria Theresa. It took less than five minutes for her to finish her coffee. She purposely drained the cup in record time. She too had no reason to stick around. A chance run-in with Kate was the last thing she wanted.

The weather was unusually pleasant that morning. For a change, it was almost balmy in this part of Germany. Fifty-nine degrees, sunny and a slight breeze was blowing from the west. It was nearly a mile from Dieter's house to Das Haus. They walked at a leisurely pace and Dieter pointed out all of the points of interest along the way. When they came upon the area, near the location of the former synagogue, Dieter purposely did not mention what happened there and kept walking. Cameron started to say something, but thought better of it. Ten minutes later they rounded the corner and came upon Das Haus.

Das Haus always had the same effect on those seeing it for the first time. It was an imposing structure. However the ravages of war were quiet obvious for all to see. Bullet holes, shell fragment damage was everywhere. Despite the visible carnage it still impressed the first time viewers.

"Is this your house?" Asked Maria Theresa.

"Yes mama, it is. I know it looks like hell now, but Dieter assures me that we can move in three months from now. We can

113

finish restoring it at our leisure. You see the property line goes all the way to the edge of the forest, and we also have a small stream at the back of our property." Stated a proud Cameron.

I can see why you like it, son! But somehow it has strange melancholic air about it." Replied Maria Theresa, as she looked up and down the street.

"It just seems to be a house of sadness." Stated a perceptive and sensitive Maria.

Both Cameron and Dieter looked at each other, not knowing how respond to her. Finally Cameron said:

"I will explain all of the details to you later on. Lets go inside for now and take a look around. Herr Jacobi the previous owner has given me the key." Stated Cameron as he walked across the street to the courtyard and the main door.

Cameron had problems with the ancient door and lock. For some strange reason it would not open. No matter how hard he tried, Cameron could not open it.

"Cameron give me the key and let me try. These old locks are tricky and you must first pull up on the handle; then turn the key." Stated Dieter as he easily opened the door.

It was obvious that Herr Jacobi had not done any cleanup. The interior was exactly as they had seen it. Dust, filth and junk everywhere you looked. Mamacita was shocked by what she saw. She unconsciously wrapped her scarf around her mouth and nose. Dieter led the way. Explaining where things would go, where walls would be moved; where new fixtures would go etc. Mamacita and Cameron listened in fascination as Dieter the architect, gave them a professional tour of the downstairs area. After a few minutes, they all went in the hallway, which led to the upper floors. Maria Theresa noticed the old wall paper in the hallway and said:

"You are going to get rid of this horrible paper? Aren't you?" Queried a curious Maria.

"Of course we are. It's very old and horrible." Replied Cameron.

Maria Theresa instinctively grabbed the corner of the

wallpaper and yanked down. Three layers of ancient dry wall covering came off in her hand. She did not realize how hard she had pulled, because a large three by three feet piece came off in her hand. Maria, Cameron and Dieter were all surprised to see a beautiful, hand painted picture underneath the wallpaper. All of them stared at the painting. It depicted a young boy of about ten years of age in a blue naval outfit. His right hand was on an old fashion bicycle and he had a matching blue naval hat in his left hand. Sitting in front of him, was a beautiful young girl of six or seven years old; holding a beautiful spring bouquet of flowers, and wearing a lovely pink summer dress. The colors were so vibrant and the painting was so well done that it appeared to have been painted yesterday.

*"O Dios mio!(*Oh my God!). That is the most beautiful thing I have ever seen!" Exclaimed Mamacita to the men.

"What, who made this? Did you know about this?" Asked a fascinated Cameron.

"Nein, nein! I mean no! But I think I know who they are. My best friend Erik and his sister. One of the former inhabitants, during the 1939 time period, was a well- known painter. Samuel Gehlen was his name and he too was sent to Poland, never to be heard from again. He could have painted this, and someone later covered it up to protect it" Stated Dieter as he ran his hand over the painting.

As he did, he tore a larger piece off the right corner, and the name S. Gehlen appeared, 1939.

"But your Erik was already gone by then? Wasn't he? Asked a curious Cameron?

"Yes he was. But I now remember a photo of Erik and his sister on the mantle in the living room. It was probably taken eight years earlier. Maybe it was Gehlen's way of saying thank you to Franz for being such a kind and helping friend." Stated Dieter.

Maria Theresa just stood there taking this information all in. She was confused and did not quite understand *"Poland," "taken away," "never to be heard from again."*

"What does this mean? What are you talking about? Who

were these people? What did they do? Where are they?" Asked an inquisitive and demanding Maria Theresa.

"Well." Cameron started to say, when Dieter interrupted him.

"You see, the previous owner was a Rabbi, and all the Jews of this village were brought here and kept here, until they were all sent away to camps." Dieter blurted out, in one long complete sentence.

"O Dios, Dios mio. (Oh God, my God). You mean all the Jews in this village were kept here and they were all killed?" Replied Mamacita in a serenely quiet whisper.

"I am afraid so, Mom! They all perished except for the son and daughter who escaped to America in 1939." Replied a concerned Cameron.

"You must tell me more, son. I need to know everything. I just, just came back, back from Israel. The Holy land! This is a sign from God!" Stated Maria Theresa a she got down on her knees and began to pray. Her prayers soon turned into sobs, and her whole body started to tremble uncontrollably.

"Mama, Mamacita, let me show you the rest of the house. You will see how beautiful it is. Common on mom. Common on!" Stated Cameron as he grabbed her by the elbow and started to push her up the stairs.

Her body suddenly became limp and she allowed herself to be pushed the rest of the way up to the second floor. For some reason the second story was not as chaotic as the first one. Someone had obviously made an attempt to clean up the place. Dieter and Cameron were showing her around when Dieter grabbed Cameron and guided him to a closet and whispered.

"Cameron, I don't think it's such a good idea if we tell you mom too much more! She seems to be very emotional, and this might harm her in some way." Said a quiet and concerned Dieter.

"Well maybe you are right? But my mother is a pretty tough cookie. She has seen and experienced worst things in her life. Maybe this is simply a flash back to her youth during the war!" Stated Cameron in a firm and decisive voice.

The most horrific scream that Cameron had ever heard came

from the attic area. Both men looked around and could not see Mamacita anywhere on the second floor. They ran out in to the landing and rushed up the last twenty-one stairs to the attic. When they opened the door to the unlit attic, Maria Theresa was standing there shaking like a wet puppy. Her entire diminutive body was gyrating like leaves in a thunderstorm. Her face was pale and lifeless. She actually had blood on the corner of her lips where she had bitten herself in fright.

"I, I, *yo, yo* (I, I) saw them. They are dead, here, here upstairs. I, I saw them!" She kept repeating, her voice shaking with emotion.

"Calm down, calm down. What did you see? What is going on Maria Theresa?" Stated a concerned Dieter.

Cameron chimed in, and tried to control his mother. Both men slowly and carefully guided her down the stairs. The whole time she could only repeat the same sentence over and over. "I, I, I saw them, upstairs. They are there now!"

After ten minutes of concerted effort, both men were able to bring her down and out in to the courtyard. Her small body was still shaking, but the bright sunlight seemed to help her regain some of her composure. However now, she started to say "No! No! No!" Over and over again.

Dieter decided, that it would be best if he ran down to his house, and returned with his car. They could then transport her to his house. Cameron agreed. Surprisingly, he returned in less than ten minutes with his car and drove them home. Mamacita was still in a coma like trance. Her features were comatose, but strained and terrified. The dried blood on her lips gave her a haunting and gruesome look.

It only took Dieter four minutes to drive them back to his house. They brought her in and carried her to her room. Cameron gently laid her down and put her in bed. Although she had calmed down a bit, Cameron was still concerned about her.

"Dieter? Is there a good doctor nearby? I would like him to come by and check my mom out? I am really concerned about her." Stated a worried Cameron.

"I think that is an excellent idea! Dr. Juergens is our family physician and lives in the next village. He can probably be here within the hour. I will call him right now." replied Dieter as he walked to his office.

Cameron went over to the kitchen and made himself a strong cup of coffee and sat down to ponder over the day's hectic events. *What a day*, he thought to himself. Just then, Dieter walked in and told him that Dr. Juergens was in fact in Niedergeyer on another call and could be here within thirty minutes.

"Great news! That is good news!" Repeated a concerned Cameron.

Both men sat in the kitchen drinking coffee and waiting for the doctor. Cameron started to make a cup of tea for his mother, when Kate eventually came down to join them, but still had that pissed-off look on her face.

"What is going on? Why all the ruckus? What has happened?" Asked Kate in her own unconcerned way.

Dieter took the time to try and explain the events that led up to Mamacita's collapse. He was very patient and calm, but Kate seemed uninterested and unconcerned. Just when things seemed to be getting tense again between them, the front bell rang. Dieter got up and answered it. Indeed it was Dr. Juergens; handsome and kind Dr. Juergens. It seemed as if every woman in the village at one time or another had a crush on him. He was tall, tan and fit. His passion was tennis and horseback riding. Both of which kept him in good shape.

"Hello doctor, how are you?" Asked Dieter.

"Thank you. I am doing just fine, and how are you guys today? What is going on, and who is the patient?" Asked a concerned doctor.

"Actually doctor, it's the mother of my son-in-law Cameron. You have met Cameron haven't you?" Asked Dieter.

"Yes of course. I know him well. He is one of the few men in this village who actually beat me at tennis." Replied Dr. Juergens as he walked upstairs.

Cameron and the doctor walked in the room. Mamacita was

sitting up in her bed mumbling to herself in Spanish. One thing that was very obvious now, was her hair. Where none existed before, a three-inch wide streak of snow-white hair was now visible. Extending from the middle of her forehead to the back of her head. Both Cameron and Dieter started to say something, but thought better of it. Dr. Juergens had never seen Mamacita before, and obviously was unaware of this phenomenon.

The doctor carefully examined her, and asked several pertinent questions. Cameron was able to answer all the previous health problems. Dr. Juergens came to the conclusion that Mamacita had suffered a severe nervous breakdown, brought on by some type of trauma. He recommended bed rest, quiet and some very strong narcotics to calm her system down. Cameron whispered to him that the white hair had not been thee a few hours ago. The white hair puzzled him, but he explained that many individuals have had similar occurrences when faced with extreme fright and anxiety. He wanted to know what had happened? However both Dieter and Cameron were at a loss, and could only repeat what they had seen. The doctor left some sleeping, headache and anxiety tablets, and also an additional prescription if needed. He said he would come by tomorrow and check in on her again.

After saying goodbye to Dieter, he asked Cameron if he was up to a re-match someday soon. Cameron agreed sometime in the future, when things were less stressful. Both men shook hands, and Dr. Juergens left the house.

Kate suggested that perhaps Maria Theresa needed a good cup of tea and one of the sleeping tablets. Cameron explained to her that he had already made some and it was brewing downstairs in the kitchen. When Cameron returned to her room, Maria seemed to be in better spirits, but was not saying anything to Cameron or anyone else. However she greedily drank the warm tea, not knowing that he had already laced it with one of the sleeping tablets. He sat there caressing Mamacita's small head, and wandering what she would say when she looked herself in the mirror.

Within ten minutes Maria Theresa was sound asleep. Her face

finally relaxed, and Cameron was able to clean it with a damp towel. Although sound asleep, the corners of her eyes were twitching uncontrollably. Her eye movement was every erratic, and her small size three feet moved from side to side. Cameron decided that he had better stay with her the rest of the evening.

Cameron went downstairs and asked Kate for a couple of pillows and a blanket. He was going to spend the rest of the day and night sleeping on the very large and comfortable lounge chair in her room. Kate had already prepared sandwiches, and offered to bring everything up to him in a few minutes. Cameron thanked her, and returned to Mamacita's room. Five minutes later both Dieter and Kate returned with two wonderful ham and cheese sandwiches, two beers, two pillows and some blankets for him. Dieter pulled him aside and whispered.

"If you need anything at all, or want a break, let me know. I will stay with her for a while. I know how concerned you must be? I am sure she will be OK!" Concluded a genuinely concerned Dieter.

"Thank you, thank you very much. This has been a harrowing day for all of us, and I will take the opportunity to get some rest. I really appreciate your concern and care." Replied Cameron as he escorted Dieter out of the room and closed the door.

Cameron laid out his blankets and pillows on the lounge chair, and sat down to eat his sandwiches. He took a few bites of the delicious sandwich, but realized that he was thirstier than hungry. He reached down and grabbed one of the two half-liter "Bittburger Pils" beers and drank a long and hard swallow. Bittburger Pils was his favorite German beer, and it really hit the spot. He thought to himself as he drank his eight percent strong beer, *"The Germans can really make good beer!"*

After finishing both beers in less than thirty minutes, a warm and cozy feeling swept over his entire body. The outside temperature had dropped drastically, and he cuddled up in his two warm blankets. Within minutes he was sound asleep. Although he was a large man, the lounge chair was perfectly suited for his frame, and he slept like a baby.

The beers must have really dulled his REM sleep, because he slept like a hibernating bear. No dreams, no memories, no movement at all. Just plain old comfortable and healing sleep. Sometime around three thirty in the morning, his mother awakened from her drugged sleep. He heard screaming again at the top of her voice. He jumped up and saw her standing in front of the mirror tugging at her hair. She kept repeating to herself, "No, No, No!"

Cameron stared at her in disbelief. Her right hand was clutching a large clump of white hair and she was trying to pull the rest of it out. Her forehead was covered in blood, and she had deep nail scratches on her face and neck. Cameron grabbed her hands and yelled at her to stop! Just then the door flew open and a pajama clad Dieter was standing there. His look of horror was only surpassed by his expression of shock.

"Oh mein Gott! (Oh my God) he exclaimed in German. Using the German language seemed to snap Maria Theresa back to her WWII trauma. She shrieked in terror and started screaming again.

"Stay away from me, don't touch me! You are dead, all of you, you are dead!" She continued to yell to no one at all.

Cameron reflected that, *"It was a good thing that Mamacita was only four foot eleven and one hundred and ten pounds!"* For a small women, she was as strong as an ox and twice as feisty. It took all of his strength to get her under control and put her back in bed. Just when it appeared that Mamacita would calm down, Kate came in and said something in German to Dieter. This small word, seem to set her off again, and she became uncontrollable and hysterical once more.

"She needs another pill!" Shouted Kate above the din.

"Yes, yes, yes!" Replied a harried Cameron. He laid his whole weight on her tiny, but struggling body and asked Dieter to put another pill in her mouth.

"OK, OK, OK, but which one? I can't tell!" Shouted an excited Dieter.

"The orange one! The orange one! The one on the end of the coffee table!" Shouted back Cameron, still struggling with his mother.

Dieter eventually found the right sleeping pill, and crushed it in a cup of leftover Chamomile tea. Kate reached over and pinched Mamacita's nose for a few seconds. This action caused an involuntary reaction on her part. She opened her mouth to get oxygen, and when she did so, Dieter forced the tea down her throat. Just then, Kate released her grip and Mamacita was forced to breathe through her nose again. The sleeping pill and tea was absorbed in her system and within minutes she was once again snoring peacefully.

"That was a neat trick, Kate." Stated Cameron to his mother-in-law.

"Don't forget Cameron, I use to be a nurse during the war! I used that trick many times with wounded soldiers who did not want to take their medicine!" Replied Kate, her chest swelling with obvious pride.

"Cameron, why don't you go take a break and I will tend to her wounds. You look like you just tangled with a lion." Asked Kate as she pointed to the door.

"That sounds good, but whatever you do, don't speak in German! That seems to set her off! Please?" Asked Cameron, as he stepped out of the room.

It took Cameron less than ten minutes to change shirts, wash up and grab a large glass of club soda and return to Mamacita's room. Kate was standing over her, gently washing her face and removing the blood from her forehead and face. She had placed a large bandage over her largest wound and disinfected the rest of them. It was obvious that Kate's previous nursing training was being efficiently and lovingly used. Cameron was surprised at the gentleness of her actions. It was the first time he had ever seen Kate in such a giving mood.

"Danke, danke, danke. Thank you Kate. I really appreciate your help and professionalism." Said a grateful Cameron to Nurse Kate.

"Bitte Schoen."(You are welcome) I am glad to help, but I think that Dr. Juergens must come by again and check her out

tomorrow. She is very ill, and has suffered a great shock. When I was a nurse in the war, I saw many such cases. It took them a while to recover." Explained nurse Kate.

"I am sure you are right. I will give him a call first thing in the morning. Thank you again for your help. I think I will try to get back to sleep now. Who knows what tomorrow will bring for us." Said Cameron, as he sat back down on the chair.

It did not take long for Cameron to fall back asleep. Although he slept for over four hours, it was a restless and fitful sleep. He kept waking up and checking on his mother all night long He was awakened by a knock at the bedroom door around eight the next morning. Standing there was Dieter and Dr. Juergens.

"Come in, come in. She is still sleeping, but I am sure you can examine her anyway?" Asked a concerned Cameron.

"I will do my best not to wake her, but I think she has had enough sleep for now anyway." Replied Dr. Juergens as he walked in the room.

That sentence seemed to have been the magic words. Maria Theresa slowly opened her eyes and touched her sore head. She wasn't quite sure of her whereabouts, but when she saw Cameron, she immediately smiled and reached out to him.

"Hijito, hijo mio." (Son, son of mine). Where am I? Why do I have bandages on my head and why is it so sore?" Asked a still groggy Mamacita.

"Mom, we are back at Dieter's house and this is Dr. Juergens. We had to call him yesterday after your incident in the attic." Replied a quiet and soothing Cameron.

"You have had quite an episode, Mrs. Clark. Obviously something in Das Haus really upset you. Can you tell me what it was?" Asked an inquiring Dr. Juergens.

Maria Theresa just stared at the doctor for at least sixty straight seconds. The corners of her mouth began to quiver again and that thousand-yard stare crept into her eyes. Cameron reached across and comforted his mother by petting her hair and face. This action seemed to quiet her down a little. She looked up at Dieter and Cameron, and in a barely audible, quaking and girlish voice said:

"You mean, you did not see them? The dead people, the rabbi, the man hanging by the neck in the corner? What about that dead German soldier near the window? He was all blown apart, his body exploded in many pieces! He had a long rifle with a scope on it, but he was dead! I saw them in the attic. All of them. They were reaching out for me; they wanted to keep me there. The rabbi was reciting the *"Kaddish!"* He reached out and touched me." Finished an unusually tranquil Maria Theresa.

"No we did not!" Replied both Dieter and Cameron in unison. We did not see anyone or anything.

"We were in the second story apartment when we heard you screaming. Your screams alerted us to your location. When we got to the attic you were totally out of control and yelling like a mad women." Replied Cameron as he slowly stroked her small hands.

"Why do I have blood on my lips and head? Why has my hair suddenly turned white? Why? Can't anyone answer me? No! You can't because I know what I saw, and no one can tell me different." Stated a slightly agitated Mamacita.

Dr. Juergens did not say anything during the entire conversation. He simply observed Maria Theresa's actions. Her statements appeared to be coherent, truthful and logical. However, he knew that of course there are no ghosts, and he assumed that Maria Theresa was imply having a nervous breakdown. In his mind, as a scientist, this could be the only explanation. She had been traveling all over the Middle East, and Europe, staying up late visiting relatives, locations and graveyards. Exhaustion set in and she simply imagined the rest. He tried to comfort her by explaining his scientific conclusions. However she would have no of it, and simply kissed it off with a wave of the hand.

Both Dieter and Cameron looked at her in disbelief! How could she know about the rabbi? Herr Hirschfeld hanging himself in the attic? Dieter was particularly shocked at the fact that she knew about the German soldier dying in the attic. Not even Cameron knew that part of the story yet! Dieter thought to himself, *"Is she a psychic, clairvoyant or possesses special powers?"* He had no answers, and was thoroughly confused. Dr. Juergens recommended further bed rest, quiet, and as much sleep as possible. Maria Theresa looked at him, but was not hearing what he was saying. She slowly got out of bed and quietly said in a soft, yet firm voice.

"I am now leaving this evil town and country. Never to return again. I can only hope that my son has enough sense to go with me, and never come back." Stated a convincing Mamacita,

"Out of the question, you are in no condition to travel! This could be very dangerous for your overall health. You must get several more days rest!" Said a resolute Dr. Juergens.

Both Dieter and Cameron chimed in. Mamacita looked at them and informed them that they could not keep her against her will and she was leaving with or without their consent. She slowly stood up and began packing her things. Cameron knew from experience that once Mamacita made up her mind, nothing would ever change it.

"OK mom! I know we can't change it. However please allow me to accompany you to Paris. We can take the overnight train from the **Köln Haupbahnof** (Cologne main train station) and be there first thing in the morning. They even have very comfortable couchettes to sleep on. How does that sound?" Asked a supplicant son.

Maria Theresa looked at her son and simply nodded her head, but continued to pack. Cameron thanked Dr. Juergens, Dieter and Kate and asked them to leave them alone for now. Everyone left Mamacita's room, but Dieter waived at Cameron as he was exiting the room.

"Do you think this is a good idea? Is she ready for such a long trip?" Asked a concerned Dieter.

"Your mother said she saw things that only I would know about. It is simply impossible for her to have found out about the German soldier in the attic. I, I just don't understand." Repeated a worried Dieter.

"What do you mean? This German soldier? What is that all about?" Asked a curious Cameron.

Dieter went on to explain about the battle over Niedergeyer and Erik Goldmann getting shot by a sniper who was hiding in the attic of Das Haus. Cameron looked on in disbelief. How could his mother know this? Herr Hirschfeld? Cameron poked his head out the door and saw Dr. Juergens and Dieter's wife whispering to each other in a corner of the hallway. The moment they saw him, they quickly separated and looked up at him. It was a look of guilt and conspiracy. Cameron wondered what that was all about, but simply thought he was imagining things.

Just then, Maria Theresa called for him and he returned to her room.

"Yes, Mamacita. What can I do for you?" Asked a concerned and worried Cameron.

"I will be ready in thirty minutes or less and I want to leave immediately. I need to get out of Germany now!" Explained a somewhat overwrought and hysterical Maria Theresa.

"OK, I will go pack an overnight bag and I will be with you shortly." Answered Cameron as he walked out the door to his room. Within ten minutes he had packed a change of clothes, toiletries and a clean jacket. When he returned to her room, Dieter was already there.

"Cameron, I will drive you to the train station in Köln. Is that OK?" Asked Dieter?

"But of course. I will be back tomorrow night. I will call you when I am one hour away and you can please come and pick me up? Could you do that for me?" Asked Cameron.

"Of course my friend, I will be glad to come." Replied Dieter.

The ride to Köln was very quiet. No one wanted to say anything for fear of breaking the ice, and reviving those haunting memories. Mamacita was particularly somber, and kept her head in her lap almost the entire journey.

The Hauptbahnof in Köln was located in the old part of the city near the river and the beautiful cathedral. The allies heavily bombed this area of the city. Almost everything was completely obliterated by a combined British and American air strike. Köln was the first German city to suffer a thousand plane raid by British and American bombers. Tens of thousands of civilians were killed and injured during this and subsequent attacks. Modern construction had totally repaired all of the ravages of WWII, and the scars of war were practically invisible.

Dieter pulled up in front of the main entrance and helped unload the luggage. Dieter and Cameron exchanged small talk for a few minutes and Dieter drove away, promising to return tomorrow night. As Dieter left the area, Cameron pondered, *"I am very lucky to have such a good man for a father-in-law."*

Cameron and his mother entered the vast hall like glass covered train terminal. Cameron purchased two first class sleeping berths tickets. Their train did not depart until ten-thirty p.m. That gave them a few hours waiting time. They went over to the elegant restaurant and had some good German coffee. Mamacita saw chocolate cake in the glass counter and expressed a desire for some of it. Cameron was at first surprised, but realized that his mother had not had anything to eat for over twenty-four hours, and besides she adored chocolate cake. They both ordered a piece and ate in silence. After they were done, Mamacita made the following comment.

"The Germans are horrible people, but they make good cake, and their coffee is not bad either." Stated Mamacita to a surprised Cameron.

It was the first smile, and or positive statement he had heard from his mother since she landed in Germany.

Cameron realized that his mother was very upset, and would always hold a deep resentment towards Germany and its people. At least she had an effort to come and visit him!

"I am glad to see that you still have your sense of humor. You will feel much better, once we are on the train. Actually, the Eurorail Express is a wonderfully comfortable train; it only makes five or six stops before Paris. We stop in Aachen, Liege, Brussels, Mons, Charleroi, Lille, and then on to Paris." Finished Cameron.

His mother made no comment other than to look at her watch again, and let out a long and mournful sigh. Cameron automatically glanced at his timepiece. He noticed that they would be departing in less than thirty minutes. He paid the bill, and pointed his mother towards the exit.

"Mom let's go over to the kiosk, and get some reading material for the ride? What do you say?" Asked Cameron?

"Good idea. Let's hope they have some American or French magazines?" Stated Mamacita as they approached the newspaper stand.

"Great, fantastic, wonderful!" Exclaimed Mamacita, as she looked upon dozens of American and French newspapers and magazines. Mamacita bough three magazines, a Paris Match, an Elle, and a Time magazine.

The fact that these were available seemed to lift her spirits. As they walked towards track number four, they passed a large mirror. She did not like what she saw. Maria Theresa was always very conscious of her appearance, and was extremely troubled by her unusually large bandage on her head. She had made a valiant attempt at disguising it, by covering her head with one of those wonderful WWII era stylish Greta Garbo hats. It hid most of the bandages and bruises, but not enough to satisfy her. She stood in front of the mirror and kept re-adjusting her hat, scarf and make-up. Cameron was keenly aware of her frustration and said to her.

"Mamacita, you look fine! Don't worry about it, everything will be OK!" Stated Cameron as he grabbed her and pulled her towards the first class compartment.

The train was beautifully painted in a bright red and yellow color. Under the windows a black sign read, "Eurorail-Paris Express." The nattily dressed conductor opened the door for her, and winked at her as he did so. She caught his flirtatious gesture and was immediately in better spirits. Cameron was also aware of his engaging move, and smiled and nodded to him as they passed. Their compartment was midway to the restaurant car and the restrooms. *Great!* Thought Cameron, as he entered their section and sat down. It was well decorated, had two folding couchettes, a small table and a private toilet and shower. *Fantastic!* He thought to himself, we wouldn't have to share the showers with anyone else. His mother was equally pleased, and asked Cameron if room service was available on the train?

"Yes, Mom! I do believe it is available. Would you like me to order something for you now?" Asked Cameron.

"No, I only wondered. I really don't feel like going out in public unless I really have to." Replied his mother as she made herself comfortable.

Within a few minutes the train was under way. Both Cameron and his mother noticed the smoothness and comfort of the ride. Unlike some of the other trains they had been on, this Eurorail locomotive was extremely quiet, and there was very little rocking. It had one of those pleasant, soft and gently relaxing motions. More like an infants cradle than a train. The sound was also very hypnotizing. It reminded Cameron of a sea voyage he had once taken with his wife. There was a great deal of comfort and relaxation , and Cameron was happy that he had chosen this mode of travel. His mother was finally learning how to relax. A few minutes later she informed him that she was ready for bed, and would like him to order a ham, Swiss cheese, mustard, butter on a Baguette sandwich.

Cameron rang for the room service attendant and ordered two sandwiches and some French fries for him. His mother crawled into her lower bunk and within minutes was snoring. It took over thirty minutes for room service to prepare their meal. When it finally arrived, Cameron did not have the heart to wake up his sleeping mother. He simply sat on his comfortable chair and ate by himself. By the time he had finished his sandwich, the train was already coming up on Liege, Belgium. He knew from experience that Paris was less than seven hours away, and he should get some sleep.

He crawled into the upper bunk and within seconds also fell asleep. A loud knock on the door, and the words, "Paris, Paris, Paris! Twenty minutes!" Woke both of them out of their deep slumber. He could not believe that they were almost there. His mother jumped out of bed and ran into the shower first. He really did not care if he took a shower or not, because he was scheduled to return to Germany within twelve hours and he could shower on the return trip. He quickly dressed and patiently waited for his mother. Nineteen minutes and thirty seconds later, a clean and well-dressed Mamacita, came out of the bathroom and exclaimed to the world, "I am ready for everything!"

Cameron was pleasantly surprised at his mothers' cheerful attitude. It was as if nothing had ever happened. She had a smile on her face and was in extremely good spirits. However she could not hide the hideous scratches, and her white hair.

Within a few minutes the train decelerated, and came to a complete stop at ***"La Gare du Nord,"*** Paris (The North Station), track number seven. The Gare du Nord was a prime example of a 19th century French train station. It had massive Corinthian columns, which were over sixty feet high. The façade was almost two blocks in width and ran parallel to the Avenue Magenta. Strangely enough the interior was in some ways similar to both the Köln and Aachen train stations. They all had large glass ceilings that allowed a certain amount of filtered light shine through. Cameron thought, *"I am sure the interior has not changed since the days of the great empire."*

Although a few modern ***accouterments*** (decorations) adorned its halls, it had remained the same for the past five or six decades. As he walked through its immense antechamber, he expected to see Humphrey Bogart waiting in vain for Ingrid Bergman from the movie "Casablanca," or some black shirted SS trooper yelling for his arrest. His mother snapped him out of his daydream.

"Cameron, what are you dreaming about?" She asked.

"Oh nothing, Mamacita. I was just remembering an old movie." He answered, as he swung his arm across the station.

"I bet it was "Casablanca," She replied.

"Yes it was. These old train stations have such wonderful character and ambience." He replied.

"Yes they do." She retorted.

By the way, have you contacted my brother Roland? He is going to pick us up, isn't he?" Asked his mother.

"Yes I did, and he assured me he would be here on time. You know Roland, he is always punctual, don't worry!" Replied

Cameron as they exited the station.

Cameron was sorry they did not have more time to spend in this neighborhood. They were across the street from one of the most popular *brasseries* (pubs, restaurants) in Paris. Brasserie de la Gare. It specialized in seafood and also in fried mussels. His mother loved this *quartier* (neighborhood). During WWII she had spent many months, both hiding and later looking for German agents in this general area. She often had secret meetings in that same restaurant, and always enjoyed the fried mussels and excellent beer. Cameron was disappointed that he could not roam around more and take in the sights. He too had a favorite nearby haunt, Hotel de Londres et D'Anvers on the Avenue Magenta. When they first started dating, he had spent many a romantic weekend with his wife there. His cousin Jeremy Grant, an ex-CIA officer, had introduced them to this wonderfully quaint hotel. This hotel had a long history with both families; both Jeremy and his father had spent many wonderful moments in it.

"Hello, hello!" Shouted his uncle Roland from across the street. It was amazing how fit he looked for an old man of eighty-six.

Both Maria Theresa and Cameron turned towards the sound, and saw him standing in a 'No Parking' zone frantically waving his arms. They waved back and carefully crossed the large street. French drivers were notorious for hitting careless pedestrians.

"I am sorry for parking here, but everything else was full!" Stated a somewhat excited Roland.

If Cameron had not known his uncle's exact age, he would of guessed fifty or sixty, at the most. In fact he was almost eighty-six years old. Roland had always been a superb athlete and at one time had actually boxed with Marcel Cerdan, the French middleweight champion. He was in excellent health and reminded him of the great American physical fitness guru, Jack Lalane. All exchanged hugs and kisses, in the typical French way.

Roland stored the entire luggage in his car, and he then pointed his new Citroen station wagon towards his home in the suburbs. He sped away from the curb at breakneck speed; burning rubber in almost every gear. Maria Theresa immediately reminded him of her fear of speeding. He mumbled something under his breath, and slowed down to a somewhat modest speed. Paris traffic is always hectic, but today it was particularly bad. It took them nearly an hour to get to Isle Adam, a small village outside of Paris.

Roland had a modest two-story house, surrounded by a large stonewall topped with broken glass and barbed wire. The main entrance was an intricate affair. A solid green steel door, topped with spikes, it was electrically operated. Cameron also noticed the many hidden video cameras placed around the house. He wondered, *why his uncle needed so much security?* Suddenly two extremely large boxers came around the corner and growled at the new comers. However the moment they saw their master enter the courtyard, they sat down and observed everyone. Cameron could tell that they were highly trained and would rip them apart at the slightest provocation.

"Don't worry, they are friendly as long as I am around. The little one is called General Foche, and the large one is General LeClerc, two of France's greatest generals.

"Just stay near us, please!" Replied Cameron. Maria Theresa did not seem too concerned; she had a natural connection to all animals, and these were just another set of friendly house puppies.

Roland's wife Victoria, an equally fit octogenarian greeted them at the main door. She was petite, but obviously fit for her age and health. Once all of the usual French kissing traditions had been accomplished they all sat down in the living room for a cup of tea. Roland was the first to ask about her white hair? Cameron started to say something, but his mother interrupted him and began to sob.

"What is wrong Theresita? What has happened to you?" Asked Roland.

Cameron held up his hand, and started recalling the events of the past three days. He started from the beginning and left nothing out.

"Oh my God, that is so terrible! How could you have seen

such things? Are you sure they were not an illusion, brought on by exhaustion?" Asked Victoria?

Both Roland and Victoria did not believe in the after life, and wanted to say something else, but saw how serious Maria Theresa was, and decided to refrain from any further comments.

This comment seemed to irritate Maria Theresa. She shouted, "Can't you see what happened to my face and head? Do you think this is normal? They were there in the attic!" She shouted!

"I, I, I am not hallucinating. I saw them! They wee trying to tell me something about Das Haus! It is a *"Casa Maldita."*(A haunted house, evil house). I can only hope my son does not move in there." Stated an obviously excited Maria Theresa.

"OK mom, I believe you. You obviously saw something, and it would be best if we did talk about it anymore. Let's move on and talk about Paris and the family." Replied a tense Cameron.

Roland picked up on the conversation, and started talking about his newest great-grandson, his daughter, and his new BMW motorcycle. Roland was an avid rider and had always driven one.

Maria Theresa noticed that everyone was trying really hard to accommodate her, and went along with their banter.

"Are you crazy? You are still on that kick? He has been driving those infernal machines since he was a young boy!" Stated a shocked Maria Theresa.

"Don't worry, he is a very good driver and has never had an accident in over seventy years!" Expressed a proud and boastful Victoria.

"I am happy to hear that. But why can't you just drive your car, like normal people?" Asked an inquiring Maria Theresa.

"Theresita, I am an old man. I have lived a full life. Survived and escaped from three concentration camps, fought in three wars and stayed married to Victoria for over sixty-five years. What else could happen to me? Don't worry I will be OK. If you want I will give you a ride tomorrow?" Replied a laughing Roland.

"Not on your life! I would rather spend the night in Cameron's evil house!" Answered an obviously shocked Maria Theresa.

Cameron looked at his aging uncle and could not help but

admire him. This man had truly experience life to the fullest and was willing to continue living it to the max. His spirit was really something special. Cameron hoped that he too could have such a fulfilling and creative stay on earth. Cameron noticed that Mamacita was now relaxing with Victoria, an appeared to be back to her old self; he took the opportunity to grab Roland and pull him into the kitchen.

"Roland, thank you for taking care of my mother. I have to be going back to Germany tonight. She is in a very fragile state and I hope you can see to it that she takes her medicine when needed." Asked a worried Cameron.

"Don't you worry? I will take care of her, and make sure she catches her flight next week. She is in good hands, and I will keep her busy for the next few days. She won't have time to think about anything else. You have my promise!" Replied Roland in a firm voice.

"Thanks, thank you once again. I would stay longer, but I have this new assignment that requires me to be in Aachen all of next week." Replied Cameron.

"I understand Cameron, she will be fine with us." Answered his uncle.

"By the way, Roland? Why do you need such strict security around your house? I notice the high walls, barbed wire, and steel doors, guard dogs and video cameras everywhere? Are you expecting trouble?" Asked Cameron in a nonchalant sort of way.

"Very astute of you, and the answer is yes to all the above questions. I have made myself very unpopular to many different factions. I write a column for several newspapers throughout the country and Europe. I use a *"Nom de Plume"* (Pen name), but by now most people know who I am. Additionally I spent many years working for the French Security Services, and I have developed mortal enemies throughout France, and North Africa.

Many of the radical Muslim groups have sworn a Holy Jihad against me. I am simply being cautious. Nowadays I am less boisterous than in the past, and I keep a low profile." Stated his uncle Roland in a calm, yet boastful manner.

"Thank you for telling that. I may call upon you for some help in the near future. I too am writing a giant expose on neo-Nazis, and I may need your help?" Replied Cameron.

"Anytime, anytime. I am usually at home or in my car. Here is my cell number. You can reach me twenty-four hours a day." Replied Roland, handing him one of his business cards.

Chapter 14

Back to Germany

His mother's visit had really unnerved him, and he was hoping to have a small respite before returning to work the following day. Cameron made his goodbyes to everyone and promised his mother to keep in contact everyday. He sincerely hoped that a few days with her family would help her. He did not wish to have Roland leave the women alone, so he took a cab to the local commuter train station in Isle Adam. From there he took a limited special electric train to La Gare de Lyons, and then another train to La Gare du Nord. The whole trip took less than two hours. He ended up back at the same location where they had arrived three hours earlier.

Cameron realized that he had almost nine hours to wait. He pondered what to do, and decided to go visit his old friend Colonel Auguste Perrin, the owner of the "Hotel de Londres et D'Anvers." The hotel was less than a two-block walk from the train station. The hotel was exactly as he last remembered; a little worse for wear, but still very presentable. It was one of those typical turn-of-the century five story establishments, which abound in Paris. The budget conscious tourist was attracted to it, by the reasonable rates, and its proximity to both La Gare du Nord and *La Gare de L'Est*. (East)

As he walked down the bustling Avenue Magenta, he greatly admired the old hotel. From a "Tactical" intelligence point of view, he gave it a five star rating. He could easily understand why both his mother and uncle Winston Grant, a WWII OSS leader, used it as a base of operations. The hotel had many secret advantages that often would befuddle German Gestapo agents or other enemy spies. It was connected through the basement with four adjacent buildings; it was also connected to the building directly behind it, which led to another street. Three of these underground entrances had inter-connecting parking areas which made for perfect clandestine ***rendezvous*** (meeting places). This maze of entrances allowed for surreptitious entry and egress. One other great advantage was its direct connection to the Paris sewer system, which on occasion offered a readily accessible, if somewhat smelly, emergency escape.

Cameron walked up to the counter and rang the beautiful antique brass. A tall and strikingly handsome elderly gentleman came to counter. He was very well dressed in a three-piece dark business suit. He sported a visible gold watch chain in his left front vest pocket, a bright red carnation in one buttonhole, and a small colored ribbon in the other, indicating he was a ***"Chevalier"*** of France (similar to the British Knighthood).

"May I be of service to you?" Asked the distinguished-looking gentleman, in impeccable English.

"Yes, I hope you remember me? I have stayed here on several occasions with my wife?" Stated Cameron.

Colonel Perrin looked at Cameron, but it was obvious that he was having problems with his memory.

"How long ago, Monsieur?" Asked the Colonel.

"Well, it has been more than fifteen years!" Replied Cameron.

"However I am sure you remember my mother, Maria Theresa and my uncle Winston Grant, and his son Jeremy?" Continued Cameron.

"But of course Monsieur. You must forgive me, I had a stroke five years ago and everything is a little mixed up in my brain right now." Exclaimed a now smiling Colonel.

"How wonderful to see you again. How is your lovely mother? Is she well?" Asked the inquisitive Colonel Auguste Perrin.

"Well as a matter of fact she is visiting her brother Roland who now lives in Isle Adam, near Paris." Replied Cameron.

"Yes, I know it well. It would be such a great pleasure to see her again. Could you give me her number?" Asked the friendly Colonel.

"I will be glad to call her on my uncle's cell phone and see what her schedule will be, in the next few days. You might even know my other uncle, Roland Gaston de Iriarte." Replied an accommodating Cameron.

"But of course! We were colleagues for many years! Your uncle is a great man and war hero. I did not know he was your uncle too. You are indeed fortunate to have so many heroic relatives!" Stated a truly impressed Colonel Perrin.

"However, I am sure you heard about my uncle's untimely death? Winston Grant that is." Asked a curious Cameron.

"*Oui, oui* of course! Everyone heard about the plane crash. How terrible, and how is your cousin Jeremy? I have not heard from him in several years? Is he well?" Answered the Colonel.

"Yes, as a matter of fact he is doing well, and still living near San Francisco with his bride and their son. He now works for the US Custom Service, and is very happy." Replied Cameron.

The lively chitchat went back and forth for over twenty minutes, until the Colonel suggested that they have lunch at the Brasserie de la Gare. By then, Cameron was famished and it sounded like such a good idea. The Colonel yelled for his clerk Mauricette; to come and take over the front desk. Mauricette was a young woman of twenty or so, and the colonel's granddaughter. Her beauty struck Cameron; she had green eyes, dark brown hair, high cheekbones and full lips. She reminded him of the fifty's Hollywood siren, Eva Gardner. Colonel Perrin noticed the stare and stated.

"I am very fortunate to have a beautiful daughter and granddaughter! *N'est pas, Monsieur Clark* (Isn't that so, Mr. Clark?).

"Yes you are. She is quite a beautiful young woman." Replied Cameron as they walked out of the hotel.

"As a matter of fact I am also fortunate to have a lovely daughter back in California. My wife and child will be moving to Germany in a matter of days. I really miss them." Stated Cameron in a melancholic way.

"I can sympathize with you Cameron. I would be devastated without my loved ones. I wish you well." Replied Colonel Perrin.

Both men leisurely walked the two blocks to the restaurant. As it was customary this time of day, it was full! However the Colonel was well known in the neighborhood and the *"Maitre"* (head waiter) was able to find them a spacious table near the front window.

After a wonderful meal, which lasted over two hours, both men sauntered back to the hotel. Cameron looked at his watch and he still had almost six hours before his train left. The good food and liberal amounts of wine has made him very sleepy. He asked the Colonel if he had a room for six hour or so?

"But of course. I will give you the same room your mother and uncle used during the war. No charge! Of course!" Replied a generous and friendly Colonel Perrin.

"Thank you Monsieur, but I insist on paying. I have a very generous expense account and I could justify this trip as a research exercise for my series of articles on the resurgence of neo-Nazis in Europe." Explained Cameron to an inquisitive Colonel Perrin.

"I am glad you mentioned that. As you know, I spent nearly thirty-five years working for the **Deuxieme Bureau** (French Intelligence), and I still have many contacts there. As you probably already know, we have our own set of fascists in France; one of the most violent group is called *"Action Directe."* They might be even meaner than the Germans! If there is anyway I can help you, just call me." Offered a gracious Colonel Perrin.

"I may just take you up on that. I can use all the help I can get. I may even have to come back and you visit again." Replied a thankful and appreciative Cameron.

"After all it's the least I can do for the nephew of the man who risked his life to save mine. I will show you to your room now. Number 105, the one your uncle and mother used throughout the war." Answered Perrin as they walked towards the lobby area.

Cameron and the Colonel took the elevator to the second floor. It was exactly the way his mother and uncle had described it him. The elevator was about the size of a large refrigerator. It was made of a large ornate cast-iron with intricate grille patterns. The effect was quite beautiful, however over the years it had been painted so often that the sides were almost touching.

His mother's favorite room was also an antique in its own right. Not more than fourteen by twenty feet, and that included a very small bathroom an shower. What made it particularly interesting was the connecting door to room 106, hidden behind a large full size *"Armoire."* Room 106 was in fact a grand suite with a large picture window overlooking the entire block, on both sides of Avenue Magenta. Colonel Perrin gave him the keys to both rooms in case he wanted to check it out.

Cameron took the opportunity to check every nook and cranny. Cameron felt at ease and relaxed in these historical rooms. His mother, uncle and cousin Jeremy had spent many a restless night looking for the forces of evil. After inspecting everything, he was sadly disappointed that no hidden secrets were found. They had been thoroughly cleaned and no evidence from the past was discovered. There was nothing there, just memories of stories from a bygone era. He called down to Colonel Perrin and asked for a wake up in six hours. It would not take him more than four or five minutes to walk to the station.

Punctually at seven P.M., his phone rang. He jumped out of bed, not knowing where he was. Within seconds he was dressed and checking out downstairs. Colonel Perrin had already left for the evening, but left a note behind. Mauricette was still on duty and wished him a safe trip home, and gave him a shy, but knowing smile.

Colonel Perrin had given Mauricette a note for Cameron. It had his personal home and cell number and once again offered his assistance. Cameron thanked her and left.

Cameron quickly walked across the street and entered the train station. At this hour of the day, things were a lot quieter than usual. His train was already there and Cameron found his stateroom without any problem. He called for room service and once again ordered one of those delicious French rolls with ham, Swiss cheese, butter and sharp mustard. He took a quick shower and awaited his sandwich. He was still drying his hair, when a knock on his door got his attention. The restaurant steward had brought him dinner. Cameron was amazed how hungry he was. That wonderful lunch had long since disappeared and he felt hunger pains again. He quickly gobbled down the entire sandwich, and drank both Belgian beers.

Even though he had just slept six hours, he was quickly dozing off again. The gentle swaying motion, and the two beers had lulled him back into lethargic trance. Cameron knew that the train would be arriving in Aachen around six-thirty in the morning, *"Great Timing!"* He thought to himself. *I can go straight to the office, and be there before seven.*

The evening sped by, like the rolling wheels of his train. Before long the German conductor, knocked on his door and announced, Aachen, Aachen, Hauptbanhof. Cameron gathered his meager belongings and got off the train. The station was alive with travelers, tourists and students. He took a cab and was in front of his building in less than ten minutes. He glanced down at his watched and noticed that it was a quarter to seven.

The ride up the elevator was uneventful, and when he grabbed the door handle to his office, he noticed that it was already opened. *How strange*, he thought to himself. When he walked in, he was surprised to see his entire staff hard at work. Everyone had voluntarily come in and was busily researching those multiple tasks he had given them last week.

"Frau Rausching, ***Bitte!***" (Please) He shouted as he entered his office

"Was ist los? What is going on?" He asked.

"Welcome back Herr Clark. I hope you had a pleasant trip? How was Paris?" Asked an unusually friendly Frau Rausching.

"I need to see you in my office, ***schnell!***" (Fast). Stated Cameron as he walked in to his office.

"What is going on? Why are you all in here so early? Did something happen?" Asked Cameron.

"Nein, Herr Clark. We heard about your incident and we all decided that perhaps we could help you out by coming early yesterday and today. We wanted to get a head start. It was important to us." Stated a collegial Frau Rausching.

"I am impressed, and grateful to all of you. Yes, I have had a difficult three days and I am glad to be back to work. Please inform the staff that we will have a meeting at nine o'clock sharp. Thank you once again; it was a pleasant surprise!" Said Cameron to an attentive Frau Rausching.

Cameron spent the next two hours reading his stack of mail and a series of emails from the home office. At exactly nine o'clock Frau Rausching knocked on the door and announced that everyone was waiting in the conference room.

Cameron entered and saw that everyone was present and ready for business. After thanking everyone for their extra efforts, he asked Frau Rausching how did they know?

"Well Herr Clark, we too have our sources." She said, a small smile on her face.

"OK then! Whatever your sources are, they are very good, and you should keep them for future use." Replied Cameron.

One by one, every member of the staff gave a report and a summary of their efforts and research. Cameron asked individual questions and made suggestions. Of particular interest to him was some neo-Nazi political membership in the German **Bundestag** (parliament) and in the military. He tasked each of them to do more research, and dig deep into any affiliation between the military, police and members of parliament. He also asked them to look into any current military and former military fraternal organizations, veterans organizations etc.

His meeting lasted a little over two hours. He announced to all that everyone could go home at noon today. This announcement was well received by all, and well appreciated. He too was glad to get back home and was looking forward to returning to Niedergeyer. He called Dieter at home and informed that he was taking the early afternoon train from Aachen and would be in Dueren around three-thirty and would appreciate a ride home.

"But of course, Cameron. I will be there exactly at three-thirty. See you soon." Stated Dieter as he hung up the phone.

Cameron finished his work and left the office punctually at twelve-thirty. He decided this might be a good opportunity to drop by and visit his old friend Wolfgang von Hagen, the Chief Editor and Publisher of the local Aachener Post Zeitung, a well- respected conservative newspaper. *The paper was very near the train station and he could kill two birds with one stone,* he thought to himself. Cameron called Wolfgang on his cell phone and was immediately put through his office.

"Hello Wolgang, how are you my old friend?" Asked Cameron?

"I am well, and how are you? Where are you and what are you doing?" Replied his old acquaintance.

Cameron started to tell Wolfgang about his new assignment in Aachen. Wolfgang asked him to come over and discuss it in detail. Cameron agreed to be there in less than ten minutes. He took a cab and in fact was there exactly nine minutes later. He entered the impressive office building and was immediately greeted by a young receptionist.

"Can I help you sir?" She asked.

"My name is Cameron Clark and I have a meeting with Herr von Hagen." Replied Cameron.

"Yes of course, he told me to be expecting you. Follow me please." The young lady got up and took him to a bank of elevators and pressed the fifth floor. The elevator door opened unto a private hallway, which led to a beautifully hand carved oak door. Cameron could tell that it was very old and obviously German by its beautiful carvings. Wolfgang greeted him at the door.

"How are you doing my friend? It has been a long time? It's so nice to see you again!" Stated a very gregarious Wolfgang.

"Yes it has. It's been too long. And how are you? Still a bachelor?" Asked Cameron?

"No, heavens no! I have been married for over six years, and I have two beautiful children. My wife is from Holland and we live across the border in Heerlen, Holland." Answered an obviously proud Wolfgang.

"That's great! It's about time you tied the knot. Two kids, I am so happy for you. Maybe we can get together sometime soon and spend time together? What do you say?" Replied Cameron.

Both men sat down in Wolfgang's lavish office. After a few minutes of friendly banter, Cameron discussed his assignment. Wolfgang listened intensively to the conversation. Not saying much, but nodding his head when appropriate.

"That's very interesting. You do realize how dangerous this might be? These Nazis have a reputation for ruthlessness, and they are still very strong in some areas of Germany." Stated Wolfgang in a calm, but serious voice.

"Yes I realize that, but I have a major assignment to accomplish and I might even make a book out of it!' Replied Cameron.

"You know I will help you! Just let me know what I can do." Replied Wolfgang as he got up from his chair and moved near the window.

"I was hoping you would say that. Thank you; thank you very much. Can you please have someone in your staff do some research throughout Germany and France. I am having my staff doing the same, and we can compare notes at a later date. I would also appreciate it if they could research any connection between the American neo-Nazis and their European counterpart. I am sure that between the both of us, we will be able to dig up some dirt? I would love to stay longer, but I have to catch a train to Dueren in forty-five minutes." Stated Cameron as he got up from his chair.

Wolfgang shook his hand and promised to get back to him in a few days. Perhaps even having him over to his house in Holland next weekend. Cameron left the building, and walked out to the curb where several taxies were waiting.

He took a cab to the station and got there eight minutes later. The train would not leave for another twenty minutes so he sat down at the local restaurant and had a beer and bought a local paper. On the front page, there was a bold headline about a high-ranking police official being investigated for neo-Nazi affiliations both in Germany, France and North America. This obviously got his attention, and he almost missed his train. He attentively read every detail, and made notes for further research.

Fifty-five minutes later he was pulling in the Dueren train station. He looked at his watch and it was three-twenty. *Great, I am early.* He thought to himself, as he scrambled down the long flight of stairs.

"Hello Cameron! Hello Cameron!" Shouted an excited Dieter.

Cameron waived back to acknowledge him. Dieter was parked on the other side of the street. In a red "No Parking" zone again. However this time there was to policeman in sight. Cameron noticed the beautiful silver Mercedes gleaming in the sun. Within seconds he crossed the street and was cheerfully greeted by Dieter.

"Well how did everything go? Is your mother OK? How was your trip?" Dieter rambled on, not giving Cameron a chance to answer.

"Slow down Dieter, I will tell you everything on the way home. We have plenty of time for that part of the trip. I also stopped by my office this morning and also went to see my old friend Wolfgang von Hagen in Aachen." Replied Cameron as he got in the car.

Dieter took the long way through the city; giving both of them to talk about everything in great detail. Dieter was an attentive listener and rarely interrupted him.

"It sounds like you had an interesting voyage? I have some good news for you." Stated Dieter with a smile on his face.

"Ingrid and your daughter will be here next Saturday. She sold the house and got a great price for it, and will arrive next Saturday at three o'clock. Isn't that great news?" Stated Dieter with a great grin on his face.

"What do you mean, sold the house? You mean lease the house, don't you?" Asked a concerned Cameron.

"No, no, no! She said sold the house, I am sure. She was able to get a rich San Francisco businessman to pay six hundred and forty-nine thousand for it! I am sure that was the price!" Stated Dieter once again.

"But, but, she never discussed it with me? We never discussed selling the house! We are returning to America in the next two years, and we need a place to stay? This was a little impulsive?

Don't you think?" Asked a surprised Cameron?

"She said something to the effect that, 'If my husband can buy a house, I can sell one too." Replied Dieter.

"Did she sound angry?" Asked Cameron?

"Well actually, yes she did! She rambled on about Das Haus, Jews, remodeling etc. I did not quite understand everything she said. Apparently my wife Kate spoke with her, without my knowledge and Ingrid is on the warpath!" Exclaimed Dieter as the car drove up to his driveway.

"I should probably call her tonight. I don't think I am ready for a long discussion, but it must be done." Answered Cameron.

The mood was very unfriendly as he entered the house. Kate was waiting in the hallway with an extremely unpleasant look on her face. She almost growled at him.

"Did your mother get to Paris OK, and has she stopped hallucinating? She really needs to get herself under control! She was hysterical and out of control!" Stated a decidedly unfriendly Kate.

At first, Cameron was shocked by her behavior, but was not going to let her get his goat.

"Thank you for your kind interest and words, she is doing fine!" He replied.

"Your wife wants you to call her the moment you walk in. She is very anxious to speak with you." Continued a still unpleasant Kate.

"Thank you for the message. I will do that immediately. Good night Dieter, I am going to my room and I won't be back down until tomorrow, good night!" Stated an obviously unhappy Cameron.

Cameron could hear Dieter and Kate arguing as he went to his room. Dieter was amazed by Kate's' behavior towards their guest. He told she had better change her tune, or she would be looking for a new home soon. Cameron was extremely upset at the turn of events that had taken place since his mother came to visit a few days earlier.

His two hour-long phone call to his wife Ingrid was even more unpleasant than his conversation with Kate. Apparently Kate had been talking to Ingrid behind his back, filling her full of hateful and harmful news. Ingrid was on the warpath and had decided on her own, to permanently move back to Germany. She had used his power of attorney and sold the house. Settled all their debts and would be arriving next Saturday. Cameron had never heard his wife so irate or irrational in all the years they had been married. She had completely made up her mind, and nothing he said could change it. Cameron was flabbergasted by her actions, but thought to himself, *"I am sure when she gets here, I will be able to change her mind and calm her down!"*

Around eight o'clock in he evening, Dieter knocked on the door and came in.

"Cameron, I am so sorry for what is going on! I do not know these women! Both Kate and Ingrid are possessed by the devil and we must try to get them back into our fold. I have made it very clear to Kate that she had better keep her barbed tongue under control or else." Stated a very apologetic Dieter.

"Dieter it's not your fault. It's mine. I am terribly sorry for all your trouble. I was thinking, it probably would be a good idea if I moved out until Ingrid gets here? What do you think?" Asked a confused Cameron.

"Absolutely not! Nein, nein, and nein! You are my son-in-law and I love you like a son! If these women can't control themselves, maybe I should ask Kate to move out for a while? What do you think Cameron." Replied Dieter with a sneer on his lips.

"Look Dieter! This is obviously causing tension among us. Why don't we do the prudent thing and just have me move out until Ingrid gets here, and then we can work things out? I am sure Kate will probably feel much better in a few days, and we can all live in harmony until Das Haus is finished? Speaking of which when do you think that might be?" Asked Cameron.

"I have hired a local contractor and a crew. They are starting tomorrow morning. These guys owe me many favors, and have promised to work night and day. I am confident you will be able to move in six or seven weeks. They will finish the rest while you are living there. It should all be done in about three months. I really don't want you to move out, but if you feel better living in a hotel for a few days, do what you think is best. However you must come in to the living room with me and have a couple of drinks? What do you say, Cameron?" Stated Dieter in a firm, but pleasant voice.

"That's good news Dieter! I am sure Ingrid will be happy. Just make sure they install two working bathrooms. I cannot envision sharing one with her and my daughter!" Replied Cameron.

"Good, I am happy that is settled, let's go in the living room and finish that good brandy, and maybe if you are interested I can continue the story about Das Haus? What do you say?" Asked a friendly and inviting Dieter.

Both men sat in their respective comfortable leather chairs, and Dieter continued on with the saga of Das Haus.

Chapter 15

Buchenwald
(Beech Woods)
Concentration Camp

November 27th, 1938

The ride from Niedergeyer to Dueren was extremely long and frightening for all concerned. Under normal circumstances the twenty-kilometer ride to the main train station would have taken less than thirty-five minutes or so. However the military transport trucks kept stopping every few miles along the way. Loud screaming and shouting punctuated each stop. The already frightened Niedergeyer Jews became hysterical and uncontrollable. Every time the green canvas tarp was pulled aside by the vicious Stormtroopers, a new batch of equally terrified German Jews were violently thrown in. Menacing *Sicherheitspolizei* (Security Police AKA SIPO). Could be heard outside the truck screaming filthy obscenities and insults.

The closer they got to Dueren, the more desperate they became. The truck was filled to capacity. Over forty scared and petrified human beings were crammed in a truck meant for fifteen or twenty at the most. Many of them had urinated and defecated on themselves. The stench was unbearable and unforgettable. Erik, his sister mother had taken a protective position towards the back of the truck near an area where some fresh air came in. This really helped them survive the journey into hell. Erik could not phantom what was going on? How could any civilized nation treat its innocent citizens in this matter? He was really worried about his mother. She was already acting delirious and frenzied. His sister was in more of a shock than anything else. She held on to Erik's hand and would not let go! When they thought it would never end, the truck suddenly braked, and the vicious soldiers started screaming again.

"Raus! Raus! Raus aus dem LKW (Out! Out! Out of the trucks!). *Aber schnell!* (Fast, but fast).

Shouted the soldiers in unison. To make things worst, over six very large German Sheppard dogs were barking as loud as they could. The dog handlers could barely keep the dogs under control. They were straining at their leashes. The whole atmosphere lent to an air of chaos and pandemonium. Because of their position in the truck, the Goldmann's were among the last to get out, and when they did they were horrified to see two young teen-agers lying dead in the corner. No one had paid any attention to them or their death throes; they had been crushed by the mob. Their bodies were horribly bruised and battered. A large pool of blood covered the entire area of the truck. The *Unterscharfuehrer* (non-commissioned officer in charge) was screaming obscenities at them to hurry up and get out or else! Erik tried to point to the two dead youngsters, but was rewarded with a kick in his backside for his concern.

All of the Jews were finally gathered in a group near some cattle cars on a nearby track. They all looked at each other in horror! There still was horse or cattle manure all over the floor, and the odor was so repugnant that they had to cover their faces with whatever they had handy. They were roughly handled and shoved inside the cars. At least fifty to sixty human beings were manhandled until there was no standing room left. As the last man entered, he was given two buckets. One was filled with water, and the other was to be used as a toilet. It was so crowded in there, that the buckets could only be hung on the ceiling! Every time the train swayed it hit some poor soul in the head causing them even more discomfort.

The heavily overcrowded train chugged eastward and then northward for was seemed like an eternity. After four hours they finally arrived at the Aachen main train station. They were all allowed to get out and stretch their legs, and given more water and a loaf of bread. Unfortunately, six more individuals had died and were unceremoniously carried off. They were all given new instructions.

"You will be traveling for the next two days and you will not have the opportunity for any more breaks! Shouted the **Sturmbannfueher** (Major of the Waffen-SS Guard unit).

"My God mother, how can they treat us that way? Why are they such animals?" Asked Erik. His mother just stared at him, and did not respond. Before he could ask her again they were herded back into the cattle cars. Squeezed together beyond belief, they did the best they could. After what seemed like days, a voice was heard.

"Hello, hello I am Doctor Herbert Fischmann and we must try to rearrange our bodies in such a way that we are more comfortable! Does everyone agree?" He asked several times before anyone responded.

"Yes, yes of course! What is your idea?" Asked several men in the back of the car.

"Lets have every other person sit down and have the one to the left of him stand between his legs. We can then rotate these positions every thirty minutes, giving our bodies more circulation and breathing room. Additionally the women who must go to the bathroom, can go to the back and the rest of the females can protect their modesty."

That was greeted with a chorus of hurrahs! Great, and lets do it. It took several tries, but within ten minutes every other person was seated, and someone else was standing between his legs as prescribed by the clever doctor. This had relieved their immediate discomfort, but it did not help the cold. The sun had gone down, and the temperature had dropped to around freezing.

The cattle cars were not meant to be watertight or insulated; to the contrary there were gaps between the wooden slats, and the cold German November wind was blowing through them like General Guderian through Poland. It was at this point that Erik appreciated his mothers sewing skills. She had padded all of their coats with an extra thick old wool blanket, and it really helped with the biting cold. Erik patted himself and remembered that his parents had hidden the gold coins in the lining of his coat. It gave him a small amount of comfort to know that he had something to fall back upon. His mother had also hidden some hard cheese, and pieces of dried beef in various pockets. Although it wasn't much, the meager rations kept them going until such time they arrived at their final destination. He stared in wonderment at his still quiet mother, and shocked sister.

"I am so glad, I can finally sit down, and stretch my legs!" Stated a somewhat confused Mrs. Goldmann.

Erik looked at his mother, but she turned away and refused to talk any further. He was confused by her actions, but did not press the matter; instead he cared for his sister, and made sure she was as comfortable as possible. This horrific nightmare continued for over two days. It was then that a horrible thought crossed his mind! *"My sister is a young innocent girl, what would happen to her in this environment? I need to do something in order to protect her!"* He thought to himself.

"Mother, mother, mother! Listen to me! Snap out of it! We have to do something to protect Esther." He screamed at his mother.

"What, what? Asked a confused Sarah.

"Mother, mother! Listen to me! We have to make her in to a boy now! Who knows what will happen to her down there? Do you understand?" He stated.

His mother suddenly seemed to snap out of it, and a look of horror spread across he face.

"Yes, yes you are right! What can we do? What can we do?" Asked a knowing and abruptly awake Frau Goldmann.

"Let's cut her hair, smear dirt on her face and turn her fancy shorts inside out and soil them!" Answered Erik.

"Yes that is a good idea! But how do we cut her hair?" Asked a confused Frau Goldmann.

"Maybe I can help? I am a doctor and I brought my medical bag. I have some medical scissors, and I even have an extra pair of pants." Offered a kind and caring Doctor Fischmann.

He bent down and pulled out the scissors and men's pants. They were fortunate that Dr. Fischmann was a slight man and they only had to cut off four inches from the bottom of the cuff. Frau Goldmann grabbed the scissors and started to trim her daughter's hair. Esther made a single glance upwards at her mother, and started to cry!

"Don't worry baby, it's for the best. It will grow back someday soon. We need to fool them, until we can figure out what to do?" Replied a concerned mother.

Esther acquiesced to her mother's wishes, and stopped crying. It took less than five minutes to cut her hair, and turn Esther in to cute young boy. They picked up the excess hair and threw it out the side of the wagon. Due to the cramped quarters, many of their neighbors were aware of what was going on, but only smiled and nodded their heads in understanding and collusion.

Once they were finished, they coached Esther on how to act like a boy and not a girl. That would probably be the most difficult part of the charade. Esther was and always would be, a cute, feminine, and coquette young lady. Erik decided to name his sister, Franz. He figured, she would respond better to a name that she knew. It would also add to the confusion, in the event anyone asked about the missing girl? After all Franz's name was on the original deportation order.

Chapter 16

"Jedem das Seine"
(To Each His Own)

The trip into hell continued for another forty-two hours. The further south they went, the colder it got. By the time they arrived in Weimar, there was four or five inches of snow on the ground. To add to their misery, the wind was howling with such force, that the snow was now blowing across the landscape perpendicular to the ground.

Erik was totally unaware of his exact location, or the fact that they were less than eight kilometers from the famous city of Weimar. This wondrous town was known for many centuries as a classical and cultural hub in southeast Germany. It had been the home to many famous German writers, scientists, poets, and many of Germany's elite nobility had also made it home. Such notables as Bach, Goethe, Franz Liszt and Schiller had lived there. One of its prominent features was a hill known as the Ettersberg. It was approximately 800 hundred feet high and dominated the countryside for miles around.

Many of Germany's greatest minds found its romantic countryside, beech forest and ambience, irresistible. Germany's elite and nobility would spend countless hours walking through the woods and villages; enjoying the beauty it offered. For decades it was the go to place in that part of southeastern Germany. No one ever dreamed that someday, the Nazis would turn it into hell on earth.

In 1936, the Nazis decided to transfer the concentration camp of Lichtenberg to a new site, and Buchenwald was the chosen location. The Ettersberg location was chosen in May 1937, and on July 17, 1937 the first 375 or so prisoners arrived at "Konzentrationslager Ettersberg." Initially it was called

Ettersberg, but later changed to Buchenwald by the Inspector of Concentration camps, SS General Eicke. Buchenwald unlike many of the other concentration camps was a detention and work camp, and not an extermination camp like many others.

The leaders of Buchenwald had but one goal in mind, "The destruction of the inmates by forced labor through the use of torture, whippings, lack of nourishment and of course horrible hygiene." However during the Nuremburg trials after WWII, the Allies estimated that over 56,000 prisoners were killed or died in detention from 1937 until April 1945 when the Americans liberated it. This does not take into account the other 13,486 prisoners that were sent to other camps for execution.

The entire camp was built by prisoner labor, and the SS were hard taskmasters. One of their favorite past-times was to have the prisoners haul heavy rocks from the quarry while singing famous SS marching songs. The SS called them the "Singing Horses." Those prisoners, who were thought to be shirking their responsibilities by the SS, were immediately shot on the spot. It was to this horrific nightmare that the Goldmann family was first exposed to Buchenwald.

When the train stopped, Erik thought it would be in a train station, depot or a camp. Instead it was in the middle of a field, 1.7 miles from Buchenwald proper. The poor inmates had not yet finished the track, and the camp was still a ways off. It was ten-thirty at night and the surrounding countryside was invisible to all. However when the doors swung open, they knew that the Nazis were close by. A loud chorus of shouts, curses and orders were screamed at them. Once again the German guard dogs chimed in and began to viciously bark and growl at them. The snow and general weather conditions made going very difficult. There was a sheet of frozen ice under the snow and it made walking a treacherous affair. The only visible lights were the small handheld flashlights carried by the guards, and an occasional headlight from one of the trucks.

After what seemed like an eternity, the weary group of approximately one- thousand new inmates were shuttled through the gate of Buchenwald. Above the main gate was a large iron sign with following inscription, ***"Jedem das Seine."*** (To each his own).

Erick wondered the meaning of the inscription. *What could it mean? It did not make sense.*

All of the new arrivals were marched to the main gate and brought in front of a large set of barracks. The men and women were immediately segregated. At first Esther was confused and just stood immobilized by fear. Erik saw her confusion and yelled at her.

"Franz, Franz, Franz come here right now." Eric's shouting brought her back to reality and she ran over and stood next to her brother. Her entire body was shaking like a leaf in a windstorm. By now Mrs. Goldmann had already been sent on her way, and she was headed for the women's detention barracks. Erik squeezed Esther's hand, and whispered to her.

"Don't worry, everything will be OK! I promise you!" Before Erik could finish his sentence a very tall and scary looking man approached them and whispered in Erik's ear.

"Do you have any money? Money? Do you hear me? Money?" He asked.

"What, what? Who are you? What do you want?" Responded a disturbed Erik, tightly gripping Esther's hand as he did so.

"Are you deaf as well as stupid? Do you want to live? You must bribe the right person if you expect live! What skills do you have? Can you do anything? Are you trained?" Peppered the questioning man.

At first, Erik was hesitant to answer simply because he feared the man. He then thought about it, and gave an affirmative answer.

"Yes! Yes I can. As a matter of fact both my brother and I are butcher trainees. My father was the village butcher, and I am in my last year of training. My younger brother is in his second year, and we are both equally well-trained and hard workers." Lied Erik. He knew this man meant business, and he knew enough about butchering from observing his father over the years, to be able to fake his way through.

"That is good! Very good for both of you! Now do you have any money, jewels, anything?" Continued the persistent stranger.

Eric was unsure what to say. He feared giving away his secret stash of gold.

"What if I did? What could you do for us? What guarantee do I have that you will help brother and me? Whatever you do for me, you must do for my brother! We stick together or no deal! Is that understood?" Replied a now confident Erik.

"Well, well, well! What a tough guy! I like that in you. Do you know who I am? No! I am sure you don't. My name is Ludwig Winter, and I am a Senior KAPO. That's right a KAPO! Not only a KAPO, But the head KAPO for this section of the camp. Do you know what that is?" Asked Ludwig.

"No, no I don't. What is it you do here? Why do you have an inmate uniform and have such much power?" Asked a curious Erik?

"Well for your information, my young friend. I am one of the oldest prisoners here and the SS have appointed me to watch over you scum Jews! I am a sort of overseer." The harsh words shocked both Erik and his sister, but they wisely said nothing.

"I am not a Jew, just a common criminal from Berlin. I was arrested last year for being an out of work hooligan and sentenced to three years in this wonderful establishment. I am now in charge of the kitchen for block 17, and I can pick anyone I want to work in my kitchen."

"OK, OK! I believe you. Lets say I can give you something valuable? Something worth around four or five hundred Reich Marks! What will that get me? Can we both have a job in the kitchen? Can you find my mother and help her?" Asked Eric.

"My friend, my young friend! For four hundred Marks, I will kill the camp commandant, Colonel Karl Otto Koch! Do you have such a sum? Do you? Do you?" Asked a greedy and dangerous Ludwig.

"If you can arrange for my brother and I to work in the kitchen, and help us find our mother I will arrange for you to get that sum within a day or two? Is that understood?" Asked Erik.

Ludwig pulled a hidden hard truncheon and hit Erik across the neck. The blow was so fast and unexpected that Erik was completely taken by surprise. He fell to the ground like a sack of cement. The excitement got the attention of the SS *Scharfuehrer* (Staff Sergeant) in charge.

"Was ist los" (What is going on?) Asked the curious Staff Sergeant.

"Nothing Sir, I was just showing these Jews how to show respect for the staff. I have everything well in hand, Sir!" Snapped the KAPO, clicking his heel and bowing as he did.

Ludwig reached down and yanked Erik to his feet. The blow to his neck was still very painful and his ears were ringing. He had never been struck with such force or violence in his entire life.

"Let that be a lesson to you my young wise-ass friend! You had better watch your tongue and do what I tell you or you will end up hanging from one of the lampposts around here! Is that understood?" Asked Ludwig, still holding Erik's shirt collar in his right hand.

The gravity of the situation struck home, and he decided to follow orders, and never pissed this guy off again.

"Yes sir, I understand! I am sorry sir! It will never happen again." Replied a shaken Erik. His sister just stood there, not knowing what to do or say. Her whole body paralyzed by fear. She too understood the power this stranger held.

"That's more like it! From now on, you and your brother will work for me and you had better pay me, what you owe me by tomorrow morning! Is that understood Jew boy?" Asked an irate Ludwig.

"Yes sir! I sure will. I promise to pay you by tomorrow morning, sir." Replied Erik without looking him in the eyes.

"Herr Scharfuerer! May I have permission to take these two pieces of scum to the kitchen? I have chosen them for my new help?" Asked Ludwig to the growling Staff Sergeant.

"OK, KAPO Ludwig, you may leave my formation. However, don't forget to bring them by tomorrow for in-processing?" Yelled the *Scharfuerer.*

"Absolutely sir! Tomorrow morning sharp! Let's go you two, move faster! Screamed KAPO Ludwig Winter at Erik and his sister.

Both Erik and his sister Esther followed Ludwig, who was almost running through the night. They had a hard time keeping up with him as he was extremely tall and obviously knew his way around the compound. Ludwig suddenly stopped and yelled.

"You had better learn to keep up with me. Every one around here is always expect to double-time. Is that understood? If you don't, you might end up as a guest of Frau Ilse Koch, the Commandant's wife, and she is even more violent than he is." Screamed an irate Ludwig.

After what seemed an eternity the silhouette of a brightly lit building appeared in the distance. Five minutes later, Ludwig opened the back door to the kitchen. A warm and comforting smell enveloped them as they walked in. Giant pots and pans were neatly stacked in the corner. Three large industrial size stoves were busily cooking the evening meal. The smell of food reminded both of them, that they had not eaten in two days, and sharp hunger pains begged to be quenched.

"Are you hungry?" Asked a suddenly friendly Ludwig.

"Yes, yes of course. We have not had any really food in two days. Than you sir!" Replied a ravenous Erik.

"Sit there in the corner, and I will bring you some food. You must never, handle any food in the cooking pots! That food is strictly reserved for the SS troopers and they will kill you on the spot, if you forget! That soldier over there is always in here; making sure we don't poison them!" Stated a now very serious Ludwig pointing to a fat and sleeping SS camp guard.

Ludwig walked over to a large refrigerator and pulled out a large chunk of Munster cheese, some Liverwurst, two boiled eggs and grabbed a large loaf of freshly baked bread. He brought it over to the two starving children and gave it to them. As the two sat down and greedily ate everything in sight, Ludwig walked over to the rest of the kitchen staff and informed them of his two new helpers. He also made it clear that they were under his personal protective custody, and warned everybody to stay away or else. They nodded their collective heads in unison; unlike some of the other prisoners these seem to be fairly well fed and dressed.

By the time he got back to the kitchen, both kids had eaten the entire tray of food and were lazily squatting in the corner. They rose when he came in.

"I hope that makes you less irritable? I will show you where you sleep. Don't speak to anyone or touch anything else! Is that understood?" Asked KAPO Ludwig?

"Yes sir, Yes sir!" They replied in unison.

He took both of them to the back of the kitchen where a small store was kept for non-perishable items, such as rice, noodles, flour, sugar, coffee etc. The door was locked with a heavy padlock and bolt. Ludwig took out a large set of keys and opened it. In the corner near the window was a small wooden cot with a straw mattress and an Army wool blanket.

"You will both sleep there! One of your jobs will be to catch and kill the rats that come in here to eat the provisions! I have to account for every single gram of food! For every rat you kill, I will reward you and your brother. Be sure to keep track and show me the dead rats at the end of each day. Only the head German cook and myself have the right to come in hear, do you understand?" Stated KAPO Winter. Not waiting for a reply, he continued.

"Don't get any ideas about stealing or bartering with anyone else! Is that understood? Any violations will cause me to send you back to the general camp population and quick death! Is that clear? Tomorrow I will show you your duties. There is a sink over there to wash yourself, and a bucket for your bathroom needs. Do not allow anyone in here!" Goodnight and try to get some rest. Don't forget my four hundred Reich Marks!" Stated Ludwig as he walked out of the supply room.

Both of them let out a collective sigh of relief and sat on the bed. For an old straw mattress, it was actually pretty comfortable and clean. They both laid on the bed and waited for things to calm down. Erik did not trust Ludwig, an he wanted to give him time to get away from the kitchen.

Erik then looked around for a spot to stash his gold coins. He knew Ludwig would not be satisfied with one coin, and would be after them for more. He reached down into his coat and pulled the seam apart. Their neatly sewed in groups of two's, were fifteen gold coins and the two diamond rings. His sister wanted to know what he was doing?

"You need to do the same thing I am. Ludwig must not find them and we must never tell, our lives could very well depend on it. You must never, never tell anyone. If you do, we might be killed! Tomorrow we have to in-process, and if they find our coins we will die." Replied a concerned Erik.

"Oh, I see what you mean! He may try to steal them from us? OK, I will take them out. I notice everyone is wearing a uniform and we are not!" Stated his sister Esther.

"That's right! And maybe tomorrow they will make us take our clothes off, in front of everyone and put on a uniform. Just leave your undershirt and underwear on, and pretend to be shy." Replied Erik, as his eyes continued to scan the room for a hiding place.

After a while his eyes scanned upwards and he saw a rusty sewer pipe protruding from the wall. The pipe was about five inches in diameter and stuck out from wall at least a foot. The only problem was it was at least eight feet high! He grabbed ten of his sister's coins and his fifteen, wrapped them in an old cloth he found on the floor.

"Esther, climb up on my back and stuff the rag with the coins in it as far as you can down that pipe." Said Erik pointing to the pipe.

"Good idea! No one will think to look there!" Replied Esther as she jumped on his back.

She had to stand on his shoulders and reach up as high as she could go. The rag and coins were shoved down the pipe and were out of view. Both of them looked up from the ground and could not see anything at all. Satisfied with his cleverness, he pondered what to do with remaining five coins. Ludwig would expect payment in the morning, which would leave four coins and the two diamond rings. He decided he would do what his father had recommended, swallow them one by one except for the coin for Ludwig. He would also hide the two rings under a broken stone near the sink, hoping to fool anyone casually searching the area.

He searched around the supply area for something he could use to swallow the coins. Near one of the stoves, he found a large jar of cooking oil. That would do just fine, *he thought to himself as he grabbed the jar.*

"What are you doing Erik? Why do you need that jar of oil?" Asked an inquisitive Esther?

"Do you remember what **Vater** said? He told us to swallow the coins if we were in danger! And I want to have them somewhere safe." Replied Erik as he drank a small amount of oil with each coin.

Surprisingly enough, they went down smoothly and without difficulty. However the cooking oil left him slightly queasy, and wanting to throw up. He quickly pinched his nose, and breathed through his mouth; his mother had taught him that trick when he was a child.

"How do you feel? Are you OK? You look pale and green at the same time." Asked a prying Esther.

"Oh, I will be OK. I am sure it will settle down soon enough. Never mind that, we need to get some rest; we will need it in the morning. Let's go to bed now!" Replied Erik as he crawled into the bunk clothes and all.

It wasn't long before both of them were sound asleep. The events of the past three days had completely exhausted them and rest is what they needed. Erik had no idea how long they had been sleeping, but he heard a voice screaming at him.

"Get up! Get up! It's time to get up!" Shouted Ludwig as he shook the bed from side to side.

It took them a few seconds to realize where they were, and who Ludwig was.

"Good morning sir, how are you today?" Replied a now wide-awake Erik.

"I really hope you are awake this morning! I must take you to the reception center to be identified and registered. After that we will return and settle our business? Right? You do have the money don't you?" Asked Ludwig sticking his hand out and rubbing his palms together.

"Yes sir! You kept your part of the bargain, and I will keep mine. Would you like it now or later? Asked Erik reaching in his pocket for the gold coin.

"Now would be fine, if you like." Replied a greedy Ludwig, smiling as he did.

Erik reached in his pocket and pulled out the shiny new 20 Reich Mark piece. He opened his hand and handed it to Ludwig in one smooth motion. Ludwig's reaction was not what Erik expected.

"Oh my God what have you done? Do you want to get us killed? You have a gold, gold, a gold coin? Don't you know that it means immediate execution if they find it on you? You did not tell me you had a gold coin!" Screamed an excited and scared Ludwig.

"What do you mean Herr Ludwig?" Asked a shocked and scared Erik.

"No one, but the German staff members is allowed to possess gold. They will hang us for sure! Replied a petrified and shaking Ludwig.

This revelation caught Erik and Esther by surprise. Erik quickly thought of a scheme that might help him and Esther.

"Herr Ludwig, is there any way that we can somehow get one of the SS guards to accept it and give us cash for it? In the process he could perhaps earn himself a commission? Maybe 10% for the coin?" Asked Erik, hoping that Erik would not flip out and turned them over to the SS guards.

"You are clever young man! Very clever indeed! This is a very delicate situation. I have to think about it. Let's go to the in-processing center and get that over with; we will then reflect what to do. You need to take those coats off if you want to keep them? You will have to give up all your clothes and belongings this morning. Is that a problem? You don't have any more of those beautiful coins hidden in there? Do you? Remember they will execute you on the spot if they find anything of value hidden on your person." Replied an obviously worried Ludwig.

Erik did not have a chance to answer; they both silently took their warm coats off and dropped them on the cot.

Ludwig, as was his custom, raced over the camp towards the processing center. Both of them had a hard time keeping up with the lanky Ludwig Winter. The journey very uncomfortable, not wearing a coat made it miserable and cold. Six or seven minutes later they came upon a large brick building. Ludwig told them to wait in the doorway for a minute or so. Three minutes later, he came out the door with the SS **Sharfuehrer** from yesterday evening.

"Come on! Come on!" Screamed Ludwig for no particular reason, other than to impress the SS Staff Sergeant.

They were led down a long corridor that eventually ended up in a large warehouse. The warehouse was divided in different sections, and various prisoners were sorting items of clothing, shoes, bags, suitcases etc. Everything was neatly stacked and accounted for. Four or five heavily armed SS guards were keenly observing the entire operation from a catwalk. A voice rang out!

"Hey you two step forward!" Growled an old man in a prisoner uniform.

The first thing Erik noticed was his green hand, the right hand was green in color. From the tip of his fingers to his wrist, they were totally green. Erik wondered, *"Why on earth would his hand be so green?"*

The man was sitting at a small table with several green inkwells and metal instruments in front of him. When they approached him, he thoroughly questioned them. Asking them, age, place of birth, names of father and mother etc. He noted all of this information on a large diary like book. After this was done, he told them to approach the table and put his left arm through a leather strap, and not to move, or else!

Ludwig bent down and whispered to Erik.

"You better go first. Your brother might get scared. They are going to give you a number, a tattoo. Don't scream or resist otherwise they might shoot you!"

Erik knew he could stand the pain and humiliation, but he was concerned about Esther. He bravely stepped forward and stuck his arm in the strap and smiled at the old man. This sudden gesture caught him by surprise. The old man stopped what he was doing, looked up at him and wiped a tear from the corner of his eye.

"Good! You are a brave young man." Stated the tattoo artist.

The whole procedure lasted less than ten minutes. One could tell that he had done this type of thing a thousand times before.

"I hope I did not hurt you too much?" Asked the man with the green hand.

"No sir! You did not, thank you sir. Stated Erik as he walked away from the table looking down at this left forearm. The number **1287959** was now etched forever on his arm and his soul. He tried not to show Esther that in fact it did hurt by biting his tongue and turning his head away from her.

The old man made an entry next to his name, and said, "Next!"

"I am next!" Said a courageous Esther. Her girlish voice sounding more like a little girl than she wanted. Everyone noticed her mistake, but no one said anything.

She stepped to the table, put her arm through the strap and only winced a couple of times when the old man now tattooed her number on her left arm. She now had **1287960** on her left arm! She had the next number in sequence, and instead of crying, she proudly stepped forward and showed her brother. Erik bent down and gave her a big hug. Ludwig then took them to the other side of the warehouse, and asked them to strip. Esther was actually able to take all but her underwear off, and get fitted with her stripped camp uniform.

Although Esther was thirteen and a half years old, she had not yet developed as a young girl, and there was no evidence of feminine protuberances. The hall was completely empty and no one paid attention to a young boy hiding behind his older brother. Once they both had changed in to their uniforms, a sad looking

165

frail old lady came over and took their clothes. Unlike the kitchen staff, she was extremely thin and haggard looking. She immediately began searching their clothes for contraband.

Erik smiled to himself, thinking that he had outsmarted the Nazis. He turned to his sister and gave her a knowing wink and smile. She at first did not understand, but eventually caught on and winked back at him.

After this ordeal, Ludwig took them back to the storeroom. The walk back seemed even longer than the earlier journey. Both of them drug their heels on the way back, and felt lost and confused. These uniforms gave them a feeling of hopelessness and finality. Up until this event, they still hoped that their father was going to come charging into the compound, and rescue them from these evil Nazis. They were going to need some time to get accustomed to their new life style.

Ludwig led them back into the kitchen, and introduced them to the rest of the day shift kitchen staff; a combination of German SS cooks and prisoners. Erik noticed immediately that they were the only two Jews in the crowd. Their bright yellow star, sewn on their shirt jacket, stood out. Everyone else was sporting a red, pink, black or no star at all. Each color denoted their category or reason for imprisonment. Ludwig introduced them to two other prisoners. Both of these men were wearing white coveralls completely covered in blood. Their hands, faces, hair and everything else were entirely covered in blood. Some of it was dry, and the rest was still dripping from their coveralls and bodies.

"Hans and Lothar, these prisoners are brand new, and they claim to be butcher apprentices. They claim to have several years of experience, working with their father in a local village butcher shop. I will let you use them as you see fit to help you, however they are to be well treated, and not abused in anyway! I will need them to work for me, as well in the storeroom. You can have them from six-thirty until one- thirty. Afternoons are strictly mine, and I can change my mind anytime I want to! Is that understood?" Stated Ludwig in an official and preaching manner.

Both men nodded their heads, but did not say anything.

Ludwig walked away and left them alone with Hans and Lothar. Both Erik and Esther did not know what to do or say; they were unsure how to handle their new situation. Finally Hans broke the ice and said.

"OK you two, just follow me and do what I tell you! OK? Can anyone make sausages?" Asked the butcher.

"Yes, of course! We are specialists in sausages. My father had his own shop in Niedergeyer, and was known all over the region for the best Bratwursts, Wienerwursts and Blutwurts." Replied an anxious Erik.

"That's terrific! We need some help with the sausages. These damned SS seem to live on them. Three meals a day if they can get it." Stated Lothar, smiling as he did so.

Erik noticed that Lothar had a pink star on his left side, denoting that he was a homosexual, and Hans had a red star showing him to be a communist. Erik did not really know or understand what this meant, but both men appeared to be friendly, and definitely not underfed. Erik quickly realized that working in the kitchen was a good thing; at least they would not starve to death, like some of the other unfortunate ones. He immediately thought of his mother; *"Wondering how she was doing?"*

They were taken over to an area of the kitchen where large meat grinders were used to grind up the meat for sausages. They were given different chores to do, Erik because of his larger size, was tasked with carrying the large chunks of animal remains from the freezer over to a table where Esther stood working a large manual grinding apparatus. The meat and fat had to be cut in usable pieces and then fed into the machines. The process was easy enough, and after a few hours both of them had an easily manageable system going on.

Before they knew it was one-thirty and Ludwig came back to pick them up. The first thing Erik noticed was the appearance of **KAPO** Ludwig Winter. His face was all bloodied up. Blood was streaming down from several large cuts on the head, nose, lips, and cheeks; just about everything seemed to be bleeding profusely. Despite his horrible appearance, he had a smile on his face, and seemed pleased with himself.

"None of you, say anything at all, or you will have a price to pay!" Screamed an extremely irate Ludwig Winter.

Everyone stood around looking at the disheveled and bloodied KAPO. Erik finally took it upon himself to say something.

"Herr Winter let me clean your wounds for you!"

Ludwig stared at the young man and simply nodded his head, as he turned around and walked back towards the storeroom. After opening the cage door he grabbed a bucket and filled it with clean water. Erik grabbed one of the pillowcases, and used it to clean his wounds. Ludwig allowed Erik to work on his face, the whole time he had a silly-ass grin on his face. Erik was thoroughly confused by this strange attitude; why could Ludwig be so happy after such a horrible beating? The more he thought about it the more confused he got.

"I bet you don't know why I am smiling, do you? Well young man, you may have done us the biggest favor of our lives. It was well worth getting beat up by the SS Staff Sergeant." Replied a still smiling Ludwig.

"Please, please tell us what happened? Why are you smiling? What happened?" Asked a curious Erik.

"After I left here, I thought about what you said, and I decided to talk to the Staff Sergeant and sort of feel him out about the gold coin. At first he was very attentive, and interested, but suddenly he turned vicious and accused me of stealing the coin, and he was going to have me shot etc." Finished a spirited Ludwig.

"OK, sir. But why are you smiling?" Asked Erik again.

"Just as he was beating me up, the Camp Commandant, SS Colonel Koch came around the corner and surprised him. The Colonel wanted to know why I was being beaten? Not knowing what to say, he simply lied, and told him I had been late for work. The Colonel was suspicious and questioned him further. Unfortunately for him in the scuffle, the gold coin had fallen out of his pocket, and unto the courtyard. Colonel Koch spotted it and claimed it for himself. He held it up in his hand and waived back and forth in front of our eyes." Stated Ludwig, staring at both them with a grin on his face.

"The Colonel has a serious gambling and drug addition problem, and is continually stealing from the inmates and the staff. The Staff Sergeant could not claim it for himself, because possession of that coin by anyone but Colonel Koch, could mean instant death for the possessor." Continued Herr Winter.

"But what is to prevent the Staff Sergeant to kill you, or make you disappear? Have you thought of that?" Asked an inquiring Erik.

"Yes I have. But God was on my side today. Two other individuals witnessed this incident; Colonel Koch's wife and another KAPO. How he could explain my disappearance? Not only that, he casually made the comment that, 'he would be very appreciative if anyone would find any more coins.' The Staff Sergeant then lied again and said he had won it in a card game, thereby incriminating himself again. The Colonel asked the Sergeant to report to his office tomorrow morning." Finished a pleased Ludwig.

"How does that help you? Us?" Asked a confused Erik?

"Listen my young friend. You cannot fool me! No one carries such a valuable coin into a concentration camp, unless he has more than one. You, you will give them to me and I will buy our way out of here. All of us, that's right. These Nazis will send you out of the country if you can pay them and never come back!" Replied a happy Ludwig.

"What makes you think, I have any more of these coins? That was it! You promised to take care of my brother and me; and if you don't, I will tell everyone that you are the owner of the coin and have a secret stash. They will torture you, and you will die." Replied a spirited Erik.

Ludwig looked down at Erik and smiled again.

"You have only been here two days and you are handling yourself like an old veteran. I have but one goal! To get out of this place in one piece as soon as possible. And you my friend are my first class ticket out of here. I don't care what lies you tell me now. All I want is the truth at the right time! I can make your life pleasant or have you killed! You are at my mercy, and don't ever forget it!" Stated a somewhat somber Ludwig.

Erik reflected on that last statement and was unsure as to what to say or do. He decided to keep quiet for now, and wait for a better opportunity. Ludwig told them to stay in the storeroom for the rest of the day; he wanted to go and get some rest now. He locked them in the room and left the kitchen area. Both of them took the opportunity to wash up and get some rest. They hoped he would return soon, because they had not eaten since yesterday and the stomach monster was making noises again.

Around seven o'clock, Lothar the butcher came into their area and asked them if they were hungry?

"Oh yes sir! We have not eaten since yesterday! Thank you very much! Thank you sir!" Answered a starving Erik and Esther.

Lothar brought a large plate of hot potatoes, two bratwursts, grey bread and sliced apples. The kids could not believe their good fortunes. Lothar carefully slid the food under the mesh door and wished them a good evening. It did not take long for them to scarf down the food. Just when they were about done with their meal, Erik had a sudden urge to use the bucket. His coins and whatever else he had in his stomach was making a quick exit.

Once the deed was completed, he immediately checked the contents. He was pleased to know that all four coins gleamed at the bottom of the bucket. He was not quite sure what to do with them. One thing was for certain; he had to clean them immediately, otherwise Ludwig would know where he was hiding them. Giving them to Ludwig was out of the question right now! However he thought about stashing them under the sink with the two rings. He looked around the room and spotted an area, right beneath the sink was a drain hole covered in a strong mesh wire. He unscrewed the cover and looked inside the five-inch wide hole. It was absolutely the most disgusting sight he had ever seen. The entire hole was filled with grease, filth, human waste etc. About four inches down there was a circular grove carved in to the side of the hole. It was over three inches in depth and could easily hide the coins and the rings.

Erik took the four coins and the two rings and wedged them tightly; he then covered the entire area with his own feces and other filth. He looked at his handy work, and was positive that no one would dream of looking there. He hoped that the sight would discourage anyone from sticking his or her hand down this stink hole.

Unless someone was really looking for them, they will never find them, *"He thought to himself."*

Chapter 17

"Homecoming"

Back in the present.

Both Cameron and Dieter finished their brandy and once again smoked a good cigar. Dieter had an unlimited supply of excellent Cuban, Dominican and German stogies. His personal connection to the Archbishop in Aachen, made it easy for him to acquire them. He did not smoke them very often, but on special occasions such as this he enjoyed taking a time out. The unpleasantness with Kate and Ingrid was quickly forgotten and both men relaxed and enjoyed the moment.

"I cannot believe how lucky Erik and his sister were. They really fell into a great position. Somebody upstairs really must like him." Stated Cameron, pointing to the ceiling with his right index finger.

"It is only fair, after such a miserable and hideous time, that good fortune smile upon them." Replied Dieter.

"You are right. They really deserved it!" Answered Cameron, blowing large smoke rings as he did so.

"Dieter, I am now going to drive back to Aachen and go to a hotel that I know near my work. I will call you everyday, and I will go and pick up Ingrid on Saturday at the airport. If you would like we can go together? I think she would like it? Don't you?" Asked Cameron as he headed out the door.

"I think that's a great idea! And don't worry about Kate, I will control her and I promise she will behave when you return next week with Ingrid and Jennifer." Answered Dieter in a friendly and caring tone.

Both men shook hands and said goodbye. By the time Cameron got to the northbound A3 Autobahn it was already very late. Cameron really appreciated the no-speed limit at this hour of the night. He drove the fifty-five miles to Aachen in less than thirty minute!

He took the Aachenerplatz exit and drove to his favorite hotel in Germany. *"Zum Quellenhof,* was its name. It was small in size, maybe 24 rooms, but it had the best restaurant in town, and the bar was out of this world. It was built around the 1870's, and still possessed a style and grandeur seldom seen today in hotels. The owner, Herr Heinz-Gunther Schmitdt, also known as 'Heinzie', was a friendly and wonderful host. Cameron had spent many a wonderful night in the bar sharing old stories and quite a few beers with Heinzie.

He parked his car around the corner and walked to the hotel. Cameron was disappointed when the night clerk was not Heinzie.

"Guten Abend! (Good evening), he said to the young man.

"Guten Abend, Mein Herr! What can I do for you? Replied the friendly clerk.

"I need a room for about five days, maybe longer. Preferably one of your large ones with the two queen beds and the double bath." Asked an inquisitive Cameron.

"So you know your way around our hotel? You have been here before, Herr?" Asked the young man, a questioning look on his face?

"Yes, of course! I have stayed here on many occasions. My name is Cameron Clark, and I was a very good friend of the owner, Herr Heinz-Gunther Schmidt." Replied Cameron.

"How wonderful, this is great! I am Klaus Schmidt, the son of Heinzie." Replied the smiling, and now very cheerful young man. He reached across the counter and shook Cameron's hand like a pump.

"I will go get and my father immediately. He would be very upset if I did not wake him. He speaks of you all the time, and has very fond memories of the old times. Please excuse me sir, I will go get him!" Answered Klaus, as he ran behind the counter and disappeared into a hallway.

"Wait, wait! Don't wake your father up!" Cameron was

unable to finish his sentence; Klaus was long gone.

Cameron just stood there waiting for over ten minutes. A disheveled and pajama clad Heinzie, came running down the hallway, closely followed by an excited Klaus.

*"**Mein Gott!** (My God)* I can't believe it, it's really you, Cameron my old friend!" Without waiting for an answer, Heinzie threw himself on Cameron and hugged him repeatedly.

Cameron was caught by surprised. It was very uncommon for Germans to show such emotions. Especially Heinzie; he had always been very friendly, but never prone to show physical or emotional sentiments.

"Heinzie, Heinzie! So glad to see you again! How are you? It's been a long time, my friend. How is your lovely wife, Heidi?" Asked Cameron, as he stepped away from Heinzie's embrace.

The question seemed to freeze both men in their tracts. Heinzie lowered his head and began sobbing uncontrollably. Cameron started to walk towards him, but Klaus waived him off, and put his hands in a prayer form and pointed upwards. Cameron now understood, something must have happened to Heidi.

"I am so sorry Heinzie! I did not know, how terrible! What happened?" Asked a disconsolate Cameron.

"Cameron, it was all my fault, my fault! We had a car accident two months ago, and she was killed. I had just purchased a new BMW 745i and I was showing off on the Autobahn. I lost control and hit a bridge at over 240 kilometers an hour. A large piece of metal was jarred and came crashing through the windshield. She was killed instantly! At least she did not suffer; it was instantaneous!" Replied a tearful Heinzie.

"My gosh, I am so sorry. You must be devastated? How are you coping? Is there anything I can do for you?" Asked a caring and concerned Cameron.

Heinzie paused in mid-sentence and quietly looked at Cameron. "Yes you can, my friend! Have a couple of beers with me and help me forget? What do you say?"

Before Cameron could reply, Heinzie was already behind the bar tapping two large half-liter frosted mugs. Cameron pointed his finger towards Klaus, Heinzie shook his head and said, "No, I am sorry, he is on duty, and no drinking allowed!" Replied Herr Schmidt.

"No problem, you are the boss. Maybe tomorrow when he is off duty we can toast to your wonderful wife Heidi." Stated Cameron.

Heinzie nodded his head, and began tapping a second round; even before the first one was finished. Cameron had a feeling that this would be a long night. After the third and final round, Cameron was feeling light headed and begged Heinzie to stop, but he continued for another hour. By then seven or eight large beers and three or four German Schnapps had been consumed. Both men were feeling no pain, and Cameron was definitely ready for bed. It was nearly midnight, and he had to get up at six-thirty. Cameron finally told Heinzie.

"My friend we can continue tomorrow evening if you would like, but I really must get some rest." Without waiting for an answer he grabbed the key that Klaus had pressed in his hand and started walking towards the elevator. He checked the key and saw it was room 224, his favorite suite. It was at the end of the hallway and overlooked the parking area; normally the quietest part of the hotel. By the time Cameron got to the room, Heinzie was well on his way to alcohol paradise and did not notice Cameron's quick exit.

The evening went faster than he expected. It seemed like he had just lain down on the soft goose feather comforter, when the wake up call from Klaus woke him up. He quickly showered, and went downstairs for some coffee. German breakfasts are not like the American ones; you usually have a poached egg, a small crunchy bread roll with butter, marmalade or cheese.

Cameron was not up to a big breakfast anyway. He drank some coffee, had the egg and a small slice of bread. He got a cup of coffee to go and walked to his office. The ten-minute walk did him good. It was very cool and blistery this morning. The fresh air perked him up a bit. The fall leaves were blowing around adding to the winter like landscape.

"Good morning Frau Rausching!" Stated Cameron as he walked in.

Good morning to you Herr Clark. I hope you have a much-needed rest? Because we have some serious concerns today! We had a break-in yesterday, and they ransacked everything. Strangely enough only a few portable computers, and some of the documents we were working on were stolen. However you must see what they did in your office." Stated an obviously excited Frau Raushing!

"Are you serious? Have you called the police yet? How did they get in?" Replied Cameron as he rushed over to his office.

He opened it and was horrified at what he saw. Every bit of furniture was smashed to pieces; the computer was destroyed beyond repair. The chair and couch were slashed and the stuffing was spread all over his office. However the large black swastikas were the most terrifying of all, they were spray painted on every wall. Behind his desk the burglars painted a death head and crossed skeleton leg bones and the words, ***"Juden Raus!"*** (Jews Out!)

"Well we must be doing something right! If they took this much trouble and time in here, they must have really wanted to know what I was up to? We are succeeding and we must continue full speed ahead." Replied an exhilarated Cameron.

"Frau Rausching? Is everyone here? Have they showed up yet? If not, called them at home and ask them to get here as soon as possible. We have deadline to meet. Have you called the police yet?" Asked Cameron, as he quietly and efficiently went around picking up his office furniture and papers.

"Nein Herr Clark! I wanted to wait for you! Do you think it wise? After all we do not know who to trust yet?" Asked Frau Rausching?

"You must call them immediately. I also want you to call Herr Wolfgang von Hagen in Aachen, Herr Kunstoff in America, Colonel Perrin in Paris, the Associated Press (AP), and the Reuters Press Agency, Le Monde in Paris, the Financial Times in London etc. I also want you to call every major German paper, magazine T.V. and radio station in Europe. As soon as the staff comes in, get them to help you. I want everyone to know about this and maybe we can finally get to bottom of this debacle. I will accept all and every interview they need, just work out a schedule for me. *Ist das klar?*" (Is that clear?") Ordered a determined and excited Cameron.

The phone calls started to come almost instantly after Frau Rausching called the **Kriminal Polizei** (Criminal Police) in Aachen. Just like in America every police department is on the payroll of most major newspapers and the news spread like a wildfire. Cameron's firs call was to his boss in the USA, Jerry Kunstoff.

Frau Rausching was able to get Jerry on the phone first.

"What? Really? That's great! Your whole office was destroyed? Fantastic! How did you do it? My God, someone must really be pissed at you? Email me some photos immediately. I am going to try to get all set up for the morning edition. Keep up the good work, Cameron. Listen to me, keep up the pressure, but be careful. You have obviously hit a nerve and they are pissed!" Finished a concerned Jerry Kunsoff.

"Don't worry boss, I have all under control. However, you could do me a favor? Can you try to get a hold of my cousin Jeremy Grant, formerly of the CIA, now with the US Customs Service in San Francisco, I might need his help?" Asked Cameron as he hung up the phone.

Thirty minutes later Frau Rausching announced that every one was present, and they were waiting in the conference room.

"Good to see you all in such a cheerful mood." He announced to the gathered employees. They all looked at each other, not knowing what to say or do.

"Has the cat got your tongues?" He asked, a smile spreading across his face.

Most of them did not understand what he meant. This was an American expression and their American colloquialism was not that good yet.

He began questioning all of his employees one by one, and took copious notes as he did so. They in fact had been busy little beavers. Every single one of them had dug up some dirt on someone in Germany or France, however the American connection was still tenuous at best. He wanted them to dig up some more intelligence on the North American relationship, and how they were all inter-connected.

In fact they had overwhelmed him with facts, figures, photos and data. It would take several days or weeks to sort it all out. He was fortunate that because they were such good journalists; his staff had copied all of their data on both mini-computer drives and also still had their hand-copied notes at a separate location. Therefore the burglars had not accomplished much with their break-in. He pondered to himself, *"If this was more of a demonstrative act; than an actual burglary."*

However Cameron was still puzzled by the fact, that they had somehow gotten access to his office without any physical evidence being present? He was going to follow-up with the building owner, and hope that they had some type of video monitoring system in the lobby? Perhaps the **KRIPO** (Criminal Police), might also have other outlets nearby; Cameron hoped that their investigative techniques were better than their response time. It had been several hours, and still no police presence.

Cameron wanted time to put this data into a format that made sense. He informed Frau Rausching not to disturb him unless it was the police or another journalist wanting an interview. He also ordered his colleagues to continue digging for dirt, but warned them to stay safe and be aware of their surroundings at all times.

Part of his new safety policy was to institute an innovative measure. It required that at least two of them stay in the office past normal business hour twenty-four hours a day. He also required them to have all their cell phones fully charged, and also asked them to limit their private conversations to a minimum, so that they could always be available. They could work out the schedule among themselves. He authorized Frau Rausching to spend up to a thousand Euros on cots, blankets, pillows etc. At first, this decision was not very popular with some of the staff members, but when he told them they would accumulate two extra paid vacation days per week of duty, they all cheered in unison, and were later on fighting with each other to volunteer for the late shift. Eventually Frau Rausching worked out a satisfactory schedule for all concerned. Every one of them would have to work a double shift every third day, and still have two days off a week.

Frau Rausching was extremely pleased that Herr Cameron Clark had given her this additional responsibility. It made her feel needed again, and she reveled in the attention. *She was at her best under pressure, and by God she would prevail,* she thought to herself.

Frau Rausching buzzed Cameron on the intercom.

"Herr Clark, Herr Clark! Sorry to disturb you! You have Herr von Hagen on line two."

"Hello Wolfgang, how are you, my friend?" Answered a friendly Cameron.

"Well it's not me, I am worried about! How are you? Is everything OK? Anyone hurt? Please tell me all about it?" Asked an obviously concerned Wolfgang.

"Everything is fine. Don't worry about it. They just damaged the office, and vandalized some equipment, but everyone is fine. You can come over and take some pictures if you like. It would make great copy for the paper?" Asked Cameron, extending an invitation to his friend.

"I will be right over, if that's OK with you?" Asked Wolfgang?

"Sure, come on over any time you want. I will be here the rest of the day." Replied Cameron.

Within seconds the phone rang again, and it was another interview from a local radio station. He was busily occupied with the radio station correspondent, when Frau Rausching knocked on the door.

"Excuse Herr Clark, but the KRIPO have finally shown up." Stated an obviously upset Frau Rausching.

"That's OK, these gentlemen are almost done? Are you not?" Stated Cameron pointing to the two radio station personnel.

"Ja, Herr Clark. Thank you for your time. I hope everything

works out for you." Both men got up and walked out.

Frau Rausching, escorted the police officers in.

Cameron looked at them, and thought to himself, *"Cops are cops all over the world."* They looked like American detectives, slightly overweight, balding and wearing ill-fitting suits. They could almost be movie extras from a bygone era. As a matter of fact, the shorter of the two had an uncanny resemblance to Humphrey Bogart.

"Guten Tag Herr Clark! My name is **Hauptkomissar** (Chief Detective) Schleptke, and this is my colleague **Komissar** (Detective) Noelke."

"Yes gentlemen, please come in and have a seat." Said Cameron, as he stood up and pointed to the two chairs near his desk.

Both men came over and sat down. Detective Noelke had a notepad in his right hand and was taking notes of the entire affair.

"Well Herr Clark, please tell me what happened? From the beginning please?" Stated Chief Detective Schleptke, as he pulled out a long black cigar.

"Do you mind Herr Clark?" He asked as he lit it.

"No, please go right ahead. I don't mind. I too smoke an occasional cigar myself." Replied Cameron, expecting the Chief Detective to perhaps offer him one.

Chief Detective Schleptke just looked at him and smiled. Cameron did not know what to make of it. It was not a friendly smile, more like a lion stretching his lips prior to devouring his prey. Cameron decided he had better be careful with his statement; the Chief Detective could have an ulterior agenda and Cameron needed to feel him out.

Cameron told the detectives everything he knew, but did not volunteer anything about his first hand knowledge of Nazis, the holocaust or fascists etc. He wanted them to provide answers, not the other way around. The interview lasted over an hour, and was only interrupted when Wolfgang von Hagen came in the office to say hello. Up to now the questioning seemed more like an interrogation, than an investigation.

Both detectives sat in silence, and waited for Wolfgang to leave before saying anything.

"So you know Herr von Hagen? Do you?" Asked the Chief Detective?

"Yes as a matter of fact, we are old friends, going back almost twenty years." Replied Cameron.

The fact that Wolfgang and Cameron were friends seemed to interest the detectives more than the crime itself. They immediately asked more pertinent questions and took photos of the crime scene, fingerprints and gathered other evidence. Twenty minutes later they finally decided to leave his office.

"Well Mr. Clark, we will be getting back with you as soon as we find out anything new or interesting." Stated the Hauptkomissar as he walked out the door, without even looking back.

The younger Komissar followed suit, and shook his head as he exited the room. Cameron just sat there staring at the closed door, not knowing what had really happened. Were they really interested? Or were they only they only filling out paperwork to make him happy? Cameron had always prided himself in being able to clearly evaluate the situation, but these guys were hard to follow. Just when he was about to get up, the phone rang again.

"Hello! Clark here." He answered.

There was a small lapse of time, a click and a heavily accented man responded.

"Hello, hello is this Herr Clark?" Asked the man with the accent.

"Yes, yes it is. With whom am I speaking?" Asked Clark, leaning forward and turning his automatic voice activated recorder.

"My name is Johanson, Sygurd Johanson." Replied the man with the now definable Norwegian accent.

"Well Herr Johanson, what can I do for you? Have we met before?" Asked a curious Cameron.

"No we have not. But I know who you are and what you do!" Replied Sygurd Johanson.

Cameron reflected on the past six months, and could not

remember ever hearing the name Johanson mentioned in anything he was doing, and yet the man seemed very convincing and assured.

"OK, you have my curiosity peeked. What is it that you want to discuss with me? Why don't you come to my office and we will talk about it?" Replied Cameron, hoping the man would get to the point.

"No, no Herr Clark. That would not be wise. I would like you to come to me. Do you know where the 'Storyville' Discothèque is? In Köln, on Bismarkstrasse?" Asked Johanson.

"Yes I do, but why should I drive that far, why can't we meet here in Aachen?" Asked a suspicious Clark.

"I have to take certain precautions, and I don't know my way around Aachen. Believe me you won't regret it. It's a hell of a story!" Replied Sygurd Johanson, a hint of excitement in his voice.

"I might just do that, but you have to give me a hint? Otherwise I won't drive that far!" Replied Cameron, leaning back in his chair and wondering what this was all about?

"I guess I could give you a clue. U.S. Army soldiers stationed in Germany are selling large quantities of automatic weapons to fascists groups in Europe, and some of these weapons are even finding their way back to the USA?" How does that sound Herr Clark? Interesting?" Answered a now seemingly excited Johanson.

"You have proof of this?" Clark asked.

"But of course, Herr Clark. I have proof of collusion between the thieves and members of the German *Zollamt*. (Customs Service).

This last bit of information really excited Cameron. This was exactly the type of stuff that he was looking for, but somehow it seemed too easy? Was this a set-up? How did Johanson know what he was doing in Germany? As tempting as it was, he had to be careful. He agreed to meet Johanson at 8 p.m. that evening. They agreed to both wear a white carnation in their coat lapel, and meet in the bar. Cameron thought, *"How 1940's is this meeting in a bar; wearing a white carnation? Something right out of a black and white espionage movie."*

Although Cameron was extremely interested in the tip, he still was leery of the whole set-up. He decided to take precautions and called both Dieter and Wolfgang von Hagen and asked for their help. Just to make sure that nothing was compromised; he did not inform either one of them of their presence. He would do so later on with his cell phone; once they got on scene.

Cameron spent the best part of an hour explaining to both men what to do and where to meet etc. Dieter was very excited and ready to get started immediately, but Wolfgang showed some reluctance or disinterest. Eventually he agreed to meet Clark in the underground parking area beneath the Storyville at 7:30 that evening. Dieter's job was to follow him there and watch his back. Just to make sure that all bases were covered, he also informed his staff of who he was meeting and where. Most of them were concerned, but knew it might be a good lead to follow, and eventually went along with the idea. Cameron promised to keep in touch at least once an hour with his employees.

Cameron reflected back to his days as a counter-intelligence special agent and had a bad feeling of what was about to happen. The hairs on the back of his neck were standing up like a porcupine in heat, and his nerves were all on edge. He had many years of first hand knowledge in the arena of intelligence and this was not going to go well. His premonitions were usually right, but he hoped for the best. However this lead might be exactly what he was looking for, and he had to go through with it.

Cameron went to a large steel cabinet in his office and took out a set of night vision devices, binoculars, video camera and a D-cell, five-cell flashlight. Past experiences had taught him to be well prepared, and he was an avid practitioner of this craft. He made sure that all batteries were fully charged, and just for fun, he threw in an extremely sharp four inch folding knife. He taped it in its sheath to his right ankle. At first he felt kind of silly with the knife, but experience had taught him that it's better to look silly than dead. He was satisfied that he had everything he might need, when he remembered that he also had an extremely small pen-tape recorder. It had a two-hour recording time, and it might come in handy.

He looked at his black canvas -traveling bag and was satisfied with everything he had brought. Just then the phone rang again.

"Hello, Clark here!" He answered. It was Johanson again; he wanted to change the time to seven p.m.

"No way! I can't leave my office that early. It's either 8 p.m. or no deal!" Replied an angry Cameron.

"OK, OK! Eight is fine!" Replied Johanson and hung up.

Cameron wondered why Johanson had tried to change the time? *Was it a diversion? Was it a trap? Were they trying to prevent him from providing contingency plans? Who was Johanson?* Cameron had so many unanswered questions. In the past his innermost instincts had served him well, and he hoped that he was wrong this time.

Chapter 18

The Trap

Cameron called both Dieter and Wolfgang prior to leaving his office. They were both ready, and would meet him at the Kerpen Autobahn west-side exit in exactly thirty-five minutes. Before leaving his office, he decided to call Jerry Kunstoff in America and advise him of the situation. Frau Rausching was able to call him at home.

"Hello, hello? This better be good? Do you realize its four a.m.?" Asked a disgruntled Jerry.

"Sorry boss! I have something hot going on and I wanted to keep you abreast of the situation." Answered a worried Cameron, not knowing if calling his boss at this hour was such a good idea?

"Oh, it's you! I guess it's all right. I gave you permission after all. What's going on?" Asked a curious Jerry. Cameron went on to explain what was happening and asked for advice?

"Use your own best judgment, but I am glad to see that you are taking precautions. Just be safe and keep me apprised of everything." Stated a sleepy and drowsy Jerry.

"One again, I am sorry for waking you so early! But I thought you might want to know?" Replied Cameron.

Oh, by the way! Have you been to contact my cousin Jeremy Grant? I really need to speak with him?" Asked a concerned Cameron.

"No, I haven't! He is apparently out of town, but his Deputy Director knows to call me as soon as he returns. He is on some type of 'Secret Mission' and should return in a few days. Replied Jerry.

"Great! It's really important that I speak with him. Please call me night or day, if he contacts you? Thanks, and I will keep in touch." Finished Cameron as he hung up the phone, and reflected on the day's events. He had been so busy that he had forgotten all about his wife and daughter. They were coming in less than a week and he had to start concentrating on that fact.

His wife was obviously going through some type of emotional crisis and he had to be there for her, regardless of her negative attitude. Cameron could not focus on the task at hand due to the concerns about his wife and her sudden change in attitude and demeanor. Cameron wondered, *"I wonder if Kate had anything to do with it?"*

A loud knock on the door snapped him back to reality. It was Frau Rausching.

"Herr Clark, I have some more reporters waiting in the foyer wanting to interview you, and the building manager, Herr Dittmar is also wanting to see you." She finished with a long sigh.

"Good! You handle everyone, but Herr Dittmar. Show him in, and don't disturb me until I call you back in the office! Is that understood?" Ordered Cameron to a surprised Frau Rausching.

"You mean, you mean I should give interviews to the press?" She asked with a large grin spreading across her large face.

"Yes, that is correct! You probably know more about the break-in than anyone else. Just don't say or do anything that might embarrass Herr Jerry Kunstoff. Is that clear? Please send Herr Dittmar in." Ordered a somewhat bossy Cameron Clark.

Frau Rausching was somewhat taken back by his dictatorial commends, but she soon realized that Herr Dittmar was standing behind her, and maybe Cameron was trying to impress him with managerial skills. She did not really mind because; he had just made her the de-facto director in his absence, and she was overjoyed by the additional responsibility.

"Come in Herr Dittmar. Come in, Please. Have a seat." Said Cameron, pointing to the large brown leather chair in front of his desk.

"Thank you Herr Clark. It is a pleasure to finally meet you in person. I am truly sorry about what has happened? It is a disaster!" Stated a somewhat excited and apologetic Herr Dittmar.

"Please, please Herr Dittmar. It is not your fault. Let's move on. Do you have any videotape I could look at? It's very important for us to try and identify these scumbags!" Replied Cameron in a voice stronger than he had expected to project. The sudden harshness of his tone caught Herr Dittmar by surprise.

"Well I think so. I have analyzed the entire tape for the past three days and these two gentlemen are the only ones that we can't account for. Do you have a recorder?" Asked Herr Dittmar.

"Yes, yes of course. There is one over there by the television." Replied Cameron as he pointed to the large 42" screen TV in the corner of the office.

Cameron stood up and grabbed the video from Herr Dittmar and stuck it in the recorder. After several minutes of non-descript images two black clad individuals walked in the main entrance of the building and walked towards the elevator. Unfortunately the quality was not very good, and both men kept heir faces hidden from the camera. They purposely turned away or secreted their faces with a newspaper. They obviously knew they were being recorded, and were very adapt at concealing their identity.

"I am sorry Herr Clark, that is all we have. These men were very good at hiding their true personality." Stated a concerned Herr Dittmar.

"It's not your fault! Don't worry about it. At least we know that they are Caucasian, about one meter eighty-five in height, and approximately ninety to one hundred kilos in weight. I would also guess their age to be somewhere between thirty- five and fifty? What do you think Herr Dittmar?" Asked Cameron as he stood up from behind his desk.

"I must confess, I did not see as much as you have, Herr Clark! You obviously have more experience than I do in these matters." Replied a sheepish looking Herr Dittmar.

"I must sincerely thank you for your assistance, Herr Dittmar. I will call the Hauptkomissar and give him a copy of the tape." Stated Cameron as he walked to the office door.

"That is not necessary, I have already done so." Stated Herr Dittmar as he walked out of the office. His answer caught Cameron by surprise. Why would Dittmarr give the KRIPO a tape before him? He was the one who had requested the tape in the first place.

"Great, that saves me some time, then." Replied Cameron as he escorted Dittmar out the door.

"Frau Rausching, please get me the Hauptkomissar on the phone?" He asked.

A few minutes later the office phone rang, and Hauptkmissar Schleptke was on the phone.

"Yes Herr Clark, what can I do for you?" Asked the Haupkomissar.

"You saw the video? Were you able to detect anything?" Asked Cameron.

"We were not able to detect anything special, the images were blurred and the men were hiding their faces. However we are still working on the case and we will advise you of any changes, Herr Clark!" Replied a somewhat gruff Hauptkomissar.

"Please stay on top of this matter, I am seriously concerned and would not want it to vanish into oblivion." Replied Cameron, wanting to make a point to the Hauptkomissar.

"What are you suggesting Herr Clark? Are you claiming that the KRIPO would somehow not do their duty? We are professional police officers and we always follow our leads until they are exhausted!" Continued a now upset Hauptkomissar.

"No sir, I am not suggesting anything of the kind. However I know how busy police officers are and I wanted only to ask for your assistance. Please don't be offended, Hauptkomissar." Replied a somewhat apologetic Cameron.

"Good, as long we understand each other." Finished the grouchy officer.

Cameron hung up the phone and grabbed his black canvas bag and started to walk out of the office, when Frau Rausching came up to him and informed him that Herr Wolfgang von Hagen had called, and informed her that he would not be able to go to Köln, and sincerely apologized. He had a serious family emergency, and would not be able to meet with him. Cameron was surprised and disappointed, but he understood. After all, family came first.

Cameron decided to call Wolfgang's office to check on him. "Hello, hello, Herr von Hagen is not in the office, can I help you? Stated the young secretary.

"Please let him know that I called, thank you." Replied Cameron, hanging up the phone.

Cameron decided to make one more call. His gut instinct told him to do so. He called Wolfgang at home. It rang four or five times and Wolfgang's youngest son, Adrian answered.

"Hello, hello, hello! Who is this please?" Asked four years old Adrian.

"Is your father home?" Asked Cameron, hoping to find out what was really going on.

"No, no he is at the office with my mother and sister." Replied the very cute and intelligent Adrian.

"Who is watching you? Are you alone?" Asked Cameron.

"Well, my Nana, Joanni is watching me until my father comes home. And I have to hang up now, because my father told me not to answer the phone!" Answered Adrian, as he slammed the phone down. Cameron was puzzled by this sudden turn of events.

Chapter 19

Lucky?

Cameron's BMW cruised along the Autobahn towards Kerpen at over one hundred twenty miles an hour. Traffic was flowing smoothly and it took less than forty minutes to reach the Kerpen exit. He pulled in to the McDonald's parking lot and waited for Dieter. Cameron thought to himself, *"My how times have changed?* They even have a drive-thru McDonald's in Kerpen. The one time residence of Ludwig Beethoven had grown in to a medium size thriving community between Aachen and Köln. When he was stationed near here, it was a small size community of fewer than six thousand souls and 21 pubs! The reason he knew there were twenty-one of them, was everyone in his unit had at one time or another gone to everyone of them and had a beer or two, before moving on to the next one. It was a kind of ritual that every "newbie" had to perform. Now it was a modern middle-sized thriving city, with a McDonalds, a theater, shopping centers and a movie theater, etc.

Cameron went inside and bought a large Diet-Coke and went back outside. Just then, Dieter's silver Mercedes pulled up next to his car.

"How are you Cameron?" Greeted the always-friendly Dieter Johannes.

"I am fine, thank you! Glad to see you here so punctually," replied Cameron trying to pull himself away from Dieter's usual crushing bear hug.

Both men sat in Dieter's car and discussed the upcoming mission. Cameron informed Dieter of Wolfgang's no show, and also mentioned his uneasiness about the whole affair. His apprehension was growing by leaps and bounds, but he knew he had to go through with the meeting. Dieter informed him that his cousin Jeremy Grant had called the house trying to reach him. This bit of information made him feel better already. Jeremy was an animal in every sense of the word; a former Green Beret captain in the Special Forces; past CIA agent and currently Chief of Intelligence for the US Customs Service in the San Francisco Regional Intelligence Center. Six foot five ex-football player and martial arts expert, and all-around badass.

Cameron knew that Jeremy could possibly provide some of the intelligence he needed on any USA based neo-Nazis, or for that matter anywhere in the world. Cameron excused himself from Dieter and went over to the nearest pay phone, and after a long and boring procedure; called his cousin Jeremy in San Francisco. The conversation lasted nearly twenty minutes, but he was satisfied that Jeremy might be able to assist him in more ways than one. Jeremy even volunteered to come over to Europe and directly help. Jeremy had accumulated over sixty days of leave, and if he did not use it, he would lose it. Cameron was grateful for the offer, but preferred the assistance from stateside, right now.

Cameron gave Jeremy his satellite, and regular cell number and promised to check with him every forty-eight hours. Cameron reminded Jeremy of their once 'Secret' password arrangement in the event of an emergency. Both men had picked a coded word, which would notify the other to charge up the hill and bring the Marines! At the time it seemed kind of silly, but now it might be useful.

Dieter waited patiently in the car and was happy to see Cameron return.

"Dieter, I was able to reach my cousin and he is all set to help us. We will be checking with each other every other day. If you receive a call from him, be sure to let me know as soon as possible, OK? I think it's time for us to go? Do you know how to get to the Storyville? Asked Cameron."

"Yes I do! I think however, it might be more prudent for me to go first and park down in the parking garage. You could arrive ten minutes later; we won't attract undue attention this way. What do you think?" Stated an excited Dieter!

"Sounds good to me, lets go. You lead the way." Replied Cameron.

Dieter led the way down the A-3 Autobahn. Cameron kept his distance, yet stayed a few minutes behind him. In less than thirty minutes both cars approached the outskirts of Köln. The great cathedral of the city could be seen in the distance. It was a spectacular sight; dozens of brightly colored lights reflecting on the large twin towers.

The cathedral was situated right on the Rhine River, and Cameron knew from previous experience that the Storyville was only four or five long blocks away. He took the Kaiser Wilhemstrasse to the Bismarckstrasse and noticed the Storyville down the block. Cameron pulled over and parked for a few minutes; he did not want to get there too early. He glanced at his watch and noticed that it was already seven forty-five. He looked around for Dieter, but he was nowhere in sight. After waiting for a few minutes he decided to leave. He pulled out from his street parking spot and drove the block down to the parking garage.

The first thing he noticed when he drove in was the absence of any lights, except for a door exit sign. The entire underground garage was totally and absolutely pitch black. Thank God he had Halogen lights on his car and they lit up the area fairly well. Off to the left, he could see a sign, which read, ***"Ausgang"*** (Exit).

"That must be the underground exit to the club." He thought to himself. Cameron waited for a few minutes and got out of his vehicle. When he shut-off the engine lights it was very difficult to see. He started walking towards the **Ausgang** sign, but had to be careful because of the many invisible parking curbs. After stumbling a few times, he finally approached the subterranean entrance to the club. Before he went in, he stood in front of the door and looked around, hoping to see Dieter's car somewhere nearby. His one hundred and eighty degree glance did not reveal the silver Mercedes or Dieter. He was concerned as to what happened to him.

Cameron began to worry. *"What could have gone wrong?"* He thought to himself? He stood there a few more seconds and finally opened the door to the discothèque. The back entrance was located at the rear of the establishment, and right next door to the restrooms. The noise as usual was deafening, and the cigarette smoke even worse than the din. He walked past the really old female restroom attendant, who did not even look up at him, and walked into the main part of the bar.

The only two customers at the bar were females, both in their early thirties and fairly attractive. The brunette was closest to him and the blonde was to her left. A quick glance revealed no one else in the vicinity. Just then his cell phone rang.

"Hello, Cameron here." He answered.

"Cameron, Cameron! It's me Dieter! I am near the railroad station. I had two flat tires! Two of them at once! I have never had a flat in thirty years, and now two of them at once! I called a tow service, but they won't be here for thirty minutes or so. Strangely enough, both tires had two perfect little holes in each of them! I can't imagine what caused them? Please don't do anything until I get there! You must promise me!" Blurted a highly agitated Dieter.

"OK Dieter, I promise! But, please hurry? I will be in the bar downstairs waiting for you. Hurry please!" Responded a concerned Cameron.

His cell phone call had distracted him; he did not notice the two skinhead looking individuals who had come down the main stairs and wandered over to the bar. They both were very tall, of medium build and wore black leather coats and black jeans. Both of them had clean-shaven heads, and multiple visible tattoos on their necks and hands.

When Cameron finally glanced up, they were right next to him, and the two good-looking women had suddenly disappeared. Cameron had an uncomfortable feeling; his instincts were usually right, and he knew something bad was about to happen. The younger of the men brushed up against Cameron and produced a large caliber silenced automatic and pressed it against his ribs. The suddenness of the action caught him totally by surprised.

"Don't move or squeal! If you do, you will die here and now!

Is that understood?" Growled the gunmen.

"Don't worry Buddy, I have no wish to die here or anywhere else. What now?" Asked Cameron, as he took his time; looking around the bar for help.

The bartender was at the end of the bar and had his head turned away from them. The women had disappeared and the rest of the customers were on the dance floor and not paying attention. Cameron knew that his chances were very slim and decided to stall for time and hope for the best.

"Let's go now!" Stated the same unfriendly gunmen, shoving the gun harder against his already sore ribs.

Both men pushed Cameron towards the restroom and the back entrance. They straddled him and literally carried him out the back area. As they passed the ever-present attendant, one of the men tossed a twenty Euro bill on her table, and rushed him out the back door.

The quiet and darkness was a sharp contrast to the interior. Cameron decided if he was going to do something, now was the time. He attempted to duck down and kick the gunmen with a silencer in the nuts, but when he did so all three men tripped in the darkened garage and they fell on top of each other. The last thing he saw was one of the men raising his gun and bringing it down on his head.

The blow was hard enough to temporarily knock him out, but after a second or two, he regained consciousness and was able to hear scuffling and fighting near him. His injury had dulled his senses, and he was not quite sure of his surroundings or condition. His body curled up into a ball and he passed out again. Cameron had no idea where he was or how long he had been unconscious. All he knew was, that he was in the trunk of a car, and they were traveling at a high rate of speed down some unknown highway.

It seemed like an eternity; the blow on the head had caused him to lose all perception of time. It could have been ten minutes or an hour. He felt around for his watch and noticed it was missing. He moved his hand down to his jacket pocket and noticed that both cell phones were gone as well. However his hand moved downwards towards is ankle and noticed that his knife was still in its sheath attached to his calf. He was surprised that these men had somehow overlooked his weapon; maybe they did not feel threatened by him, or it was simply an oversight?

As he lay there not knowing what to do; a million ideas popped in and out of his aching and throbbing head. Just when things seemed to spin out of control; the car suddenly accelerated and took defensive actions. It swung from left to right as if trying to avoid something or somebody. Cameron was in an awkward position, there wasn't much he could do, except await the outcome of this high-speed chase.

Cameron heard what sounded like five or six muffled and silenced gunshots. From inside the trunk the silenced gunshots were barely audible, but they were definitely bullets. He felt very frustrated, but there was little he could do. The car suddenly braked and he slid forward hitting his already injured head on some protruding piece of metal. He immediately began to bleed heavily all over himself again, and the blood squirted all over the trunk of the car. Within seconds he could feel the warm and sticky blood spray all over his shirt, face and neck. He tore a piece of shirt and applied a temporary compress to his wound. This seemed to do the trick, and he stopped bleeding almost immediately. He thought to himself, *"Head wounds have a tendency to do that, but they often stop as fast as they start."*

Just as suddenly as it started; the action came to an abrupt end. Cameron could hear strange voices outside the car, but he was not sure what language they were speaking? *Arabic? Greek? Albanian? No!* He thought to himself. They are speaking *Hebrew!* Yes Hebrew! This new bit of information really surprised him. What were Jews doing in Germany, and why would they kidnap him? After all he was on their side. A few minutes passed before anyone opened the trunk and spoke to him.

A heavily accented voice stood in the shadows and pointed an extremely powerful flashlight in to his eyes and told not to move and keep his hands in plain sight. Cameron did as he was told, not wanting to antagonize the already pissed off strangers.

"We are going to put a blindfold on you and transfer you to another car! Is that understood? Please, for your own safety do not try anything stupid!" Stated the unknown voice behind the flashlight. His enunciation was not as accented as the first individual.

Two sets of hands picked him up and carried him to another nearby vehicle. Cameron could tell that it was a large car. Unlike before, he was put in the back seat and blindfolded. Two men sat next to him and the vehicle took off at a high rate of speed; destination unknown. Cameron tried to listen for clues, but the vehicle was traveling too fast for him to detect anything. However he was able to notice that a fourth stranger occupied the front passenger seat and was apparently the leader of the group. Cameron tried to ask a question, but was rewarded with a sharp blow to the head. Not only did it hurt like hell; it started his head wound bleeding all over again.

The apparent leader of the group said something to the one who had struck Cameron. Cameron could not speak Hebrew, but he could tell that the man was being chastised. His reply was apologetic and meek.

"Herr Clark, please don't move or say anything else. My men don't have much patience with Nazi sympathizers." Stated the hidden voice, in the front seat.

"What did you say? Nazi sympathizers? Are you crazy? I am not, Aaaah!" Before Cameron could finish his sentence he was rewarded with another tap on the head. However this time it was not as hard as before. It was more of a push rather than a blow.

"I told you not to speak! No more talking until you are told to do so!" Stated the voice from the right front passenger seat.

Cameron thought about his situation, and got very angry. He did not care who these bullies were; he was not going to let them slap him around. Obviously if they wanted him dead; he would be dead by now! He decided to address the leader of the group anyway.

"Excuse me sir? You must have me mistaken for someone else?" He replied. Before they could reply, he continued.

"My name is Cameron Clark and I am an American journalist. I am doing an investigation on modern day Nazis in Germany, France, Europe and the USA. Where do you get off thinking I am a Nazi? To the contrary I am trying to prove the resurgence of fascism in Europe." Stated Cameron, hoping not to be hit again.

There was a long pause and finally the front seat passenger replied.

"So you say that you are not a fascist? You have a funny way of showing it? Everyone who hangs around you was or is connected to the Nazis!" Answered the unknown front seat passenger.

"What is that suppose to mean? I do not hang around Nazis! I resent that!" Continued Cameron, his anger beginning to boil over.

"Don't tell me you did not know those men in the disco? They were just strangers to you? You just happened to bump into them? What about your father-in-law in the silver Mercedes? Tell me you did not know about his past? Did you know that his wife had been a leader in the German Women's Youth Nazi movement, and was actually almost brought to trial by the Allies?" Stated the voice.

"I, I, I knew about Dieter Johannes; he told me he had been a member of the Hitler Jugend as a young boy. He further stated that he developed stomach cancer as a teenager, and never saw service during the war, but I did not know those men in the disco, not did I know about Kate's high party affiliation." Replied a stubborn Cameron, raising his voice as he did so.

I was there to meet a source. He allegedly has information on American soldiers in Germany selling large quantities of weapons to right-wing radicals and Muslim neo-fascists both here and the Middle East.

"If that is true? Why is it, that your best friend Herr Wolgang von Hagen is a known right wing sympathizer and is the son of SS General Peter von Hagen, a known personal friend of Adolph Hitler? Don't tell me you did not know this bit of information? I sure find it interesting that everyone around you is or was a member of the Nazi party?" Responded the front seat passenger.

Cameron was completely taken by surprised. How could he have been so foolish? Of course, his every move was being broadcast all over the world. Before he could regain his composure, they threw one more bit of information at him.

"I almost forgot! Your office manager Frau Rausching, she is the daughter of the wartime Nazi **Gauleiter** of Kreiss Aachen, **Doktor** Willhem von Struebenz. In 1946 the Allies executed the Herr Doktor for war crimes. Rausching is her married name; please don't tell us, that no one informed you of this bit of information either? You are about the worst investigative reporter I have ever met! The only conclusion I can reach is that you are lying to us Herr Clark." Concluded the voice in the front seat.

"I am totally flabbergasted by this news. I truly never realized that the problem was a great as it is. It's not that I am stupid, but a trusting fool. You must believe me when I tell you, I was taken completely by surprise!" Replied an incredulous Cameron.

"This may be true? But until we know all the fact we can't allow you to run around the countryside. You will be our guest for a few days. At least one thing is true, some American soldiers are involved in selling guns, and that is why we are here." Continued the unknown voice.

"I am tired of all this nonsense. You have no right to hold me. Your methods are as bad as the other side. I demand that you let me go right now! I am tired of talking to an unknown voice in the dark. Please tell me your name, so I know how to address you!" Screamed an irate Cameron.

"I would strongly advise you not to move or do anything stupid. We are not in a very good mood, and don't react well to your type of people. Our names don't matter, but it makes you feel better, you can call me Mr. Jones; the others are Mr. Smith, Mr. Brown and Mr. Green." Replied Mr. Jones, a snicker in his voice.

"OK Mr. Jones, what now? What can I do to prove who I am? What will it take to let me go? People will be looking for me." Finished a somewhat less boisterous Cameron.

As an afterthought, he blurted out one of the few Hebrew

words he knew. At one time in his past, a young Israeli intelligence officer had been assigned to him, and had taught him the words.

"Ha-Mosad le-di-Modi'in u-le- Tafkidim Meyuhadim." (The Institute for Intelligence and Special Operations). Stated Cameron in a slow and deliberate way, not knowing what reaction he would get. After all the MOSSAD, as it was often referred to by western intelligence, was actually called the "Institute" by those in the know. Cameron was fishing for a bite, but none came.

No one responded in the car. There was total silence. It was as if everyone was holding their breath; waiting for the first word to be spoken. Their silence was actually an acknowledgement of his suspicions. Finally Mr. Jones said something.

"What makes you think that we are part of the MOSSAD? And even if we were, you know we could never admit it and let you live? Do you really want to die Mr. Clark?"

Cameron carefully thought about is answer. He did not want to force the issue and force them to do something they were not necessarily going to do. He had to call their bluff, and hope for the best.

"Well you see, Mr. Jones I am a poker player and I had to play the only hand left for me to play. It was a really weak hand, but you called my hand and I have to fold." This rather ambiguous answer, momentarily stunned Mr. Jones; he quietly reflected on his retort.

"I have to give you more credit than I initially suspected or wanted to, Mr. Clark. Let's just call this a tie hand and let it go at that? What do you say?" Replied Mr. Jones.

Cameron decided to remain silent for the rest of the trip, and hoped for the best. As it was the journey only lasted another thirty minutes or so? The vehicle came to a complete and sudden stop. The rapid stop caused Cameron to slide forward and once again strike his already sore head on the front seat. He let out a curse!

"Shit! Shit! Jesus Christ, be careful!" He screamed at the invisible driver.

"Sorry Mr. Clark, we have finally arrived. We will be

transferring you to a building, and please don't try anything foolish! Is that clear?" Asked Mr. Jones.

"No problem! Can you please release my hands; I desperately need to go to the bathroom? My bladder is full and if you don't allow me to relieve myself we are going to have an accident!" Stated Cameron in a forceful, but pleading voice.

Mr. Jones gave Mr. Green instructions to remove the restraints, but not before he placed his revolver against Cameron's right kidney, and pulled back the hammer for emphasis.

"Mr. Clark, I am placing my silenced .22 cal. Beretta automatic where it will do the most damage. Is that clear? These hollow-points will blow away your kidney and most of your stomach; if you as much flinch! Please don't make me do it? We are in the middle of nowhere, and no one will hear the shots!" Said a menacing Mr. Jones.

"Hey, all I want to do is a take whiz; not get killed, don't worry!" Replied an anxious Cameron.

One of the men reached down and released his handcuffs. The relief was instantaneous as the blood came rushing back into his numb hands. Cameron took the opportunity the rub his wrists and stretch his arms along the back of the cushion; when he did so he felt a cell-phone crammed in the back of the seat. The sudden braking motion must have jarred it loose. He knew it was dark, and hoped no one would be the wiser; he coughed as loud as he could, hoping he sound would divert their attention, and crammed the phone in his left sock.

No blows came raining down on his head; nor did he hear anyone say anything. *"So far so good,"* he thought to himself.

"Get out! Get out! Go ahead and relieve yourself." Shouted one of the four men, as he was pushed out of the car.

The sudden movement caught him by surprised and he stumbled forward. When he did so, his black ski mask jarred itself upwards, and for a split second he was able to see the car. It was a dark colored four door Mercedes. He was even able to see the first letter of the license plate. **'M'** stood for Munich, Cameron knew from previous experience that all cars in Germany are registered to the home address city of the owner, and start with the initial of the city, '**B**' for Berlin, '**AC**' for Aachen, '**F**' for Frankfurt etc.

Cameron was pleased with himself, but just when he thought how clever; he was suddenly shoved forward and his blindfold was shoved down to below his chin. Once again his vision was blocked and two of the men grabbed his arms and guided him forward down a gravel path. After a few minutes of tripping and stumbling along, they stopped in front of what must have been a large wooden door. He heard one of the men produce a key and a squeaky door creaked open.

"Watch your step! Three steps upward, and then a dozen steps downwards. Go slowly and carefully, we would want you to hurt yourself." Snickered one of the four men. All four of them joined in and started laughing uncontrollably. Cameron was not very amused, but decided to keep his mouth shut for now.

Mr. Jones said something, and the rest of them stopped laughing on command. They roughly pushed him down a set of musty and damp stairs. Cameron could tell by the moldy smell that this was an obviously old and unused building. He was pushed along an obviously long corridor. After a few seconds they stopped in front of a door. Mr. Jones opened it, and Cameron was unceremoniously shoved in.

"Mr. Clark, you will be our guest until we check out your story. Here is a blanket, a bucket for your necessities and a plastic jug with water. I hope you enjoy your solitude." Mr. Jones slammed the door shut and left him alone.

Cameron surveyed the room by feeling his way along the edge of the walls and counting the number of steps it took him to cross it. The cell appeared to be approximately ten by twelve feet. The only visible light came from under the cell door, and a tiny twelve by twelve inches window high up on the wall. At the north end of the room stood a small straw cot, and a three legged wooden stool. Although it was very dark, his night vision finally kicked in, and he was able to see most items in the room without much problem.

He realized that he must take immediate action before his situation deteriorated beyond control. He felt down his left leg and was comforted to feel the cell phone still stuck in his sock. He prayed that it was still working and that there was a cell signal in this area. He pulled it out and flipped it open. Cameron was pleased to hear and see the working signal light up and turn green.

At least it was working, but for how long? The signal strength indicator showed that it was less than half full, and it was only on the lowest signal indicator. *"What to do?"* He thought to himself. *"Should I try now, or in the morning? When are signals strongest?"* All of these ideas ran through his mind. He knew that they might find the cell tomorrow and he would not get a second chance.

He sat down on the short wooden stool and pointed the phone towards the window and said a short prayer. Although Mr. Jones had said that all of his acquaintances were dirty, he still trusted Dieter Johannes and believed him to be an honorable man. Besides calling Germany would be easier than calling the States. He might only get one chance, and his gut instinct told him to go for it.

He took his time and carefully dialed Dieter's home number in Niedergeyer. It rang once, twice, three times and finally on the fourth ring a sleepy Dieter answered his phone.

"Ja, bitte?" (Yes, please?) Answered a sleepy Dieter Johannes.

Chapter 20

Rescued?

"Don't say anything and just listen! My cell phone will probably die on me! Don't speak! Just shut up and listen!" Stated a very excited Cameron.

Dieter was very surprised by the tone of voice and the obvious excitement in his voice. Cameron had never spoken to him like that before. Dieter had so much to say, but he could tell that Cameron was extremely agitated, and he had better just listen.

"Dieter! I have been kidnapped by four men. They are driving a large dark colored Mercedes, maybe black or blue. The license plate first letter is **M** for Munich. I heard them speak in Hebrew, and I believe them to be from the Israeli MOSSAD! Did you understand me?" Questioned Cameron?

"Yes, yes of course! Are you sure about the MOSSAD? Why would they want to kidnap you?" Asked Dieter?

"I cannot explain everything right now, but you must swear on your father's grave never to repeat this story to anyone, but my cousin Jeremy Grant. Do you know what to do? No one at all! Not your wife Kate, my wife, Wolfgang von Hagen, Frau Rausching! No one at all! My life could depend on it. Not even the police, I can't trust anyone, but you Dieter.

"Why such secrecy? What is going on Cameron? I am really worried about you!" Finished an anxious Dieter.

"Please just do as I say and everything will be OK! One more thing, I am within approximately two hours driving time from Köln in an old building out in the country, maybe in a castle, probably in the basement twelve steps down. I have to hang up now. Keep calling my cousin and give him the password **"CONTAFLEX"**, he will know that this is a real emergency and react accordingly. You must give him all the help you can, and he knows to trust you because of the password. Please repeat the password?" Finished an out of breath and agitated Cameron.

"Listen! Tomorrow at sun-up, I will call you one more time. I hope that this phone has a built in GPS tracking system like most modern phones do. Contact my cousin and have them monitor this general area and maybe they can pick up a signal. I will not get too many chances; be sure they are listening! Is that understood?" Stated Cameron in a firm tone of voice.

"I promise I will do everything you have instructed me to do! On my honor, and as your father-in-law, I swear!" Promised a solemn and confused Dieter.

"Who was that? Why are they calling so late?" Asked Kate from her side of the bed.

"Oh, it's one of my business associates, he just got into a serious car accident and needs some help. Just go back to sleep and I will handle it. Goodnight, dear!" Said Dieter as he got up and put his robe on.

Dieter walked downstairs where he could have some privacy. Cameron had left all of Jeremy's phone numbers in his office. It took him a few minutes to find them; he looked at his watch and realized it was past midnight in Germany. *"California time would be around nine o'clock in the morning,"* he thought to himself. Dieter systematically dialed the country code; the 415 area code and finally Jeremy's direct office number. On the third ring Jeremy answered.

"Halo Jeremy, hier ist Dieter von Deutschland. (Hello Jeremy, this Dieter from Germany!) I am so sorry, I forgot who I was speaking to. Excuse me!" Stated a confused Dieter.

"That's OK Dieter, I too speak fluent German. Is everything OK? Is Cameron OK? What can I do for you?" Replied a surprised Jeremy.

"CONTAFLEX! CONTAFLEX! Do you understand me? Did you hear me?" Asked Dieter.

"Yes I did! Who told you that word? And are you sure of the word?" Replied Jeremy.

"Yes I am! **CONTAFLEX**, that's what he said for me to tell you! He was very specific. He said you would understand and react accordingly." Repeated an excited Dieter Johannes.

"OK, OK! I hear you and I understand the meaning. Please tell me exactly what he said; don't leave anything out!" Answered Jeremy as he reached over and turned on his tape recorder.

For the next twenty minutes, an overly excited Dieter repeated every word three times until Jeremy was satisfied that he had all the facts. He instructed Dieter to rent two separate rooms side by side in two separate cities under his name and prepay them for at least one week; he also needed two large rental cars under Dieter's name as well. He instructed Dieter to leave one car at the airport in Köln under the long-term parking lot; he should put all the keys inside the fuel tank cap. The other car should be parked at the guest parking spot near the hotel in Köln. Dieter was also given instructions to text-message all the details to Jeremy's cell phone.

After being satisfied that Dieter was in complete control of his end of the mission, Jeremy hung up, and made reservations for the first direct flight from San Francisco to Germany. As luck would have it, there was a flight leaving in four hours and twenty minutes from San Francisco; arriving in Köln Germany eleven hours later. He had enough time to go home and pack a quick bag. Jeremy lived in Fremont, which was in the South Bay area of San Francisco. It took him less than an hour for the round-trip back to the airport. Jeremy was fortunate to be able to use his duty vehicle to cruise around the city using his lights and sirens. It really helped to get around San Francisco's murderous traffic. By rolling code three; he was able to get to the airport over three hours early. This allowed him time to do some more coordinating with his overseas contacts.

Jeremy also spoke with his boss and informed him of his emergency. Director Brown was very understanding and offered his assistance, and also made some valuable suggestions. Director Brown made the Homeland Security Dispatch Control Center available to Jeremy on a twenty-four hour basis. Jeremy took the immediate opportunity and contacted the Foreign Surveillance Branch of the NSA in Frankfurt, Germany, which the nearest consulate office in that part of Germany. He informed the Foreign Surveillance Branch duty officer of his dilemma and asked for assistance in monitoring transmissions starting in four hours and running for the next twenty-four hours. The duty officer was more than willing to help, but he needed the assistance of the German Intelligence Services, and that took a special high-level approval. Jeremy contacted Director Brown and he offered his immediate assistance, and contacted the State Department in Washington, who in turn contacted their man in Germany.

Jeremy's wife was a little surprised by his sudden departure, but she understood it was an emergency, and had always been very understanding of his many previous adventures.

Due to his high-ranking position within the Homeland Security Department; the State Department had issued him a Red diplomatic passport that would facilitate his overseas travel, and at the same time protect him from nosy inquiries.

Because of his federal law enforcement position and connections, he was able to be carried on the manifest as an extra Air Marshal, and thus was able to carry his duty .45 cal. Sig-Sauer with three extra magazines, and a back-up Sig-Sauer, just in case. Knowing that he probably would not get much sleep in the next seventy-two hours, he immediately chose the sleeping birth in the first-class section. Jeremy asked the good-looking redheaded stewardess not to wake him until they were two hours out from Germany. Not wanting to offend anyone in the Air Marshal Service, he tracked down the resident Air Marshal and informed him where he was and what he was doing. Past experience had taught him to avoid stepping on other colleagues' toes, and it always paid off to be careful and prepared. The duty Air Marshal was appreciative of the heads-up and also offered any assistance he could. Pleasantry over with, Jeremy decided to rest as much as he could.

The good-looking red-haired stewardess brought over a large glass of wine. Jeremy took a long swig from a glass of champagne; put his black eye cover on and promptly fell asleep. Sleeping was one of his specialties. His many years as a field agent and Special Forces officer had conditioned him to sleep whenever he could. The body was like a battery, it could store energy up to a certain point, but sleep was essential to that process.

Jeremy slept like a baby throughout the rest of the flight. The same attractive redhead stewardess woke him up exactly two hours prior to landing. Jeremy began immediately calling his contacts in Germany, and France. They were unable to provide any new information, but he wanted to wait before he called his buddy at the Israeli embassy in Bonn. He obviously needed their help if the MOSSAD was involved, and they would not reveal any information on the phone.

Jeremy dialed Dieter just to let him know that he would be landing within a few hours, and wanted to know of any updates.

"Hello Dieter, any news?"

"Ah hello, Jeremy how are you? No, I have not heard anything, but he should be contacting us shortly." Replied an excited Dieter.

"I hope you are right. Otherwise we won't have much to go on." Stammered an equally upset Jeremy.

"Do you really think we have a chance of finding him? After all, Germany is a big country, and he could be anywhere? I am so worried!" Finished a visibly upset Dieter.

"If he calls, we will find him. We can triangulate the cell phone calling towers and come within a few hundred meters of his location." Stated a positive sounding Jeremy.

Jeremy hoped that Dieter believed his show of confidence. Past experience had shown that just the opposite was true. Jeremy knew that everything was being done that could be done. The entire power of the American and German governments were being utilized; something was bound to come up. He knew that patience was the best policy right now.

Chapter 21

Desperation

The plane landed on time and Jeremy rushed through German Customs. His "Red Passport" helped him through the customs area. He went out to the street level reception area; there waving frantically, was Dieter Johannes. Jeremy walked towards him, and was prepared for the usual Dieter assault. Dieter was known for his hugs and enthusiasm, and Jeremy was not disappointed. Dieter attacked him like General Guderian marching through Poland in 1939. Dieter hugged him so violently that Jeremy had his breath knocked out of him. Taking a few seconds to recover, he looked down at his cousin's father-in-law.

"Hello, hello Jeremy! How are you? How was your flight?" Asked Dieter with a genuine smile on his face.

"Great! Thank you Dieter. Let's get out of the street and try to be less conspicuous." Explained Jeremy, while trying to release Dieter's bear like death grip.

"Sorry, sorry, I was happy to see you again." Replied Dieter, as they walked towards the parking garage.

Dieter brought Jeremy up to date, and gave him all the keys and paperwork for the rental car and hotels. After a ten minute long debriefing from Dieter, he was completely up to speed and ready to proceed. His first order of business was to contact his NSA Foreign Surveillance Branch representative in Frankfurt. Jeremy dialed the direct access number to Brian Berrymann, the NSA intelligence man in Frankfurt.

"Hello Brian, this is Jeremy Grant, I hope you are up to date on what is going on with my cousin?" Asked an inquisitive Jeremy.

"I will let you be the judge of that? You are currently standing in the underground parking garage at Frankfurt International Airport, and there is an elderly man with white hair and a matching goatee near you. There is a mint condition silver Mercedes next to him and your international cell number is 024-22-863001? Should I go on?" Asked Berrymann?

"No! Not all. I am very impressed. Let's just hope you can do as well with my cousin." Replied Jeremy, raising his eyebrow as he did so.

"Don't worry buddy. It helps when you know the arrival time of a target, his general description etc. Your boss in San Francisco gave us the entire scoop and we were waiting for you. As a matter of fact, our German friends are giving us their full cooperation and are assisting us in the mission." Stated an overly confident Berryman.

"Was ist los?" (What is going on?) Asked a concerned Dieter, not knowing what was happening?

"It's OK Dieter. I will explain it to you in a second!" Replied Jeremy.

"Listen up Brian, I will be floating around the Frankfurt area until I here from you. Call me the moment you here anything? OK?" Stated Jeremy.

"It's a deal!" Finished Brian as he terminated the conversation.

"Let's go driving around." Replied Jeremy with authority.

"Which car?" Asked Dieter.

"I think we should use the rental car. Your Mercedes is too visible and it attracts too much attention. Are there any high areas around here?" Requested Jeremy.

"Define high? We have some mountains and hills near the Autobahn?" Asked a curious Dieter.

"That sounds good. Let's go to one of those Autobahn rest areas, and wait for

Brian to call us." Replied Jeremy, as he started up the large four-door Opel rental car, and headed south towards the main north-south autobahn.

Locked up alone in the dark and cold cell, Cameron reflected on some of the events that led him to his present situation. He racked his brains in an effort to find a possible solution. Regardless of his efforts, he could not think of a way out of his dilemma. His only hope was his cousin Jeremy Grant and Dieter Johannes. The sun was already up above the horizon, and he estimated that it was somewhere between eight and nine a.m. At least fourteen hours had passed, since his last phone call to Dieter. He wondered to himself, "Should I call now, or wait a few more hours?"

He reached down into his sock and pulled out the hidden cell phone and glanced at the time. It was exactly, 8:52 a.m. Pretty good guess, he thought to himself. Before he could further reflect on his situation, he heard footsteps coming down the stairs. Someone inserted a key into the lock and his cell door was opened. Standing there was Mr. Jones.

"Good Morning!" Stated Mr. Jones.

Cameron glared at him, not wanting to answer, but his solitude forced him to reply.

"Guten Tag."

"Aren't we the grumpy one?" Asked a rather surprised Mr. Jones.

"Well, what do you expect me to be? A cheerful happy camper, after being tortured, kidnapped and abused." Replied Cameron, noticing that Mr. Jones had a large tray with what seemed to be a large and good smelling breakfast.

"I can always take it back to the kitchen, if you are not hungry, that is?" Inquired a smiling Mr. Jones.

"No, that's OK. I am feeling much better now." Replied Cameron, as he stood up and reached for the tray.

"That's better! You must be hungry by now." Answered a seemingly sympathetic Mr. Jones.

Mr. Jones appeared to be in good spirits and actually smiled at Cameron. This unexpected demeanor caught Cameron completely off-guard. It was totally out of character for him. Cameron was so hungry, that Mr. Jones's current state of joviality was really inconsequential to him. He grabbed the tray and proceeded to wolf down the breakfast. Someone had taken a great deal of care in preparing his meal. It included a large pot of good German coffee, three freshly baked breakfast rolls, butter, marmalade, an assortment of cheeses, and German sliced delicatessens. The smell was so powerfully inviting that he forgot where he was, and what his circumstances were.

It took Cameron less than ten minutes to devour this sumptuous breakfast. Cameron sat on his bench and reflected on his situation. Hopefully Dieter notified the authorities and his cousin Jeremy, Cameron thought.

Cameron glanced at his watch and noticed it was nearly ten a.m. He decided it was time to try calling again. He bent down and grabbed the cell phone from his sock and stood on the stool near the only window in his cell. He extended his arm skyward as high as he could go, and pressed the redial key. The phone rang, once, twice and on the third ring a breathless Dieter screamed.

"Halo, halo? Wer ist das? (Who is there?)" Answered Dieter in German.

"It's me Dieter, can you hear me?" Replied a concerned Cameron.

"It's me, Cameron!" Dieter replied as he handed the phone to Jeremy.

"CONTAFLEX, CONTAFLEX!" Afraid of alerting Mr. Jones and his crew, Cameron whispered.

"I hear you buddy. Do you know where you are? Can you give me any clues?" Asked an inquisitive Jeremy.

Cameron slowly gave Jeremy all the indicia he could remember. Step by step he explained the distances, the license plate, the color of the car, the pathway, the number of steps etc. Jeremy assured him the both the German intelligence service and NSA were now tracking his signal and they hopefully could get a fix.

"I hope you are right. This will probably be the last chance I will have to call you. My phones battery is just about dead, but I will leave on and hope you will be able to track me." Answered a visibly nervous Cameron.

"Don't worry Cameron, we have the best guys in the world working on it, and you will be home before you know it." Retorted Jeremy, hoping to cheer up his shaken cousin.

"Oh, one last thing before I go. I must be near an apple orchard and cows are also nearby. I can hear them mooing all night, and when I drove up I smelled a strong smell of apples." Cameron finished the conversation with confidence in his voice.

"That's good intelligence. I am sure the Germans will know how to use it. Hang in there, and don't give up. Keep the signal going as long as you can." Stated Jeremy.

Just when his chances for survival seemed to be increasing he heard something outside his door. A key was inserted in the rustic lock and three of his kidnappers were standing there looking at him with anger in their eyes.

"Whom were you talking to?" Asked an obviously angry Mr. Jones.

The other two men just stood there and glared at him. Cameron noticed that one of them had an electric cattle prod and was pressing the on and off switch, which caused it to spark. The thought of being zapped again brought back vivid memories and he unknowingly flinched and retreated to the furthest corner of the cell.

"I will not ask you a second time, tell me or you will pay the consequences!" Screamed an obviously irate Mr. Jones.

"I was talking to myself. I was bored!" Replied Cameron in a flippant way. He was tired of being tortured and he decided to resist as best as he could, DEFIANCE!

He glared at Mr. Jones, and gave him the finger!

"I am sorry you feel that way. Mr. Brown, do your job!" Screamed Mr. Jones at Mr. Brown.

Cameron knew that he was about to get tagged again and he decided to go down fighting. He waited until Mr. Brown got close enough; and lunged at him with the heavy wooden stool and caught him by surprise. Mr. Brown stepped away and was only lightly struck on his right shoulder. Brown now stepped forward using the cattle prod like a spear and managed to catch Cameron right in the chest. The shock was the most painful thing Cameron had ever felt. The shock was so violent that he bit his tongue and urinated on himself. The warm fluid caused him to freeze in his tracks, and he looked down at the large stain now spreading between his legs. It also caused him to drop the stool, and unfortunately the cell phone was jarred loose from his pocket.

Everyone in the room stood still. The gray phone clanked on the floor and it broke in four pieces. Cameron's eyes were glued on the phone and he did not see the second strike which caught him right in the crotch. The wetness caused the electrical intensity to be magnified and he collapsed to the floor writhing and twitching like a fish out of water.

"Well, well aren't we clever? Where, where did, did get that phone and who were speaking with?" Demanded Mr. Jones, as he stared at Cameron. His eyes were squinting so tightly that he actually looked like a Chinaman.

Cameron knew that it was now useless to hide or lie to Mr. Jones.

"I found it in the backseat cushion of your car, and I stuck it in my sock after you searched me." Replied Cameron, slowly regaining his composure.

Mr. Jones walked over to the phone. He slowly picked up all the pieces and attempted to put them together. After a few minutes, the green light came on Mr. Jones smiled again.

"Now tell me, who you were speaking with? There is no use denying it. All I have to do is press the last call button and it will tell me." Stated a now confident Mr. Jones.

"Since you are so clever, you figure it out." Cameron slowly snickered, regaining his confidence as he spoke.

"Well mister tough guy, it looks like you called a number in the Dueren area. And if I am not mistaken you live in that district, don't you?" Asked a sinister looking Mr. Jones.

Cameron debated whether or not he should tell Mr. Jones. It could either scare him off or make him angry. Cameron was in no mood to take any more abuse, and he decided to play his hand.

"OK, Mr. Jones! The U.S. Marines, and the GSG-9 are on their way here, and if I were you, I would scurry back to whatever hole you crawled out of." Cameron now stood up to his height and looked down, on Mr. Jones.

Mr. Jones debated what Cameron said. Deep in thought he glanced down again at the phone and noticed that it appeared to be the same type issued to his men. He froze in horror and ordered Mr. Brown to get the rest of the men. A few minutes later, they all showed up, Mr. Smith, Mr. Brown, and Mr. Green. All of the men had a look of fear in their eyes, they knew that one of them had screwed up, and they all hoped it was the other guy. Mr. Jones did not lose his temper very often, but they could tell he was extremely agitated. He held menacingly the cattle prod in his right hand and pointed at them one by on as they entered the cell.

"Would you please show me your cell phones?" Asked Mr. Jones, his angry voice now squealing as he spoke.

All of the men reached for their individual phones. One by one they produced them; holding them in the air, with a sigh of relief, all of them except Mr. Green. His faced had suddenly turned really green, like his name. He vigorously patted his pockets; turning them inside out in desperation. No matter how hard he searched, he knew the inevitable; he was in deep shit. He held up both arms in desperation, slowly shaking his head.

"I am so sorry! I don't how it could have happened. I must have lost it in the struggle in the car? I really don't know how it happened? Please forgive me? I, I, I." Finished a now desperate Mr. Green.

"Do you know how bad this looks for us? You have compromised our entire mission. Both the German government and the Americans will want our blood! Not even our compatriots in Jerusalem can help us? There is no way I can protect you.

Mr. Green looked up one more time and silently pleaded with his boss for forgiveness. Mr. Jones slowly shook his head from side to side, and laughingly said.

"Well Mr. Green, the only thing you will be doing in the next few years is guarding the border with Lebanon, if your lucky that is." Smiled Mr. Jones.

Before Mr. Green could respond to that last comment, Mr. Jones adroitly lunged forward and jabbed Mr. Green in the chest with the cattle prod. He held the button down until Mr. Green passed out. Every one in the room stood transfixed by this shocking event. Mr. Jones said something in Hebrew to his men, and they silently bent over and picked up their unconscious colleague.

Before Cameron could react to these new events, Mr. Jones left the cell and locked the door. Cameron stood in complete silence for a full two minutes. He stood transfixed staring at the now closed cell door. Five minutes later he heard two vehicles departing at a high rate of speed. *What now?* He thought to himself.

Two hundred kilometers away in Frankfurt, Jeremy and Dieter were still standing in the garage waiting for Berrymann to call them back. Their conversation with Cameron ended abruptly. The last thing they heard was the angry voice of Mr. Jones. They did not have long to wait. Berrymann called a few minutes later and gave them the good news.

"Guess what? I have good news for you. The Germans and the NSA were able to track the signal to a small village north of Stuttgart. It's called Boeblingen and there is an old abandoned sixteenth century castle nearby. According to the local gendarmes, the only thing near the castle is a large pasture full of cows, and several large apple orchards. We have already dispatched a helicopter and some GSG-9 Bundesgrenzschutz officers, and they should be on scene within minutes." Finished a proud and boastful Berrymann.

"My God! That was fast. What should we do." Asked an excited Jeremy Grant.

"Nothing for now. We will fly him back to your location, as soon as we locate him. Stay where you are, please!" Stated Brian Berrymann.

"You don't really expect us to sit around and do nothing? Do you?" Asked Jeremy with anger in his voice.

"That's exactly what I expect you to do! You will only be in the way. Stay where you are and we will notify you when we have something." Replied Berrymann, hanging up the phone as he did so.

Jeremy stood there in silence trying to regain his composure. Who in the hell did Berrymann think he was? Jeremy turned to Dieter and said.

"Let's go now, we don't have any time to spare. Now!" Shouted an obviously angry Jeremy."

Dieter knew better than to argue with him. He got in the Opel and strapped his seatbelt on. The rental car was a beautiful new five door Opel Astra GTC, 200 H.P. Turbo. Jeremy got in and looked at Dieter and smiled; the smile of a cat about to pounce on an unsuspecting mouse.

Dieter felt slightly uncomfortable as Jeremy pulled away; burning rubber as he did so. In less than five point six seconds, the Opel was accelerating at over sixty miles an hour. Ten seconds later he was cruising at over a hundred and twenty and still going strong. Jeremy was really impressed with this jewel of German engineering.

Jeremy glanced at Dieter once more and asked him to verify the GPS directions given by the built-in dash screen.

"Dieter, make sure that we are heading southward towards Stuttgart. We can't afford to make any mistakes now!" Stated Jeremy.

"Don't worry, I know my way around this neighborhood. Besides German manufacturing is pretty good." He replied, pointing at the in dash GPS monitor.

"OK, OK, OK! Just don't get me lost. Cameron is depending on us, and we can't let him down. Do you really think this car can do 260 kilometers per hours?" Asked Jeremy as he floored the accelerator.

The response was immediate, this expertly manufactured German car screamed ahead, rapidly reaching 260 Km plus!

"Wow! She is doing over 136 M.P.H.! At this speed we should be there in less than an hour." Said Jeremy as they flew down the autobahn.

Dieter sat in the right passenger seat not saying a word. He always enjoyed driving fast, but only when he was driving. He did not know how well Jeremy could drive, and it made him slightly uneasy. Jeremy settled down in the number one passing lane and did not take his foot off the accelerator. It didn't take long for Dieter to relax. Although Jeremy was driving extremely fast, he always kept a safe distance and did not take any unnecessary chances. The rest of the trip was driven in silence.

Dieter occasionally glanced at the map and back up at the GPS monitor. The only sound heard in the speeding car was the wind and the sexy female voice of the monitor. Her English accent was a pleasant addition to the trip.

Dieter suddenly shouted at Jeremy!

"Slow down! Slow down! We are approaching the exit near Boebliggen." Screamed Dieter, louder than he intended to.

"OK, OK! How about we pull in to a local gas station and ask some questions? They might give us some clues? What do you think?" Replied Jeremy.

Chapter 22

Savior?

The Opel came to a screeching halt in front of the ESSO gas station. It was one of those brand new gleaming station, lots of windows and glass, but no character. Dieter turned to Jeremy, and told him.

"Why don't you stay in the car and I will ask around if anyone knows of an old castle or building around here?" Stated Dieter without even waiting for an answer. He walked the few yards to the front door.

"Gruess Gott!" He said as he entered. He was greeted by a chorus of, **'Guten Tags'.**

Dieter approached the front counter and was greeted by an extremely attractive blonde clerk. If this had been the 1940's, and Hitler was still in power, she would have been the poster child for German womanhood. She was extremely tall, about five-feet nine, one hundred and fifty pounds and had a very large buxom. Long blonde hair in a ponytail, and also had beautiful white teeth. Dieter was awe struck by her beauty. She reminded him of a long lost love. Claudia was her name, and she had been killed in a bombing raid in 1943. He could not help but, stare at her. She could have been a twin sister of his Claudia. She noticed his intense stare.

"Can I help you?" She asked with a smile.

Her simple, yet beautiful voice snapped him back to reality.

"Pardon my staring, but you resemble someone I knew years ago in another life." Replied a somewhat embarrassed Dieter Johannes.

"Oh, that's OK! I get that a lot." She replied.

"I am looking for an old castle, building, monastery with an orchard and cows. Do you know of anything resembling that description in the vicinity?" Asked Dieter.

"Funny you should ask? I had some members of the KRIPO (German Police) ask me the same question, less than five minutes ago!" She replied with a look of puzzlement in her face.

"Were you able to help them?"

"Yes, yes of course! There is an old castle called, Schloessburg not more than five kilometers from here, on the other side of the autobahn." Replied the clerk.

"Can you tell me if there is a quicker way to get there? A shortcut maybe?" Asked Dieter.

"Well yes there is, but it's down a muddy track behind the station. It will get you there before the KRIPO!" She exclaimed with exuberance.

Dieter ran back to the car and gave Jeremy new instructions. He tore thru the parking lot and drove down a muddy field for about two miles before he saw the old castle. Jeremy was amazed by what he saw. It could have been a back-lot image of a Hollywood monster movie. A large stone tower overlooking a mote and a high stonewall. Jeremy expected Frankenstein to come marching out of the front door. It was sitting on a slight rise and surrounded by apple groves and many cows. Both men knew this was it.

On the other side of the field, they could see many German police cars with their blue lights flashing. Above them two GSG-9 German helicopters were providing escort duty for them. Jeremy wanted to get there before Brian Berryman and his cohorts. He drove his car as fast as he could, and came to a screeching halt in front of the main gate to the castle. Thirty seconds later the posse showed up. They all came with their guns drawn, ready for action. They had no way of knowing that Jeremy and Dieter had beaten them to the punch.

"Halt! Halt!" Yelled a burly German officer pointing an H&K MP-5 at them.

Jeremy could tell that this officer meant business, and knew what he was doing. The weapon was properly held and pointed right at them. Jeremy had seen that look before, and he was not about to move. He slowly raised his hands and spoke.

"Hey Brian, call off your dogs! It's me Jeremy, and Dieter Johannes!" Stated a concerned Jeremy, keeping his raised hands high above his head and in plain view.

"Jeremy, Jeremy Grant? What in the hell are you doing here? I thought I told you not to interfere? The Germans won't like this?" Blurted an angry Brian Berrymann.

"Slow down partner! Let's get something straight! You do not or cannot tell me what to do! Cameron is my blood, and we take care of each other. Is that understood?" Replied an obviously highly agitated Jeremy, shaking his index finger in the air like a spear. Dieter just stood there like a deer in the middle of the road not knowing what to do.

Berrymann looked at Jeremy and reflected on what his reaction should be? After all, his German compatriots were staring at him waiting for instructions? Brian bit his lip and walked towards Jeremy. At first it looked like a showdown at the OK Corral. Both men felt their blood pumping and their hands twitching. Eventually both men realized that this was very unprofessional, and Jeremy extended his arm in a peace offering. At first Brian hesitated, but he too extended his arm in a harmonious gesture. Jeremy took the opportunity to grab the hand and pull him forward. It appeared to be a friendly gesture, but Jeremy's grip was so tight that Brian actually winced and he felt his knees buckle under him. Jeremy leaned down and whispered. His voice growling like a bear ready to pounce on a enemy.

"Listen you piece of shit! The only reason you are still alive is my cousin needs help now! His life is more important than your worthless carcass. If you ever address me in that tone or interfere with one of my missions, you will disappear forever! Is that understood?" Snarled Jeremy, to a barely conscious Berrymann.

Brian was in a quasi-kneeling position, holding his breath unconsciously. Jeremy's iron grip was so powerful that it made him whimper. Finally Jeremy relented and allowed him to stand back up. Brian stood up and took a large breath of air.

"Enough of this nonsense! Lets go look for Cameron."

Finished a now relaxed Jeremy.

Brian grabbed his now numb hand and shook it vigorously. He turned around and spoke to the GSG-9 troopers and they immediately deployed in a V-shape squad formation towards the castle. The helicopters continued to circle the area looking for the kidnappers. Jeremy and Dieter brought up the rear and waited for the GSG-9 agents to enter the castle.

Less than two minutes later a disheveled, dirty and smelly Cameron walked out of the front door. Cameron's eyes had a hard time adjusting to the light. He covered them with his hands and slowly walked towards Jeremy and Dieter. Both Jeremy and Dieter ran forward. Dieter as was his custom, gave Cameron a giant bear hug; causing him to exhale all of the air in his lungs, and nearly passed out.

"Hello Dieter, you are worst than the torture these idiots inflicted upon me." Stated a now breathing Cameron. Dieter smiled and stepped back.

Jeremy walked up to his cousin Cameron and shook his hand, and patted him on the back. Both men intensely stared at each other. No words were necessary. The family bond was stronger than any spoken word or actions.

"Glad to see you in one piece!" Stated Jeremy in a matter of fact tone of voice. Cameron slowly nodded his head and smiled.

Brian Berryman broke up the family gathering by suggesting that Cameron be taken to a local hospital for a routine check-up. Cameron objected, but was over-ruled by Jeremy and Dieter.

"Don't argue with us, you need to see a doctor! You look terrible!" Stated a caring Dieter Johannes.

Jeremy looked at his cousin and nodded his head.

"If you had a mirror, you would be horrified! You definitely need to see a doctor. If for no other reason than to clean you up a bit. God only knows what awful critters are crawling all over you." Said Jeremy as he mockingly brushed himself off.

"All right, OK! But I am not spending the night there. No way Jose!" Replied a now rambunctious Cameron.

Brian Berryman said something to the police, and one of their vans pulled up in front of the men and escorted Cameron to the hospital. Jeremy, Dieter and Brian all followed the police van to the hospital in Boebliggen. The rest of the GSG-9 troopers continued their investigation of the crime scene; along with the remaining KRIPO officers.

The drive to the hospital took less than fifteen minutes. Both Dieter and Jeremy were initially not given entry to Cameron's room, but twenty minutes later they were all allowed in. Cameron found himself hooked up to a saline I.V., and was devouring a plate of spaghetti and meatballs. The attending physician, a man in his sixties or seventies was at the foot of the bed writing on a pad.

"Hello Doctor! How are you? Is the patient going to live?" Stated Jeremy extending his hand as he did so.

"Oh, yes! He has a few bruises, burns, and is dehydrated, but overall in pretty good shape. However I wish to keep him here for observation for one or two days. Just in case something unforeseen happens." Finished the Herr Doctor Ramerstein.

"Will we be allowed access to his room until he is discharged?" Asked a concerned Jeremy.

"I don't see why not? Company will probably make him feel better and accelerate his healing." Replied Doctor Ramerstein.

"Great! Thank you for your professionalism." Replied a gracious Jeremy.

Chapter 23

Back Home in Niedergeyer

Less than two days later Cameron, now feeling fit and none the worst for wear; was en route to Dieter's house. The ride home was made almost in total silence. Everyone had questions to ask, but no one felt comfortable enough to ask them. Although Jeremy was the least talkative of the three, he initiated the conversation when the vehicle approached the outskirts of Köln. It was about an hours drive to Niedergeyer and Cameron was now in a talkative mood.

"So tell me Cameron, what happened?" Asked an inquisitive Jeremy.

Cameron looked up at his cousin Jeremy and started to recount the story from the beginning to the end. By the time he was finished, his timing was incredible. Dieter drove into his driveway just as Cameron was telling them about his adventure that same morning. Cameron had mixed emotions about returning to Dieter's house. Before he had a chance to continue this train of thought, his daughter Jennifer came running out of the house followed by his wife.

"Daddy, daddy! How are you? I missed you so much! Are you OK?" Blurted out a joyous Jennifer Clark. Her embrace was almost as strong as her grandfather Dieter Johannes. It was the first time in years that his daughter had shown him such affection. He held on to her shoulder and relished the strong feeling between them.

Cameron was overwhelmed by the emotional greeting from his daughter, but was confused by the lack of sentiments from his wife. Ingrid just stood in the doorway and gave a slight wave of the hand and a nod. Cameron pulled away from Jennifer and walked up the few steps to door and grabbed his wife.

"Hello dear! How are you?" Stated Cameron as he attempted

to kiss his wife.

Her response was very cold and noncommittal. Cameron could not understand her reaction. Ingrid had always been a very loving and giving wife, and now she was greeting him like a stranger. Cameron was confused and hurt at the same time. Not wanting to start a fight right now, he simply pulled away and stepped into the foyer. Jeremy and Dieter followed him in. Dieter ushered both men into the living room and asked to sit down and get comfortable. Dieter returned a minute later with a large tray full of sandwiches, beer and a bottle of his best wine. Both men helped themselves and awaited his return. Suddenly they heard a large commotion coming from the kitchen area. Dieter's voice was heard screaming orders at his wife and Ingrid.

"You will listen to me, and not contradict me! I don't know what has gotten over you! Both of you are acting like a pair of bitches, and I will not tolerate that in my house. You especially Ingrid! How could you treat your husband like a stranger; after what he has been through? How dare you? I want both of you to go inside and greet our guests properly! I will not allow my son-in-law and his cousin to be treated in this manner!"

Not waiting for an answer, Dieter left both women in the kitchen staring at each other. He returned to the living room, where Jeremy and Cameron were still eating their sandwiches.

"Is everything OK? I am sorry about all that screaming and yelling, but I had to get a message across, and unfortunately, screaming is the only thing they understand." Stated a somewhat irate Dieter.

Both men looked at him and nodded in unison. Two minutes later, both women came in and apologized for their poor behavior. Instead of waiting for answers they turned around and went upstairs without any further comments. Cameron had the urge to go after his wife and demand an explanation. Dieter looked at him, and quietly shook his head from side to side.

"Cameron, I don't know what is going, but I will find out and put an end to this nonsense! Enough of this!" Stated Dieter, a serious look on his face.

"OK, I will follow your advise for now, but I am not happy at all. I have enough to worry about without this complication, don't you think?" Replied a concerned and irate Cameron.

Jeremy just sat there not knowing what to say or do. The uncomfortable silence was broken by the shrill sound of the telephone ringing. Dieter jumped up and dashed over to the stand.

"Hallo, hallo! Hier ist Johannes!" (Hello, this is Johannes) Answered Dieter in German.

"Who is this? You are who from where, the Israeli consulate in Frankfurt? You wish to speak to Herr Cameron Clark? Please wait just a second." Acknowledged Dieter, handing the phone to him.

"Yes, can I help you?" Replied a curious Cameron.

He signaled for his cousin to pick up the other receiver and listen in on the conversation. Cameron waited for Jeremy to be on the other line before he began speaking.

"What can I do for you? What is it you wish to speak to me about?" Asked a rather gruff Cameron.

"The ambassador would like to speak to you in person. Can you find some time for him in the next few days?" Asked a very apologetic sounding secretary.

Cameron glanced over at his cousin Jeremy. He shook his head and held up his fingers. He mouthed in silence, two or three days!

Cameron understood and informed the young secretary that he would contact them in the next few days, and advise them of his schedule. She hesitated and asked if he could be more precise.

"Well young lady, just because your ambassador wants to speak with me; it doesn't mean I have to jump to his command. Give me a number and I will call you back with my schedule." He waited for an answer for over twenty seconds.

Although he could not hear clear voices; someone was obviously giving her instructions. She finally responded.

"OK, Sir! The number is 02321-84887. We will be expecting to hear from you as soon as possible." Without waiting for an answer, she hung up the phone.

Jeremy looked at him and winked; giving him the thumbs up as he did so. Dieter who was not privy to the conversation, looked on with a quizzical look. Finally Cameron acknowledged him.

"Dieter that was the Israeli ambassador's office wanting to meet me as soon as possible. No, I don't know what they want, but I can assume it's about what happened to me in the last five days." Replied Cameron.

Jeremy looked at Cameron and smiled once more.

"We've got them by the proverbial balls! Let's squeeze them and see what comes out?" Stated a now jubilant Jeremy.

Both Cameron and Dieter did not quite know why he was so happy about.

"Don't you see? They fucked up big time and now they have to try and make it up to you? Let's try to get as much as we can from them? I will call my pals at the State Department and see if there is something we really need from them. The Israelis are very good negotiators, but we now have a trump card and they might come around to our way of thinking!" Exclaimed a jubilant Jeremy.

"I don't really follow you? What are you mumbling about?" Asked a curious Cameron.

"Don't you see, my cousin? We may want to exchange something with them that they were unwilling to give up in the past?" Replied Jeremy with a flair.

"Like what?" Asked both Dieter and Cameron in unison!

"I don't really know? But I am sure that my friends at the State Department or the CIA will think of something." Stated a confident Jeremy.

"Well why don't you make your phone calls, and I will go in the office and use the other phone and call my boss Jerry Kunstoff, and my office staff in Aachen." Replied Cameron as he stood up and walked out the living room.

Jeremy immediately began calling everyone he knew, and informed them of the situation. Both the CIA and the State Department wanted to get involved in the meeting with the Israeli ambassador. Jeremy lied when he told them that the Israelis specifically refused any co-operation with those two agencies. Jeremy assured them that they would be kept in the loop.

Ten minutes later Cameron returned to the living room, and had a smile on his face. His editor had been extremely excited and wanted an immediate story. Cameron was able to calm him down for now and promised him an exclusive editorial within forty-eight hours. His cousin Jeremy looked at him and asked?

"Are you sure you can keep him under control? It would not be a good idea if your boss leaked the story to the world? Stated Jeremy.

"Don't worry Jeremy, he is a professional and would not jeopardize our safety, for a story." Replied Cameron with a smile.

"I hope you are right? It could raise some very serious problems for us. Stay on top of it little cousin." Stated Jeremy, in a firm voice.

"I have it under control Jeremy, not to worry!" Replied Cameron as he walked over to the liquor cabinet and grabbed a bottle of German cognac and poured himself a healthy triple shot. He turned around and offered the men some cognac as well. Both Dieter and Jeremy nodded their head in unison.

Dieter got up and pulled out a large box of Cuban cigars and passed them around. The cognac and cigars were the catalyst that Cameron needed to completely relax and unwind. He looked at his cousin and asked him he had heard the incredible story of Das Haus? Cognac and good cigars were always consumed prior to storytelling.

"No, no, not really! But I am sure you will tell it to me?" Replied a curious Jeremy.

"Actually, I should have Dieter tell it to you. He has all the facts, and I wouldn't want to leave anything out? What do you say Dieter?" Asked Cameron in a pleading way.

"Ja, Ja OK!" Dieter responded and started telling Jeremy the story from the beginning. All three men sat back in the large and overstuffed chairs and listened intensely.

Chapter 24

Freedom?

Back in Buchenwald 1939

KAPO Ludwig returned from the morning formation with an even bigger smile than on the previous day. He walked in the pantry and greeted Erik and Esther like an older brother. Both of them were caught by surprise. Erik knew that Ludwig wanted something from him and he had to be very cautious when dealing with this skilled wheeler and dealer.

"OK Erik, I think we can work together and get out of this hell hole? What do you say my young friend? Yes you heard me right, out of here!" Stated a gleaming Ludwig.

"How can you be so sure that we can buy our way out of here? What guarantees do we have? Can you trust anyone here?" Asked a suspicious Erik.

"Well you are right, no one can really be trusted, but when it comes to gold; it can be trusted above all else, and you seem to have a supply of it." Answered a still smiling KAPO Ludwig.

"What makes you think I possess more gold?" Asked Erik.

"Well my young friend, I have been here too long not to be a good judge of character, and you have some coins stashed away somewhere. If you don't tell me, I will send your little brother back to general population, and he won't last long without you or me?" Snickered an evil looking Ludwig.

Erik carefully reflected on what to say. Perhaps it was time to make a deal with Ludwig after all. He looked down at his sister and thought of the million evil things these thugs could do to her.

"Herr Ludwig, what would it take to ensure that a letter got out of here, and mailed to the U.S.A.? I have an uncle in America who could possibly help us get out of here. I need to write him and ask for help, and you need to ask how much it would cost for us to get out?" Asked a now confident Erik.

CAPO Ludwig looked at the young man, not knowing what to say or do.

"Do you mean all of us? Me included?" Asked a surprised Ludwig.

"But of course Herr Ludwig. If you help us, it would be only right that you too enjoy the benefits of freedom. However you would need to find out where my mother is and what her status is? That would be part of the deal, understood?" Stated a suddenly grown-up Erik.

"We are talking about two different things now! One is getting a letter out of here, and the other is getting all of us out. There would be expenses involved; that must be paid in advance. The Staff Sergeant for example is in deep trouble, but I am sure we could bribe him. He then might bribe the colonel and get out of hot water. Do you have the means to bribe him now?" Asked Ludwig, a slow grin appearing on his face.

"I am not saying I do, nor am I saying I don't. Let's suppose I would find another gold coin, would you be able to get the letter out of the camp? I would have to have a guarantee that it was mailed?" Stated a confident Erik.

"You are a clever and intelligent young man. I am sure we could work something out, but I cannot make any guarantees until I see the proof. If I commit myself to this mission, I have to be assured of success." Replied Ludwig, looking down sternly on both of them.

"OK Herr Ludwig, I am going to trust you enough to make the initial contact with the Staff Sergeant and we both can hope for the best. Why don't you go and speak with him and see if he is willing to help us." Replied Erik, glancing at his sister as he did so. She nodded at him, and smiled.

"When can you have the coin available? Asked KAPO Ludwig.

"I am sure I can have one by tomorrow morning. However I will need some paper, an envelope and a pen." Stated Erik.

"No problem, I will go and fetch those items right now. I should return in less then ten minutes." Explained an overly anxious Ludwig.

As Ludwig left the storeroom, Erik waived at his sister and put his finger to her mouth then to her ears. He wanted her to be quiet and not say anything. She nodded and winked at him. Although Ludwig was now a possible ally, he still did not trust him completely. It was a good thing he did so, because his instincts were correct. Erik climbed on a wooden floor barrel and looked over the door to the kitchen, and there crouched down and listening to the keyhole KAPO Ludwig.

"I can see you and hear you, Herr Ludwig! I thought we were allies, Herr Ludwig? Don't you trust me? I cannot gain access to the item unless you leave the barracks and allow me free reign throughout the building. Is that understood?" Stated a bold and confident Erik.

"Oh, aah, ohhh! I am sorry I dropped something. I am leaving now and you can see me from the window." Stated an embarrassed KAPO Ludwig, as he swiftly departed the barracks through the front door.

Erik asked his sister to climb on the ledge on be a lookout. She quickly climbed up and looked out the top windowpane. She then observed the KAPO walking away at a fast pace towards the SS barracks.

"OK, he is really gone this time! He's halfway to the SS quarters." Finished a joyful Esther.

"Good! Just stay up there and keep watch for anyone coming our way." Replied Erik as he knelt down under the sink and reached down the sewer opening.

A few seconds later; he took two of the gold coins in his possession. He looked around the storeroom for something to clean them with. On the top shelf was a large bottle of medicinal alcohol. Not wanting to leave telltale clues around; he refilled the alcohol bottle with a little water and it looked good as new. A few minutes of hard cleaning cleaned the coins better than new.

Erik knew that KAPO Ludwig would want to know where he

got the coins. Erik made sure that everything was exactly as it had been when Ludwig left. He double and tripled checked everything for correctness. When he was done, he asked his sister to re- check his work. He then had an idea to confuse Ludwig by going next door and spilling some flour on the floor. There were twenty or more large burlap bags of flour stacked up against the wall. Erik purposely opened several of them and spilled some floor around the floor and sacks. Additionally he stepped in the flour with his shoes, giving the impression that someone had recently been there. He also made sure that his shoes were covered with flour. He looked around and was satisfied that everything looked original. His sister screamed in a loud voice.

"Erik he is coming back and the Staff Sergeant is with him. I am worried. This was not part of our plan? What do we do?" Asked a petrified Esther.

"Don't worry little sister, we have him where we want them. I will handle the whole situation. Just stay calm and cool, and don't say anything at all." Replied a confidant Erik.

Before either one of them could say or do anything, the door swung open and the SS Staff Sergeant and KAPO Ludwig burst through the door like a couple of tornadoes gone wild. The sound was so loud that it startled both children.

"You scum! You rats! You discussing filth! Holding out on me? Trying to get me killed? Do you know that the mere possession of gold coins will get you executed." Screamed the Staff Sergeant.

The initial shock was very effective, and Erik wondered, *"Was this such a good idea after all?"* KAPO Ludwig was standing behind the Staff Sergeant and gave Erik a big smile and winked at him. This made Erik feel better and he started to relax a little, for he knew it was all a charade.

"Yes, yes sir!" Replied a now confident Erik.

For a moment everyone just stood around looking at each other and not saying anything to one another. Finally the Staff Sergeant pointed to Erik and then to a stool in the corner, and started to speak in a quiet voice.

"KAPO Ludwig tells me that you no longer wish to remain in our beautiful camp? Is that true? Don't be afraid, you can tell me the truth?" Inquired the grinning sergeant.

"Well, well sir! That is true, I have an uncle in America, and he has on previous occasions offered to pay our passage over there. We feel it would be a good time to take him on it!" Replied Erik, feeling more confident as he did so.

"Well let's say I could make this happen? What would be in it for me? After all I am risking my life by helping you!" Stated the somewhat calmer Staff Sergeant.

"Do you have any more gold coins? I mean readily accessible that is!" Asked the greedy sergeant.

"If I did, I would want my mother and KAPO Ludwig to also be released." Asked an overly confident Erik.

"You are asking way too much. How many coins do you have? Do you have that many? You realize it would take many coins to bribe everyone, including the camp commandant?" Finished the Staff Sergeant, a little less confident now.

"Could you perhaps tell me how many you would need?" Asked Erik.

"I don't really know for sure, maybe eight, maybe ten, maybe twelve? It all depends on the commandant. He is the one who is pushing me for money. As a matter of fact I have to meet with him tomorrow and it would be nice if I had something to show him?" Finished the almost pleading sergeant.

"Give me an hour and I am sure I will be able to come up with something for you." Finished a very self-assured and cocky Erik.

The Staff Sergeant looked down and the young man and almost wanted to say something to him, but decided against it and walked out. They all looked at each and Ludwig finally said something.

"You have moved me beyond words! Never in my entire life has anyone done anything so selfless for me. You have given me hope in humanity. I want you to know that I appreciate it with all my soul." Stated a now crying Ludwig.

Erik and Esther stared at each other; not knowing what to say. Finally Erik spoke to Ludwig.

"We hope that our actions will help you, and in return you will help us. That is the way life should be? Don't you think so?" Replied a now grown-up Erik.

"Yes I agree, but in this hell hole, no one has ever shown me any compassion. What are you going to do for the sergeant?" Asked an inquisitive Ludwig?"

"I am going to leave it up to you Herr Ludwig. I can give you two gold coins, and let you decide how best to deal with the sergeant. I don't think he particularly enjoys having to deal with me." Replied Erik.

"That is very trusting of you Erik. I promise to do what is right for all. Why don't you write the letter to your uncle in Chicago, and I will make sure it gets mailed as soon as possible." Replied a very friendly Ludwig.

Both Erik and Esther had the first good nights sleep since they got there. Visions of a long sea voyage; plenty of food and a clean environment whirled through their collective heads. As the sun broke over the horizon and lit up the storeroom, they were awaked by noises coming from the hallway where the sacks of flour were kept. Ludwig and two of his flunkies were ankle deep in flower. Their faces, arms and hands were covered in a fine white powder. Ludwig looked very irritated and once again was bloodied and beaten. Ludwig turned around when he heard the door to the storeroom open.

"As you can see, I had no choice! The Staff Sergeant insisted that I search this area and try to coerce you in to revealing the location of the rest of the coins! He was very adamant and told me not to return unless I found the coins! I had no choice. He can make our lives very uncomfortable. Please forgive me Erik? I really had no choice!" Pleaded a sobbing Ludwig.

"Don't worry Herr Ludwig, I suspected something would happen and we hid the coins elsewhere. They are not anywhere near the flour. Stop looking there." Stated Erik in a calm, but firm voice.

"OK men, stop looking and return to your duties. Please?" Asked a very serious Ludwig.

Both men walked away from the hallway and returned to the kitchen without saying another word. Erik looked at Herr Ludwig and motioned to him to come in the storeroom. KAPO Ludwig did so and closed the door.

"Well it's obvious that we can't trust the Staff Sergeant, and the chances are that he won't be alive beyond tomorrow? We need to contact Colonel Koch ourselves and make a deal with him directly? Do you agree with me or not?" Asked a somber KAPO Ludwig.

"I agree with you, but how do we go about it?" Asked Erik looking straight at Herr Ludwig.

The commandant knows me already; one of my friends works in his house as a housekeeper and she has direct access to him everyday. I can get word to her and she can inform the commandant of a possible goldmine? What do you think?" Asked Ludwig.

"I think it's a good idea, but can you trust her? After all the sergeant was not reliable, and how well do you trust this person?" Asked a concerned Erik.

"This women is my lover, and she loves me very much. She would do anything for me. I trust her with my life." Replied a boasting KAPO Ludwig.

"I hope you are right! But what will she do when she finds out you are leaving this wonderful place?" Asked Erik, a smirk on his face.

"I know what I am doing, and I want both of you to lay low today. Stay here and lock yourself in the storeroom. I will be back this afternoon." Stated Ludwig as he walked out of the building.

"What do you think Esther? Asked a concerned Erik.

"I believe in Herr Ludwig. I think he will do whatever is best for all of us, but maybe we should always have a secondary plan? What do you think?" Stated a now talkative Esther.

"Let's get some rest until he gets back." Stated Erik as he walked over to his cot and sat down.

Four hours later a jubilant KAPO Ludwig came rushing in the room. Completely out of breathe and panting like a dog.

"Children! Children! Get up! Get up! He shouted at the top of his lungs. My friend was able to arrange a meeting with Colonel Koch and he was extremely pleased. He agreed to mail your letter directly through the Red Cross and he would ensure that we all get out of here within a few months. However, he insisted that you pay him at least six more gold coins now, and the rest when you leave! Isn't that great? Aren't you happy? We are going to leave this hole!" Screamed an overjoyed Herr Ludwig.

"Herr Ludwig what's to prevent him from murdering us and keeping the gold?" Asked a concerned Erik.

"I have a plan. You need to finish writing your letter and we will take it in person to the Red Cross and ask that Colonel Koch be present. After handing over the letter, we can then hand him the six gold coins; in plain view of the Red Cross workers. If anything were to happen to us, they could be our only witnesses." Finished Ludwig, with a wide grin on his face.

"It sounds probable. Right now it's our only option. By the way Colonel Koch informed me that the Staff Sergeant would be court-martialed and executed in a few days. We won't have to worry about him anymore." Said Ludwig with a smirk on his face.

"That will surely relieve one of my biggest worries. I will be able to sleep in peace; knowing that the animal is caged, and put away for good." Stated a concerned Erik.

"Let's quit worrying about it and wait for the big day! You can come up with that many coins? Can't you?" Asked a worried Ludwig.

"You get the letter out of here and I will come up with the coins. However you still have not said anything about my mother? Do you know anything about her? Her whereabouts? You must give me news, or we don't have a deal." Stated Erik firmly.

"I will do some research tomorrow. I have a friend who works in the reception warehouse and he knows where all inmates are located. He should be able to tell me something tomorrow." Answered a nervous Ludwig.

"By the way, you have not told me how many coins Colonel Koch wants?" Asked Erik.

"Oh yeah, he wants at least twelve gold coins. I gave him the two you gave me, and we will have to come up with another ten coins, when you are released! I should say, when we are released!" Finished a smiling CAPO Ludwig.

"So let me get this right. He already took the one coin, and you gave him two today and he wants ten more when we are released?" Asked Erik.

"That is correct! You do have ten more coins? Please say you do? By the way your uncle in Chicago will have to pay an additional $1,500.00 each in gold for your release!" Implored a now whimpering KAPO Ludwig.

"$1,500.00 in gold? Wow, that is a lot of money? My father always said, his rich American brother had plenty of money. I don't think it should be a problem for him to come up with that sum! I guess we will have to wait and see what happens?" Stated Erik in a matter of fact tone.

"I hope for your sake that he does! Otherwise we will all go straight to the firing squad and the ovens!" Replied a now gloomy Ludwig.

"Don't forget to inquire about my mother? I need to know what has happened to her? Please Herr Ludwig?" Begged Erik.

"Believe me my young friend, I am just as concerned as you are. I will do my best to find out? Why don't we call it a day? Get some rest and stay here!" Finished Ludwig as he walked out of the storeroom.

Erik and Esther were exhausted by the events of the day. They both took the opportunity for getting some much needed sleep. KAPO Ludwig took the opportunity to go to the IN-PROCESSING center and speak with his old friend Herr Klaus Kaminski. Klaus was one of the oldest residents of Buchenwald. He had been of the original three hundred transferred from other camps.

Klaus was the unfortunate soul with the green hands. He tattooed everyone upon arrival in the camp. Herr Ludwig went in to the kitchen and took a large chunk of cheese, a piece of roast beef, a freshly baked loaf of bread and some dried fruits. Ludwig put everything in a backpack and ran over to the center. Klaus was still processing the last prisoners of the day, and was happy to see his old friend Ludwig.

"How are you, my friend?" Asked Herr Kaminski.

"I am just fine. How are you? Replied Ludwig, as the chitchat went back and forth.

"What can I do for you?" Asked Kaminski.

"I have brought you a few provisions. I hope you can use them?" Asked a smiling Ludwig.

Herr Kaminski grabbed the heavy bag and looked inside, and let out a loud gasp!

"**Mein Gott!** There is enough food here, for two or three weeks or more.

I really appreciate it, but what can I do for you? No one gives me this much food for reason? What is it you need?" Asked a serious Herr Klaus Kaminski.

"You are a very wise and intelligent man! I need to know what happened to a certain Sarah Goldmann who came in with her two children? Where was she sent? Can you tell me?" Asked a now serious Ludwig.

"Well, let me see? Goldmann, Goldmann? Not a very common name!" Said Herr Kaminski, his wrinkled and green finger scrolling down the ledger.

"Here, here she is! She was sent over with the other Jews to work in the mines. The mines, yes she was sent to the mines!" Finished a somewhat saddened Herr Kaminski.

"Oh, No! She is surely dead by now. No one lasts very long there!" Exclaimed Ludwig, as he turned around and walked out of the center.

All the way back to the storeroom, he pondered whether or not he should tell Erik that his mother is most likely dead? *No!* He told himself. *"Not a good idea! I should wait until our journey is assured."*

KAPO Ludwig was very traumatized by the news of Mrs. Sarah Goldmann. The average inmate lasted less than a week in the mines. Conditions were so horrible that just about every inmate caught pneumonia, dysentery and other contagious diseases within days of arrival in the mines. Their life expectancy was practically zero, and if they survived their time in the mines was worst than hell. Even the German SS guards dreaded working there. They usually reserved these duties for either the brand new troops or their SS *Hilfestruppen*. These were usually foreign allied soldiers who volunteered for the SS.

Chapter 25

America at Last!

The days dragged by slowly like a snail going uphill. Every new day brought hope and despair at the same time. Erik could not understand what was taking so long? He often wondered if, *"Colonel Koch had simply taken the coins and never forwarded the letter to his uncle in Chicago?"*

The sun was beating down on the tin roof of the barracks. The heat was unbearable as there was not a breeze for a hundred miles. Although it was very hot, it felt good. All of the bones in his body were finally thawing out from the deep freeze of winter. This past winter had been exceptionally cold, and the hot sun was a form of microwave helping him to revitalize his core. Erik envisioned himself somewhere in America on a hot desert basking in the sun, and not in a concentration camp in the middle of Germany. Weather like this was very uncommon for this part of Europe, and even the brutal guards seem to mellow out a bit, in the temperate climate.

A loud voice seems to wake him up from his daydreaming. An out of breath and heavily panting CAPO Ludwig ran into the barracks and yelled his name, Erik, Erik, Erik!

"I am here Herr Ludwig, I am here. What is it? What is going on? What is going on?" Replied a concerned Erik.

"Common, lets go now to the commandant's office. He has received the money from America through the Cuban Embassy and the Red Cross. You and your sister are leaving immediately! Now!" Shouted an excited Ludwig.

Erik stood frozen in terror! Ludwig had said, "Sister!" Was it just a slip of the tongue or did he know that his brother was in fact a girl?

"Yes, you heard me correctly! I said sister! You don't think that little charade of yours fooled anyone? It doesn't matter anymore. Your uncle specifically paid for his nephew and niece. Colonel Koch was a little surprised at first, but as long as he gets his money, he will let her go!" CAPO Ludwig finished, in one long sentence.

Erik just stared at Ludwig like a deer in the road. All of his attempts at concealing his sister's sexuality had not been a secret after all.

"Don't look so stupid Erik! I had an ulterior motive for not turning you in! I wanted out of here, and you were my ticket out of here. Lets go! Don't forget to bring your coins, or you won't get out today!" Stated a smiling Ludwig.

"What about you and my mother?" Asked a more serious Erik.

"The only thing I know about your mother is that she was sent to the mines within weeks of arriving here. I have no further news from her since that date! Don't be too hopeful; few if any survive that hell!" Stated a morose Ludwig.

Erik stared at Ludwig and understood what he was trying to say. His emotions were overwhelming him, but he knew he had to maintain his composure for Esther's sake.

Ludwig went on to say.

"As far as I am concerned, my chances are pretty good, as long as I come up with the gold coins, the colonel will reduce my sentence, and let me go home today or tomorrow as well. Please tell me you have enough coins for all of us? Please?" Begged Ludwig.

"How many do you need?" Asked Erik.

CAPO Ludwig was taken by surprise by the question. He had not really thought about it! Colonel Koch had wanted twelve coins for the three of them six months ago and he assumed that the price was still the same.

"I suppose six? Is that too much? Do you have that many? Please tell me you do?" Pleaded a concerned Ludwig.

Erik stood in the middle of the room and tried to mentally calculate how many he still had. One plus two, plus ten that would be thirteen? He started with thirty and that would leave him with seventeen? Plus the two diamond rings? If he gave Ludwig six coins, he still would have eleven for his trip to America. *"Not bad,"* he thought to himself.

"OK, Herr Ludwig! I have enough for all of us." Erik shouted with joy!

CAPO Ludwig fell to his knees and thanked God for this small mercy. He hugged Erik thanked him for his generosity, but insisted that they leave immediately.

"OK Herr Ludwig, but you need to help me to retrieve my coins. Please let me climb on your shoulders?" Asked Erik.

"What did you say? My shoulders?" Asked a surprised Ludwig.

"Yes, they are hidden in the pipe above you head. I need a boost to get them out!" Replied Erik with a smile.

Erik scrambled up KAPO Ludwig's tall frame and stood on his shoulders. He reached up and pulled out the coins from the pipe. Standing on Ludwig's shoulder was easier than his sister's attempt. Ludwig shook his head in disbelief. How easy it had been?

"Do you know how many times I have been in here looking for them." Said Ludwig.

Erik smiled and nodded his head. He told Ludwig to reach down in the sewer drain hole and retrieve the other coins and rings. While Ludwig was busy doing just that, Erik quickly and quietly swallowed the other coins, with the exception of the six he was going to give to Ludwig. There was no need to now relax and trust anyone. He remembered his father's instruction and decided to take a few precautions.

When Ludwig finally managed to retrieve the coins and rings, Erik had managed to swallow his coins. He kept Ludwig's coins separate.

"You are a clever young man. I never would of thought of anyone putting anything down this shit hole! OK, we now have the coins; lets go the office and get the hell out of here!" Stated an ebullient Ludwig.

Erik grabbed his sister, and started to run out the door when he suddenly stopped in mid-stride and spoke to Ludwig.

"How do you know that Koch is not going to double cross you?" I will give you the six gold coins and one of my rings as an insurance policy. The ring is worth at least three or four gold coins, maybe more? If I were you I would swallow them and give them to him; when he is alone and you can guarantee your exit?" Stated a suddenly very adult thinking Erik.

"Yes, I think you are right. Yes, I will do that. What did you use to swallow your coins?" Asked a pensive Ludwig.

"Kitchen oil, kitchen oil! It works great." Said Erik, handing him the bottle of oil.

It took Ludwig less than two minutes to swallow the coins, and the one ring. All three ran across the parade field to Colonel Koch's office. They announced themselves to SS guard on duty and were escorted in to the inner-sanctum.

"KAPO Ludwig, are these the prisoners in question? Erik and Esther Goldmann?" Asked a stern Colonel Koch.

"Yes Sir!" Replied KAPO Ludwig.

The two Red Cross representatives were standing near the colonel and were quietly observing the whole procedure. Both men were neatly dressed and appeared to be in their mid-thirties. The colonel read an official Nazi Proclamation, "That for humanitarian reasons blah, blah, blah, blah they were being released to their uncle in America and were to never return to Germany, and would from this day on, lose their German citizenship etc." Bla, bla, bla finished an out of breath Colonel Koch.

The Red Cross representatives stepped forward and handed both children an international identification card and a refugee passport. Before the Red Cross personnel could assume control of the two inmates, the colonel ordered the two SS guards to take them into his private office for one last search. After all, he did not want them to steal anything from the camp. Both Red Cross representatives strenuously objected to this procedure, but were overruled by the colonel on the grounds of national security.

Erik smiled to himself. Thank God he had listened to his father. The colonel was trying to steal from them, but Erik had been too clever. Both of them were rudely searched and in addition to the ten coins, they found the other ring. The colonel chastised them for trying to steal government property and readily pocketed the coins and the ring in his private safe. After admonishing them for this crime, he once again allowed them to enter the outer foyer. He brusquely asked the Red Cross representatives for the three thousand American dollars from their uncle. They in turn handed it to the colonel and made him sign a receipt. The colonel wanting to protect his ass, asked the SS Senior Sergeant to sign on his behalf. The SS man was at first reluctant to do, but a direct gaze from the Colonel, convinced him to do so.

KAPO Ludwig took this opportunity to inform the Red Cross representatives of his name and prisoner status. He also stated that the colonel would be releasing him in the next two days, and he would appreciate it if they could escort him out of Buchenwald. They both acknowledged his presence, and stated that they would check back on him, and assure that he was released as promised.

Once all the formalities were completed both Erik and Esther were escorted to a waiting large Mercedes sedan. They could not believe that were finally free! Nine long months of hell and torment, had seemed like nine years. Although by some standards their confinement had been relatively easy. Two hundred in eighty-nine days in Buchenwald could never be considered painless, but thanks to KAPO Ludwig they managed to survive.

Erik realized that Ludwig had in fact been their guardian angel, and he was glad that they were able to save him as well. His only concern was the lack of information about his mother and her whereabouts? His father's lack of communication was less worrisome; he knew that his father was stronger and better able to take care of himself. Erik hoped for the best, and prayed that his uncle might be able to help him find out more information about his parents.

KAPO Ludwig had to spend another two days in hell, until his bowels cleared the coins, that is. Colonel Koch kept his word and released him as promised. Although released from Buchenwald his luck never really changed. When the Germans invaded Poland in September 1939, Ludwig was drafted in the German army, and reluctantly served until the end of the war.

Erik, his sister and the two Red Cross representatives drove out of Buchenwald and headed south towards Switzerland. It would be the first stop in their journey to freedom. The Red Cross representatives first needed to stop at another two locations before they finally headed towards the border.

Chapter 26

Delay en Route

The trip south to the Swiss border took forever. The Red Cross representatives stopped in a little village to purchase clean clothes for them, and allow them to take a bath. It was the first time in over nine months that they sat in a real tub, and used bubble bath. Just when they were enjoying it, someone knocked on their door and asked them to please hurry-up.

"Herr Goldmann, Herr Goldmann! We have to hurry if we are going to make the border before nightfall. Please hurry!" Stated the Red Cross representative. Erik was initially shocked to hear, Herr Goldmann. This was the first time anyone had ever called him Herr Goldmann. It brought back memories of his father, Niedergeyer and home.

"Yes Sir! We are just about finished, and we will be out in five minutes." Shouted Erik to both the Red Cross man and his sister in the next room.

His sister Esther was almost dressed in her new dress and fancy shoes. She was looking herself in the mirror and liked what she saw. It was the first time Erik had seen her smile in a year, and it was a good feeling. Erik jumped out of the tub and ran over to the bed, and started to put his clothes on. He could not believe the quality of the suit they had bought for him. This was the first time he had ever worn an adult suit, and it fitted him very elegantly. His new two-tone shoes were very classy and matched his suit, a topcoat and a hat topped off the ensemble. He looked at himself in the mirror and did not recognize himself.

Erik had aged by ten years! He was haggard, had sunken cheeks and hallowed out eyes. He finally remembered that he had not seen himself in a mirror since he'd left home. The change was incredible! He left as a young man; he now looked like a grown man.

"Herr Goldmann, we need to go!" Shouted the Red Cross man; with a little more impatience this time.

"Yes sir! I am done and I will be right out." Replied Erik as he opened the door and stepped out in the hallway.

"My, you sure look different! Let's go now!" Stated a somewhat irate Red Cross man.

Everyone got in the large waiting Mercedes and sped off towards the Swiss border.

"Why, why are we in such a hurry? Why do we have to rush? I just don't understand?" Asked a confused Esther.

"That is a very good question Esther." Replied the driver.

"The Nazis have only given you a twenty-four exit transit visa, and if you are still on German soil by eight o'clock this evening, they may not let you go until you pay a fine!" Said the driver.

"You mean, you mean they could take us back?" Asked both kids in unison?

"They can do anything they want until we cross the Swiss frontier. Don't worry we are only less than ten kilometers away and should be there in fifteen minutes or less." Replied the driver.

"By the way, my name Bernard de Cotili and my friend here is Mannfred Schultheiss, and we are both Swiss nationals. We will be your escorts until we reach Switzerland; after that we will pass you on to your next hosts.

"We are very pleased to meet you, and you already know our names." Replied a smiling Erik.

Exactly twenty-two minutes later, they reached the Swiss frontier. The Swiss soldiers looked very much like German soldiers, but spoke German with a funny singsong accent. However, they acted in a polite, but efficient manner. The Red Cross officials arranged for a speedy transit and within less than ten minutes they were at last free of the Nazi yoke.

It wasn't until much later that the Goldmann children realized that they were actually at liberty to do whatever they wanted. They were put up in a beautiful five star hotel. Their suites were almost as big as their entire house in Niedergeyer had been. When

Erik asked how much this all cost, he was politely told not to worry about it. Their new Red Cross representatives, Herr Goesling and Monsieur Marchant were also Swiss, but one was of German descent and the other French. Both of them were equally gracious and obliging.

Monsieur Marchant made it a point of explaining the rest of their planned itinerary. They would stay in the hotel for two days and rest. Subsequently they would be taken by train to the airport in Geneva and flown to Lisbon, Portugal where their Cuban representative would pick them up and fly them to London. From London they would catch the French ocean liner "SS Normandie."

"Excuse me, Mr. Marchant? Did you say Cuban representative? Why Cuban? And why must we go to Portugal and not directly to London? And why a French ship? I just don't understand?" Asked a confused Erik.

Esther just stood there in silence, looking like a deer caught in the headlights.

"Well you see Erik, international politics are a very complicated matter. This is the way that diplomats worked things out to help you and other refugees get out of Germany and rejoin your relatives in America. Cuba has agreed to act as a go between and expedite your travels. Do you understand?" Replied a smiling Monsieur Marchant.

Erik reflected for a few minutes before answering.

"I guess so! I guess that makes sense, but when we will be able to speak with my uncle in America?" Does he know we are coming? Will he be there to pick us up in NewYork? Can you please check on my mothers' status? My father is still in Niedergeyer and probably does not know our whereabouts?" Replied Erik, unsure of his current status?

"Your uncle has made arrangements for his attorney to pick you up in New York. The attorney will then place you on a train and you will go directly to Chicago, arriving less than a day and half later? Your uncle has covered all of your expenses, and he has sent an extra five hundred dollars in emergency funds. I will do my best to find out what I can concerning your mother and father." Replied a satisfied Monsieur Marchant.

"Well it sounds like he has thought of everything? Don't you think so Esther?" Asked Erik?

"Yes, I believe he has, but I have a question? I wish to speak to you privately?" Stated Esther pulling her brother aside.

"Since we have the extra money from our uncle, maybe we could give one or two more of our coins to Herr Ludwig, and perhaps he could look for our mother, or maybe the kind Red Cross representatives could look on our behalf? What do you think?" Requested a suddenly very adult sounding Esther?

"My God! That is brilliant! Excellent idea, I will ask Monsieur Marchant to help us?"

Erik approached Monsieur Marchant and asked him if he would take three of their remaining gold coins and attempt to find information on their missing mother? He left it to their discretion on how best to spend the coins. He had full trust in their actions. Monsieur Marchant was somewhat surprised by the request, but agreed to their demand on the condition that they realize how difficult this mission would be. Erik and Esther agreed and understood the full significance.

"Well now that we have settled that, why don't we go and have dinner!" Asked a hungry Monsieur Marchant.

"That is a great idea, but I think we would prefer to eat in our rooms, if that would be possible?" Asked a suddenly shy Erik.

The children stayed in their hotel, and had room service brought up to their room. It was a treat! They had never indulged in this fashion, and they really enjoyed the excellent food and service. They were not accustomed to this type of luxury and it did not take long for both of the Goldmann children to fall fast asleep. Erik slept like a bear, but Esther was very restless and had a difficult time falling asleep. Eventually she finally let the 'Sandman' into her eyes and she dozed off around one A.M.

Monsieur Marchant let them sleep in. Their flight did not leave Switzerland until two o'clock in the afternoon and he did want to wake them until ten A.M. Flying time to Lisbon was less than five hours time in the newest B.OA.C. (British Airways) airplane, and they would have sufficient time to prepare for their journey.

After thanking the Red Cross representatives for their invaluable assistance the Goldmann's finally boarded their plane for Lisbon, but not before giving them their uncle's address in Chicago. Erik wanted to ensure that he receive news from them in the event they were able to do something for their mother?

They were very excited, as neither had ever flown before. The last ninety-six hours had been a series of adventures beyond their limited scope of comprehension. The plane promptly took and before long was cruising at fifteen thousand feet over the French Alps towards Spain and then on to Portugal. A very beautiful B.O.A.C. stewardess approached them and asked if they wanted anything special to drink or eat? At first they were somewhat confused and embarrassed. However, they finally asked for a glass of orange juice. Within minutes the hostess brought a pitcher of juice and some delicious chocolate biscuits. The children ate the biscuits, drank their juice and promptly fell asleep. The droning noise of the propellers had a hypnotic effect, and just about everyone aboard was feeling its effect.

Within a few hours the plane was circling the large runway awaiting permission to land in Lisbon. Erik knew that their layover would not be a long one and he looked forward to continuing his journey to America. They had to disembark and go through the normal formalities with customs. They were back on board in forty-five minutes and now flying northward towards London. The flying time was about the same length of time. When the plane approached British airspace; suddenly two planes appeared alongside and escorted them the rest of the way.

The two planes were marked with a strange camouflage design, and had a light blue colored underbelly. They were a pair of British Spitfire fighter planes. Erik had never seen such a beautiful airplane; it was sleek and certainly looked very fast. The pilot could be clearly seen as he gestured with his right thumb and wiggled his wings. Erik and Esther could not understand why two fighters were escorting them to the airport. Another strange appearance over London that day, were dozens of large silver colored airships. It wasn't until much later in the day that he understood the significance of this moment.

Once they cleared customs, they took a taxi to the docks at Southampton. The taxi driver was extremely pleased to have such a good fare. After all it wasn't everyday that he took someone all the way to Southampton.

"Did you here the news? It looks like we are about to go to war? The bloody Krauts are probably marching on Poland as we speak. We have a treaty with Poland to protect them in the event of an attack from Germany! Isn't that something?" Asked the driver with his heavy Cockney accent.

"Did you say war? *Mit Deutschland*?" Asked a scared Esther!

"Well my little one, do I detect a slight German accent?" Asked the suddenly curious driver.

Esther noticed her mistake and clammed up. Her brother answered in her place.

"No sir! We are Swiss, and we are on our way to America to live with our uncle in Chicago!" Replied a quick thinking Erik.

"OK mate, just be careful out there and have a safe journey." Replied the now friendlier taxi driver.

It took them over an hour to get to the docks in Southampton. The French cruise ship SS Normandie was easily spotted. It was docked in the first berth near the harbor's entrance. She was beautiful, *Erik thought!* Her sides gleaming white, and her large chimney funnels had green stripes around them.

Erik stared at the ship and could not believe how beautiful she was. No sign of rust anywhere, not even on the anchor. She was huge! Over a thousand feet in length, she was a ship of superlatives and adjectives. Nothing in the world could match her size, luxury and speed. She was over 80,000 tons and could still manage over thirty knots; she held the transatlantic speed record in both directions. Erik had purchased a guidebook in Portugal and knew all of the pertinent facts about her.

The SS Normandie's career as a luxury liner; unfortunately

was cut short by the beginning of WWII. Erik and Esther would have the privilege of being on her 139th and last voyage. A bad string of luck would haunt her until the day she was finally decommissioned.

As the taxi rolled towards the magnificent ship both of the children were awe struck by her grandeur and majesty. Erik imagined that a great French painter had designed her. She was incredibly beautiful and majestic.

"She's a beauty, isn't she?" Stated the taxi driver?

"Yes sir, she certainly is! I have never seen anything as striking." Replied an admiring Erik.

The taxi stopped a hundred yards or so from the ship. The driver helped them with their meager belongings. Erik tipped the taxi driver with some of the money from his uncle, and decided to board the ship immediately. They both were afraid that someone might change their mind and send them back to Germany.

The anxiety grew into a terror and they both started running towards the ship.

Chapter 27

Crisis at Home

Back in Niedergeyer
Present Time

"Wow! What a story! I can't wait for you to finish it! Please tell me how it ends?" Asked a curious and suddenly excited Jeremy.

"Well I can tell you all I know, but the story is still not finished! Only Cameron will be able to finish this story. He is still working on it, aren't you?" Asked an inquisitive Dieter.

"I don't really know the facts, Dieter? You are the great storyteller. Maybe someday we will together tie-up all the loose ends into one great story. It is prophetic that my current crusade has somehow interwoven itself into my existing assignment?

I have so much to do, and don't forget my trip to Frankfurt and the Israeli Consulate?" Replied Cameron.

"Yes, yes of course! We need to make arrangements and follow-up with the State Department, the Central Intelligence Agency, NSA and the Germans. Dieter, can I use your office for a few minutes?" Asked Jeremy, walking away from them towards the front of the house.

"But of course, makes yourself at home! Replied a smiling Dieter.

While Jeremy made his phone calls, both Dieter and Cameron stayed in the living room and relaxed. The topic of conversation turned to the two females in their lives and their existing poor attitude.

"I need to know Dieter? Can you tell me the truth about Kate? Was she in fact arrested after the war and almost executed as a war criminal?" Asked Cameron.

Dieter stared at Cameron, not knowing how to answer him. The question caught him by surprised. He thought this was a great family secret, and how did his son-in-law find out?

"Cameron there are many things in life that are better left alone, and I think this is one question that I should not answer! We have a very good relationship, but I cannot betray my wife! It would probably end our marriage! Considering the way the girls have been acting; it might not be a bad idea, but I have too many years invested. Please don't push the issue? You might not want to know the truth?" Replied a nervous Dieter.

Cameron stared at him for a few seconds before answering.

"I don't know how to say this Dieter? I think it's time for all secrets belonging to that time in history to be expunged forever. Even if it means exposing the ones we love the most. Realistically, it probably won't affect our lives too much? I have a pretty good idea of her and your past. The individuals who kidnapped me, they gave me a pretty good rundown on all of you. There is no longer any need to hide her past, Dieter!" Finished Cameron, as he looked at his visibly upset father-in-law.

Dieters' face suddenly grew red in color. The vein over his left eye began to swell and pulsate. The seconds grew into a minute or more; still no answer! Cameron was worried that Dieter was going to have a stroke and die on him. He got up and walked over to him. Cameron put his hand on his shoulder and stared at him.

"Dieter, only tell me what you want to! I am not pressing you for more information than you want to tell me. Eventually the truth will come out, and it would be better if you told me now." Stated a now serious Cameron.

Dieter got up and walked over to the bar and grabbed another brandy. He poured himself a healthy double shot. He turned around and pointed at the bottle with his free hand. Cameron silently nodded his head and held up his glass. Dieter walked over and nearly filled it to the rim.

"If I drink all of that, I will not be able to walk up the stairs and properly greet my spouse. Although that may not be such a bad idea after all!" Replied a sneering Cameron. Dieter looked at him and grunted an acknowledgement.

"The truth is Cameron, I am embarrassed of our family's past, but you are right; we should finally get rid of this terrible burden! My wife was an active member of the Nazi Party. She was and still is a brilliant chemist and she assisted the A.G. Karbon chemical company in developing the poison gas used in their extermination chambers! She was just a chemist, and never knew the extent of her participation until she was shown a film of the chambers in 1943.

She was so emotionally devastated that she decided to quit her prestigious job. She took up nursing under the guise of helping the war effort. However her allegiance to the Nazi Party remained as strong as ever, but she did not wish to continue developing such horrible weapons." Stated a barely audible Dieter. His head was hanging down and he was gently sobbing.

"Wow, that is indeed some secret! But you can't blame yourself for her deeds?" Replied Cameron in a gentle and soothing way.

"Well, I did not know of her complicity until after the war; when the American MPs came looking for a Kate under her maiden name. We lied to them; we told them she had died in a March 1945 bombing raid in Mainz. As you know records of civilian casualties were not very accurate, and we got away with it until recently. We in fact had been evacuated to the Mainz area and were caught in an American Air Force bombing raid. When we returned to this area at the end of the war; we simply obtained papers using her new married name. Until the arrival of modern computers, it was almost impossible to trace anything that occurred so long ago." Finished a very desolate Dieter.

The silence in the room was overwhelming. Cameron was overcome with emotions and sentiments. He looked at his poor father-in-law and sympathized with him. After all, he was not the one who had committed those atrocities; it was Kate! This whole circumstance was putting him in a very awkward situation. Here he was right in the middle of a nest of Nazis. How could he do his job without revealing what he knew? He could now understand why the MOSSAD suspected him of being a co-conspirator. What would his boss Jerry Kunstoff say when he found out? *"I will have to deal with that problem when it happens"*, he thought to himself.

Finally Dieter broke the silence. He took out a handkerchief and blew his nose. The sound of it snapped Cameron out of his daydream.

"Cameron, I beg you not to say anything to anyone right now. Things will somehow work themselves out. After all we are both very old, and don't have long to live!" Begged a now crying Dieter!

"I can't promise anything right now. Let me think about it, and we will talk about it in the next few days." Replied Cameron, turning his head away not wanting to look Dieter in the eyes.

"Thank you Cameron! Give it some time and hopefully you will have a change of heart. I have always tried to be a good man and make up for my family's indiscretion." Finished a very somber and obviously upset Dieter Johannes.

Just when things seemed to be getting less emotionally charged, Jeremy came back in the room. Dieter quickly turned away and tried to wipe the tears away from his eyes.

"Well everything is all set! I spoke to all parties concerned and they have a plan worked out for us to get something out of the Israelis! Seven years ago a United States State Department employees gave Top Secret documents to Israel. Jaimy Behrens was his name, and he was convicted in absentia for giving away Top Secret documents to a foreign power.

Unlike most spies; he did it for patriotic reasons, not for money! He was a devout and religious Jew, and believed that the United States was not being forthcoming with the State of Israel. He approached them and gave the Israelis some very vital Top Secret documents concerning American foreign policy in the Middle-east." Finished a smiling Jeremy.

"And how does that affect us?" Asked Cameron, standing up and walking towards Dieter.

"Don't you see? We have them by the short ones." Replied Jeremy; as he grabbed his crotch.

"Short ones? **Was ist Das**?" (What is that) Asked a confused Dieter Johannes.

Both Jeremy and Cameron laughed out loud simultaneously. They looked at each other trying to decide which one of them would explain it to Dieter. After a short and uncomfortable moment, Cameron explained it to Dieter in German. Within a few seconds Dieter smiled and nodded his head.

All three men were standing around in the living room trying to analyze what Jeremy had said. Their silence was interrupted by an absolutely hysterical and out of control Kate. She entered the room, like a tornado sweeping across Greensberg, Kansas. Her eyes were bulging like a Chihuahua in heat. Her large index finger was wagging back and forth like a conductor leading a philharmonic. Everyone present stood transfixed and shocked by her behavior.

"Calm down, calm down! What is going on?" Replied a disconcerted Dieter.

"You, you know what is going on! How dare you tell anyone about my past! It's none of their concern what my political affiliations were sixty years ago! How dare you tell them?" Screamed a frenzied Kate, turning her body and anger in the general direction of Jeremy and Cameron.

Both men stood transfixed and horrified by her behavior. They both wanted to say something, but were shocked to say the right thing. Finally a brave and courageous Dieter, spoke up.

"Dearest Kate, you need to take a deep breath and calm down! You are totally out of control, and if you continue in this fashion you will have a stroke! Go upstairs and take your medicine!" Stated an upset Dieter.

Just when they thought things might begin to quiet down, Ingrid burst into the room and started yelling at her father, husband and poor Jeremy. Not wanting to aggravate matters, all three men just stood there, and said nothing. This attitude seemed to anger the women even more.

"Please Ingrid stay out this! This is no concern of yours! Please don't make matters worst!" Repeated a somewhat more belligerent Dieter Johannes.

"What do you mean? Stay out of it? I am right up to my elbows in it! I am the only one who is taking Mama's side! You should be ashamed of yourself! How dare you protect these inhuman beasts! Mama is a good person and does not deserve to be treated this way!" Finished an equally irate Ingrid.

In all his years of marriage, Cameron had never heard his wife act in this fashion. Her mannerisms, gestures and vocabulary were more fit for a drunken sailor than his wife, *"He thought to himself."*

"OK ladies, that is enough for the day! I don't know what is going on, but we must try to regain our composure, and work this out." Stated a somewhat more conciliatory Dieter.

Both women just stared at him and walked out of the room in a huff. Their footsteps and irate voices could be heard stomping up the stairs. Dieter looked directly at Cameron and said.

"It is obvious that our presence is not wanted here, lets go to Aachen and spend the night there. Hopefully the women will have regained their decorum." Stated Dieter as he walked out the room.

Jeremy looked at Cameron for guidance?

"I guess that's OK? I am in no mood to argue with anyone right now." Replied Cameron, walking out the door as he did so.

"Hey Dieter! Don't forget I left my car in the parking lot near the Storyville Disco. It's been there several days and we need to pick it up? Why don't we go there first, and then on to Aachen?" Asked Cameron.

"Ja, Cameron! Let's do that. It will give us time to talk and forget our troubles.

Chapter 28

SS NORMANDIE

Dieter continued his story, as the three men drove to Köln and then on to Aachen. He would have plenty of time to tell his story, as it was a three or four hour drive.

September 1st, 1939 Southampton, England

Erik and Esther were back on the docks in Southampton walking towards the massive ship. The long walk to the gangplank took forever. Hundreds of men with carts, trucks, dollies were all working in unison to get the ship ready for her epic voyage. Erik was unsure which gangway to use. They walked towards a large white gangplank in the middle of the ship and approached an important looking man in a dark blue uniform with two gold stripes on his sleeves.

"Excuse me sir? Where do we board the ship? Is this the correct spot?" Asked a somewhat nervous Erik.

The tall, forty something officer turned around and looked down at the Goldmann's.

"Well it depends where you are going. Let me see your ticket?" Replied the kind officer, with a big smile on his weather beaten face.

"You see sir, we are going to America, Chicago that is! Our uncle will be picking us up in New York! And we will then go to." Stated a suddenly vivacious Esther. Dieter cut her off in mid-sentence.

"Please forgive her sir! This is our first sea voyage and we are very excited. Can you please show us the way to board the ship?" Asked Erik.

"But of course, just show me your tickets, and I will be able to help you." Replied once again Chief Steward Phillippe.

As Erik reached across to hand him the tickets, his sleeve creped up and his green concentration camp tattoo was plainly visible. Chief Steward Phillippe froze in horror. He had heard about such things, but had never met a survivor yet!

"Is, is that what I think it is?" Asked an inquisitive and suddenly caring Chief Steward.

"Where do you come from? Are you German? Jewish?" Asked Monsieur Phillippe in rapid succession.

"Yes to all of the above, monsieur! We are German Jews and we were just released from Buchenwald concentration camp. Our uncle in Chicago is going to take care of us." Answered Erik, unable to control his emotions.

"You are a brave young man to take responsibility for your sister and yourself. I see from your ticket that you are in the second-class section. I am sure there must be some mistake. I could swear that there is a first class suite for the Goldmann family. I will personally escort you to your suite, monsieur." Replied a smiling Chief Steward Phillippe.

"But monsieur, I don't know if that is correct? I don't think my uncle would send us first class? I, I." Stuttered a confused Erik.

"No young man, I am sure about it. There is a suite reserved for you and your sister. Should you need anything else during your voyage, please do not hesitate to call upon me for assistance." Finished the Chief Steward as he grabbed the two small suitcases and showed them the way aboard the SS Normandie.

They walked up to the main sea deck and entered the fabulous main salon. The kids had never seen such luxury and opulence. The deep maroon carpet was so thick and luxurious that it felt like you were floating on air. Everything was painted in gold or silver. There was an air of magnificent extravagance throughout the entire ship. After what seemed like an hour, Monsieur Phillippe stopped in front of cabin number 7774. Erik looked down the seemingly endless corridor on either side of their suite, and was amazed by the length of it. Chief Steward Phillippe opened the door to the magnificent two-room suite, and handed them two keys.

"Here you are, your cabin! Should you need anything just ring that red button, and someone will be here within seconds. We are here to please you. We will be departing around six p.m. Dinner will be served around eight p.m. You dining area is section C, on the second deck forward, enjoy yourselves." Finished the Chief Steward as he left the room.

"Can you believe how beautiful this suite is?" Asked a suddenly alive Esther.

"I am sure someone made a horrible mistake and they will come and move us to the hold with the cattle!" Stated a nervous Esther.

"Don't worry, I am sure that even the cows sleep well on this ship!" Replied Erik, smiling as he did so.

"I hope you are right. I just don't want to wake up and find myself peeling potatoes again in the kitchen?" Answered Esther.

Both of the kids took the opportunity to thoroughly examine the spacious suite. They were shocked to find out that they had two complete bathrooms, two master closets; in fact two of everything. They even had stereophonic music throughout the cabin. They also had a small refrigerator filled with delicacies. A large assortment of cheeses, sliced turkey, butter, biscuits, cookies, jellies fresh fruit, and chocolates filled the refrigerator. Various drinks both alcoholic and non-alcoholic were also available. Everything one could wish for was there for the taking.

Both of the Goldmann's settled in, and took a nap in the luxurious beds. They were so exhausted that they fell into a deep and comatose sleep. The children were suddenly awakened by the loud noise of the main engines starting to move the ship away from the docks. The foghorn blew a long and mournful sound; it sounded like a giant beast of prey roaring in anger.

Erik jumped out of bed and glanced down at his watch. It was exactly 6 P.M. Both of the children looked at each other and decided to go out on deck to watch the ongoing festivities. It took them less than a minute to run up to the next deck and go outside. There were hundreds of passengers on deck gaily waving and smiling. Some of them were throwing brightly colored streamers and confetti as the ship slowly pulled away. Both the docks and the ship's railing were covered with colored paper. Other passengers were actively taking pictures of each other and of the docks.

Several bands were playing martial music on the docks, and on board the ship. The whole atmosphere was very pleasant and festive. It reminded him of Karnival(Mardi Gras) in Dueren during the happier times. It brought back a sudden feeling of nostalgia for his home in Niedergeier and his parents. How were they surviving? It was the first time in weeks he had thought of them. His sister noticed the sudden silence on his part and asked him if everything was OK? Not wanting to worry her, he lied and told her he was feeling a little queasy. She laughed at him, and told him he was a sissy.

Erik now stood near a lifeboat and silently looked towards land. The giant ship slowly pulled away from shore. Within fifteen minutes the SS Normandie was more than five miles away and the green English horizon was slowly disappearing in the night. Erik glanced once more, and wondered, *"Will this would be the last time he would ever see Europe again."* He became nostalgic and tears came to his eyes. As he wiped them away his younger sister noticed the tears and asked?

"Why are you crying, brother? You should be cheering and not weeping!" Said a suddenly adult Esther.

Caught by surprised, an embarrassed Erik replied!

"You silly girl, I am not crying. I just got something in my eyes. Perhaps some of the soot from the ships funnels? I will be fine, don't worry." Finished Erik as he turned and walked away from her.

The walk back to their cabin only took a few minutes, and when he opened the door, his sister had already caught up to him. They both marched in to their room and were surprised to find some beautiful new clothes laid-out on the bed.

"Oh my God!" Screamed a delighted Esther as she fondled the three beautiful dresses, shoes and stockings.

"This must be a mistake, these are not our clothes!" Exclaimed Erik as he looked at the three new suits, matching shirts and shoes in his closet.

He could tell that these items were of high quality by the feel, and the fancy labels. Someone had gone through a lot of trouble for them. Erik was still trying on his new wardrobe when a knock was heard.

"Hello, hello." Erik replied.

"It's me Chief Steward Phillippe." Replied the voice from the other side of the door.

"Just a second please, I am getting dressed." Answered an excited Erik.

It took him less than thirty seconds to get ready and rush to the door. There standing with a big smile on his face was Monsieur Phillippe.

"I am sorry to disturb you Monsieur Goldmann, but I thought you might be able to use these clothes. Dinner aboard the ship is formal, and I perhaps thought you did not have sufficient time to purchase evening wear?" Asked Monsieur Phillippe with a shy smile.

At first, Erik was somewhat perplexed by the statement. Never having been aboard a cruise liner before, he was not familiar with their habits, and did not know what to say or do.

"I am very grateful for your thoughtfulness, but I don't think we can afford such fine clothes. Our budget is pretty limited." Stated Erik looking back at his closet.

"Not to worry Mr. Goldmann, this is a present from Monsieur Richter, your dinner companion." Stated Monsieur Phillippe, smiling as he did so.

"But, but why would this gentleman wish to buy us such beautiful clothes? We do not even know him?" Replied Erik, as he waved his hand towards the closet.

"Monsieur Richter is a very wealthy American gentleman of German origin, and he is trying to assist you in any way he can." Finished Monsieur Phillippe.

"That is very generous of him, but how can I thank him?

Asked a somewhat perplexed Erik.

"Not to worry young Mr. Goldmann, Mr. Richter is your dining room companion, and you can thank him personally tonight." Answered Monsieur Phillippe as he backed out of the door.

Erik looked at Esther and she shook her head and smiled.

"Don't worry big brother, there are some good people left in the world. Lets enjoy our presents and thank him later on." Stated a very mature Esther.

At exactly 7:55pm a very strange sounding gong alerted them to the fact that dinner was being served. Mr. Phillippe knocked on their door and personally escorted them to the correct dining room. Both Erik and Esther were impressed by the long lines of well dressed ladies and gentlemen patiently waiting their turn. The headwaiter asked them for their room number and looked down a seating arrangement chart.

A few seconds later, the waiter guided them over to their table. It was a corner table overlooking the main deck and a view of the horizon. Sitting at their table was a very handsome gentleman. He was in his mid-fifties, tall and thin. He had silver hair and a pencil thin black moustache. Erik could tell that he was a very wealthy individual by the clothes he wore and the gold Cartier watch he wore on his wrist. His suit was obviously tailored made on Saville row in London. Erik thought to himself that, *"He looks like an American movie star."*

As they approached the table, he stood up and greeted them.

"Good evening Mr. Goldmann, and you too Ms. Goldmann. I am Abraham Solomon Richter, your dinner companion for the next seven days. I am really looking forward to our trip." Stated the friendly Mr. Richter.

Erik nodded his head in silence not knowing what to say or do. Mr. Richter pulled a chair and pointed to Esther. Slightly embarrassed she sat down and smiled at him. Erik sat on the opposite side of the table and stared at Mr. Richter.

"Thank you very much for your generosity. We don't know what to say or how to thank you." Blurted out a suddenly shy Erik

Goldmann. Esther stood up and reached across the table. She extended her hand to him and smiled.

"Yes, yes, yes! You are a very kind and generous gentleman." She stated, not wanting to stare at him as she did so anyway.

"You are most welcome. It is nothing. I wish I could do more for you someday." Replied Mr. Richter.

"By the grace of God, and my late fathers' wisdom, we were able to get out of Germany in 1932 and move to America. My father was a very successful jeweler, and he opened three shops within two years. He was very happy and content until his untimely death a few months ago. He lived the American dream, and never regretted leaving Germany." Stated Herr Richter, his eyes suddenly turning dark grey as tears gathered at the corners of his eyes.

"Erik thought for a second." Before replying.

"You are a lucky man. I hope that we can have such success in America?" Replied a now more confident Erik.

"I am sure you will young man, America is a land of great opportunity and freedom. All you have to do is work hard; have a goal and never look back. Whatever horrors you experienced in Germany, they are now behind you. Make today the first day of your new life and cherish the ideals of democracy. You probably don't realize how close we are to a World War?" Asked Herr Richter.

"Well no sir! We have been out of contact with just about everything for the past nine months or so. Is it that eminent?" Asked Erik, looking at his younger sister with concern in his eyes.

"Yes! Yes it is! Germany is probably going to launch a preemptive strike any day now. You are lucky to have escaped Germany when you did. When you get to America you must do everything in your power to help those poor souls left behind, and whatever you do become an American citizen as soon as possible." Stated Herr Richter with a flourish.

"Of course we will! We will do everything in our power to help our parents, relatives and friends. Becoming an American citizen will be our main goal." Replied Erik, his chest bulging in pride.

"That kind of attitude will help you in life, and don't ever forget those left behind. Let's not talk politics and eat our dinner. Tonight we are having Lobster-tails, a Nicoise salad, steamed baby carrots, green beans and a wonderful potato salad. And if you eat all of your dinner we will have an assortment of cakes, ice cream and sherbet! How does that sound?" Asked Herr Richter, smiling as he did so.

"Don't worry Monsieur Richter, I am sure we can devour everything you put in front of us." Replied Erik pointing to his sister as he did so.

Chapter 29

War in the Atlantic

The next twenty-four hours had been filled with promenades on the decks, games of shuffleboard and wonderful meals with Herr Richter. The days were filled with great moments of pleasures and enjoyment. Never in their hectic lives had they experienced such bliss and harmony. They had almost forgotten the horrors of Buchenwald; it seemed like a bad dream. The only bad reminder was that appalling green tattoo on their arm. Whenever they took a shower, that horrible memory would flash back in to their consciousness. No matter how hard they tried, they could not wash away the green numerals on their arms.

A sudden change of course woke up both of the Goldmann's. The ship's engine was no longer quiet; it was revving at a high rate of speed and the ship was zigzagging across the Atlantic at top speed. A very loud alarm bell was heard throughout the ship. It was a persistently piercing and annoying ringing. People were heard screaming and running outside in the corridor. Erik jumped out of bed and looked outside. Dozens of passengers were scrambling up and down the stairwells with no particular place to go. Finally Monsieur Phillippe, out of breath and panting came to their door. He was wearing his life preserver, and held a large flashlight in his hand.

"Hurry, hurry! Put on your life jacket and follow me! Quickly now!" He almost screamed at them.

"What is going on Mr. Phillippe?" Asked a concerned Esther.

"I don't really know, but we have orders to have a practice abandon ship drill! However I believe it is more serious than that. I heard on the BBC radio this morning that Germany had invaded Poland yesterday and that France, Belgium and England were at war with Germany!" Stated an excited Mr. Phillippe.

"Did you say war? Do you think we are in some sort of danger? Are the Germans going to sink us?" Asked an incredulous Erik?

"No, I don't think so, but the Captain of this ship is not taking any chances. The SS Normandie is the fastest passenger ship afloat; I don't think any German naval ship could catch us. After all the SS Normandie is now a French naval vessel. In time of war the command has reverted back to the French Navy. We are now considered a ship of war, and not a passenger ship." Finished a now very serious Monsieur Phillippe.

As they gathered around the lifeboat on 'C' deck, Herr Richter appeared next to them and gleefully said.

"Isn't this fun? Such excitement? Common on children don't be scared, nothing is going to happen to us. The Normandie can cruise at between 28-33 knots; the fastest German U-Boat, can only do 18-20 knots on the surface! They will never catch us!" Finished a very confident Herr Richter.

His confident mannerism had a soothing effect on the Goldmann's and everyone else around them. The crew responded in a very professional manner and this also had a calming effect on all the passengers. After five minutes the passengers were released to return to their cabins, and the drill was terminated. However Erik noticed that some crew- members were now painting all of the portholes with dark grey paint. Additionally, signs were placed on certain doors prohibiting them from being opened during the hours of darkness. The ship was rapidly converting itself from a peacetime pleasure cruise boat to a naval auxiliary ship of war.

There still was an air of excitement throughout the ship. As the passengers returned to their cabins, most of them talking about the war, the boat drill and what might happen to them. Esther and Erik quickly returned to their cabin, only to be greeted by Monsieur Phillippe.

"Children, please listen to me. The next time we have a drill it may be the real thing and you won't have time to gather your belongings. Be prepared at all times. Should the alarm sound again have an extra set of warm clothes, socks, shoes close by.

Don't panic and follow instructions! Is that understood?" Stated a serious Monsieur Phillippe.

The sudden reality of war made them anxious and nervous. Erik started to say something, but thought better of it and just stared at the Chief Steward instead.

"I don't mean to scare you, but it is always best to be prepared?" Finished a concerned Monsieur Phillippe.

Both of the kids silently looked at the Chief Steward before Esther finally said something to him.

"We thank you for your help Monsieur Phillippe, but I am quite confident that my brother Erik is capable of taking care of us. He has done so for the past year, and I am sure he can continue to do in the future." Stated a suddenly adult sounding Esther.

This powerful statement on her part caught them off-guard. Esther was growing up! *"Thought Erik, as he stared at his little sister."*

"Well that is very kind of you Esther! I will make sure nothing happens to us. Thank you for your confidence and support." Replied a now smiling Erik and Monsieur Phillippe.

The Chief Steward left their cabin smiling. Erik started packing some warm clothing and his rain gear just in case. Esther nervously watched him; without saying a word. After a few seconds of staring at Erik, she started doing the same thing. Within five minutes each of them had all they would need packed in their small suitcase standing near the front door. Erik finally said.

"I guess that's about all we can do for now? What do you think Esther?" Asked Erik?

"Yes I guess that's all!" Replied Esther walking towards her bed.

"I am really tired and this continuous swaying is making me sleepy. I am going to take a short nap before dinner; why don't you do the same?" Asked Esther as she flopped down on her bed.

Erik stared at his sister and was amazed to see her sleeping already. It had taken her less than ten seconds to fall asleep. She had a girlish smile on her face, and seemed to be without a care in the world. Erik was suddenly tired himself; he glanced at his watch and it was nearly five-thirty. Dinner was not until eight p.m.; that would give him plenty of time for a nice nap before dinner. He set his alarm clock for seven-thirty and promptly fell asleep.

His sleep was interrupted by one continuous nightmare after another. He dreamt about Niedergeyer, and his parents, the long train trip to Buchenwald, Herr Ludwig, the camp Kommandant, Oberst Koch, the trip to Geneva, Southhampton etc. It was as if he was watching a black and white newsreel of his life. His nightmare was interrupted by the alarm clock. It was exactly seven-thirty.

"Come on Esther, get up and get dressed. We can't keep Herr Richter waiting." Stated Erik as he waggled his finger at his sister.

Exactly twenty-five minutes later the dinner gong sounded. Both of them made their way up to the dining area. Herr Richter was already there waiting for them. The Goldmann's were getting accustomed to his daily presence, and really enjoyed his company. They almost looked upon him as a substitute father.

All of sudden Erik had a crushing feeling in his chest and collapsed in his chair. He began sobbing uncontrollably. The gravity of the situation finally caught up with him, and he felt very vulnerable and scared. His sudden and shocking action caught every one by surprise. Herr Richter and Esther were quite concerned and reached out to him.

"Are you OK? Asked Herr Richter.

"What is wrong brother?" Inquired his sister, with a pleading look in her face?

Erik stared at them for about ten seconds without saying anything. He needed time to gather his thoughts and regain his composure. He took a deep breath and reclaimed his self-control. He stared at both of them and quietly said.

"I am sorry for my outburst. We have been under incredible stress for almost a year, and I simply had some sort of uncontrollable anxiety attack. Look across the room; sitting over there is a man who looks exactly like Colonel Koch, the camp

Kommandant of Buchenwald. For a few seconds I imagined they were coming to get us again." Stated a panicked looking Erik.

It was the fact that we survived Buchenwald and everything else; only to possibly be taken away or sunk in the middle of the Atlantic was more than my brain could endure! I am better now, thank you!" Stated a now calm Erik.

His statement was not well received by Esther. She stared at her brother and started to cry. She was silent except for the long stream of tears running down her face. Her sobs were getting louder by the minute.

"Now, now, now! Don't worry we will make sure that nothing happens to any of us. I will personally guarantee that you get to New York on time! I will protect you as if you were my own children." Stated a kind and gentle Herr Richter.

Erik stood up and embraced his sister. They hugged each other for more than a minute; Erik bent down and kissed Esther on the forehead. She quickly and quietly stopped sobbing and resumed her position at the table.

"Well now children, let's have a wonderful dinner and not worry anymore about the war, or anything else. I have looking forward to this dinner all day, and I am not going to let some bad dreams spoil our evening." Finished Herr Richter as he too sat down.

After a sumptuous meal of veal, rice, asparagus, onion soup and a delicious chocolate soufflé, they were all ready for a walk around the deck. The ship was clipping along at over thirty knots, and the wind was coming in from the north; this combination made the huge liner sway from side to side. They had to hang on the side of the railings to keep from being swept overboard. After ten minutes of intense battering they all decided to go back inside.

"Let's all sit in the lounge and have a coffee, chocolate or a nice cup of soothing tea?" Asked a concerned Herr Richter.

"That's a great idea, I could really use a cup of hot chocolate about now." Replied Erik and Esther almost in unison.

The lounge was nearly full of passengers, but there was a cozy booth in the far corner, near the bar. The waiter promptly took their order and returned less than five minutes later with their steaming hot cups of chocolate. Everyone sat around sipping and enjoying their beverage. After a few minutes of silence, the conversation returned to the impending war. It seemed as if everyone in the lounge was talking about the war.

"Well what do you think Herr Richter; will America enter in to the war?" Asked an inquisitive Erik?

"Well I don't think so right now. England, France and the rest of the Europeans have very large armies and can probably take care of themselves for now. However, there is no way that an American citizen of our present day Republic, or for that matter any other government can "Abdicate" his or her responsibility. Nor can we deny the self-evident truth of evil, as demonstrated by that Bavarian Corporal, now or in the future.

Herr Richter continued. "Fascism is a force against human decency, and must be eradicated and destroyed at all costs; regardless of the rat hole they live in; whether it be in Germany, Italy or Spain or any other place on earth. It is our duty to help those who can't help themselves, or through circumstances cannot or won't change their future.

We must be the standard-bearers and lighthouse keepers of Democracy and freedom. Regardless if the cost in human suffering and pain is more than we can stand; we must march on and conquer evil. Our 'Statue of Liberty' must always be there, lit to greet, all those souls seeking liberty. We must reflect our true values and encourage all freedom seekers around the world.

We are citizens of a great "Republic" and cannot escape our duty. We are obligated to protect, defend and if we must conquer all of those who are trying to destroy our liberties, ideals, and our independence. Future historians will judge all of those who pretended to be liberals, but in fact were cowards, traitors and collaborators.

Had all the weak and liberal leaders of the world stood together under one united flag of democracy; listened to Winston Churchill, we would not be where we are today!" Stated Herr Richter in a firm voice.

Erik looked at Herr Richter and reflected before replying.

"I think I understand what you are saying. Freedom is part of our soul and our life, and we cannot renounce our responsibilities? Is that correct?" Answered Erik.

"Yes, yes! You understood exactly what I was trying to say. For a young man of your age, you have a grasp of the situation." Replied Herr Richter with a big smile on his face.

Ether just sat there, not knowing what to say or do. She just stared at both of them. She finally spoke.

"I am not quite sure what you men said, but I think I understand? We basically can't let them get away with it?" Replied Esther, slightly embarrassed by her ignorance.

"Oh don't worry little one, I will explain it to you later on in our cabin. However, I do think you understand the concept." Replied Erik in a serious tone.

"I am so pleased that you children understand what is going on in the world today. You are the future, and without you fighting for our liberties and independence; we are doomed to failure." Stated Herr Richter in a solemn tone.

"I am sure we will do our best. We have already experienced the evils of fascism, and we are not anxious to ever see it again. All we want is to see our parents and relatives again." Replied Erik as he got up from his comfortable chair.

They bid Herr Richter a good evening, and returned to their room. Esther was slightly confused by the whole speech, and just grabbed Erik by the sleeve and hung-on.

The walk back to their cabin was done in silence. Both of them were somewhat exhausted by the events of the day. It was wish to go straight to bed and sleep well without interruptions. Just as they were undressing, someone knocked on the door.

"Who is it? Asked a somewhat annoyed Erik.

"It's me, the Chief Steward Monsieur Phillippe. I have a surprise for you. Please open up!" Replied the steward in a pleasant voice.

"OK, Monsieur Phillippe I will be right there." Replied Erik as he tried to run to the door.

Monsieur Phillippe stood in front of the door with a large dessert cart. It was filled with every imaginable dessert. To include fresh strawberries and cream, a lemon sponge cake, raspberry tarts, a chocolate mousse and so on, and so on.

"Thank Sir! I don't know if we can eat all tonight?" Replied a grateful Erik.

"If you cant' eat it all, just put it in your refrigerator, and maybe you will finish it tomorrow!" Without any further comment the steward left them alone.

It did not take them long to scarf down many of the delicacies. However they were so full, they saved a majority for the next morning. They crawled in to bed and hoped that everything would not come out during the night.

Chapter 30

Return to Aachen

Back in the Present

The ride to Köln was very slow. Traffic was almost to a standstill due to a major four-car collision on the Autobahn near the Kerpen area. For a change, conversation was kept to a minimum. It was as if all the men had enough talking for one day. When they approached the **Bahnhof** (Train station) area in the city center, Jeremy finally spoke.

"We need to retrieve your car, but not get ourselves in a pickle again. There is a good possibility that some of your evil friends are still hanging around. Let's approach with caution. What do you say?" Stated a concerned Jeremy.

Both Dieter and Cameron agreed in unison. Cameron spoke next.

"Don't you think we should have some type of plan in the event of trouble? The last time I came here, the shit hit the fan with a vengeance. I want to be prepared this time." Replied Cameron.

"Good idea." Stated Dieter as he pulled off the main street and parked in an alley near the disco.

"Dieter I want you to park your car near the main exit facing outwards, in case we have to get out of here in a hurry. Keep the motor running and wait in the car. Cameron and I will approach his rental car from opposite sides and scope out the neighborhood. Dieter, don't move until we are safely in the car and moving towards the Autobahn. Also everyone make sure that your phones are charged up and operating!" Stated Jeremy in a bossy manner.

Both men agreed, and prepared for the entrance to the underground parking area. Dieter drove his car to the entrance, and the other two men quickly got out without making any noise. Dieter pre-positioned his Mercedes as instructed. Cameron took the right parking entrance and Jeremy the left one. Both men stealthily walked in to the structure. Cameron pointed to Jeremy trying to tell him that his car was on the right side. Jeremy acknowledged and started walking over to Cameron.

The very dusty BMW was sitting exactly where Cameron had left it. It was completely covered in a fine powder. Cameron approached the vehicle, and looked inside. Everything appeared to be the way he left it. He started to grab the door handle and Jeremy screamed at him.

"Don't move! Step away from your car. Step away from your car now!" Blurted out Jeremy looking very serious.

"Cameron, you were the last one to drive your car? Correct? Then why are there fingerprints on the dust near the door handles and trunk? Someone other than you has been messing with your car?" Go tell Dieter to park at least one hundred meters away from the entrance and tell him to call the German *Feuerwehr* (Fire Department.) and *Polizei* (Police). This does not look kosher, there is a wire going in to your fuel tank from the rear brake light. The moment you step on the brake pedal, an electrical current will set off the fuel tank and then, Kaboom!

"I am sure someone has tampered with your car." Stated Jeremy after he very carefully checked the car over.

Cameron walked out to the entrance and instructed Dieter what to do. Dieter parked his car at the end of the block and followed Jeremy's instructions. Dieter started to walk back towards the entrance when both Cameron and Jeremy came running out of the building.

"Get back! Get back! The car is rigged to explode. Wait for the Polizei! Shouted an excited Jeremy.

All three men ran to the opposite corner of the block and waited for the cops to show up. It took less than two minutes for the first unit to respond, and within five minutes the whole neighborhood was overrun with cops and fire engines. Jeremy waived them down and explained the situation. The senior German officer called for the bomb disposal unit.

While waiting for them to show up, the German cops were giving Jeremy the third degree. Jeremy had enough of this type of questioning and whipped out his red diplomatic passport. The red passport impressed the German official and he backed off. Within five minutes the bomb disposal unit showed up with their very large bomb hauling truck in tow. They first off-loaded a tracked miniature robotic device. It was the newest on the market and it had the capability to sniff -out any known explosives in the world.

Everyone seemed to stop breathing, as the small tank like device crept in to the garage. Inside the command vehicle, the bomb incident commander was moving a small radio controlled joystick. The robot approached the vehicle from the right rear. The close circuit television camera zoomed in on a wire sticking out of the gas cap. The wire ran parallel to the trunk lid and disappeared inside the car.

Inside the command post the bomb disposal expert smiled when he saw the crude device.

"No problem Hans! Just put your blast suit on and cut the wire. That should solve the problem, don't you think?" Stated the overconfident bomb expert.

"I guess so? Are you not worried about a booby trap with a reverse current tripping device?" Asked Hans, as he was putting on the blast proof suit and helmet.

"No, I don't think. They are not usually that clever, but just in case be sure to ground the cable." Replied the supervisor.

The bomb technician replied, "OK, boss!"

Once again everything came to a standstill as the bomb disposal specialist walked in the garage. The robot stood back and videotaped the whole episode. Meanwhile Cameron, Jeremy and Dieter stayed near their car and hoped for the best.

Hans approached the BMW, wire cutter in hand, and checked out the entire exterior area. Everything seemed to be in order, except for the wire from the taillight to the gas tank. He remembered to ground the wire before he cut it.

"Hello Command Post, this is Hans. Everything appears OK,

and I am going to cut it on the count of three! Standby! One, two and three."

Those were the last words that Hans ever spoke! The car was booby-trapped. The moment Hans cut the wire, a different electrical circuit was activated, and the detonator set off. Over four hundred pounds of military issue

C-4 explosives, and twenty-five gallons of gasoline were detonated.

Hans never knew what hit him. They never found his body. The largest piece ever recovered was less than three inches in diameter. The concussion was so great that the entire front of the building collapsed on top of the garage entrance. Flying debris killed two other officers, who were standing out in the street near the entrance. The entire neighborhood shook like it did during WWII, when a thousand Allied planes bombed this same neighborhood into oblivion.

Jeremy, Cameron and Dieter were uninjured but badly shaken up. Due to the enormity of the explosion, total chaos dominated the street. Fire department personnel were trying to put out the multitude of small fires started by the blast. Search and rescue experts were combing the area for survivors. The cops were trying to rescue their comrades. Everyone was moving at once in different directions. Finally, a middle-aged battalion chief fireman blew a very large and extremely loud air horn. Everyone stopped where they were.

"Halt, halt, halt!" He screamed as loud as he could.

It had the desired effects, he wanted. All of the different squads stopped doing what they were doing and quickly returned to the command post for instructions.

"Gentlemen please! Let's have some order! You are all running around like a bunch of chickens with no heads. Lets all take a breath and calm down a little. We can't help anyone like this!" Stated the irate battalion fire chief.

All of the different crewmembers were assigned specific duties. Group leaders were allocated and given exact tasks, which they in turn gave to particular officers. Within minutes they began to accomplish them in a less disorganized fashion; with an emphasis on safety rather than speed. The whole operation began to look like a military operation, rather than a brawl.

Although the scene began to look like a more controlled enterprise, the **Kriminalpolizei Inspector**, began questioning Jeremy, Cameron and Dieter once more. He was very suspicious of the strange circumstances surrounding the explosion. He was particularly interested in the reason why anyone would want to kill them?

"So tell me, why does anyone want to kill you? Whom did you piss off?" Asked the inspector.

Jeremy thought about his answer, before he replied.

Jeremy replied. "We don't really know inspector. My cousin is a world famous reporter. He is currently writing an expose on the resurgence of Fascism in Europe. Maybe that has something to do with it! He was recently kidnapped by them and barely escaped with his life."

"This very well could be the answer. We need to stay on top of this! We lost three good men today and someone will have to pay for it!" Replied the obviously irate Inspector.

After fifteen more minutes of extensive questioning, all three men gave the inspector their information and asked permission to leave the area. Although not quite satisfied with the situation, the reluctant inspector gave his approval. They quickly returned to Dieter's car.

Dieter said.

"Wow! That was some explosion? What do you think it was Jeremy?"

"Most likely C-4 military explosives. Maybe related to those rogue American soldiers that we heard about earlier in the week. Those guys were selling guns, rockets, and explosives to the Nazis?" Answered a pensive Jeremy.

"But why was there a wire in the gas tank and not a simple detonator?" Asked an inquisitive Cameron.

"Actually I think the gas tank was a sort of primitive timing device that is commonly used by terrorists all over the world. Once the brake pedal is depressed it sends a current through the wire. Simple, but effective." Replied Jeremy.

"Primitive Hell! There was nothing primitive about that explosion! They knew what they were doing and wanted to ensure that no one survived!" Stated an angry Cameron.

Cameron said. "We should get out of here and go check on the girls. I have a bad feeling about his whole affair. If they are crazy enough to do something like this broad daylight; they might to the same in Niedergeyer.

Within minutes they were cruising on the Autobahn towards home. Dieter was pushing the pedal to the metal. He was driving so fast that even Jeremy had to tell him to slow down.

"Slow down old friend, otherwise we will never get there alive." Jeremy stated as his knuckles turned white from squeezing the dashboard!

"I am very anxious to get there, I have a bad feeling about this." Stated Dieter, as he slowed the Mercedes from one hundred and forty miles an hour to a comfortable one hundred per hour.

Cameron said. "I am going to call the girls and warn them to be on the lookout for anything suspicious."

Cameron dialed the home number and the line was busy, busy! He tried Ingrid's cell number and it too just rang and rang. Which meant that someone was talking on the cell and couldn't or wouldn't answer the phone. He then decided to call the Niedergeyer Chief of Police at home, and ask him to go check on the girls. The home number rang, rang, but no one picked it up. Cameron tried the cell number and it too just rang. *Could it be that Ingrid was talking to the Chief of Police?* He thought to himself.

Maybe she was somehow notified and was trying to find what was going? Cameron tried all the numbers again in the next thirty minutes and always got the same response. He informed Dieter and Jeremy of his lack of success and urged Dieter on. As the vehicle approached the entrance to Dueren, Ingrid finally answered the cell phone.

"Hallo, hallo wer ist das?"*(*Who is there?) She asked?

"It's me honey, are you OK?" He hurriedly asked?

"Yes we are fine. I thought you guys were going to go to Aachen for the night? Where are you now?" She asked?

Cameron suspected there was something wrong, but he could not tell what exactly? Instinctively he knew to lie to her.

"Yes we are in Aachen, and won't be back until tomorrow around noon. I have some business to take care of and I need your father's help. I will call you when we leave. Bye." Finished a concerned Cameron.

"Pull over, pull over Dieter!" Shouted Cameron to a shaken Dieter.

"What is going? What is happening? Why are you shouting at me?" Replied Dieter as the car skidded to a halt near the shoulder.

Cameron explained his misgivings and suggested that they sneak up on the house and check it out before making a grand entry. Dieter and Jeremy both agreed. Dieter suggested they use the back road and park in the forest behind the house. They all agreed, but Jeremy brought up the point that they might need wheels to get out of town in a hurry. Everyone concurred that they would drive to the crest of the hill behind the house, and coast down with the engine turned off.

Dieter noticed several lights on in his house, and at least four cars parked in or near his driveway. This activity concerned him and every one else. His car glided to a stop less than twenty yards from his backyard. Jeremy pulled his pistol and Cameron armed himself with a tire iron. Dieter had a large five-cell flashlight in his right hand and could use it as a weapon.

Dieter waived at them and pointed to the back gate near the corner of his yard. All three men stealthily approached the house. They opened the back gate, which was totally covered in green ivy, and walked into the back yard. From their location they could see the kitchen area.

"Sshussshhh! We can sneak in this way and no one will be the wiser." Stated a very agitated Dieter.

As the men approached the back deck near the kitchen, voices could be heard arguing in the kitchen.

"*Nein*! *Nein* it's not a good idea! You can't do it here; there will be too many questions! Killing three at once will raise too many eyebrows. Not even you can cover up a murder of this caliber in such a small village!" Stated an unknown voice in the dark.

"I guess you are right, but Dieter and his son-in-law are causing way too many problems for us. How do you think Kate and Ingrid will react?" Asked another darkened figure.

"Quite honestly I don't really care anymore. The mission comes first! If they can no longer stand the heat; we will have to take matters in to our own hands! Realistically we must protect him. Both Kate and Ingrid are the weak link in our mission. They have become excess baggage, and maybe it's time to eliminate them, but what will Dr. Juergens say? He won't approve of this?" Whispered the anonymous voice.

"He will have to go along with the program. This eliminates any trace of his and their past." Replied another unknown voice.

Cameron thought he recognized the last speaker, but he was not quite sure yet. There was too much background noise. They needed to get closer. *Did he hear right?* Were they talking about murder? Cameron whispered to Dieter.

Cameron asked? "Isn't there another way in the basement? I seem to remember a basement staircase that comes out in the kitchen?"

"Ja, that is correct! We must however be very quiet, the basement is full of junk and we might make some noise!" Replied a concerned Dieter.

Dieter led the way through the back door. They had to ease their way through a multitude of old junk. Once the initial entry was made, the path cleared up rapidly. Dieter crawled up the stairs on his hands and knees. At the top of the stairs a kitchen light shone through the glass door. Dieter was able to put his head against the glass door, and listen to the conversation.

"Cameron, Cameron! Come up here quietly. Do you recognize any of these voices? My hearing is not as good as it use to be!" Asked an excited Dieter.

Cameron snuck up to the door and listened! He heard several

voices he recognized. Herr Baume, the (New) Chief of Police, Dr. Juergens, the village doctor, Reinhold Niederholz, the village ex-**Burgermeister** (Mayor), Ingrid and Kate and some else from his past. He could not quite make out the voice, but he was sure he knew it! The voices continued to speak in the kitchen.

"We need to do something now! We cannot wait any longer. It might be too late! Now is the time for action!" Screamed the unknown voice in the corner of the kitchen.

Cameron, Dieter and Jeremy had heard enough. Whatever was being hatched in the kitchen was definitely not good news for them. It was mutually agreed to withdraw from Niedergeyer and go back to Aachen.

After sneaking back to their car, the ride to Aachen was made in almost total silence. Both Dieter and Cameron were shocked and terribly upset. The news that possibly his wife and mother-in-law were involved in some type of conspiracy against them was unimaginable. A thousand scenarios swirled in his exhausted brain; none of which had happy conclusions.

Dieter strained his memory; that mysterious voice was so familiar and yet he could not quite place it. Maybe it would come to him later on in the evening. He knew whom this person was, but he was not able to focus just now.

Dieter took the downtown cut-off and drove to the hotel. They went to the bar and ordered some drinks. They brought their drinks to a corner booth and sat down. He asked the waitress if Heinz-Gunther Schmidt was in, but he had apparently gone for the evening.

Cameron decided to call his boss Jerry for some moral support and advice. Cameron was totally confused and could not think straight. Too many factors were interrupting his train of thought. He needed some comforting words from an old friend; an unbiased recommendation from his boss was needed.

Cameron was able to wake Jerry up. Once again, Cameron forgot the time difference and manage to wake up Jerry at 04:45 A.M. Jerry was in his usual grouchy mood. However, when Cameron started recounting the events of the past few days; Jerry just listened and remained silent.

"Are you sure? Can it be that your wife is somehow involved in this? I find it very hard to believe? She was always so non-committal and reserved." Stated an unhappy and concerned Jerry Kunstoff.

A tired and alarmed Cameron Clark replied. "I don't really know anymore! Things have been so hectic since my kidnapping, first by the Nazis, then by the Israelis. Thank God for Jeremy and Dieter. I could not have survived my adventures without their assistance."

"It sounds like things are rolling along. Do you want to come back now? Or do you want to see this puzzle to its conclusion? I will back you up either way. My only concern is your safety! Whatever you do, please send me some notes on the whole story!" Stated an uneasy and worried Jerry Kunstoff.

"Well boss, let's just play it by ear. I feel pretty comfortable at this stage of the game. I will keep you up to date of any new developments. In either case my cousin Jeremy will know as much as I do, and he can always keep you informed in the event of a disaster! He has been a great friend and a perennial ally throughout this ordeal." Finished a much-relieved Cameron Clark.

Jerry had a way of calming him down. He felt a great sense of relief and renewed confidence. Jerry was almost like a father confessor to Cameron. Cameron suddenly felt liberated and released from this heavy burden.

The three men sat down in a booth; in a dark corner of the hotel bar. Cameron mentioned how much this current adventures reminded him of Erik Goldmann and the Nazis of sixty years ago. Time did not seem to alter the events of history.

Cameron stated. "Nothing much has changed!

The Nazis had tormented Erik and his family; and now Cameron was also besieged by the same foe. Cameron hoped for a better ending than the Goldmann family.

The three men consumed a large quantity of beers and schnapps. After a few hours, a more jovial and relaxed mood permeated the hotel. All of a sudden, Dieter became more outspoken and started to cry. His tears turned into sobs, and he finally broke down.

"I am sorry, sorry Cameron! I have a confession! I have not been telling you the whole truth. There is something in our past that has haunted me my whole life. I was so ashamed, I just could not tell anyone!" Finished a very emotional Dieter.

"I am sure it can't be that bad, Dieter." Replied a caring and concerned Cameron Clark.

"Oh yes, yes indeed. It's not something to be proud of. I always thought I could hide our past, but it has come back to haunt us so many years later." Finished a still crying Dieter.

Jeremy interrupted the conversation by attempting to console a distraught Dieter, but to no avail. Dieter cried like a newborn baby with a wet diaper. Jeremy finally gave up.

"You both have no idea what the truth is? Many years ago I did something, which has haunted me forever. I was in love and I thought I was doing her a favor. Do you understand Cameron? I lied to everyone and it will now cost me my family!" Stated an inconsolable Dieter.

"Dieter it can't be that bad. You don't have to tell me, but it will probably relieve some of your depression. I promise I won't be judgmental. I love you and I care very much for you. You are a good and decent man." Finished a caring Cameron.

"Do you remember me telling you that my first child was born in March, 1945 in Mainz am Rhein? Well all of that was true enough, but that child was in fact my daughter Ingrid! My wife was in fact already two months pregnant when I married her. She had been engaged to SS General Peter von Hagen. His first wife, Patricia von Hagen, the mother of Wolfgang was killed during an air raid in 1943. Kate and Peter were due to be married in January 1945, but he tragically died on the Eastern front. She came to me and asked if I would do her a favor? I was always in-love with her and took the opportunity to marry her. The war helped us hide the birthdays and wedding date. After my wife and I returned home, we had to hide her real name, and who the father of her first child was." Finished an emotional Dieter!

"Wow, wow and wow! Does Ingrid know who her real father is and how old she really is?" Asked Cameron?

"Yes of course! But I have treated her like my own for all these years, and no one else knew the truth; except Kate of course." Finished a severely distraught Dieter.

Cameron stuttered and replied! "Let me understand you correctly. My wife Ingrid is the daughter of an SS General and a high-ranking Nazi mother? No wonder she now has those fascist sentiments! How can I possibly explain any of this to my daughter?

"I am sure it is difficult for you, but believe when I say, it's also difficult for me!" Answered Dieter.

"Not only that, but my best friend Wolfgang is the son of the SS General and a half-brother of Ingrid? No wonder the Mossad kidnapped me and thought I was somehow involved in this witches brew?" Replied a stunned and speechless Cameron.

"My god Cameron, you are really screwed! No matter what you do, someone is going to be pissed at you forever! I would not want to be in your shoes cousin!" Replied Jeremy; grinning as he did so.

"Don't be such a wiseass, this is serious stuff! My whole life is revolving through my head and this is the only thing you can say? Asshole!" Replied a very upset Cameron.

Chapter 31

Going to War

1939 Finally in America

The remainder of the sea voyage had been full of excitement, fear and pleasure. On at least three occasions, over-zealous lookouts had spotted non-existent U-boat periscopes and the ship took radical evasive actions. Although the thought of being torpedoed by a submarine was extremely nerve-racking; it somehow added an element of dread and excitement to this adventure.

Erik had never experienced such horror; even Buchenwald was not as frightening as the thought of drowning in the North Atlantic. Erik's sister was more ad-ease and did not seem to particularly mind the adrenaline rush, one way or the other. She was very stoic and happy at the same time. Esther rarely concerned herself with the daily routine. At times, it appeared that she had suffered such trauma in Buchenwald that nothing could ever affect her again. Erik worried about her long-term physical and mental effect. He hoped that coming to America would help her regain her normal physical and mental perspective on life.

When the SS Normandie finally arrived in New York; there was a great deal of fanfare and jubilation. Martial music was playing on the docks. The fireboats were shooting large streams of water in the air. Passengers and crewmembers were throwing colored confetti overboard. It seemed as if everyone was happy to be alive, and grateful to be in America. Thousands of family members, friends and complete strangers, stood on the dock and waived handkerchiefs, scarves and hats at the docking of the SS Normandie.

Monsieur Phillippe and Herr Richter came by their cabin and

bid farewell to them. Erik could tell that Herr Richter had grown fond of them and he was finding this parting very difficult. Both Monsieur Phillippe and Richter gave them their home address and phone number; in the event they should ever need their assistance again.

The children had also grown attached to both Monsieur Phillippe and Herr Richter. They too were very sad to see them go, and had grown to care and respect the men. At times they had almost forgotten their real parents, and slipped into this make believe world of fantasy that was the SS Normandie. The love and care bestowed upon them by their *ersatz* (Make believe) parents; allowed them the luxury to fantasize and deny their past.

Despite all of this, Esther and Erik were extremely excited to finally arrive in New York. They could not identify this strange sentiment; it was similar to the feeling they had on their birthday. They were excited and yet anxious at the same time. They did not know what to expect from their uncle and his family. Their parents had very rarely spoken about uncle Samuel; other than he was a rich American uncle who owned a chicken farm.

The skyline of New York was most imposing to them. Never in their lives had they seen such grandeur. Everything was extremely large and elevated. The Empire State Building loomed above them all. So many giant structures, packed in a compact area. It was something out of a Hollywood movie. After a few moments, of intense staring, they eventually regained their senses and looked down on the dock.

Erik and Esther walked down the long gangway, not knowing what the future would hold for them. They were pleasantly surprised when they saw a large sign that read:

Erik and Esther Goldmann, welcome to America!

Maurice Goldmann held the sign high above his head and was waving a large American flag in his other hand. Erik noticed that his uncle resembled his father very much, except he was seven years older. They both waved and shouted at each other, but due to the large crowd and loud music very little could be heard. They waited in line until it was their turn to walk down the gangplank.

287

As they approached their uncle, Erik had a mixture of strong sentiments. He was very happy to be in America, and yet saddened at the fact that he had left his real family behind in Germany. He had mixed emotions, but hoped that Esther could handle the ordeal better than he could.

His uncle was extremely tall, and yet the family resemblance was uncanny. Uncle Samuel was well dressed and had the appearance of a wealthy businessman. As they grew closer, Samuel shouted!

"Welcome to America! Welcome to America! I hope you had a pleasant voyage? How was your passage?" Asked a concerned uncle Samuel.

"Thank you, thank you it was wonderful. But we are glad to be in America! Have you had any news from Vater?" Asked Erik?

"I am glad you had a wonderful trip, but I have not heard from you father in almost eight months. He was the one who informed me of your detention in Buchenwald. A neighbor managed to smuggle a letter out through Holland. I have not heard from him in a long time. I tried sending him some letters, but they were all returned." Stated Samuel, a sad look on his face.

"I will make it my main goal to reach my parents. We were fortunate to meet some really nice Red Cross personnel in Germany and Switzerland. They promised to try and help us. I will try to write them when we get to your house." Stated an adult sounding Erik.

Uncle Samuel informed the children that they would be spending the night in New York and catching the 'Silver Bullet Express' to Chicago early tomorrow morning. Erik and Esther were excited to ride on a train all the way to Chicago. They had heard so much about the great American trains. They had no clue that it would take them almost two days to arrive in Chicago.

Spending the night at the Waldorf Astoria with their uncle Samuel was an even a greater treat. They would have the opportunity for some one on one time with him. Just as they expected, the hotel was magnificent. The front lobby was very ornate and ostentatious. White marble counters, and floors throughout the entrance. The main hall had crystal chandeliers and a beautiful crimson carpet in the lobby area. A nattily dressed porter took their luggage up to their room. Their rooms were even more luxurious than the SS Normandie. They took a quick shower and changed into something more comfortable.

Although they were exhausted, uncle Samuel suggested a carriage ride through Central Park. They had heard so much about the park and couldn't wait to see it. Uncle Samuel was waiting in the lobby for them and greeted them with a smile.

"Hello children, I am so happy you are here with us now. Starting today you life will be filled with pleasure, love, and excitement! I promise to take care of you as if you were my own children!" Stated a somewhat saddened uncle Samuel.

"That is most kind of you. We in turn will do the same. Thank you again for getting us out of that horrible place." Replied a teary eyed Erik. Esther did not reply directly, but simply nodded her head in approval.

As they stepped out unto the street, a beautiful while carriage pulled by two magnificent black horses pulled up to the curb. The driver an elderly black man dressed in a long dark grey trench coat and matching hat. He sported a magnificent well-trimmed white beard, and somewhat resembled a black Santa Claus.

· "Good evening Sir? What is your pleasure? Do you want the deluxe tour? A two -hour ride through the entire the entire park?" Asked the friendly driver?

"Yes, yes that sounds magnificent!" Replied Uncle Samuel, as he helped the children aboard the carriage.

The friendly coachman, whose name was Adam, introduced the two horses as "Springer and Spaniel."

"That is an odd name for such beautiful horses. Why would you name them Springer and Spaniel?" Asked an inquisitive Erik.

"Well, I love all animals, and I use to have two dogs with the same name. They were killed in a tragic car accident about the same time I acquired these two beautiful horses. I figured I would always remember my dogs if I called the horses with those names! Does that make sense?" Asked the old man with an inquiring look on his face?

Erik paused for a second and eventually nodded his head. The old man talked the entire two hours, he sounded like a recording; he hardly took a breath between sentences. He explained in great details all of the pertinent and trivial facts concerning Central Park and the surrounding neighborhood. As the carriage returned to the hotel the old man asked them if they had fun?

"Yes, yes! It was very exciting. I did not know how big it was. It was extremely interesting, thank you Adam." Stated an excited Erik.

"Well children it's getting late and we should have dinner before we go to bed. What do you say? After all, our train leaves very early, and you should be rested. Don't you agree?" Asked uncle Samuel?

Both of them answered in unison! The long day had in fact exhausted them and they were ready for a warm bath and a good night sleep.

Uncle Samuel took them to the hotel restaurant where they had a marvelous dinner and relaxed prior to going to rest. The dinner was as good, if not better than the meals aboard the SS Normandie. They politely excused themselves and went straight to bed. Uncle Samuel decided to stay in the bar, for a few minutes and have a nightcap.

They were both awakened by a loud knock on the door. Erik looked at the alarm clock and saw that it was already six a.m. Their train left at seven and they had to hurry. They were ready and out the door in less than ten minutes. Uncle Samuel was patiently waiting in the lobby. He had a taxi waiting and they sped off towards Grand Central Station.

They arrived exactly at six-forty a.m. and had sufficient time to grab a quick breakfast in a coffee shop.

They boarded the 'Silver Bullet' and immediately found their stateroom with the help of two very friendly Pullman conductors. Erik and his sister had a private berth with a toilet, and Uncle Samuel had the neighboring suite. They agreed to meet up for an early lunch. Samuel felt comfortable enough to allow them the freedom to explore and search the train, without interfering.

Erik and Esther took advantage of this opportunity and truly discover every nook and cranny of the Bullet. In less than an hour they had walked up and down twice and were ready for a nap. Uncle Samuel as usual punctually knocked on their door, and took them to lunch as promised.

As the gentle rocking motion of the train hypnotized them, the day quickly sped into night. Time was in fact moving faster and faster for them. The whole journey from Germany to here was, but a blur. So much had happened in the past weeks that it almost seemed like a dream. Erik expected any moment to wake up back in Buchenwald with Kapo Ludwig screaming at him.

"Chicago, Chicago, Chicago." Brought him back to reality. The conductor was shouting at the top of his voice!

"We are ten minutes from Chicago," he repeated. Uncle Samuel punctually knocked on their door and prepared them for the arrival.

Erik and Esther were nearly at the end of their odyssey. Almost two weeks had passed, and six thousand miles later since their departure from Deutschland. So much had happened to them, and they were not quite sure what to expect in America.

Samuel could feel the tension and tried to comfort them as best he could. He hugged both of them and told them not to worry. He promised them peace, tranquility, and prosperity. They looked up at their tall uncle and sighed. His comforting words were well received; yet they still felt some fear and anxiety.

"Come on! Come on! Let's get off the train and meet the rest of the family!" Shouted an anxious Uncle Samuel.

Chapter 32

Chicago 1939-1941

The entire Samuel family was at the station ready to welcome them home to America. There was Mrs. Sally Goldmann, Samuel Jr., and little Anna Martha the youngest of the bunch. Anna was extremely tall for her age, although only ten years of age she was as tall as Esther. She obviously took after her father, and so did Samuel Jr. Erik thought to himself, *"What do they feed the kids in America?"*

Both Erik and Esther were very self-conscious of their height difference with the rest of the Samuel family. Uncle Samuel noticed the envious looks and said.

"Don't worry children, six months from now you will all be the same size. The diet here is healthier than where you came from. Once you get enrolled in school and start playing sports again you will grow like a weed." Stated uncle Samuel with a smile on his face.

That simple statement seemed to make them feel better. Erik really hoped that his uncle was correct. He never truly realized what nine months at Buchenwald had done for his physique. He was of average height before the incarceration; this trauma had stunted his growth, but he hoped he would resume growing again shortly.

They all got into uncle Samuel's big four door red Cadillac, and headed down the highway towards the outskirts of Chicago. Erik was amazed at the size of the buildings, and the distances between properties. The further they got from the city, the larger the farms got. Forty-five minutes later they made a hard right turn down a wide dirt road. The sign over the entrance said: "Golden Chicken Ranch."

There was one thing that Erik and Esther noticed right away; it

292

was the rather pungent odor coming from the large wooden buildings that lined each side of the road. The closer they got to the huge house, surrounded by a large pond and graceful trees, the worst the smell got. Uncle Samuel noticed how uncomfortable the children were.

"Don't worry, you will eventually get use to it! We have over a hundred thousand chickens, and we produce around fifty thousand eggs a week. It takes a while to adapt to the smell. Don't worry, within days you won't even notice it!" Said uncle Samuel with a wink.

"I am sure we will!" Replied a less confident Erik, pinching his nose as he did so. Esther simply held her handkerchief to her face and gagged.

The house was immense by German standards. It was four stories high, with both a basement and an attic. It had ten bedrooms, six baths, two kitchens, and two of everything else. The first thing that Erik noticed was the temperature inside the house; it was a comfortable sixty-eight degrees and smelled wonderful.

"Well as you see children, we have installed a cooled air filtration system. It also has a scented fresh pine odor throughout the house. We are the only building within our property that is completely free of that smell. We have to work here, but we do not want to smell like chickens all the time." Waving his arms in a grandiose manner, uncle Samuel pointed to the upstairs bedrooms.

Samuel stated to the children. "You will both have your own room, near each other, and you will not have to share a bathroom. Each of you will have your own space! I hope that is OK?"

"Great, great! We are very thankful uncle Samuel. Compared to where we came from, your home is like a palace. Thank you again for helping us!" Replied a teary eyed Erik.

They moved into their luxurious quarters and were happy to find that Aunt Sally had filled it with dozen of new clothes, shoes, shirts and coats. They each had their own desk, two closets and a large walk-through bathroom. Everything had been organized and well prepared in advance. Erik could tell that someone with great love and care had prepared their rooms for them. He sensed he would get along with his aunt Sally Goldmann. In many ways she reminded him of his mother.

Days turned into weeks, then into months. Erik kept himself busy by going to high school and working on the farm during the week. He started a soccer program at his high school, and really enjoyed the game again. It brought back memories of Niedergeyer and the good times he had as a youth.

On weekends he had found employment at a local aircraft plant as an assistant machinist. Although he was in his senior year of high school, he still managed to do all of his chores around the house and work twenty hours at the factory learning a trade. His life was so busy between school, the plant and his chores that time just flew by.

Just as Herr Richter had promised, life in America was good to him and Esther.

He had, but one goal in mind, to save enough money for his father, mother and grandfather. He estimated that he would need around five thousand dollars to buy their way out of Germany. He was so busy earning money that his personal and social life really suffered. His uncle had on several occasions offered to give him the money, but Erik insisted in doing it on his own. He felt that Uncle Samuel had done enough for them. He often pondered on his decision, but felt very strongly on this issue. He was the eldest Goldmann now and he had to make the decisions.

The outbreak of war on the European continent in September 1939 worried most Americans and especially President Roosevelt. He instituted many changes to the military and declared a limited state of emergency throughout the country. He and the Congress passed measures to augment our national defense budget and make long-term plans for a six million-man army. As many as eighty-four new training camps were being built, throughout the nation. Although America had not officially entered the conflict, we were preparing for the future.

As the months rolled by in Chicago, the war in Europe grew in intensity. Denmark and Norway quickly fell to the Nazi onslaught. In quick succession, the Germans rapidly overran France, Belgium,

Holland and Luxemburg. Within a year, Hitler dominated all of central Europe. England was the only defender of democracy and bastion of freedom in that part of the world. Although America had not officially entered the war, it managed to supply England with most of her needed war goods. Officially America was a neutral power, but leaned very heavily on England's side.

On June 1941, Hitler made one of the biggest mistakes of his military career; he launched 'Operation Barbarossa'! Over two million German and allied soldiers marched into Russia. Although Germany and Russia had a mutual non-aggression pact, Hitler bowled through Russia like General Sherman through Atlanta. By early December over a third of Russia was in German hands, and the Nazis were within ten miles of Moscow. Once again Russia's best friend and ally came to her defense, 'Mother Winter.' It was one of the coldest winters on record, and the Nazi armies were stopped within viewing distance of the Kremlin.

The Goldmann family followed the news of the war in Europe with great interest. They were all aware of the possible significance of a defeated Russia. It was a common topic at the dinner table every evening. Erik in particular was an avid history buff and followed every battle with great interest. He analyzed and read newspapers, journals, magazines, and listened to the radio almost every day. Over time he became quite an expert on the war, its battles and their leaders. He had a giant map of Europe in his room and followed the war with colored pins. If anyone in the family wanted to know anything on the war, they simply had to ask Erik, and he would help them.

Erik graduated high school in 1940 and worked full time at the aircraft plant building bombers for America. Working full time, he was able to earn a decent salary and by December 5th, 1941 he had the required $5000.00 to set his parents free, or so he thought. At dinner that evening, he brought up the subject to his Uncle Samuel.

"How do I get the money to the Nazis, Uncle Samuel?"

Uncle Samuel asked Erik? "Do you have the required amount?"

Erik replied. "Yes I do, and I want to go to Cuban Consulate

General as soon as possible and take care of this matter. My parents have suffered so much, and I only hope that it's not too late."

"I still have the number of the Consulate General in my office. If I remember correctly his name is: Dr. Diego Ferreria Adorante. Let's go and call him right now." Replied an excited Uncle Samuel.

"Hello, hello? Is this Dr. Diego Adorante? My name is Samuel Goldmann and you once helped me to free my nephew and niece from Germany! Do you remember me?" Asked an excited Samuel.

"Yes, yes of course, Mr. Goldmann! I hope everything went well for you?" Replied the friendly Dr. Adorante.

"Yes all is well, however we are trying to liberate my brother, his wife and her father now! My nephew has the required five thousand dollars, and we would like to start negotiation as soon as possible. Could you be of further assistance?" Asked Samuel.

"But of course my friend. Come by tomorrow at ten o'clock and we will get started. Do you remember where we are located Mr. Goldmann?" Asked the Consulate General?

Samuel answered. "Yes I do! It is near Madison Avenue and Sixteenth Street? Is that correct?"

"Exactly! I will see you then, goodbye!" Finished Dr. Adorante.

"I am so excited, I can't wait to go. Let's go and tell Esther." Erik ran upstairs to tell Esther of the good news.

Esther was overjoyed by the news. Deep in her heart she had given up all hope of ever seeing her parents again. She now had a glimmer of anticipation, and prayed that she might see them again.

Erik woke up at six o'clock, ran down stairs and ate a quick breakfast. He was the only one in the kitchen, and debated whether or not to wake up his uncle. He looked at his watched and it was only six-twenty. No! He decided to wait another thirty minutes or so. Time went by so slow, the minute hand acted like the hour hand. He finally could not stand it anymore and ran up the stairs to his uncle's bedroom, just as Samuel was coming out the door.

"Slow down! Young man! It's only seven o'clock! We have plenty of time! Lets go back down stairs and have some coffee? OK?" Replied a smiling uncle Samuel.

"Yes, yes, yes! I am just so nervous. I can't wait! Please hurry!" Replied Erik, as he ran down the stairs.

Both men drank some coffee, and uncle Samuel had toast and a poached egg. Erik just paced up and down the floor. Samuel finally yelled at him.

"Slow down Erik, you are driving me crazy with your pacing. We will get here in time. Why don't you go outside and get the car ready?" Said uncle Samuel as he tossed him the keys to the car.

The ride to the consulate was made in almost total silence. Finally Erik could not stand it any more, and shouted. "Are we there yet?"

"Yes we are, Erik! Do you see that large grey office building on the corner? That is the Cuban Consulate.

The whole affair took less than thirty minutes to arrange. They provided all pertinent information and gave Dr. Adorante the five thousand dollars. He in turn promised to get back to them as soon as he heard from the German Department of State. The ride home was not as cheerful as the ride to the city. Erik was extremely nervous; yet silent. Uncle Samuel did not wish to upset him, and also did not speak until they arrived at the house.

"All we can do now is wait for the Germans to get back to us. Don't worry everything will be fine." Stated Uncle Samuel as he walked towards the house and up the porch.

Erik was not in a speaking mood, and ran straight to his room. He ignored the entire Goldmann family who were waiting for him to say something. His sister Esther was waiting for him in his room.

"Well, well how did it go? Are we going to see our parents again? Did, did you give them the money?" Stuttered a confused Esther.

"I did everything I could! All we can do is wait! It is

completely out of my hands!" Replied an equally upset Erik, embracing Esther, as he did so.

They were both so emotional that they continued hugging each other for a full three minutes or more. They were both so physically drained, after this experience that they eventually collapsed on the bed and just lay there. Esther was the first to begin sobbing uncontrollably. Erik tried hard to maintain his composure, but was unable to do so. They both ended up weeping and reminiscing at the same time. The emotional outburst helped them to forget their sorrows for now.

Uncle Samuel managed to inform the rest of the family. They all wanted details, facts and he tried to fill them in, as best he could. Everyone in the house seemed to be on pins and needles, and very irritable. There was a certain amount of edginess in the air; like a moment before a thunderstorm when the air is heavy and full of static.

The rest of the weekend was filled with chores for the kids and cleaning house for mom and girls. It seemed like everyone wanted busy work to make to time go by faster. They were all trying very hard to forget what was really happening in Germany, and to the rest of the family. However, the daily news bulletins kept them on edge and frustrated.

Back in Washington D.C., negotiations with the Empire of Japan were not going well. President Roosevelt was still trying to come to terms with the Japanese. However the warlords in Japan had already decided to attack the United States and would launch a large naval armada to simultaneously attack Pearl Harbor, the Philippine islands and the British territories of Hong Kong and Singapore. An overwhelming force of both naval and ground forces would strike the Dutch territories of Indonesia and Malaysia.

Sally Goldmann got up early on Sunday, December 7th, to prepare an extra special meal for the family. She thought it might be a treat to eat turkey, rather than the usual chicken dinner. However turkey took a long time to cook, and she put it in the oven at around six a.m. Later on in the day, she decided to bake a pumpkin pie for the boys. She knew that the men really enjoyed her pies, and this might just the thing to calm everyone down. Suddenly and without warning, Samuel Jr. came running down the stairs and shouted!

"Turn, turn, turn on the radio! We are at war! Japan has attacked us! They bombed Pearl Harbor and sank all of our ships! Listen! Listen!" Shouted a nearly hysterical Samuel Jr.!

"What did you say? Asked a stunned Sally.

"Mom, we are at war! They attacked us!" Screamed an out of control Samuel Jr.

Sally turned on her kitchen radio, and they all heard of the horrible sneak attack on Pearl Harbor. Sally looked at her watch and the time was around one-thirty p.m., Chicago time. She tried to calculate what time it would be in Hawaii. One, two, three, four, five hours earlier! Yes, it was around eight-thirty Sunday morning in Honolulu!

The Goldmann's all gathered around the radio for the rest of the day. The attack was so unexpected and barbaric that the entire family was glued to a chair and did not budge for hours. It was incredulous that the Japanese could have attacked us while we were still negotiating peace with them.

They were so excited that they forgot all about the turkey. Sally had taken it out of the oven and saved it for a later time. At around eight p.m. they finally all sat down in silence and ate a wonderful meal. However due to the disturbing news of the day, no one seemed to be very hungry! There was absolute silence at the table, until Erik looked at his uncle and said.

"I am going down tomorrow and join the Army! I need to do something! I can't wait!" Blurted Erik in on long sentence.

"Why don't you wait and see what happens? They might not take you; you are not an American citizen yet?" Replied Uncle Samuel in a soothing and calm voice.

"I may not have my citizenship yet, but in my heart I am just as much an American, as anyone else. I am sure they will want someone with my language skills. I will go down tomorrow and enlist. I am sure that America will need every soldier they can get." Stated Erik in a firm and authoritative voice.

Uncle Samuel looked at Erik and said. "Well, if that's the way you feel, I can't and won't stop you. You are a grown man and I am positive you know what you are doing. Your father would be very proud of you if he were here."

Erik looked at his uncle, and nodded his head in silence.

"I will drive you down to the enlistment center in the morning. It's about a forty-five minute drive and we should all take it easy this evening. Tomorrow will be a long day for all of us." Stated Uncle Samuel in a fatherly way.

Uncle Samuel continued. "Well now that, all of that is settled, I think it would be a good idea for all of us to go to bed and get some rest."

Everyone understood his meaning and did not argue with him. Samuel Jr. started to say something, but Sally gave him a dirty look and he shut up like a clam on steroid. Samuel Jr. silently went upstairs to his room! The rest of the family followed Samuel to bed except for Esther. She lingered downstairs for another ten minutes or so. Eventually, a worried Erik went back down and found her still in the kitchen.

"What are you doing down here? Come on its time to go to bed!" Ordered Erik.

"I don't want to! I want to stay here and drink some milk! You can't make me go to my room!" Screamed an enraged Esther.

"Calm down little sister there is no reason to act this way! Everything will be OK!" Replied Erik in a stern voice.

Erik walked over to the fridge and grabbed a large pitcher of milk and poured his sister and himself a large glass. He remembered that Aunt Sally had baked some fresh chocolate chip cookies and brought some over as well. Esther looked at the cookies and started crying.

"I am, I am just not ready! I, I, I." Stuttered Esther as she ran upstairs and slammed her bedroom door. Erik stood there and pondered what to do?

Chapter 33

"You're in the Army Now!"

Erik followed her upstairs and confronted his confused sister. The first thing out of her mouth was.

"Are you going to leave me? I don't want you to go in the Army! Who is going to care for me? That's not fair! I don't want to be alone again! Please don't go! I will miss you so terribly much. I would not do this to you!" Finished a hysterical and out of control Esther.

Erik looked at his crying sister and realized that he needed to comfort her now. She was sixteen and very emotional. Most girls her age had raging hormones and an over-active imagination. She was confused and hated being neglected. It had taken her almost three years to stabilize herself in her new environment, and now her beloved brother was going away to war.

Erik reached down and gently patted her on the head.

Erik looked at his sister and said. "Do you remember when we were little, and you were afraid? I use to tell you stories to calm you down? Well now you are a big girl and a lot has happened to us. I will always be with you, and I promise to write you everyday. In return you must study hard and write me also. I will always be there for you, and Uncle Samuel and Sally love you very much as well. Don't worry, I will always protect you."

' Those comforting words seemed to somewhat calm her down, and within five minutes she was sleeping. Her body was finally relaxing. It wasn't a peaceful sleep; she tossed and turned the whole evening. Nightmares of Niedergeyer, midnight train rides and Buchenwald overwhelmed her thoughts and dreams. Eventually her body stopped trembling, and she fell into a deep sound REM sleep.

After a fitful night of tossing and turning, a loud knock at the door woke both of them up!

"Get up, get up it's time to go join the Army! You can't snooze now, get up, up, up!" Shouted Uncle Samuel in a laughing sort of way.

Erik jumped out of bed, took a quick shower and ran downstairs. His sister took her time and mopped around the room. Everyone else was sitting around the table having breakfast. The mood was somber and no one wanted to say anything to him. He finally broke the ice.

"Hey I am only joining the Army, not getting killed! I promise I will take care of myself and come back soon."

Even those comforting words did not seem to help matters much. They all stared at him and Aunt Sally started to cry.

Samuel looked at Sally and slowly shook his head from side to side. Sally immediately stopped crying, but continued whimpering.

Uncle Samuel finally said.

"Let's go Erik, I am sure everyone else in Chicago has the same idea! They might run out of soldier slots, before you get a chance to enlist!" He laughed and that seemed to break the ice.

The ride in to Chicago was a long one. It seemed as if everyone was on the road this morning and they were all in a hurry to join the Army. The Army recruitment center was at the local YMCA, near Twelfth and Grand. They had no problem finding it. Even though it was only nine o'clock in the morning, there was a line around the entire block. It seemed like every young man wanted to enlist. Uncle Samuel dropped him off and told him to call the house when he was ready. Erik waited for over four hours before he was able to see a Recruiting Sergeant.

"So you want to join the Army, do you?" Asked the obviously overweight, grouchy and exhausted Sergeant.

"Yes Sir, I do!" Replied Erik.

"OK then, fill out these forms and when you are done, go stand in line over there." Replied the still grumpy Sergeant.

It took Erik less than thirty minutes to fill out all the forms. He did as the cranky Sergeant told him to do and stood in line with the rest of the young men. Another half an hour passed by before he saw another tired and overworked clerk.

"Goldmann, Goldmann, Erik Goldmann!" Shouted a young officer from a neighboring office.

"Sir, yes Sir, that's me. I am here!" Shouted Erik and stepped forward.

Erik and the young officer went into a private office. Erik was given the bad news. Because he still was not a citizen, he could not volunteer for enlistment! However, he could go down to his local draft board and volunteer for the draft!

Erik looked at the officer and said. "So excuse me Sir! I can't join here, but my draft board can draft me today? That does not make sense?"

"Well I am sorry, but that's the current law!" Replied the overworked officer, as he dismissed Erik.

Erik left the Army recruitment center and took a taxi to the draft board office, which was all the way across town. To his horror a long line ran around the block. He quickly got his place in line; then called Uncle Samuel to inform him of these new developments.

Actually this line moved pretty quickly. His name was eventually called and he went before a four-man draft board committee.

"Well Erik, let me make sure I understand this? You are volunteering for the draft? Is that correct?" Asked the most senior board member.

"Yes, yes, yes! America is my country now and I wish to repay her for everything she has done for me, and my family. I won't be a citizen for another eighteen months or so, but I wish to do my part." Stated a proud Erik Goldmann.

"You are a very patriotic young man and I am sure we can help you. America needs citizens like you, and I am sure we will be able to assist you. Please step outside for a moment so that we may come to a decision." Said the senior member.

Erik replied, as he stood up. "Yes Sir, of course!"

Erik waited in the hallway for less than five, before he was called back in front of the assembled board.

"Erik Goldmann, you are hereby qualified **1A**, and are immediately eligible for the draft. Go outside to the clerk's office and he will issue you a set of induction orders! I would like to commend you for your patriotism." Stated the same senior board member.

"Thank you Sir! I will do my duty and proudly serve this country. I have never shown this to anyone else since I have been in this country, but I wish to let you know how strongly I feel about this Democracy." Erik slowly raised the sleeve on his left arm and showed them his green tattoo.

For a moment there was complete silence in the room. The four board members were speechless and simply stared at each other, not knowing what to say or do! Finally one of them asked?

"Is, is that what I think it is? Did you have that done in Germany?"

"Yes Sir! I was one of the lucky survivors of Buchenwald. My sister and I were saved by my uncle and brought to America. I have had a good life here and I wish to repay her in kind." Said Erik, as he stood up and started to walk out the door.

"We are proud to have you in our Armed Services and we are sure that you will make us proud someday!" Stated the senior board member.

Erik left the room and walked into the next office, where he had to wait forty-five minutes for his induction orders. Finally a young clerk called his name and handed him six sets of orders. Erik nervously grabbed them and looked at them. He was expected to report to Camp Croft RTC (Replacement Training Center), South Carolina, no later than December 18th, 1941. His orders allowed travel by train or bus, as long as he arrived no later than 0600 hours December 18th, 1941. Erik left the Draft Board building and called Uncle Samuel.

"It's me, it's me! I am in the Army now. Really, I was drafted today and I have to report to Camp Croft before the 18th of this month!" Shouted an excited Erik Goldmann.

It took Samuel less than thirty minutes to pick Erik up. The Draft Board was closer to his farm than the Army Recruitment

Center had been. All the way home, an excited Erik could not stop talking. He asked Samuel one question after another.

Samuel said. "Slow down Erik, you will get there soon enough! Let's go home and find out where this Camp Croft is? Did you ever ask them?"

"Actually no! I was too excited and I could not wait to tell you. I only wish Vater was here to share in my excitement." Finished a suddenly pensive Erik.

The fond memories of his family and Niedergeyer brought back childhood memories and he became silent. Samuel sensed that Erik was struggling within himself and decided not say anything. The rest of the trip was made in absolute silence. When they finally arrived at the house, Samuel asked a question of Erik.

"Are you going to say anything to the rest of the family? They all would like to share your excitement? I think it would be the right thing to do? Don't you?" Asked a rather pensive Uncle Samuel.

Erik calmly said. "I guess you are right, I am a little nervous to be truthful. I am overwhelmed by the whole affair, but I am sure I will be calmer tomorrow morning. Let's go inside and tell them everything."

As Erik entered his house, the entire family was waiting in the kitchen. They all started speaking at once; the din was almost beyond belief. One after the other they raised their voices in order to be heard. Finally Uncle Samuel raised his voice, and they all suddenly fell silent.

"Quiet now! Let the poor man speak his peace. Go ahead Erik, I am sure they will now show some respect for Private Erik Goldmann." Uncle Samuel spoke in an authoritative voice.

"Yes that's right, I was drafted into the United States Army. I am to report to Camp Croft on or before December 18th, 1941. I don't even know where it is, but I am sure I will find it. I am so excited! But first I must go to the Reception Center and get processed in, and tested like everyone else. I am very lucky that the Reception Center is right here in Chicago. It should not take more than three or four days, and then on to Camp Croft."

Finished an exuberant Erik.

Several days after the sneak attack on Pearl Harbor, Germany declared war on the United States. This event was very traumatic for the Goldmann's. They were proud Americans; yet had ties to Germany and felt conflicted by the whole situation. Even though they were Jews, their German roots were very strong, but after a decade in America they had become Americanized; however they still felt some familial ties to Deutschland.

Uncle Samuel sat them all down at the dinner table, and explained to them the ramifications of the Declaration of War.

On December 11th, 1941, Dr. Adorante called the Goldmann residence to pass on the bad news. The state of Cuba was an ally of the United States and therefore they declared was on Germany. It was no longer possible to negotiate any political matters with Germany. All diplomatic relations had been terminated; only the International Red Cross could possibly relay communications between the two powers.

Erik was totally devastated! All of his hopes and dreams were rapidly and suddenly dashed. His hard work and long hours were all in vain. The five thousand dollars were gone forever.

Dr. Adorante stated. "I will try to recover your money, but it is no longer in Chicago. We sent it on to Switzerland already, and the chances are very small of ever seeing it again."

Erik was shocked and chagrined beyond belief. All of his efforts had been for nothing. He started to say something, but realized it was useless to discuss it any further.

He hung up the phone and went upstairs to his room. He did not want Esther to find out. It would be too much for her to handle in one day. This was something he had to handle himself. She could never stand the separation from him, and now the permanent loss of her parents. He would wait for a more opportune time to tell her. Uncle Samuel came up to his room to discuss the phone call with Dr. Adorante.

Uncle Samuel tearfully listened to Erik. Samuel tried to comfort him, but the news was too horrible to bear. This was the only remaining hope, and he finally realized that he would never see his family again. He asked Uncle Samuel to please not discuss this with anyone in the family. He did not want Esther to accidentally find out.

Erik made up his mind to concentrate all of his efforts on his Army career, and hope for the best. After his three days at the Reception Center and not wanting to be late in reporting to the base, Erik left three days early. He took a train to New York, which took thirty-six hours or so. From there he took another connecting train the next day to Spartanburg, S.C. Arriving exactly thirty-four hours early at Camp Croft.

Erik took a taxi to the camp. As they drove up, he was amazed at the size of the camp; it took almost twenty minutes to drive around the perimeter. He could see dozens of neat wooden barracks, and a large parade ground and other buildings.

The MP at the front gate checked his orders; then escorted him to his company area. The Army had managed in a year to convert large areas of farmland into a giant military installation. The cantonment area was approximately 167 acres, and eventually was expanded to over 16,900 acres, which included an artillery impact area, firing ranges and a large training area.

Arriving over a day and a half early caused the company clerk to assign him to temporary quarters until he could be officially checked-in with the rest of the new recruits. He was in fact the first soldier in his company, 1st Platoon, Company "C", 1st Battalion, 7th Infantry Training Regiment. Most of the men in the 7th Regiment would learn the same basic infantry skills, however many others were trained to be members of various platoons, such as Heavy Weapons, Cannon, Antitank, Service and Headquarters etc.

The Company Clerk had assigned him to building 1409, which was in the northwest corner of the parade ground, near the base theater and the canteen. Erik did not know that it would be many weeks before he ever saw those two facilities again.

The first night was a memorable one to say the least. Army regulation required that a CQ (Charge of Quarters) and a Fire Guard had to be present when a barrack was occupied. Even though he was the only one in the building, he had to have two other soldiers watching him.

Private Erik Goldmann finally fell asleep around one a.m. Around two o'clock a very loud siren sounded. It was extremely deafening and could be heard throughout the base. It was a persistent tone and had distinct ring to it. The CQ and Fire Guard came running in Erik's room and did not know what to do. They looked at Erik and panicked!

"What do we do? What does it mean? I don't know where to go?" Stated both soldiers to a bewildered Erik.

"Well don't you think it means something bad? I have only been in the Army for two days, but I am sure it means take cover, or something similar to that. Don't you think? Is there a basement in this building? If there is, why don't we go down there, and wait until someone tells us what to do? Stated a confident Erik.

"That sounds like a great idea! The basement is at the other end of the building. Lets go!" Shouted the CQ!

All three men ran down the corridor, until they reached the staircase. The basement was directly under the stairwell. Thirty minutes later another siren sounded. This time the siren changed pitch, and lasted five minutes longer. The men assumed correctly that this was the all clear. Erik recommend to the CQ that he call the Company HQ and notify someone where they were, and that everything was OK!

"Great idea! You are pretty sharp for a private!" Stated the obviously overwrought CQ.

"Thank you Sir, it's just common sense." Replied a proud Erik Goldmann.

"Listen Private Goldmann, don't call me Sir! I work for a living. Is that understood?" Growled the CQ.

"Goldmann, Goldmann! What kind of name is that? German? Asked the somewhat nosy CQ?

"Well actually yes, it's a German name, and it means 'Man of Gold.' " Replied Erik, embarrassed by the question.

"I kind of suspected that? What is a Kraut doing in the US Army?" Asked the now pushy CQ."

"For your information, I was born in Germany and came over here in 1939 as a refugee. I volunteered for the draft, and the rest is history." Replied the now confident Erik.

"You volunteered for the draft? Seriously? Volunteer? Why?" Asked a confused and bewildered CQ?

"Yes I did! It's the least I can do for the country that gave me back my freedom, and taught me the spirit of democracy! I will be a citizen in eighteen months, and until then I will do the best I can for my adopted country! Don't you know how lucky you are?" Replied Erik, staring down the CQ.

"All I know is that I was drafted against my will! I can't understand you? I guess everyone has a calling in life? You would not catch me volunteering for this Army or any Army!" Finished a visibly upset CQ.

The next morning, the company First Sergeant came by the barracks to compliment the CQ for his action on the previous evening. However, the CQ was honest enough to tell him about the Kraut who had led them to the basement, and suggested calling company HQ.

"You mean he knew what the siren meant? How? We wanted to test the recruits, and he was the only one who reacted properly. Let me talk to him, this kid is sharp!" Stated the First Sergeant with a grin.

Erik was somewhat confused by the request to report to the First Sergeant. As far as he knew, he had not done anything wrong. He walked over to the 'Company' area and entered the building. He immediately saw a sign on the wall, "First Sergeant." Inside the room, on the right of the doorway, sat a young soldier behind a large desk. The young soldier could not have been more than eighteen, but he already had Corporal stripes.

"Excuse me Corporal, my name is Goldmann and I was told to report to the First Sergeant." Replied Erik.

"Hold on a second, I'll see if he's free! Replied the Corporal.

The Corporal returned and showed him into the office of the First Sergeant. The Corporal whispered into Erik's ear the proper way to report at attention. Erik did exactly as he was told, and stood attention in front of the First Sergeant.

"Private Goldmann reporting as ordered, First Sergeant!" Snapped Private Erik Goldmann.

At first the First Sergeant did not respond; he simply kept looking at his paperwork. Thirty seconds elapsed before he said, in a booming voice.

"At ease soldier! Take a seat." Pointing to a large wooden chair next to his desk. Erik did as he was told.

"Well Private Goldmann, you did a hell of a job last night! The base commander had ordered a simulated air raid to test our response. Out of all the new recruits, you were the only one to respond correctly! I am proud of you! It also makes me look good, since I am the only company that notified higher HQ. Job well done Private!" Stated the smiling First Sergeant.

"Thank you Sir!" Replied Erik, overwhelmed by the compliment. After all he had only done what came natural to him.

The First Sergeant asked him if he was born in Germany? "Well yes, as a matter of fact I was born in Niedergeyer, near Dueren." Replied Erik, wondering where the First Sergeant was heading with this line of questioning?

"So you are a Rheinlander from the Eifel region." Replied the First Sergeant in German!

Erik was caught by surprise. He had no idea that the First Sergeant spoke German, but was amazed that he too had a *Rheinische* (Someone who came from that region) accent.

"Yes, I too was born in Germany. My name is Ryan Kreutz, formerly known as Reiner Kreutz. My parents migrated from Monschau in the Eifel in 1911 when I was seven years old.

Erik was too dumbfounded to speak. He just sat there, and looked like a deer in the woods. He did not know whether it was appropriate for a private to speak with the First Sergeant on a personal basis. Sergeant Kreutz broke the ice by extending his hand. Erik stood up and shook the hand of the man that would teach him more about being a soldier than anyone in his life.

First Sergeant Kreutz was a Regular Army soldier, RA as they were called, rather than a conscript or a reservist. He had enlisted in 1923 and nearly had nineteen years of service. He was a professional soldier and did not particularly care for draftees. They really had to prove themselves to him before he would accept them.

"I understand you volunteered for the draft? Is that true? Why would you do that? Your papers indicate that you are not yet a citizen? Why did you rush to act so rapidly? Is there some ulterior motive?" Asked the inquisitive First Sergeant.

Erik hesitated at first, but he once again lifted up his shirtsleeve and revealed his green tattoo. The First Sergeant did not say anything to Erik. He reached under his shirt and pulled out his dog tags and showed it to Erik. Beneath his service number was the religious inscription. It said Jewish! Erik stared at the dog tag and nodded his head.

"You are a very brave and intelligent young man. The Army is going to need people like you, now that we are at war with Germany. I have a policy of awarding temporary "Acting Corporal stripes" to those that deserve them. You have shown courage and patriotism, and I am now awarding you, your acting Corporal stripes. If you do a good job in the next thirteen weeks, I will make them permanent upon graduation from Basic Training. How does that sound Corporal Goldmann?" Finished a jovial First Sergeant.

"Thank you Sir. I am not sure I deserve them, but I will do my best to honor your trust in me. However, I do have one simple question? What does an acting Corporal do?" Replied the overwhelmed Erik Goldmann.

First Sergeant Kreutz answered Erik. "You basically follow my directions and your Drill Sergeants orders. I will have the young Corporal issue you a set of orders and give you a copy of the Drill and Ceremonies Manual. The rest you will learn as you go along. Any more questions Corporal? Your Drill Sergeant, will be reporting in two days. Staff Sergeant William is his name. I am sure you two will get along fine."

First Sergeant Rainer Kreutz was correct in every way. Staff Sergeant William was a great leader and taught Erik how to be a good soldier and a Corporal. Erik was amazed how fast time flew by. Between early morning reveille, physical training, marksmanship, field maneuvers, drill and ceremony and everything else in the world, time flew by. As the weeks turned into months Erik became more and more a professional soldier like the First Sergeant and SSG William. One week before graduation, 1SG Kreutz called him into his office.

"Private Goldmann you have done an outstanding job in the past twelve weeks, and SSG William has recommended that you be promoted to the permanent rank of Corporal. The Company Commander has endorsed my recommendation, and as of today you are officially a Corporal. Congratulations!" Stated the 1SG as he stood up to shake Erik's hand.

"Thank you very much. I appreciate the confidence in me." Replied Erik, still not believing the honor bestowed upon him.

"Now what about your future? Have you thought about what you would like to do? You have great language skills that the Army could use? Obviously German and French as well, I think you would be ideally suited for the Intelligence career field! What do you think?" Asked a smiling 1SG.

"Actually I thought along the same line of thinking. I think I would be a great asset to any field intelligence unit. However, I would like to work with a maneuver unit and not get stuck in some office. As soon as I become a citizen in three hundred and ninety seven days, I would like to apply for Officers Candidate School (OCS). What do you think?" Replied Erik.

"I think it's a great idea! I believe they now have a program to expedite your citizenship application? I will look into it and let you know before you graduate next week. What do you say?" Asked the 1SG?

"Thank you very much for all your help 1SG! Replied a grateful Corporal Erik Grossman.

1SG Kreutz kept his word, and upon graduation Corporal Erik Goldmann was sent to the Military Intelligence Training Center (MITC) at Camp Ritchie, Maryland, which was a former National Guard installation. Camp Ritchie was set up to train various types of intelligence personnel.   Once their initial schooling was completed they were then sent on to other camps for further training or overseas deployment.

Erik satisfactorily completed his advance training and was now promoted to Sergeant. He had graduated top of his class at Camp Ritchie, and Sergeant stripes were his reward. His next assignment was at Fort Hunt, Virginia where a joint Prisoner of War (POW) interrogation unit was established. This combined Army-Navy unit was established to assist in the mutual cooperation between these sometime opposing intelligence services. Its primary purpose was to interrogate and process high-ranking German officers. Initially, these German POW's were mostly U-boat and Naval officers, but as the war dragged on, different types of POW's were captured and brought to Fort Hunt.

Sergeant Goldmann really enjoyed his time at Fort Hunt. It was a pleasant environment, plenty of time off, and a very interesting job. After a period of six months had elapsed he was promoted to assistant team leader, which earned him another stripe. He now was a Staff Sergeant, and could pretty much dictate his work schedule. His Lieutenant, 1LT Brian Jonas, was very dependent on Erik and allowed him a great deal of freedom. After all Erik was the only native born interrogator on the team and was very good at his job.

Towards the end of 1942 Erik had served nearly a year in the Army and was anxiously awaiting his notification for US citizenship. Strangely enough on the eve of the anniversary of the attack on Pearl Harbor, SSG Goldmann was sworn in as a citizen of the United States. It was one of the proudest moments of his young life, and it afforded him the opportunity to go to Fort Benning, Georgia to attend the ninety-day Officer Candidate course, better known as OCS. He immediately called his uncle and sister and informed them of his new status.

His family was very proud of him and wished him well in his future career as an officer. Despite the passage of time and continuing efforts on their part, no information was ever heard from his parents. He swore to himself that he would never give up.

Many years later he would find out the eventual fait of his father.

Upon graduation he was immediately sent to Camp Sharpe, Pennsylvania. Camp Sharpe was a staging area for personnel being deployed to an overseas combat theater. Here they received additional combat training, and were formed into smaller and more manageable interrogation squads. Most individual team members did not know their final destination until they were halfway across the Atlantic.

2LT Erik Goldmann was no exception. After twelve long days at sea; he was called into the captain's office and handed a large sealed yellow envelope.

Chapter 34

From Bad to Worse

Back in the Present

The men were still sitting in the hotel bar; by now they were feeling no pain. The copious amount of German beer and Schnapps had dulled their worries. However Dieter suddenly raised his head from the bar and looked straight into Cameron's eyes and said.

"I have one more confession Cameron. Your daughter Jennifer is not really your birth daughter! She is the daughter of Ingrid and Dr. Juergens!" Stated a still intoxicated and crying Dieter.

The silence in the room could have been cut with a knife. It was as if all of the alcohol had evaporated from their blood stream. All of the men were stone sober. Everyone's eyes focused on Dieter's mouth waiting for the next sentence.

Cameron exploded! "What do you mean? Jennifer is my daughter, and always has been! How can that be?"

Dieter replied. "Do you remember when your wife came to visit us nine months or so before Jennifer' birth? She had an affair with Dr. Juergens and got pregnant. At the time it was felt that it would be better to make you believe that you were the father, and when the time was right, you would be told the truth!" Continued a still crying Dieter.

"I, I, I don't believe it. Why, why? She is my daughter, and I will always love her! This can't be, I don't believe it!" Finished an emotional Cameron.

Dieter continued. "Dr. Juergens was being groomed for political office, and it was felt that a daughter and granddaughter from pure Aryan parents would increase his chances in any future election. The time is getting closer for him to run for office. The political climate is now more receptive in Germany. A recent article in Das Bild (German paper) newspaper showed that as many as forty-five percent of Germans feel that Hitler had some positive influences in Germany. They are ripe for some hardcore right-wing politicians."

"What kind of crap is that? Jennifer is a pure Aryan Nazi child? Please don't tell me I've been a patsy for all these years? It just goes to show that the Mossad was right in kidnapping me? Everyone here but, Jeremy and I are the only non-Nazi in our group of family and friends!" Stated Cameron with a deep sorrowful voice, as he stared at his cousin seeking solace and comfort.

Jeremy started to say something, but thought better of it. After all there really was nothing that could reassure Cameron in his current situation. Jeremy got up and sat next to his cousin; putting his large arm over his shoulder. Cameron was touched by the gesture, but was in a total state of shock and could not utter a single word. His mind raced over the past eighteen years trying to pick out indicators, but nothing really stood out.

"Now what? What do I do? Is my life over? My job?" Stated a totally dejected Cameron. His head slowly shaking from side to side, as large tears trickled down his face.

Dieter and Jeremy stared at him not knowing what to do or say. They both had no solutions for this tragic event. Dieter was particularly touched by this drama. He felt partially responsible for this incident, and did not really know what to do?

"Cameron I don't really think we can solve anything this evening. Let's all go to bed and we shall talk about it again in the morning." Stated a now suddenly awake and sober Dieter.

Jeremy nodded in agreement and all three men got up and retired to their respective rooms. Cameron walked up to his room like a zombie. He was totally mesmerized and devastated by the events and was not conscious of his actions. He did not even try taking his clothes off. He just fell into his bed like sack of potatoes.

Cameron attempted to fall asleep, but all of the actions of the past few days kept him awake. His consumption of large quantities of alcohol would have normally put him to sleep, but the incredible revelations kept him wide awake. He tossed and turned until three a.m. Eventually fatigue and alcohol overcame his restlessness, and he fell into a deep sleep; interspaced with horrible nightmares about Adolph Hitler, Hermann Goering and concentration camps.

The loud banging on his door awoke him from his terrifying ordeal. The entire bed was drenched in sweat, and Cameron was covered in vomit. He must have puked during the night, but the alcohol level kept him from waking up. He yelled at Dieter.

"Hold on, I will be right there. Just give me a minute; I need to take a quick shower. I will meet you down stairs in a while." Stated a foul smelling Cameron.

The hot and steamy shower finally brought him back into a state of semi-consciousness. Cameron slowly regained his thoughts and memory. They all had way too much to drink last night, and they were going to pay the price today. Fifteen minutes later he stumbled down the stairs, and joined the other men in the restaurant for breakfast.

As Cameron sat down at the table, he observed that both Dieter and Jeremy also had massive hangovers, were not very talkative and had their heads propped up by the their palms.

Cameron said. "Someone has to say something! What are we going to do? This will end up killing all of us.

Dieter replied! "You are absolutely right! We must confront the devil, before he swallows us up. It's my entire fault; I never saw it coming! Had I only known, I could have prevented it? I was like an ostrich for the past sixty years. I put my head in the sand and hoped that they would not swallow me up! It's time to do something!"

Jeremy looked at the other two men and felt sorry for them. They were both in a horrible predicament. No matter what they did, their spouses would hate them; or even worse they might turn them over to their Nazi friends. He suddenly said!

"You guys are royally screwed! It doesn't matter what you do, the Nazis or their masters will have a major hard-on against you! You won't be able to sleep in peace for the rest of your life!" Stated a gloomy sounding Jeremy.

"Thanks buddy! With friends like you, who needs enemies? Don't be so negative and give us a positive idea. You are supposed to be the intelligence expert. Think!" Stated Cameron, almost screaming at his cousin.

For a moment, there was complete silence. No one said anything for at least sixty seconds. Suddenly Jeremy looked up and shouted.

"Mossad, the bloody Mossad! Remember they owe us big time. We need to somehow get them involved in this mess. If anything goes wrong; we can always blame them for the whole mess." Stated a smiling Jeremy, waving his arm like a symphony conductor.

"That sounds feasible, but we have to be very careful. After all we are not dealing with amateurs. They have a long memory, and have a history of being very vicious." Replied a careful and somewhat skeptical Cameron.

"Don't be such a silly girl! If we do it right, they will fall for it, hook, line and sinker! We must set a trap that cannot be traced back to us, and let them sink the hook." Replied a confident Jeremy.

"That sounds like a possibility, but who can we trust to act as a go between for us? Do you know anyone who you can trust?" Asked a somewhat skeptical Dieter Johannes?

"Yes and so do you! Your current boss, Jerry Kunstoff is the perfect candidate." Replied a self-assured Jeremy!

"Do you think he will go for it? After all it's very dangerous? He has a lot to lose if this blows up in his face." Stated a somewhat somber Dieter.

Cameron replied with enthusiasm. "He is the only man in the world who could pull this off, without being too obvious about it. He has contacts all over the world and could even use my friends in Paris. That will help to cover our tracks!"

"OK, OK Cameron! You know him better than anyone; call

him and make the arrangements. This has to be done as soon as possible and without delay." Replied Jeremy.

"I'll call him immediately, however you two need to disappear for a while. Don't disappear forever? If I need to contact you, I have to be able to reach you in a few hours. Why don't you go and visit our old friend Colonel Perrin in Paris? He has contacts with the French press and he too could drop a bomb from the French point of view. If they all do it at the same time, no one will know where the true source is. Besides, I am sure he would be glad to see you again Jeremy?" Stated a smiling Cameron.

"Great idea! The train station is right across the street and we could catch the TVG Express to Paris. From Köln or Aachen, it's less than five or six hours. Just hang around Colonel Perrin's bar or the restaurant, and I will be able to contact you. After all you two are good at hanging around bars." Finished a now smiling Cameron.

"That is a wonderful solution for us, but what about you? What are you going to do? Where are you going to hide for the next few days?" Asked a concerned Jeremy Grant.

"Don't worry friend, I have a spot that no one will ever find me, and I will be safe. It would be better for your safety, that I not divulge anything to anyone!" Replied Cameron a big smile on his face.

"Good idea, just stay in touch." Replied Jeremy as they walked away from the restaurant area.

Dieter and Jeremy went back to their rooms and packed for the trip. In order to confuse those looking to do them harm, they left a dummy forwarding address in Vienna. They made a point of telling the clerk that they would be there for at least a week.

Cameron got on the house phone and spoke with Jerry Kunstoff for over an hour. Jerry understood what had to be done and agreed to contact his old friend General Gabriel Golan, formerly of the Israeli Defense Forces. General Golan had at one time been the chief of the Mossad and owed Jerry several favors. It was decided that the general would mysteriously release information to several Jewish tabloids in Tel Aviv and Jerusalem.

They in turn would write scathing stories about the revival of Fascism in modern Germany. The general would drop a dime on all the participants in Niedergeyer, Dueren, Aachen and Köln, including their names and how they were connected.

Cameron realized that by doing this, he probably would ruin his chances of ever getting back together with his wife, and possibly losing his daughter forever. He felt very strongly that this was the only way out. Ingrid had chosen her battlefield, and he was determined to win the war.

Jerry Kunstoff would release a similar story a few hours after the Israeli newspaper did. Cameron also decided to really stir up the shit by going back to his Aachen office and have them do a follow-up story in German. In order to protect his plan he had to make sure that the Israelis published their story first.

Once the story was on the international AP (Associated Press) and the Reuters wire, it was guaranteed to get everyone up in arms. Cameron did not know who he could trust or not trust in his office, but he was determined to go for broke.

Cameron walked to the corner, outside the hotel, and used a public phone; he advised both Jeremy and Dieter of his scheme. By then Dieter and Jeremy were already on their way to Paris. Jeremy thought it was an excellent idea, but Dieter Johannes was not quite ready to give up his family.

Dieter begged Cameron to reconsider, there was too much at stake, and he pleaded with Cameron to find another way. Cameron explained to Dieter that this was 1938 all over again, and he had to choose this time. There would be no second chances. Those who picked the wrong side; had to pay the price. Dieter hesitated for more than thirty seconds, and eventually gave his blessings. Dieter knew it was the right thing to do; however it would surely tear his family apart.

Upon further reflection, Dieter was convinced that if more Germans and Europeans had taken a stronger stance in 1938, WWII would not have happened. Although he was sure that he was doing the right thing, he shivered at the consequences. Everything he had worked so hard for would be swept away.

Dieter sat in his first class compartment staring at Jeremy. Jeremy seemed to be in a deep sleep; without a care in the world. Dieter wondered how Jeremy could remain so calm?

Dieter finally spoke to Jeremy, and said.

"Doesn't this bother you? Are you not concerned what might happen to Cameron and the rest of us?" Stated a somber Dieter Johannes.

"Well my friend, I have been around the world too many times to let something like this bother me! Whatever happens? It happens! I can no longer control the circumstances, so I will simply flow with the tide and hope for the best. I hate to be crude, but you guys have a lot more to lose than I do. I am just here for the ride, and help protect my cousin." Replied a stoic Jeremy Grant.

Dieter replied. "You are right, I wish our positions were reversed. I do not want to see my family shattered this way."

Chapter 35

Combat in Africa, Sicily, Italy and Normandy

1943 on the High Seas

2LT Erik Goldmann excitedly opened the large manila envelope. It contained his team's orders. His POW Interrogation Team would be landed at Algiers, Algeria and proceed by truck to Al-Quatar, Tunisia where they were to join up with soldiers of the 1st Infantry Division, the Big Red One, on their push westward.

Their ride westward on a five-ton truck was not the most pleasant accommodation they had ever undertaken. It seemed as if the Algerians or Tunisians did not ever repair their potholes. Erik and his men felt every single bump along the way. It was as if the Rommel had purposely exploded landmines en route. By the time they arrived at their Battalion Headquarters, they all felt like they had earned the Purple Heart.

His Battalion Commander, Colonel Michael James Brigdon, a West Point graduate, class of 1923 was anxiously waiting for them in the Command Post HQ.

"Well lieutenant, you sure took your time getting here? Where in the hell have been? Your orders stated you were to have been here two days ago? Where have you been keeping yourself? I sure hope you did not in stop in one of the whorehouses along the way?" Stated the colonel, with a smile on his face.

Erik was shocked by the insinuation. He started to reply with a smart-ass answer, but thought better of it.

"No Sir! We only landed two days ago, and have en route since then. The roads are not exactly made for speedy advance, Sir!" Replied a somewhat dismayed lieutenant.

Everyone in the room stood in silence. Not a word was said for thirty seconds. Finally, Colonel Brigdon broke the ice.

"I am glad to see you have a sense of humor lieutenant." Replied the now smiling commander. Everyone else in the tent started laughing out loud.

"LT Goldmann, you seem to have a slight accent? Where were you born?" Asked his commander.

"Sir, I was born in Niedergeyer, Germany, but I am now a proud American citizen." Replied Erik, as he snapped to attention.

"Well that's great! A Kraut as my translator and interrogator!" Replied the still smiling colonel.

"Sir, I am a United States citizen and I resent being called a Kraut." Replied Erik, as he stared the colonel right in the eyes.

"Well, I admire your spirit. Now let's get back to the war! There is a hill being held by the Germans near the Plains of Mateur, and we have been ordered to take it. I am confident we will, and subsequently you will have many POW's to interrogate for me. I want you to go with the advance detachment, and please leave as soon as possible. Is that understood Lieutenant Goldmann?" Stated the now official sounding commander.

"Sir, yes Sir!" Replied Erik in a loud and booming voice. He hoped he didn't sound too childish, but he was anxious to get going.

Erik went outside and told his team what their mission was. A few minutes later a young looking Captain Enids came forward and identified himself as the 'E' Company Commander.

"OK, LT. Just follow my lead and stay close to me. We will set a Command Post (CP) and you can start doing your thing, after we attack. Is that understood?" Asked the friendly looking CPT.

"Absolutely! However Sir, I have one small favor to ask? Do you think we could be issued some ammunition? We were never given any." Asked a somewhat embarrassed Erik.

"Shit! Those rear echelon pukes! You mean they sent you in a combat zones with no ammo?" Retorted the visibly upset captain.

"Yes Sir! We managed to steal twenty rounds between us, but that is all Sir!" Replied a somewhat sheepish Erik.

The captain turned around and pointed at a burly sergeant and said, with an authoritative voice.

The captain ordered. "First Sergeant, give these men a combat load, and plenty of hand grenades. Also don't forget some regional maps, and the communication codes for the day. Who knows? They might need them.

Erik looked at the sergeant and nodded. He then turned around and said to the Captain.

"Thank you, sir." Erik said, feeling a little more confident.

A few minutes later, two privates returned to the area with twelve bandoleers of rifle ammunition, twenty-four hand grenades, six illumination flares, some .45 caliber ammo and a field radio. For the first time since their arrival in Africa, the team felt like real combat soldiers. Erik made sure all his men had the correct amount of ammo, and asked the young privates if they could have some food, K-rations?

"Yes Sir! Just send a couple of your men with me, and I will take care of you." Replied the pimpled-face private first class.

Erik assigned his NCO and another man the job of picking up the K-Rations for his team. They returned ten minutes later with twelve sets of rations for each man, and an three extra rations for any captured POWS.

"Great idea, Sergeant! I never would of thought of it." Replied a smiling Lieutenant Erik Goldmann.

Easy Company moved out and soon ran into trouble. The Germans had powerful 88mm canons on the hill, and they could observe the entire valley for miles around. Every time the men moved out, the Germans attacked them. Captain Enids eventually called for divisional counter-battery fire from their 155mm artillery pieces, and soon had the Germans running for their lives.

Shortly thereafter, the first German POWS were brought to Erik's location. The MP's had set up a small holding area, and within two hours over fifty German POW's were confined in the small area. Erik knew from experience that the best time to interrogate prisoners is immediately after their capture. They are vulnerable, tired and possibly hungry; and at their most fragile state. The battle flowed back and forth for several days, but the allied forces were making headway against Rommel and the Afrika

Korp. Erik and his team soon earned their combat ribbon the hard way.

After several more months of hard fighting, Lieutenant Goldmann and his team were sent back to Algiers for additional training and some R&R (Rest and Recuperation). It was a much-needed time-off for all concerned, however they were only given seven days before the training started all over again. Four weeks of difficult boat landing exercises and night maneuvers got them in top physical condition, and the were ready for their next theater of war, SICILY.

Not only did the 1st Division have to face the battle hardened Panzer divisions in Sicily, but Lieutenant Goldmann was caught up in the political wrangling between the American forces and the British 8th Army, under General Montgomery. The delays in taking North Africa put additional strain on General George Patton and his commanders. The Brits wanted to run the show, but he would have none of it.

Patton eventually managed to convince General Eisenhower and his staff to allow him to use the battle hardened 1st Division to assault and hold the southeastern side of the island. The battle off Gela Beach was one of the toughest of the war. The experienced Hermann Goering Panzer Division fought with desperation and nearly overran General Roosevelt's Regiment. Some of his panzers actually fought all the way to the edge of the beach. Some lucky hits by American 105mm artillery and accurate naval gunfire saved the day for the allies.

The Germans tried one more time to punch through, but by then naval forces had the whole area under deadly fire, and the allied air forces rained terror on the German and Italian defenders.

Sicily was a good training ground for Lieutenant Goldmann's unit. The amount of prisoners taken was in the thousands, and he and his men were under constant duress trying to extract valuable intelligence from enemy. It was here that Goldmann was promoted to First Lieutenant, and given command of an intelligence unit, approximately one hundred men in total. By now Goldmann and his men, had been in almost continuous combat for seven months.

They were all getting tired, but the excitement of the chase was pushing them onwards.

Patton and his troops shoved the Germans all the way back to the Italian mainland, and the allies began chasing them up the entire length of the Italian boot. Towards the end of 1943, now First Lieutenant Goldmann was transferred to his battalion intelligence headquarters, and later sent to England for further training.

At first he was puzzled by the sudden move, but after a few months in England he surmised what was about to happen in the near future. His language skills were soon to be a great asset in the upcoming invasion of France. After all he was both fluent in French and German.

The Normandy invasion was and still probably is the greatest military achievement in history. Through this magnificent military coup, the allies were able to defeat Hitler and eventually bring the Nazis and their cronies to their knees. However, once again the Big Red One had to be on the front lines. The American military commanders felt that only the 1st Division could pull off this landing. Not everyone felt as convinced as General Omar Bradley that they should once again lead the way.

The many original surviving soldiers of the 1st Division were openly hostile to another beachfront landing. Many of them, were convinced that they would not survive another foreign shore assault landing. Many of the veterans were taking bets, and offering odds who would survive, and who would not.

On June the 6th, 1944, the dawn broke grey and overcast over the beaches at Normandy. The weather was miserable and all the boats rocked in the waves. 1st Lieutenant Goldmann thought, *"How ironic it was that he would be landing back on free French soil in Normandy. The same ship's name that took him to freedom, a mere five years ago."*

Goldmann and his men felt somewhat re-assured by the largest naval armada ever assembled in history. They were surrounded by more than 5000 ships; which included 9 battleships, 25 cruisers, 79 landing craft, destroyers, mine sweepers, and of course a whole bunch of merchantmen and Liberty ships. At exactly 0550 hours the naval bombardment started hitting Normandy and surrounding area.

The first wave of Americans suffered terribly. The naval shelling had done little damage and the Germans were quite willing to fight back. Goldmann and his unit were on the second wave and they landed about six hours after the first wave. What they saw was worst than anything they had seen in nearly eighteen months of combat. The Germans were still heavily resisting, and only small squads of men had made it off the beach. Everywhere they looked, complete devastation reigned supreme. Dead bodies, wounded men, both American and Germans were milling about, looking for help. Explosions and gunfire still ripped a deadly path across the beach.

Initially Goldmann and his men could not find their battalion headquarters, and were simply fighting as infantrymen trying to survive this disaster. Eventually the men managed to push inland and get around the German beach defenses. However the price had been heavy for the 1st Division, over 3100 casualties were incurred on that horrible day. This figure only included the killed and wounded from the 1st division. All toll, over twenty thousand allied soldiers, sailors and airmen fell victim to the German war machine on that infamous day.

1st Lieutenant Goldmann and his men had been among the lucky ones. They suffered only two minor wounds; however many of his men had incurred shattered nerves on that day. On day three, they managed to regroup and start doing their jobs again. Several thousands German POW's needed to be processed and interrogated.

Goldmann and his teams worked eighteen to twenty hours a day. Somehow the men did not mind; they were able to extract valuable and important intelligence. They sensed that their long hours were helping to win the war, and help them get home faster. Many of the Germans captured were from older reserve units, or foreign conscripts. They were more than willing to spill the beans for a few extra rations, or a chance for better treatment. The problem now was sorting out the good intelligence from the bad.

The days turned into weeks, as the Allied war machine rumbled through the beautiful French countryside. Within less than two months, they had passed Paris, and were rushing towards the Belgium, German frontiers and the Ardennes.

Erik became aware of a gnawing feeling in the pit of his stomach as they approached the Dutch, Belgium-German borders. It was one thing to fight on foreign shores, but how would he act in his own backyard? It was about this time that his battalion commander called him to their headquarters, near the small Belgium town of Eupen. He was promoted to Captain and given the additional duties of identifying key terrain targets for the divisional intelligence section.

Eupen was a small scenic town near the German frontier and had an important railroad crossroad that led to the German town of Aachen, and also to Liege, Belgium and beyond. It was imperative that the allies glean as much operational intelligence as possible. Their immediate shot term goal was the city of Aachen, also known as Aix-la-Chapelle by the French.

Napoleon Bonaparte occupied that part of Germany in the early eighteenth century and as a matter of fact many of the locals still used French words in their dialect. It was the first major German city to fall prey to allied forces and the German were determined to hold on to it. Hitler once referred to this city as, "The home of the First Reich." He expected it to be held at all costs.

Chapter 36

Attack on Aachen by the Allies

Aachen was a historic city dating back to the Neolithic and Roman times. It was and is one of Germany's most beautiful cities. Right on the border of both Belgium and Holland, it has been a very special place for all Germans for more than twelve centuries. The Great Emperor Charlemagne was pronounced Emperor of Europe and Germany in the year 800 A.D.

For many centuries all German Emperors were crowned in this city. The last emperor crowned was around the sixteenth century. The Romans loved it for its natural warm springs and mineralized waters. It is still used today by many Europeans as a health and cure spa.

However in the fall of 1944 the city was the most important link in the Eastward onslaught against Germany. Winston Churchill once wrote in his memoirs, *"This potential (Nazi) spearhead had been carefully watched while it lay in reserve cast of Aachen, wrote Winston Churchill."* He further quoted, *"When fighting on that front died down in early December, it vanished for a while from the focus of our Intelligence (and General) Eisenhower suspected that something was afoot, though its scope and violence came as a surprise."* Winston Churchill further wrote in his six-part memoirs of WWII. *"In the Ardennes sector, a single corps, the VIII American, of four divisions, held a front of 75 miles; the risk was foreseen and deliberately accepted, but the consequences were grave and might have been graver."*

It was under these extremely difficult circumstances, that Captain Goldmann was selected to personally conduct a reconnaissance of the city. He was to try and obtain some up to date data and intelligence on the German defenses. Particularly the Siegfried Line defenses which surrounded the countryside around

Aachen. Some of these strong defenses were originally built in WWI, and were known as the Hindenburg Line. The modern Siegfried Line was built and improved in the thirties, and was over 390 miles long, from the border of Holland to the Switzerland frontier. It was fortified by hundred of bunkers, minefields, and concrete tank traps. The Germans felt quite safe behind their **Westwall** (German name) defenses. Hitler was convinced that it would be as secure as the French **Maginot** Line, and we all know how wrong that was. It took the German forces less than one week to go around or through the Maginot Line.

Normally Erik would have been happy for this type of mission, but he had been suffering from a horrible toothache. He was scheduled to go to the battalion dental surgeon in two days, but this mission was more important. Captain Goldmann asked the dentist for some pain pills, and went on his mission anyway.

For over three weeks, he had been warning the battalion commander of the grave danger they faced, if they simply attacked headlong into this area. Three large man-made lakes surrounded the allies and they provided power to the Ruhr industrial area. It would have been a disastrous situation to simply charge into Aachen and the adjoining area of operation without proper reconnaissance.

Up until now, no one wanted to listen to his warnings, but eventually he was given permission to try and dig up some intelligence. Erik selected a small squad of combat veterans, most of which spoke German or French. He had handpicked six men plus himself, and two radio operators. It was imperative that communications be maintained with his higher command throughout the mission.

In order to assist his team obtain unobserved admittance into the city, his battalion commander had ordered a large-scale artillery bombardment to start at exactly 12:05 a.m. It was to last exactly thirty minutes and included normal and smoke projectiles. It was hoped that it would give them sufficient time to infiltrate into the city. Erik and his men were brought up to the jump off point at around 11:30 p.m., where they received extra ammo, and had time to darken their faces and silence all of their gear. At exactly 12:05 all hell broke loose, as seventy-two 155mm and 105mm canons commenced to fire on the city. The concentration of fire had the desired effect on the German defenders; they all took cover and waited for the bombardment to end.

The artillerymen were efficient and professional; they fired their rounds at fifty-yard intervals; moving forward as the men advanced in the city. It gave Goldmann and his troops the necessary cover they needed to advance unseen. Erik and his men waited for twenty-five minutes before they started to move forward. As quickly as it had started, it stopped. The silence was as deafening as the bombardment had been.

Their advance was covered by the sound of collapsing buildings and uncontrolled fires raging throughout the imperial city. The sound of sirens, and soldiers screaming masked any noise they were making. Erik knew exactly where to go, the *Rathaus*(City Hall) was in the center of the city and probably had some valuable information.

The squad crept down the *Adalbertweg* Avenue toward the Rathaus. Using the large and imposing cathedral as a guide. Erik knew that city hall was directly behind it. *So far so good*, he thought to himself.

' Five minutes later they were in front of the massive door that guarded the city hall building. A direct hit from a 105mm shell had blown it off the hinges, and it lay on its side. Erik posted two men to guard the entrance, and the rest of the squad entered the still burning building. Rubble was strewn everywhere, and most of it was still on fire. Erik found a building directory sign that gave him directions to the *Burgermeister's* (Mayor) office. He and his men crawled over the rubble towards the office, and were suddenly startled by a loud voice.

"Halt, halt!" Shouted a German soldier, half buried in debris. His body was barely visible under the piles of rocks and wooden beams.

His next sentence was, *"Hilfe, hilfe."* (Help)!

Erik and his men quietly approached the area, their weapons

ready for action. Captain Goldmann signaled his men to be quiet, as he approached the rubble where the man was last seen.

"Halo, halo wer ist da?" (Who is there?) Asked Erik as he crept closer to the man. Hearing no answer, he asked again, and still no answer.

He kept crawling closer to the last known sound of the voice, but now there was an eerie silence throughout the large room. His Thompson .45 caliber sub-machinegun was at the ready and pointed downrange. Just when he thought the soldier had vanished, he felt a soft and squashy arm under his foot. He immediately froze in his tracks and tried to identify the rest of the body. He grabbed his red lens flashlight and shone it down on the body. The German soldier was now completely immobile and obviously dead; the arm in fact was two feet from the body and no longer attached.

The German soldier had obviously bled out, but had had enough strength to cry out prior to dying. His right hand clutched a German Potato Masher grenade in a death grip, and his listless eyes staring blankly into the ceiling. Erik waved to his men to come forward. They continued to search the room, but found no one else. One of the sergeants called out to Captain Goldmann.

"Sir, Sir! I think there is a large safe here. All the men came running over to look at the extremely bulky metal safe.

"Well done!" Replied Captain Goldmann.

"How in the hell do we get the damn thing open? Asked Erik as he looked as his men.

"Don't worry, I have some plastic explosives and we can just blow it up!" Replied Staff Sergeant Barlow, as he produced a two-pound satchel of explosives, and smiled.

"Great, great! Did you ever do this professionally, Sergeant Barlow? Let's do it, and get the hell out of here! You men take cover behind the door." Replied the Captain, as he pointed to the men.

The squad ran for cover, as SSG Barlow pulled the friction detonating cord and ran like hell the thirty yards to the exterior door. Everyone ducked down and waited the fifteen seconds before the explosions rocked the entire room. The explosive force was greater than they needed; the entire front door of the safe was ripped off, and peeled back like a can of sardines. As a matter of fact some of the contents were beginning to burn, and Erik ran over and stomped down on the burning paper.

"Come on, men! Let's grab all this stuff and get out of here." Finished an excited Captain Goldmann. Within minutes his men had put out all the fires, and were picking up all the scattered documents. The amount of stuff in and around the safe was overwhelming.

Erik gave orders to his men, "Take everything, and we will sort it out later!"

In less than five minutes the men had collected every document and maps of the area, Erik then ordered his communication team to relay a message to HQ. Goldmann wanted to make sure that his unit knew who they were, and that they would be coming back the same way on Adalbertweg Avenue. He did not want any trigger happy G.I.'s to confuse them for Germans. It took them less than twenty-minutes to make it back to their lines, using the tall cathedral spire as a guide.

Dawn was breaking over the eastern part of the city, as the remaining elements of his squad climbed over the last trench, and back into American lines. Even though it was a cold morning, they were all covered with sweat as if they had just crossed a river. The stress of the mission had them all soaked through and through.

Erik and his men had hit a goldmine of information. The documents showed the entire defensive fortifications for the city and the surrounding area. It also showed that the Germans had plans in place to blow the dams on the Roer and Ruhr rivers causing widespread loss of life and property. The Aachen region of the Eifel mountain range fell sharply down to the Rhine River seventy miles away. If the Germans blew the dams, everyone and anything in its way would be swept away. The Nazis were willing to sacrifice their own population in order to delay the Allies.

Erik and his men were awarded Bronze Stars for their action. Originally Erik was put in for the Silver Star, but his Regimental

Commander, a known anti-Semitic downgraded it without reason.
Erik's Battalion Commander attempted to intercede, but was
harshly told not to meddle. Erik quickly learned that not only
Germans were anti-Semitic, and was deeply hurt by this hateful
action.

The fighting in and around the city of Aachen continued for
over forty more days and was eventually secured after a high
number of casualties on both sides. The battle in the region of
Aachen was considered part of the Huertgen Forest (Green Hell),
the Germans called it, **Schlacht im Huertgenwald.** It was an area
from Aachen to the Rur (Roer) river. A series of vicious battles
was fought between the Germans and American forces in the
densely and thickly wooded forests. These battles took place
between September 19, 1944 and February 10th, 1945. Amazingly,
it was the longest continuous battle fought in WWII between
American and German forces. The entire area was a corridor of
barely fifty square miles east of the Belgium-Dutch-German
borders, but due to the hilly and mountainous terrain it was often
referred to as the "Green Hell."[1]

Most of the men were convinced that they would be home by
Christmas, and were already planning their homecoming. Erik
tried in vain not to let them get their hopes up, but they were
insistent that the war was almost over. After what seemed like an
incredibly long break, Captain Goldmann and his unit were
marched forward to an area just southwest of Aachen. This was a
'quiet sector' and the men enjoyed the respite.

Patrols still went out everyday, but the amount of prisoners was
comparatively small, and they did not have that much to do. One
thing did strike Erik as being unusual; many of the POW's were
from Panzer and SS units. This concentration of SS units was
rather strange in this part of the western theater. Erik tried really
hard to figure out the meaning of these obvious indicators, but
none of his superiors would listen to him. The weather had turned
really ugly and he was not able to order up any reconnaissance

---

[1] *Wikipedia free Encyclopedia, Battle of Hurtgen Forest.*

flights; to verify his suspicions.

After what seem like a year of just sitting around; he grabbed a jeep and two of his best NCO's and decided to go and check for himself. The roads were all covered with a thick layer of freshly fallen snow. The dirt roads were normally almost impassable, even with the ever-reliable Jeep, but the two feet of snow made it very challenging. Many of the tall trees had fallen across the roads, and made perfect roadblocks.

Additionally, the Germans had set explosive charges along the forest roads and the going was extremely rough, but Erik was determined to find out what was going on in this sector of the front. Erik kept thinking of his men and their prediction of going home by Christmas. The deeper he drove into the forest, the more he became convinced that America was a long way off and they would never leave this place before spring at the earliest. Just then the road ahead was blocked by a series of earthen bunkers and logs. They were over twenty feet high and covered with dirt, leaves and green branches for camouflage.

"SSG Barlow! Pull over and let's go check it out. This does not look healthy!" Uttered a now concerned Captain Goldmann.

It was December 15th, 1944 and Captain Goldmann and his men were about to become the very first victims of the Battle of the Bulge. The full moon gave them some sort of visibility, but they were equally visible to the Germans. The full moon cast long shadows on the glistening snow. They cautiously drove up to the blockade and stopped. They intently listened for any sounds, but all they heard in the distance was the muffled sound of what sounded like large tanks, armored personnel carriers, and trucks, an occasional artillery piece. The sound was too subdued to be able to identify the direction or the numbers. Erik waved to his men not to move. Everyone crouched silently behind the Jeep. Nothing was heard for ten seconds, and Erik stood up and went forward to investigate. His men followed at five-yard intervals behind him. The only sound they now heard were the pounding of their hearts and snow crunching beneath their boots.

Ten minutes later they had managed to walk about fifty yards or so, when a sudden shout made them freeze in their tracks.

"Halt, halt! Wer ist das!" (Halt, who is there!) Came a loud voice from behind a tree.

Erik and his men froze in their tracks, hoping they could sneak away. Their silence drew an aggressive response from the sentry. He fired his MG-42 machinegun in their general direction. The tracers seem to come right at Erik, but he managed to hug the snow and they passed right above his head. He heard his two men cry out in pain. After the initial noise there was total silence behind him. He crawled back to where his men had been, and to his horror they both were not moving. Large stains of blood surrounded their lifeless bodies. Small amounts of steam escaped from their bodies; it was the last vestiges of life. It appeared to him as if was their souls escaping the Earthly bond of earth, and floating in to heaven.

Captain Goldmann reached out with his hand and managed to find an artery on SSG Barlow neck. There was no use, he checked both men, but they were already dead. The machinegun had caught both men across the chest, and they died almost instantly. He tried to crawl away from the area, but he once again heard the same gruff voice. A voice he had heard before.

"Stop, stop or I shoot!" Screamed the tall German soldier in English.

Erik was sure that the voice he heard was that of KAPO Ludwig Winter formerly of Buchenwald, and now a German soldier. *This can't be*, he thought to himself!

Erik was undecided how he should play his hand. Was Ludwig alone? What were his intentions? Erik had always been a good poker player, and decided to try his luck once more.

"Achtung, achtung." (Attention, attention) Shouted a now confident Captain Goldmann in German. For a moment the confused German soldier, stood there not knowing what to do or what to say.

"You, you! I know who you are!" Replied the soldier to Erik.

"Is that possible? Is it you? How can it be? What a co-incidence? *Mein Gott*, you are a Captain in the American army?

What, What?" Ludwig stuttered as he stepped from behind the bunker, not knowing how to properly express himself.

Erik took the opportunity to pick up his weapon and point it at Ludwig. KAPO Winter, or currently known as **Gefreiter** (Private) Winter of the 351st Pioneer Battalion. It took Ludwig a few seconds to react.

"What are you doing? It's me, KAPO Ludwig. Put down that weapon! I would never harm you, not after what we have been through?" Stated a very confident Gefreiter Winter.

Erik slowly lowered his weapon, but kept it clutched in his right hand. Erik stared at his old friend and former nemesis.

"Can it be? You, KAPO Winter in the middle of the forest? What are you doing? Why are you here?" Asked Erik, still a little uncomfortable with the situation.

"Well one thing I know for sure, I am now your prisoner and let's get the hell out of here! Do you know how long I have been waiting to give myself up? Unfortunately for the past three years, I have been fighting the Russians, and they don't take prisoners!" Finished a now out of breath Gefreiter Winter, a small smile spreading across his long and bony face.

Captain Goldmann replied. "That sounds good to me, but how are we going to find our way back to our lines? You shot our only transportation, and my Jeep is full of holes!"

"Let's pretend you are my prisoner if a German patrol comes by, and vice versa? What do you say?" Asked a smiling Ludwig.

"Great idea! Let's start putting some distance between us and that bunker." Stated a now more confident Erik.

"Don't worry about the bunker I was the only one on guard duty. The rest of the unit is at the point of departure. We need to hurry now, in less than ten hours the whole German Army is going to attack in this sector, and you will be overrun. We don't have much time." Finished Gefreiter Winter, as he tugged on Captain Goldmann's sleeve.

Erik stared at him in disbelief. "What do you mean attack in force?"

"No offense dear friend? But where have you been for the past six weeks? We have been moving heavy tank units, artillery and infantry divisions in this whole area. Tomorrow morning a major offensive will blow right through this area, and if we don't hurry we will be the first victims!" Stated a now nervous Gefreiter Winter.

"How come you know so much?" Asked a confused Captain Goldmann.

"Well it just so happen that I am the Plans and Operations clerk for the **Kommandant,** and I have access to such information. I just so happen to have the misfortune of having guard duty this evening. Maybe it was my good fortune? Let's quit talking and start hiking!" Finished a rather pompous Ludwig Winter.

"Let's follow the tire tracks back towards our lines." Stated a more commanding Captain Goldmann.

Just as they started walking westward, the full moon disappeared behind some dark clouds and it started snowing again. Gefreiter Ludwig Winter nodded his head and they both headed off in a westerly direction towards the American lines. The going was pretty rough, and even though they were walking at a brisk pace; they only managed to advance two miles in four hours. The snow was falling so heavily that it was beginning to cover the tire tracks.

"How much further to your front lines?" Asked a worried Ludwig.

Erik started to respond, but thought better of it. How well could he trust this German soldier? Maybe he had a conversion and now was a true Nazi?

"I would estimate another few miles or so should get us to the nearest LP/OP. From there we can probably hitch a ride to the battalion headquarters." Responded Captain Goldmann without turning around, trying to be as vague as he could be.

Ludwig replied. "If we are lucky we should make it on time, but only if we pick up the pace."

The further they walked, the colder it got. The snow had almost entirely covered up the road and the vehicle tracks. Erik glanced at his watch and it was nearly two in the morning. By his estimation they had walked nearly three or four miles closer to the

American lines. They stopped behind a large fallen oak tree to take a quick break. As they squatted down, they heard German voices off in the distance. Both men tensed up, and waited to see in what direction they were going. It appeared that they were coming straight towards them. The path would lead them within a few feet of the hidden men. Ludwig squatted down near Erik and said.

"What do we do? Do we fight or hide?" Stated a concerned Ludwig.

"Nothing for now! Let's see where they go?" Replied Erik as he snuck a peek at the German soldiers in the dark.

Not more than ten yards away, a squad or more of soldiers coming towards them, but these were American uniforms, not German ones!

Chapter 37

Battle of the Bulge

The **Ardennes Offensive**[2] (16 December1944 - 25 January 1945) was a major German offensive on the Western Front. This attack was called, *"**Unternehmen Wacht am Rhein**"*, (Operation Watch on the Rhine) by the Germans. The US Army called it the Battle of the Ardennes, or the Battle of the Bulge. It was a series of coordinated offensive operations by the Germans, whose main goal was to split the British and American line in half; capturing Antwerp Belgium in the process. They then hoped to encircle and destroy the four Allied armies and negotiate a separate peace treaty with the Allies; leaving the hated Russians out in the cold.

It was in this mess that Captain Erik Goldmann, and Gefreiter Ludwig found themselves in. The Germans had in fact disguised many English speaking German soldiers as American MP's, in the hope of confusing the Americans and creating havoc behind the lines.

"Ssshhh, don't say anything or do anything! I think they are Nazis disguised as Americans. We don't have the firepower to take them on!" Erik whispered holding his index finger over his lips.

Gefreiter Ludwig Winter quickly hid in a snow bank, and did not say a word. Erik followed the lead German pointing his Thompson at him, until they were out of sight.

"I think it's safe now. They are going south of us, and as long as we keep going in a westerly direction we should not run in to them again!" Stated a somewhat confident Captain Goldmann.

Ludwig was almost invisible in the snow. His well-camouflaged white ski smock was perfectly blended, and Erik had

---

[2] *Wikipedia free Encyclopedia Battle of the Bulge.*

a hard time seeing him.

Ludwig replied. "You lead the way!"

Erik took the point, and occasionally glanced down at his compass for assistance. After what seemed like an eternity, they finally arrived at the crossroad near the American lines. Erik glanced down at his watch and it was exactly five in the morning. They continued a few feet further and were immediately challenged by an American sentry.

"Halt! Who goes there! Advance and be recognized." Shouted the American guard. He then said, **"Cincinnati!"**

Captain Goldmann replied! **Reds!** The guard, feeling confident that the challenge was correctly answered, screamed out!

"Step forward, and identify yourself!"

Captain Goldmann stepped forward and looked at the sentry.

"I am Captain Erik Goldmann, and I have a German prisoner with me." Replied Erik.

"I urgently need to be taken to your battalion headquarters. Do you have a vehicle available?" Asked a concerned Erik.

The guard looked at Erik, and slowly raised his weapon. The barrel of his M-1 Garand pointing right a Erik's chest and waving back and forth between both men. Erik and Ludwig did not dare move or make any sudden gestures.

"You know buddy, for an American, you sure sound like a Kraut to me! Don't do anything funny, and put your weapon on the ground, until I call my Sergeant." Stated a now suspicious guard.

Three minutes later a tired and grumpy sergeant showed up and demanded to know why this idiot of a Private had dared to wake him up.

"Slow down Sergeant, this man has a German accent, and we were warned about Germans in American uniforms!" Replied the young Private.

"Let's see your dog-tags!" Asked the Sergeant, sticking his hand out.

Erik complied. The Sergeant quizzed Erik for a few minutes, and was satisfied by his answers. Erik was able to convince the

Sergeant to arrange for transportation. Fifteen minutes later a jeep and driver showed up in front of the CQ. Erik glanced at his watch again, and it was now five forty-five. Captain Goldmann gave instructions to the driver to race over to the Division CP. The driver took off like a bat out of hell. Both Erik and Ludwig Winter were petrified that this crazy ex-NY taxi driver would get them killed before the Germans had a chance too.

Erik was checking his watch once more, when a huge series of explosions began to fall behind them. The entire area was being bracketed by artillery and mortar fire. The entire horizon to the east of them was lit up like a giant bond fire. The Germans opened up with every piece of their 1900 guns and *Nebelwewerfers* (Multiple Rocket launchers, often referred to as "Screaming Mimi's" by the GI's) artillery. Every American foxhole, bunker, CP, LP/OP for ten miles inland was hit wit pinpoint accuracy. The Germans had carefully plotted all of their targets for weeks and knew exactly where to strike.

Within thirty to forty minutes the entire frontline had been pummeled by German artillery. American troops were already beginning to crack under the strain. Erik kept edging the driver onwards. Thirty minutes later they finally arrived at the Divisional Headquarters. Erik told the driver to stay put and not leave the Jeep unattended for a minute. Erik grabbed Ludwig by the collar and dragged him into hell.

It seemed as if everyone was running around burning documents, maps, screaming orders etc. Erik managed to find the Divisional G-2 Colonel and introduced him to Private Ludwig Winter. After a round of negotiations Ludwig agreed to help, if he was given a letter of recommendation, and a job in the kitchen. Erik and Private Winter were taken to the map room and Ludwig faithfully recorded every known German position, supply depots, and expected troop concentrations. However the situation was now so fluid, that many of these points of interest were obsolete. Just as Private Ludwig and Captain Goldmann were finishing their work, a series of large explosions rocketed near the Division Headquarters.

Erik managed to get a signed ***'Pass par Tout'*** (Good for everything) order signed by the G-2, and they ran out to the front of the building. The jeep was still there, but the driver had disappeared or been killed. Captain Goldmann and Private Ludwig Winter jumped into the still running Jeep and accelerated westward. Goldmann knew that Ludwig's information was only good if he managed to get it Corps HQ in Eupen, Belgium.

As the sun rose on the horizon, Erik drove like a madman towards Eupen. The situation was so fluid and chaotic, that no one stopped them for nearly twenty miles. A roadblock, manned by American MP's demanded to see orders and I.D.'s. Captain Goldmann was at first reluctant to stop, but the .50 caliber machinegun was a great persuader. After a small five-minute delay, they were allowed to proceed westward. Eupen was now less than five miles away. Erik slowed down his breakneck speed and started to relax a little. Gefreiter Ludwig Winter had not said a word since they left the Division HQ. He now turned around and spoke to Erik.

"I am sorry we did not meet sooner. I think it's too late now! There is no stopping Field Marshal Model and General von Rundstedt now!" Stated a somewhat confident Gefreiter Ludwig Winter.

"I would not be so sure if I were you. As soon as the weather clears, our bombers and fighters will wipe out your tanks, and troop concentrations." Stated a confident Captain Goldmann.

Before Ludwig Winter could reply, they arrived on the outskirts of Eupen and were being stopped by some American MP's. After checking their dog tags and questioning them, they were later directed to Corps HQ and the J-2 section. Upon arrival at their destination both men were separated. Ludwig was pumped for information for two days, and given a VIP pass in the nicest POW camp near Paris. They never saw each other again, however after the war Erik received a postcard from Ludwig from Berlin. There was no return address, but Erik was assured that Ludwig had survived the war.

Captain Erik Goldmann was temporarily assigned to the

Divisional Intelligence Unit, and remained there until after the German offensive was stopped.

The information provided by Ludwig Winter was instrumental in slowing down and eventually stopping the German onslaught. It took the Americans almost six weeks from the date of the initial attack to return to their original lines of demarcation. In late January 1945, Erik was returned to his battalion. It would never be the same again, over forty percent of his unit had been killed, captured or were simply missing. The allies continued their eastward and southward attack. On February 24th, 1945 Erik was called to this battalion headquarters and given a very important mission by his battalion commander.

"Captain Goldmann, I understand you were born in this neck of the woods?" Asked a curious Colonel Jaimerty?

"Yes Sir! I was born in Niedergeyer, near Dueren, just south of Aachen." Replied Erik, wondering what this was all about?

"Well we have a very special mission for you! That is if you decide to take it?" Asked his colonel, raising his eyebrow as he did so.

"I will be glad to do it. No matter what the mission is!" Replied an anxious Captain Goldmann.

The battalion commander smiled at him, and nodded his head. He laid out the mission, and waited for Erik to reply. Erik was overwhelmed by the plan, and the ambitious nature of the attack. Captain Goldmann was to be made temporary commander of 'B' Company and they were to spearhead a battalion size advance on Niedergeyer and beyond. 'B' Company would attack on the main line of advance through the center of town, and drive out any enemy troops westward and northward. 'A' and 'C' companies would then concentrate their forces in a pincer movement at the north end of the town. It was hoped that this maneuver would cut off the retreating Germans. Division G-2 had determined that the Germans had at least two battalions of Support Troops and some anti-aircraft batteries in the area.

"Wow! Thank you Sir! Are there any known civilians in the town? Or have they all been evacuated?" Asked Erik, his face suddenly becoming very serious.

"As far as we know, it's a 'Free Fire Zone'! The Air Corp has been dropping leaflets all over the area for the past four days. We can only assume that any remaining civilians are working with the Nazis. Are you having second thoughts?" Finished a serious Colonel Jaimerty.

"Oh no Sir! I am only concerned about my men, and any innocent civilians." Replied a pensive Erik.

"If you don't want the assignment, I will give it to someone else Captain Goldmann." Stated Colonel Jaimerty, a worried look on his face.

"Absolutely not, Sir! I will make sure that the mission is successful. Are we going to have any coverage fire from our artillery?" Asked Erik?

"We have all of the major intersections, streets and high observation points already pinpointed. If you need any support, just call for it and you will have all you need." Replied a now smiling Colonel Jaimerty.

"By the way, I may not be here when you return. I can no longer stay in command of this battalion due to my promotion last month to full colonel. I will be moving Regiment or Corps HQ in the next few days." Finished his battalion commander.

"I will be sorry to see you go Sir!" Replied Erik, extending his hand in friendship. Colonel Jaimerty extended his hand and both men nodded to each other. It was the acknowledgement of two warriors who admired and respected each other.

Erik gathered all the company commanders, platoon leaders and first sergeants for a fast briefing. It only took Erik thirty minutes to set out the plan of attack on Niedergeyer, his birthplace. Despite the many horrors and hardships he and his family had suffered and the hands of the Nazis, it was a difficult thing to do. Brief glimpses of his life flashed before his eyes. He wondered how much of the town was damaged or destroyed; were there any civilians left? All of these memories rumbled through his brain. His nostalgic trip down memory lane was quickly interrupted by his First Sergeant.

"Excuse me Captain, I have some maps for you and the other men." Stated First Sergeant Peterson.

Thank you, First Sergeant. Make sure all the men have extra ammo and hand-grenades. I hope we won't need it, but the G-2 believes that there could be close to six- hundred Support Troops in the village; let's take no chances.

"No problem Sir! Are we still meeting near the church at 04:45 tomorrow morning?" Asked the First Sergeant.

"That is correct, and make sure all of the companies have the daily 'Sign and Counter-Sign'! I do not want any of our men shooting at each other." Stated a concerned Erik.

Erik spent a restless night thinking about tomorrow's mission. It was a miraculous state of events; the coincidence was too incredible to believe. Six years ago, he was a young teenager playing soccer in Niedergeyer, and now he was about to re-capture his hometown by force. For the first time in years, Erik tried to recall what his parents looked like. He had purposely put them in a corner of his brain, because the pain was too great; now he was trying to think about them again. No matter how hard he tried, their faces just would not appear to him. He tossed and turned all night and did not get much sleep.

Erik's First Sergeant woke him up at 03:30. He had a cup of steaming hot coffee in his hand. Erik looked at him and smiled.

"1SG you would make a good wife to some lucky women." Stated a now completely awake Erik.

"I am blessed with a great wife already Sir! It's the US Army! I have already been married to her for the past twenty-two years, and she treats me well." Finished a smiling 1SG.

The company got ready for the attack on Niedergeyer. They lined up in two columns along the main road. The other two companies took positions to the north and south of the city boundary. Company 'B' was less than two miles from the city limit and the objective. At the last moment, they were given a Sherman tank for support and Captain Goldmann decided to use it as the spearhead of his attack. The tank took the lead and slowly rumbled up the main road. At the junction to Niedergeyer the tank veered left towards the center of town. Large fields of wheat and corn grew to the north of the road, and potatoes were growing on the south side of the road. It could have been an idyllic scene, if it wasn't for the horror of war.

A four men reconnaissance squad was sent two hundred yards ahead of the tank and 'B' Company. They sprinted ahead of the tank and looked for mines and ***Panzerfaust*** (Bazooka like anti-tank weapon) carrying German soldiers. At the entrance to the village, two large stone houses covered the road. The squad slowed down, and started to crawl forward. There was no sign of the enemy anywhere. Feeling confident they stood back up and advance at a faster pace. Just when they thought the coast was clear, the unmistakable sound of a MG-42 opened up on them. The MG-42 was the fastest firing machinegun in the world; it could fire over 1200 rounds per minute, and sounded like a sewing machine on steroids. The initial burst hit the first man in the leg, and he went down. The rest of the squad managed to take cover in the parallel ditches that ran alongside the road.

The M4 Sherman tank commander observed what was going on, and swung the turret around towards the MG-42. This was one of the newer models of the Sherman and had the larger 76mm gun, additional appliqué armor on the front, sides and turret. The gun barked, and the downstairs window blew up. The tank fired one more round just to make sure. The pinned down squad cautiously moved forward and threw two hand grenades through the front door. After the clearing of the house, they all moved forward with great caution.

Captain Goldmann went forward with the first squad, as they advanced up the main street. So far things were going pretty good, or so they thought. Half way up the village, were the remains of an old castle on the left side of the street. The building had crumbled on itself, but it was so large, that hundreds of soldiers could have been hiding there. Just as they approached the corner of the street, a four-barreled 20mm anti-aircraft gun opened up on them from the main gate. The high rate of fire caused everyone to take immediate cover where ever they could.

Captain Goldmann immediately called an artillery battery for suppressive fire. Just as predicted, thirty seconds later four 105mm rounds landed within ten yards of the German gun, and killed the entire gun crew instantly. Captain Goldmann called for another eight rounds to land fifty meters west and fifty meters north. The thundering fire landing on the old castle seemed to take the fight out of most the defenders. White flags started appearing everywhere. Dozens of stunned German soldiers walked out with their hands raised. The rest of the company moved up and took care of the POW's, and moved them to the rear.

Captain Goldmann and the first platoon continued northward through the village. Just as they were approaching Erik's old house, a series of 81mm mortar rounds, fired from a well-hidden GrW-34 mortar, started falling among them. Not all of the Germans were ready to surrender yet. These mortars came from the Panzer training area on the northern end of the village.

The entire platoon took off running up the street looking for cover, however Erik knew of a better spot to hide. Das Haus was immediately to the left of Erik, and he knew that the cellar was bombproof. He ran to the door and kicked it down. The mortars continued to fall as Erik ran down the stairs to the basement. He picked a spot under the stone stairs and crouched down. As a child he always hid in this same spot when he was playing hide and go seek with his sister. The shelling continued for the next three minutes, however none of the shells hit Das Haus!

Erik suddenly heard what sounded like whispering in the cellar. He could not tell exactly where the sound was coming from. He tried to pinpoint the sound, but was unable to do so. After the shelling stopped, he was better able to hear the humming, whispering voices. His vision was finally able to focus in the darkened cellar; it sounded as if it the noise was coming from the darkened sausage cellar. The sound was an eerie and spooky hum. He had never heard anything like this in his life. Erik began to wonder if there was a German soldier hidden there? He called out twice, but no one answered. Could it be someone trying to warn him?

Erik finally decided that it was his imagination getting the best of him, and he needed to get back with his men. He carefully climbed up the stairs and walked out the front door. He paused and looked around; not seeing anyone he started to cross the street.

"Pow!" He heard the sound, before he felt the pain in his right rear shoulder. The impact was so great that it knocked him to the ground. Erik debated whether or not he should move or pretend to be dead. A sniper shot him from behind, and he was still a target! The only place he could run to was an old barn across the street. Erik tensed all of his muscles and tried to will himself to stay calm.

Captain Goldmann managed to make it to the barn without being shot again. The sniper was obviously holding back; hoping for more targets. It was very common for snipers to simply wound the first target; knowing that it would take two or three additional soldiers to rescue him. Several members of his platoon had found their way to the old barn and were firing wildly at Das Haus.

Taking the opportunity offered by his men, Erik managed to crawl to the far side of the barn, and out the back door. He was no longer in the line of sight and could be safely helped. Members of his squad and the medic met him and gave him first aid. They hovered over him like a bunch of old ladies. The bullet had gone clean through his shoulder and did not hit any major arteries. The medic told him the good news, and although in severe pain he managed to instruct his men what to do next.

Captain Goldmann asked one of his men to crawl up to the third floor of the barn and ascertain where the sniper was. Corporal James Garett was the chosen volunteer. His men took up firing positions around the block and waited for CPL Garett to return. Garett managed to verify the sniper's exact location in less than two minutes. The sunlight reflected off the scope, and the Corporal managed to him through the curtain. The corporal quickly and stealthily retraced his steps and brought the intelligence back to Captain Goldmann. Erik was now satisfied that the area was secure and they could proceed with their mission.

"1SG Petersen, I want you to move all the men back from that house. At least one hundred yards to the north and take cover! I am going to call for a fire mission on Das Haus. Send the Communications Sergeant over here right now!" Ordered an authoritative Captain Goldmann.

"Yes Sir!" Replied a concerned 1SG Petersen.

Erik was carried by two his men away from the barn and brought to a safe location, a stone building which was an old Pub. Captain Goldmann called in his artillery battery to fire and got an immediate response. The first 105mm round landed directly behind the house, and the second round was a direct hit on the attic. The next two rounds landed in the courtyard and in the street. Captain Goldmann told his men to wait two minutes and then verify the situation.

Two men dashed down the street and entered Das Haus through the front door. A quick survey of the upper floor revealed the mangled body of a German soldier clutching a K-98 Mauser rifle with a Zeiss scope. The force of the explosion had torn him apart. They thoroughly examined the entire structure and found no one else hiding in the shadows.

The attic had in fact partially collapsed downwards into the third story. There was no other sign of life anywhere in Das Haus, except for those long lost spirits in the cellar. Their presence would probably never leave Das Haus alone, and would be a constant reminder of what had occurred there.

Erik could not help, but wonder if those voices in the cellar were the lost souls of the fifty-six Niedergeyer Jews? Was there such a thing as ghosts or spirits? The more he thought about it the more he was convinced that it could be possible. He had no way of knowing that sixty years later, a small and elderly lady would have an unexpected visit from the inhabitants of Das Haus.

Erik was oblivious to the fact that some day in the distant future, he would return to Niedergeyer for another tragic event.

Chapter 38

The End Is Near

Back to the Present

Cameron decided to go into hiding until things were sorted out. Cameron had an old German acquaintance living near Euskirchen. While stationed in Germany, as a young intelligence officer, Erik had met a German Luftwaffe Lieutenant; Heinrich Juenkers was his name. They had been very close friend, and kept in touch over the past two decades. Juenkers had risen in rank and was now a three-star general in the **Bundeswehr** (Military). Not even Cameron's wife or his father-in-law knew of their connection. Cameron made a call to General Juenkers, and was immediately invited over to his house. The general lived less than an hour away from Aachen.

The general was very pleased to see him and did not ask many questions. Cameron briefly explained his position, and the reason for secrecy. General Juenkers provided Cameron with a safe house, classified telephone and a government car. Cameron made himself at home and attempted to relax a little. Feeling secure and comfortable, Cameron started to develop his contingency plans. He called Jerry Kunstoff and updated him. Once that was done, he called his office in Aachen.

"Hello Beate, how are you? How are things?" Asked an inquisitive Cameron.

"Ja, Ja I am fine. Has anyone called for me in the past two days?" Inquired Cameron to a worried Beate.

"Please just listen. I am going to Austria on business and I will be back in three or four days. Don't tell anyone, and just take my messages. Is that understood?" Finished a serious sounding Cameron.

"But, but! How will I get a hold of you?" Replied an anxious Beate.

"Don't worry, I will contact you everyday. Please just take my messages and don't ask any more questions!" Finished a harsh sounding Cameron.

Not wanting to stay on the line any longer, he abruptly hung up on her. His location was safe enough, but he felt like a mouse in a trap. He did not like waiting for the trap to spring shut. Just as he was contemplating his options, his cell phone rang. He glanced down at the screen and saw it was from Dieter Johannes.

"Hello Dieter, how are you?" Asked a friendly Cameron, happy to hear from his father-in-law again.

"Please, please don't say anything! Just listen! Shut up and listen!" Screamed an almost incoherent Dieter.

"What is going on Dieter? Please calm down. Tell me what happened? Please?" Asked a now concerned Cameron.

There was silence on the phone, and Cameron heard Jeremy and Dieter arguing. Finally Jeremy came on the phone and said.

"I am sorry to tell you cousin. I have some bad news for you. A terrible accident has happened! Your daughter Jennifer is dead!" Finished a sobbing Jeremy.

Cameron was totally taken by surprise. He was speechless; his throat swelled up shut and only croaking noises came out.

"What did you say? Who is dead? My Jennifer?" Asked a stunned Cameron to his now crying cousin.

"I hate to tell you this, but 'Das Haus' has claimed two more victims." Finished a very upset Jeremy.

"Are you mad? This had better not be a sick joke? How can this be? Do you know the circumstances? What happened?" Finished a totally devastated Cameron.

His whole life was now coming apart before his eyes. First his mother-in-law was discovered to be a Nazi, his best friend was a Nazi; his wife cheated on him and had an affair with a known Nazi, and his child was not really his baby girl, and was now dead?

"We are still in Paris, but we are taking the Express back in ten minutes and should be in Aachen in less than five hours.

However, you might as well know the rest of it." Finished his cousin in a quiet and sad voice.

"You mean there is more? How much worst could it get?" Asked a scared and concerned Cameron.

"I am afraid so! Your wife found Jennifer hanging in the attic. Jennifer had left a note in which she claimed to have heard Ingrid and her mother planning evil deeds against you and Dieter. She could not believe that her mom and grandmother were Nazis, and wanted to kill you. She also found out about her real father, Dr. Juergens another Nazi. Jennifer took it very hard and simply went upstairs and hung herself. Your wife, feeling extremely guilty and shamed by her actions, also hung herself next to your daughter." Finished a now totally devastated Jeremy.

Cameron could hear Dieter sobbing in the background. He sounded like a wounded animal. His wails were like a wolf baying at the moon. Cameron continued.

"Oh my God! Why has God forsaken me? I simply can't believe it, my entire family gone forever. Please come home and help me through this chapter of my life. I need you now cousin." Begged a broken Cameron Clark.

"I will be there in less than six hours. Hold on cousin, both Dieter and I are on our way." Finished Jeremy, his voice quivering as spoke.

Cameron sat down and reflected on the past few months of his life. Was there anything he could have done to prevent this calamity? Did he push too hard? Should he have asked for help sooner? His thoughts were spinning through his mind like a kaleidoscope. He eventually calmed down and called his boss and friend Jerry Kunstoff in California. Jerry was devastated by the news and promised to be there in sixteen hours or less. Cameron knew that Jerry was a good friend and would be there for him.

Cameron phoned General Juenkers and explained the situation to him. His friend hung up and rushed right over. The general was there in less than fifteen minutes.

"I am sorry, so sorry Cameron! Did you see it coming? Why, why?" Exclaimed an obviously distraught General Juenkers.

"No, no I did not! I was so involved with my story and my problem that I did not even think about my daughter." Stated a visibly upset Cameron Clark.

The general continued. "I feel so bad for you and Dieter. What a horrible ending for both of you. Do you know what you are going to do? What are your plans? How do you go on? Are going to write your story and expose these madmen?"

"You better believe it! I will dedicate the rest of my life to it. I will not stop until all of these miserable rats are exterminated. There is no place or hole safe enough for them to hide. I will hunt them down for the rest of my life. I will become as fanatic and zealous as they are. They have awakened the modern day David, of David and Goliath fame. I will use every resource at my command until they are wiped off the face of the earth." Stated a now out of breath Cameron.

"If there is anything I can do for you, I will be there fore you and so will all of my resources. Not all Germans are like these madmen, and I will prove it to you." Replied an emotional General Juenkers.

"Than you, thank you very much. I will take you up on your offer. However, I need to get the train station and pick up my cousin Jeremy and my father-in-law." Stated Jeremy looking at his friend deep in thought.

"Sounds like a deal. Lets go now!" Stated Cameron without waiting for a reply.

It did not take them thirty-five minutes to arrive at the train station. Both Jeremy and Dieter were already waiting outside for them. After a round of emotional hugs and kisses General Juenkers drove them towards Dueren and home. The entire trip was made almost in entire silence. As they approached Niedergeyer, Dieter finally spoke up.

"Gentlemen, there is something I have to do. Please don't interfere. I have been waiting nearly sixty years for this, and today is the day!" Stated Dieter in a forceful way.

No one dared to say anything, Dieter was on a quest for justice and Cameron had a pretty good idea what was going to happen.

Deep in his heart, Cameron was happy that Dieter had chosen to take this action. As the car pulled up to the driveway, Dieter turned around and said:

"Please stay in the car until I call you." Before anyone could reply, he was out of the car running up the stairs like a madman.

Cameron, Jeremy and the general sat in silence in the vehicle. Less than thirty-seconds later they heard loud screams, crying and furniture being tossed about. The noise got louder and a small chair came crashing out of the kitchen window. More screaming and yelling followed for five more minutes. Cameron was hesitant about going to help Dieter, but he decided to stay out of it out of respect for Dieter. Dieter was settling an old score and he wanted to do it in his own. All of a sudden a disheveled and crying Kate Johannes was thrown out the front door. She tripped on the top stair and landed on her posterior. She slowly got up and shook her fist at Dieter, who was standing in the doorway hysterically laughing.

Dieter walked over to the car and told the men to come in and have a beer with him. They all quietly got out and walked inside. The interior looked like a bomb had gone off and destroyed everything. Tables, chairs, lamps, pictures, pots and pans etc., were strewn everywhere.

Dieter calmly stated. "It's over, over forever! The wicked witch is gone and never will return! Please come in and ignore the mess! This is the first day of my life as a single man!" Stated Dieter with a smile on his face.

The four men sat in the torn up living room and enjoyed a couple of beers. The conversation turned to the events of the past two days, and the future.

"We must make the arrangements and prepare for a very sad and emotional funeral. I would like to have everyone in town come and see what a passive attitude can result in. That is if Cameron has no objection?" Stated an assertive Dieter.

"That would be very nice if you could arrange this for us. I don't think I have in me right now to do anything." Replied Cameron; large tears streaming down his tired face.

Chapter 39

The Funeral

No one slept that night. Every one of the men had direct and indirect memories of Ingrid and Jennifer. Pictures in the house constantly reminded them of what had happened. It was a constant source of discussion throughout the day.

Dieter's other children came by and helped to arrange the funeral. Dieter was happy to see that they were taking his and Cameron's side. No one had seen Kate since yesterday, however no one really missed her.

Jerry Kunstoff arrived in the early morning and spent a great deal of time with Cameron. He felt somewhat responsible for the events of the past seventy-two hours. The German Polizei interrogated both Dieter and Cameron for several hours, and quickly and quietly classified the events as a double suicide.

General Juenkers made sure that the resident Nazi police-chief was not involved in any of the proceedings. He would be dealt with at a later date, along with the other Nazi conspirators.

It was decided to spread this story throughout Germany, Europe and the USA. This was their opportunity to tell the truth and let the world know about the resurgence of Fascism throughout Europe and world. Every known news media, print, satellite, cable, magazine and T.V, were invited to attend the funeral. It was hoped that this tragic event would spread the word. Jerry and Cameron used all the resources that they had, and were amazed when over 150 journalists appeared for the funeral. It was an almost festive affair as all the T.V. station had brightly colored trucks and cars. However one was quickly reminded of the tragic nature of this event by its location.

The weather was typical German fall day. Cloudy, overcast, drizzling and cold. The long procession of guests stretched for over one kilometer to the cemetery. It seemed as if everyone in the village had shown up for this tragic event. One notable exception was Dieter's wife, Kate. Both Cameron and Dieter had other things to worry about that Kate's absence.

The Catholic priest, an old family friend gave the eulogy and benediction. There was a very depressed and somber atmosphere throughout the service, except for the disrespectful news organizations. Cameron and Dieter were quietly reflecting on their lives and the love ones they had lost. They did not notice the small and elderly man walking towards them. He was well dressed and wore the usual dark suit and tie, but he had something on that no one else had, he wore a Jewish Yarmulke/Kippau on his head, and a Silver Star enameled ribbon his lapel.

The small man appeared to be in his late seventies or early eighties. He walked up to Dieter and said: "I am so sorry for your loss Dieter/Cameron. I flew all the way from New York to be here! Don't you remember me?"

Dieter stared at the man for over a minute, and finally shouted! Erik Goldmann, Erik Goldmann, you came back!

The End?

'Das Haus' the house and the Son of the Rabbi

About the Author

Sean Ryan Stuart is a Southern boy by birth and heritage, however as the only son of a professional military man, he traveled extensively throughout the world and lived in Europe, Germany, Spain, North Africa, Japan, Korea and many other countries for over twenty-five years. He is militarily retired, and 100% disabled from the Army. He also spent six years in the Air Force as an Air Policeman, and was a Counterintelligence Special Agent in the Army. Additionally he closely worked with various local civilian, state and federal law enforcement agencies throughout the world in an undercover capacity. This association with civilian law enforcement extended to, and included his last seven years in the military. He also spent over twelve years with the Sacramento Police Department as a Reserve officer.

Mr. Stuart has had extended training in the field of security, OPSEC, private investigations (Licensed in California), counter-terrorism and linguistics. He is fluent in six languages and proficient in several more. He has been used as a technical advisor in Hollywood. Mr. Stuart currently lives in California and has taught classes at the college level, and specialized in Russian Organized Crime, terrorism and other related subjects.

Previous books: *Red Snow Part One* and *Red Snow Part Two*.

www.ingramcontent.com/pod-product-compliance
Lightning Source LLC
Chambersburg PA
CBHW022146010726
47493CB00002B/357